Alta's Curse

Alta's Curse

Gerald,
great writing with you,
keep writing!
Patrick Curran

Patrick Curran

To the Reader

Alta's Curse is based on a true story. The information comes from research I conducted over a period of three years, beginning in 2014, and from interviews with those who observed or were involved in the events that transpired in Tallapoosa, Georgia from 1975-77. My research also includes public information from FBI files held at the National Archives at Atlanta on the gas tapping surveillance and trial. Two of the characters in the book, Lamar Tate and Virgil Pettigrew, were given fictitious names to protect the privacy of any remaining family in the area. Further details on my research can be found in the Acknowledgements at the end of the book.

ISBN: 1530915007
ISBN 13: 9781530915002
Library of Congress Control Number: 2016905760
CreateSpace Independent Publishing Platform
North Charleston, South Carolina

Prologue

———

WITHOUT PROHIBITION, MOONSHINE WOULD NEVER have amounted to much. It had been around forever and was rather harmless, a staple of every subsistence farmer, especially in the South. This is the story of Sam Alta Dryden from Tallapoosa, Georgia who made a fortune in moonshine.

The push for prohibition started in the early 19th century, when well-intentioned citizens urged the nation to become more temperate. By 1913, income-tax revenues were substantial, so the federal government was no longer dependent on alcohol tax. Yielding to teetotalers, they passed the Volstead Act prohibiting the manufacture and sale of liquor. There was indeed a brief dip in alcohol consumption, accompanied by a significant increase in organized crime in the big cities of the North, having to do with smuggling foreign liquor into the country.

Meanwhile the South, still reeling from the Civil War and the horrors of reconstruction, was devastated by the infestation of the boll weevil. Cotton acreage on plantations was cut in half in the 1920s, and tenant farmers lost their only cash crop. The Great Depression followed in the '30s, leaving most southerners desperately poor and struggling for any way to make a living. The Red Cross reported widespread starvation among both white and black families. Hard times indeed! Though the wincing brutality of the Great Depression, did little to build better citizens, it did foster a breed of big-hearted outlaws—Bonnie and Clyde, Pretty Boy Floyd, and Baby-Face Nelson. Alta Dryden took note.

In 1933 Prohibition was repealed, primarily because the Treasury needed alcohol revenue to end the Great Depression. Income tax, the main source of revenue at the time, had all but disappeared due to business failures and unemployment. With the repeal of Prohibition, states and counties had the right to remain dry or wet. Hundreds of counties across the Bible belt voted to enforce "dry" laws, banning the manufacture and sale of alcohol. Though it was legal to drink whiskey even in dry counties, the price became exorbitant. Federal tax on bonded whiskey rose to $10.50 a gallon, pushing the retail price to over twenty dollars a gallon. Moonshine, or "white lightening," on the other hand, sold for around five dollars a gallon. Never had forbidden fruit been so tempting.

A firestorm of unintended consequences followed. Most obvious was the creation of an enormous market for affordable, yet illegal whiskey. And when you throw into this odd equation, a dirt-poor Georgia boy like Alta Dryden, with the mind of a wizard and the heart of an outlaw, well then, you've got yourself a surefire empire in the making.

Making big money in moonshine required a corporate structure with three parts: the boss, the still operator and the distributor. They worked together like a three legged stool. By far the most critical leg was *the boss,* the man with the money. In Haralson County, Georgia, Alta Dryden was the man. No one went without a turkey at Thanksgiving or a gift at Christmas when Alta was around. Beyond funding the operation, he built relations in the community. Locals, often turned a blind eye to the "likker bidness." Some were suppliers, some were family, and most were beholden. The "local law" could be helpful as well. At times, it was no more than flashing their headlights at a bootlegger roaring down the mountain, warning of a road block. At times it was helping a supplier with a load of sugar to find his way to the still. And now and again, the county sheriff might tip off a still operator when federal agents were planning a raid. Of course, these shady alliances changed directions like the wind. A co-conspirator could become an informant, and an informant could become a co-conspirator. Tricky business.

When the three legged stool was working, a big operation could produce a thousand gallons of whiskey a day. More than a million gallons a year flowed into Atlanta alone. By 1950 the Alcohol Tax Unit of the IRS declared war on moonshiners, arresting bootleggers, seizing stills, and raw materials coming into the stills.

Many of the bootleggers became famous stock car racers "Lightening" Lloyd Seay, a close personal friend of Alta Dryden ran whiskey from Dawsonville into Atlanta. When a deputy pulled Lloyd over for speeding with a load of moonshine, legend has it, Lloyd gave him two five dollar bills. "Dammit Lloyd." the deputy said, "You know the fine for speeding ain't but five dollars." Seay replied. "Yeah, but I'm gonna be in a hurry coming back, so I'm payin' an advance."

Lloyd Seay, Daytona Beach

From 1954 to 1964, the ATF destroyed over seventy-two thousands stills and arrested over seventy-one thousand violators in the Southeast region alone, while illegal liquor sales continued to boom. The battlefield constantly shifted, as agents intensified their surveillance and moonshiners countered with new still sites and new routes to market. West Georgia nights were filled with the roar of bootleggers racing down "Thunder Road," the wail of the law in hot pursuit, and the rumble of blown stills.

Sheriff Pink Allen and Federal Agents Jimmy Satterfield and Doug Denny raiding a West Georgia moonshine still.

Alta Dryden made a fortune in moonshine in the '60s and '70s when he wasn't in the Atlanta Federal Prison. By the mid-seventies moonshine was on the way out. The high price of sugar had taken the profit out of the business. At the same time, drugs had come along and quickly proved to be more profitable with a lot less effort.

By 1975, Alta Dryden claimed he'd seen the light. When he got out of prison, he vowed, he was heading home to sell off his moonshine empire, to win back the love of his dying wife Shelby, and to revive Tallapoosa, a border town with a checkered past. He'd be returning, however, to a world that had changed, a world he'd only read about in prison. Though he was up for parole, he had two critical issues to deal with. First, he had to get out of his whisky business inside the prison, and then he had to decide if he would return to Tallapoosa. The warden had warned against returning home.

Run from the one's I love? No way!

Contents

Part 1

———

CHAPTER 1

Atlanta Federal Prison, July 1975

AT TEN SHARP, AN ELECTRONIC signal released the locking mechanism in the cellblock door, accompanied by a piercing alarm. Red lights flashed in every guard tower, sending armed guards scurrying across the catwalks. The cellblock door rumbled open, and row upon row of inmates in soiled orange jumpers shuffled into the sweltering heat. The bloom of Pine-Sol partially masked the stench of human confinement. The morning walkabout had begun.

Alta Dryden, as always, found his way to the front of the line and sauntered across the yard in a spotless, starched jumper. Half-moon glasses hung from the end of his nose. Below a full head of finely parted gray hair, he looked more the warden than the inmate. He claimed his spot in the yard, a spot that was hard to cover from above, a shady spot, a spot where business was done.

Every con in the yard stole a glance at Alta: the iron jaw, the poker face, the captain of the ship. He nodded on occasion but held the stare until they looked off.

Inside he floundered: water up to his knees, plugging leaks, bailing hard. *Am gonna do-right; am gonna get back to Shelby.*

As the morning sun moved across the yard and inched toward his spot, he edged deeper into the shade. His mind wandered more and more these days, always seeking to understand how he'd fallen into a life of crime. As Dr.

Dorothy Epstein, the prison psychiatrist, continued to remind him, "To get out of a hole, you need to figure out how you fell in." He understood the business of the hole, and in theory, he understood the concept of introspection she recommended, but he had yet to master it.

He'd grown up poor in the foothills of Appalachia, on a one horse, forty-acre farm. As a boy, he did his chores, fed the chickens, gathered the eggs, chopped firewood, and whatever else needed to be done. Then he was off to school. He was a bright student, and very gifted with numbers. Not much of an athlete, he caught the early school bus home from high school and helped out with the planting and picking, mostly cotton and vegetables. Pretty damn normal, he thought.

Those were the good times, but they never lasted. It was one thing, being warm and well fed, listening to a preacher, shouting about good and evil…and everyone in the church jumping around and chanting *Amen!* And *Hallelujah!* Alta got that. Good was good, and evil was evil, and that's the way it was. But, when the mill shut down and the crops failed, and they were all cold and hungry, then his chores had changed. Then, Daddy told him to lug big bags of sugar from the trailhead to the whiskey still deep in the hollow. And son, he'd said with a wink—*don't get caught.*

Things had changed, but he didn't know why. If he'd crossed the line legally, he never noticed. When the sugar was stacked at the still, he chopped wood for the still fire, dammed the creek, and trenched culverts to the condenser box. Later, he filled one-gallon milk jugs with moonshine, and hauled them down to the trailhead. And later yet, he loaded the jugs by moonlight into battered cars with souped-up engines. There were, after all, new chores to learn, new skills to master. Work to be done. Soon enough, while still in high school, he kept the books, ordered raw materials, and made the big deals with Atlanta bootleggers.

He put his reflections aside as Raylee Toms, a lifer, sidled up. Stooped and undersized, Raylee was far from imposing—easy to underestimate. They'd done time together, in and out, here and there, over the years. Early on, a cell warrior had messed with Raylee. They found the fool dead inside a locked cell with multiple stab wounds. Around the yard they said, "Raylee can smell fear and knew how to work it." In his prime he'd made a fortune bootlegging and robbing banks. Last fall, he had a stroke that stretched his face like a snare drum. These days he was a lifer with nothing to lose.

His head rocked fitfully as he struggled with his words. "How you…how you do-in'?"

Alta pursed his lips while scanning the yard. "Not so fine, thank you. Doc Dorothy says my heart's plugged up, may need a bah-pass. So, how you do-in'?"

"Up…up and down…mostly up…since ah got right…got right with de Lawd," Raylee said as he gazed up through razor wire and crossed himself.

Alta nodded politely. Raylee had of late declared himself saved; a born-again Christian, but he had yet to work through his occasional swings of violence.

"The stroke was…was a sign."

"What about my par-dun? Was that a sign?"

Their banter was overlapping and never ending like a braided rope. With few transitions, they'd drop a strand here and pick up another there.

"She cud…kill you…you know…young Mandy cud. Your heart…your heart can't…can't take it…to say nuttun…nuttun 'bout the rest…the rest of your 'quip-ment."

Raylee convulsed, caught, it seemed, between choking and laughing.

Alta smiled and turned serious. "Now Raylee, we been over this before. Shelby's the best woman I ever known, and Mandy, well, she's been awful kind to me. But then again, before I got locked up this last time, Shelby threw me out."

"Shelby was right," Raylee nodded. "She's way too fine…too fine a lady… to be hangin' 'round with a backslidin' hillbilly."

———

Alta knew it was Doyle before he got there: the jangle of keys, the clap of a nightstick against a flashlight, the squawk of a two-way radio, then a tidal wave of Aqua Velvet.

Doyle, the yard sergeant and a partner of sorts, was old school: no black leather cases on his duty belt, everything hanging off—a mess, but he considered himself ready. He was wide and squat like a tree trunk that had been sheared off by a twister. He got lost in the underbrush until you bumped up against him.

Both Alta and Doyle were Civil War buffs; both had lost family in the war. With Doyle every encounter was a quiz. Doyle stepped up close to Alta and whispered, "Good mornin', Captain. Does bell ring a bell?"

Alta pursed his lips and nodded slowly. "Bell! That's good. Yes sir, right up the road here, General John Bell Hood destroyed his own supply depot and torched eighty-one rail cars of ammunition. Damned if he was gonna let them blue-bellies get our supplies."

They both grumbled.

"Gawd-dam William Tecumseh Sherman," Alta spit out.

Doyle pointed up to the cupola that sat on top of the prison entrance. "This mornin' I climbed to the top."

Though Doyle was in his pocket, Alta never knew if he was telling the truth. But he was awful good at his Civil War history. "So what did you see up there, Sergeant?"

"I saw the Bell Tower at the Oakland Cemetery. General Hood's head-quarters was right there where the tower stands. That's where he made the decision to blow up the train shed and the ammunition cars. The right thing to do, but a sad, sad day for the South."

"You saw the Bell Tower, didya?"

"Hell yes, it's only two miles up the Boulevard from here." Doyle stepped back and puffed out his chest. "Anyway, the Cobras shorted the Aryan Brothers. They're formin' up across the yard."

Alta's head snapped up. "You sure?"

"Your golden boy, Lamar Tate, shorted the Cobras, so they had to short the Aryans," Doyle said, grinning.

Alta glanced at Raylee, who shook his head. "Are the Cobras packin'?"

Doyle cocked the visor of his hat to the side and nodded. "The Cobras, the Aryan Brothers, the whole damn yard. Storms a-comin'."

"Where's Fa-row Cash?" Alta asked calmly.

"Stirrin' the shit."

"Get him oh-va here."

With keys jangling and nightstick clapping, Doyle swaggered off, then turned and snickered. "Aye, aye Captain."

Raylee reached up the sleeve of his jumper and fingered his shank. "Arma...arma-geddon."

Alta's heart went into overdrive as he saw the gangs coming at each other. He caught himself and exhaled deeply. His heart thundered on.

Raylee flinched uncontrollably. "Ah said Arma...Arma-geddon. Like in the Bible."

"I know, I know," Alta frowned. "Armageddon, that's where we're headin'."

The PA system boomed: "This is Doyle. Break it up. Walk away. Separate!"

The gangs drifted apart as a troop of guards from the main block marched across the yard.

Hoping Doyle had calmed the uprising, Alta continued, "So where were we? Shelby and Mandy, right? You see, I'm stuck. Shelby being a lady and me being a felon. We had, it seems, ir-rec-on-cil-able dif-fer-en-ces. So picture this: there's poor ole me, out in the cold, and then young Mandy comes soarin' in on angel's wings, providing shelter from the storm."

"Thou shall not commit adultery," Raylee blustered. "That's a commandment of de Lawd!"

Alta grunted. "When it comes to being a felon, I don't think the Lawd cares about adultery."

Raylee raised his hand with two fingers extended. "Two things: first, it's none of my business; and second, the Lawd does care."

"You're right, it's none of your business, but I've decided. Seriously, I've decided, I'm goin' back to Shelby—that's if she'll have me. Best woman I ever known, and she's right. I'm goin' straight, strictly lee-git. You're probably right about Mandy; she's probably too young for me, and I'm not sure her divorce has gone through with Lamar, the playboy prince."

Alta's head dropped to his chest as he deliberated. Nothing set his heart to pounding like the thought of Lamar Tate, Mandy's ex. When Lamar, a heartthrob on a Harley, was on the prowl, no woman was safe.

"Worst decision I ever made, gettin' Lamar involved in the moonshine business."

Raylee nodded, pleased he'd steered Alta in the right direction. His eyes narrowed as he scanned the yard. The gangs had pushed back together and were taunting each other.

"It ain't too late...too late, to lay ole Lamar straight."

Alta chuckled. "When I hear you talk that way, you bein' reborn and all. It sounds like some of the old-you came along with the new-you."

"Could be?" Raylee shrugged. "I may...I may do it over, bein' reborn and all. Anyway, when you...when you gettin' out?"

"Twenty days—that's twenty days, eleven months and three years this time. The pardon has got-ta be a sign of some sort."

Raylee crossed himself. "If you don't go straight, you're a damn...a damn fool."

"A damn old fool."

Alta winced as the yard parted, and Pharaoh Cash stomped toward them, black, burly, and violent. An armed robbery conviction and a blown knee had ended a promising football career. These days he led the Cobras and controlled bootlegging inside the prison. He bought moonshine, of course, from Alta.

Alta nodded to Raylee. Pharaoh brushed against a set-up man as he cleared the crowd.

Raylee eased his right hand over his left, extended his fingers up under his sleeve, gripped his shiv, and whispered, "He's packin', boss."

Pharaoh lurched to a stop just short of where Alta stood, but in clear view of the rest of the yard. At his side, stood Pharaoh's lieutenants, two towering hulks.

"Hey Alta, your golden boy shorted us again, and we're hearin' 'bout another price in-crease. What the hell is goin' on?"

Alta felt the ground shifting under his feet, yet he tempered his response. "Now, now, Fa-row this is quite simply the nature of business, the ebbs and flows of the market...supply struggling to catch up with demand--a minor hiccup. We are pard-ners, are we not?"

Pharaoh stomped back and forth for all to see. "Your system is broke, old man, and you're a short timer. Things gonna change...forget about ebbs and flows...we're talkin' a rip tide."

For the first time, Alta felt alone caught between letting go and reaching out for a better life. He'd hoped to simply walk away from the past. His eyes narrowed as he looked across the yard. The Cobras, a knot of black men with dreads and red serpents inked around their necks, were faced off against the Aryan Brothers, a knot of white thugs with long hair and scarred faces. The tops of their jumpers hung from their waists. Most had AR inked across their chest. The rest, cons and guards alike, swung their heads back and forth from Alta's spot to the gangs across the yard.

Alta stepped from the shadow into full view. "I'll get you what you missed and throw in ten extra cases."

"That's the old deal," Pharaoh hissed. "The new deal is...I'm in charge, mutha-fuck-a."

Jaws clenched. Alta stepped back into the shadows.

Both gangs stood their ground, sneering and scowling, eyes tightened, teeth flashing; then the chanting and taunting began, followed by subtle shifts in weight, catlike circling, inching forward, seeking the prime attack angle. Alta had seen it all before; part of it was real, part of it was a power play, and part of it was routine violence. His instinct told him to attack. Yet he paused. His heart was pounding.

Pharaoh was a ticking bomb. His head swiveled around the yard. He paused then looked up directly into the sun. This seemed to be his signal. The gangs exploded, a blur of arms and legs, slashing and kicking. Shanks flashed in the sun. Cries and screams, mixed with the thud of lead pipes on flesh, echoed across the yard. Alarm bells screamed out of every cellblock. From the tower above the fight, Doyle barked into a bullhorn, "We've got us a situation in the southwest corner!"

A riot squad poured into the yard, another marched across the catwalks, some with guns, some with fire hoses.

Again, the bullhorn barked, "What'll it be? Water or guns?"

The gangs froze, considered for a moment, and then vanished like roaches on a linoleum floor, leaving a trail of blood and weapons.

After cuffing some of the rioters and getting the injured to the hospital, the riot squad closed in on Alta's spot.

Doyle marched up with a squad of troopers in tow and quickly cuffed Alta and Pharaoh. Everyone knew Pharaoh had set off the riot, but Doyle wanted to stage it right.

"So, prisoner Dryden, who set this thing off?"

Alta paused, trying to calm his racing heart, then lied, "I can't say."

Doyle rocked back on his heels and shook his head. "You can't say?"

Pharaoh winked at Alta as he turned to Doyle. "Sumtime shit happen."

Doyle's face tightened as he glared at Alta and Pharaoh. "If this 'shit happen' again, both of you are lookin' at hard time in solitary, and Alta, your pardon is gone. Clear?"

They nodded.

Though he couldn't explain it, Alta knew instantly: he had blinked. He also knew in a more humbling way that everyone knew he'd blinked. Things had changed.

Two blasts of the horn signaled that the morning walkabout was over. Inmates tramped slowly back through the cellblock doors. Time for lockup. Time for a cell count. Surely time for a weapons shakedown. Alta shrugged, another day in the slammer.

He struggled to calm the pounding in his chest as he shuffled back to his cell. As they got back to their cellblock, Alta whispered to Raylee, "Bring me the whiskey numbers tonight."

Raylee nodded and then went off like an evangelist at a revival, "You're right...Lamar's got to...got to go. And Mandy...Mandy's got to...got to go, too. Get back to Shelby...and get right with de Lawd."

Still shaken, Alta stretched out on his cot and puzzled through the showdown with Pharaoh His first response was anger. *How in hell did I let Fa-row bully me?"*

"I know the game," he crowed aloud. "Hell, I invented it."

In the early days, it was about the money, but no more.

I've tucked away more than I can spend. Maybe I'm broken? It's true some part of me is lured by the hunt, the clever scam, the jolt of power that comes with beating the system? And by Gawd, I'm good at it.

His mind went blank as he stared out the cell window. Then it hit him.

Shee-yet, the old game is oh-va!

CHAPTER 2

Tallapoosa Water Tank, Same Day

———

LAMAR ROARED TO A STOP below the water tank that loomed above town. *Tallapoosa: The Dogwood City* was painted in four-foot red letters across the eighty-thousand-gallon tank. He shoved his Harley back on its stand, pulled off his goggles, and brushed back his long blond hair. He stooped over and admired himself in his bike mirror, then chuckled. *Yeah that's me, a heartthrob on a Harley.*

He grabbed his pack and paused. Then stepped back to admire his new bike. African wild dogs were painted on the gas tank: ears pointed; fangs, razor-sharp eyes, red glowing embers. All in all, a savage pack of carnivores circled a statue of Lady Justice, fending off other predators. It pleased Lamar that the message was unclear. African wild dogs, he'd learned, were apex predators, the vigilantes of the African savanna.

Lamar was head smart but no student, partly a deranged dreamer, partly a cunning carnivore. He'd passed Biology 1A and little else at West Georgia College. The concept of the apex predator was his lone takeaway. Like a pig in a puddle, it was enough. He learned that when two species compete for an ecosystem, an apex predator preys on both and creates stability. His brain snapped shut on that revelation. It gave purpose and direction to a disturbed mind. After all, he was out there, in the midst of the fray, seeking stability between moonshiners and revenuers, honest citizens and corrupt politicians, local merchants and corporate retailers—all fierce contestants on an unstable planet. He was an avenging angel in the struggle for world peace.

Lamar pushed through a hole in the cyclone fence and climbed the tank. Clouds drifted to the south. The sky was a radiant blue. He would enjoy the moment before turning to business.

Tallapoosa clung to the shag end of the Appalachian Mountains, known as the Piedmont region. To the north, hills rose to granite peaks, narrow valleys, and rocky soil. Red clay covered the ground, rich in iron but none too fertile. It quickly eroded when trees were cleared for crops. Yet, cool mountain springs ran over beds of limestone, and the protection of towering trees and deep hollows made it a fine place to cook whiskey, raise pigs, and get the drop on strangers.

Lamar eased round to the south side of the catwalk. Off in the distance, a trace of the other Georgia, the Coastal Plains, could be seen or imagined. Further south, Columbus marked the western edge of the fall line that ran east through Macon and over to Augusta and on to the Atlantic Ocean. Rolling hills gave way to flat, fertile land, what had been big cotton country. Some believed that folks from the plains had better manners than those from the high hills. Everyone agreed it was ungodly hot and swarmed with tiny man-eating gnats called *no-see-ums*. To the west, Tallapoosa, the Dogwood City, was poised for action, open for business from all directions, textile mills or moonshine stills.

As the sun began to set, he edged to the west side of the water tank. Pulling field glasses from his pack, he scanned the countryside. The Tallapoosa River wandered by like a ribbon of gold. Most of the counties in these parts, Lamar recalled as he chuckled to himself, were dry. They'd voted to prohibit the sale but not the consumption of alcohol and thereby created a prime moonshine market. *Nice.* He checked the schedule he'd inked on his forearm. He had six bootleggers hauling shine into Alabama that night. They'd meet at the American Legion post later.

Raising the field glasses, he smirked. "Let's see what the good folks of Tallapoosa are up to."

Of late, Tallapoosa looked a lot like any other small town in the South: a tidy grid of four or five city blocks, split down the middle by a highway and train tracks. Mixed neighborhoods skirted the town: clapboard shacks, brick ranch-style bungalows and, here and there, a grand Victorian gem with a shaded wraparound porch. Small farms and woodlands rolled on for miles. Like the rest of the south, Tallapoosa struggled to recover from the Civil War and Reconstruction. It blossomed in the 1880s when the railroads linked it to Atlanta and Birmingham. Back then, cotton was king. By 1907, the jenny at the Tallapoosa Cotton Mill never stopped spinning. Horse-drawn wagons loaded with cotton bales lined the dusty roads leading to town. The hiss and rattle of spinning jennies blended with the click-ety-clack of trains leaving town, crammed with spools of yarn. Then, in the 1920s, the boll weevil cut cotton acreage in half. The Great Depression followed in the 1930s, leaving most Southerners desperately poor and searching for any way to make a living. They weren't the best of times. Yet, these days, as Lamar looked out on the town, there were many fine things going on in Tallapoosa: proper churches, clubs, schools and some damn fine stores: Lipham's Department Store, Thrower's Flower Shop, Hildebrand's Pharmacy. Added to that, teeming pockets of industry had arrived: the American Thread Company, Southern Can Plant, Stoffel Seals Corporation, Hoover-Hanes Rubber Corporation, Darsey Manufacturing, and more. All in all, many fine local institutions were pulling the community together.

Lamar snickered. "Let's see what's happening on the shady side of town."

Just west of town on Highway 78, lights came on in an old tin warehouse. Out front, a two-ton truck was being loaded with what looked like bags of sugar, large sheets of aluminum, and wooden mash barrels.

"Yes sir," Lamar snorted, "a new still's goin' up. Fed's blowing 'em up by day; moonshiners rebuilding 'em by night—an unstable eco-system. I got to save 'em from themselves."

He sharpened his focus as he moved the glasses into town. Club 78 was below the tank. Jacked-up trucks and juiced-up sedans were parked outside, driven by bootleggers or ATF agents on the prowl. Anything could happen in this freewheeling honky-tonk. A George Jones "she-done-me-wrong" song drifted up from the jukebox. On any given night, you could meet the girl of your dreams or get shot, plan a robbery or get busted. Neither sin nor salvation had the upper hand. Club 78 wasn't in the business of making better citizens.

Across the street, the lights shone bright out the bay doors of Smith's Garage. A Dodge Coronet howled as they tried to synchronize the carbs. The body sat low on the frame, and a tarp covered the backseat.

Lamar tightened the focus. "Well, how about that. It's Billy Chitwood and his badass Coronet."

Billy, one of Lamar's bootleggers, would be hauling tonight.

"That a boy, Billy, get that hemi tuned."

Setting aside the field glasses, Lamar tried to untangle his thoughts. Could he really save the homeland? There had indeed been ups and downs in the local economy and endless conflicts between the feds and the moonshiners: stills were destroyed, agents shot, moonshiners jailed. He had scavenged from both, making good money snitching to the feds on Alta and, lately, making good money skimming off Alta's moonshine business. How else could a po' boy afford handguns, Harleys, and pole dancers?

He ran his hands through his hair. Time was running out. With Alta's connections, he'd be out of prison soon and put an end to the skimming. And then there was Mandy, his ex-wife. He hadn't sent an alimony check in a year. He'd heard she fancied Alta. Billy Chitwood, who knew everything local, said Alta had helped her out now and then with the bills and groceries. Funny thing about Alta, he was a generous soul. You never knew what he was up to.

Lamar's lips curled. His eyes narrowed. He snarled at the rising moon and trembled with excitement. He needed one big hit, a grand slam. Then he'd pack his bags and skedaddle. Softly at first, and then louder and louder, he howled a wild-dog howl. Soon he was at full wild-dog alert and hustled down the ladder. *Let's run some likker tonight!*

CHAPTER 3

ER, Tanner Hospital, Same Day

———

It was 11 p.m. when Mandy Tate collapsed on the bench in the women's dressing room. She peeled off her scrubs, her third and final change-out of the day, and hurried to the shower. The momentary silence was shredded by the wail of an incoming ambulance. It was her week to work grave shift, but she'd swapped off with another nurse and pulled a double shift so she could get off at eleven. Struggling to avoid bankruptcy, she desperately needed to catch up with her ex-husband Lamar at the Legion Post.

She pulled on a flannel shirt and jeans, washed her hands again, removing the last traces of betadine, and shook out her salt-and-pepper mane. On her way out, she glanced in the mirror. Tightly pursed lips and a hollow stare greeted her.

Good Lawd, is that me? I'm supposed to be in control.

She crumpled on the bench, thought about crying, rejected it, and then quietly sobbed. Lately, her pain pulled her back to her youth. Unknowingly, she searched for clues to her misery, something that could get her back on her feet. She'd had her share of ups and downs. Long ago, Cyrus Chauncey, her grandfather, had homesteaded forty acres of hard scrabble land in Haralson County. Her father, Vassar Chauncey, struggled to make a go of it. The boll weevil in the '20s and the depression in the '30s, put an end to the cotton crop.

Mandy came along in '43. Sadly, her mother Elizabeth, died in childbirth. Vassar did the best he could as a single parent. He wasn't around much, but when he was, he showered her with dolls and dress-up clothes. At five years old, she'd arrive for breakfast as Doris Day with a blond bob wig. She'd be back at dinner as Debbie Reynolds in cutoff shorts and a bouncy ponytail. She'd wear any get-up to make her Daddy laugh. Doris and Debbie, her celebrity sisters, neither replaced her mother nor helped her figure out who she was.

Interrupting Mandy's childhood recollections, Bridget Mulligan, the head nurse and Mandy's relief, hurried in, all round, white, and starched. She eased next to Mandy on the bench, a swan cap on her head and a crucifix around her neck. She was the mother Mandy never had. At sixty-three she was a formidable force in the community. Everyone asked for Bridget, even whiskey haulers bleeding out from gunshot wounds. She handed Mandy a tissue and gave her a hug.

Bridget studied Mandy's shirt and jeans. Then she jumped up with a grin and said, "Lemme guess, you're not goin' dancin' tonight?"

Mandy dabbed her cheeks. "I'm tryin' to catch Lamar at the Legion Post."

Rolling her eyes, Bridget shot back, "Did that backslidin' tent show say he'd join you?"

"Not exactly. Most nights, he meets his bootleggers at the Post before they do their run."

"Sooooo…he's makin' a dollar or two. Are you gettin' your alimony?"

"Hell no, and the court is threatening to garmish my wages."

"Dear me. Let me see if I can get some help for you on that. Is he still doing his animal thing?"

Mandy blushed. "Says he's a wild dog, saving the planet."

"Seriously, Mandy, does he know when he's being a wild dog?"

"What d'ya mean?'

"Hmm. I'm not sure I'm sayin' this right, but does he know when he stops bein' Lamar and starts bein' a wild dog?"

"His eyes glaze over, and he starts ravin' about savin' the planet. But no, he doesn't start peeing on fire hydrants."

"Just wondering. He may be delusional, like he's not aware that he's not Lamar anymore."

"Delusional?"

"I'm not sure if that's the right word, but it's serious."

"Well, he's not Frankenstein. He's just a fruitcake."

The light above the door flashed red, and a siren echoed down the hall as another ambulance arrived.

Bridget pulled Mandy to her feet. "Come on, girl. Go get him."

Mandy's eyes lit up. "Here I go!"

Bridget gave her another hug and headed for the door.

Moments later, another ambulance screamed in. Mandy's head snapped up at the wall clock. It was 11:15 p.m. and she was running late. She grabbed her day-log and headed for checkout. No one was at the admission desk. She leaned against the counter, checking her log against the duty board: three overdosed teenagers; four car accidents with major lacerations and broken bones; three assaulted women, looked like domestic violence; three gunshot wounds at a convenience store holdup; two knifings, one dead on arrival. All within miles of Tallapoosa. The trauma and treatment rooms were packed, and triage was overflowing. Muffled moans and cries came in all directions.

———

It was 11 p.m. Lamar emerged from his single-wide trailer after a late afternoon nap. Ready for some midnight whiskey hauling, he hopped on his Harley and roared through town. He was cocksure he owned Tallapoosa. He was equally sure, at the ripe age of thirty-four, that he owned the hottest bike on the planet. Pleased with his grand entrance, he paused for a moment in front of the Burger Inn and wrapped out the Ironhead engine, then rumbled into the Legion Post, a cinder-block fortress adorned with American flags and Pabst Blue Ribbon signs. A rusting World War II tank stood guard out front. The solid working-class folks from the mills and farms stayed clear of the Post.

He strolled across the dimly lit back porch that reeked of stale beer and cheap perfume. Soldiers on the prowl, bad-boy bikers, conspiring outlaws, and lonely hearts of every stripe filled the tables. Fights were routine, with shootings now and again. Lamar strutted to the far side of the porch and marked a table with his leather jacket. His whiskey haulers would be in soon. Slipping off his red bandanna, he shook his hair free, and swaggered over to the bar, preening like a peacock. These moves, he'd found, gave him maximum exposure to the ladies. The lead singer from the band let go with a country favorite, "Don't Give Your Heart to a Rambling Man."

Lamar smirked and sang along. "Don't fall in love with me darlin', I'm a rambler."

It was payday, and the Legion Post was jumping. He waited in line at the bar, watching Virgil Pettimore, the bartender and bouncer, mix drinks. Virgil was a local legend, a big fellow with a gray flattop, who had done hard time in Atlanta Federal Prison. Red braces, stretched over an ample paunch and struggled to hold up his trousers. For years, Virgil had been an enforcer in Alta's moonshine army, an empire that stretched across the Southeast. Both had made money, big money, and both had done several stretches in prison for, as they say, conspiring to violate federal liquor laws. On his last stretch several years back, Virgil was found guilty of operating a handful of thirteen-thousand-gallon stills in Haralson County, Georgia, and Cleburne County, Alabama.

Lamar flashed an evil smile. He'd been heavily involved in all of this but somehow had never been charged. Sure, some folks said he'd snitched to the feds for immunity, *but hey*, he thought, *what do they know?* He nodded to Virgil as reached the bar. "Gimme a beer, old man."

Virgil scowled as he wiped down the bar. "Hey son. You haulin' tonight?"

Lamar fiddled with a bottle cap. He needed to pass on a price increase, however unwarranted, and it needed to start with Virgil. He took a deep breath and cocked his head to one side. "Haulin', yeah, we're haulin'...but we need to talk...you see, costs have gone up...sugar's up, yeast's up, copper line has never been cheap, and lately the feds are takin' down stills as fast we put them up...soooooooooo it follows that our prices have got to go up."

Virgil crossed his arms and leaned back against the cash register. "Run along, Lamar, don't be hustlin' this ole dog. Jest gimme my regular order, at the regular price, or I'll make scrap iron out of that candy-ass bike of yours."

Lamar's lips curled back as his ears perked up. Though a predatory fire roared through him, he became cool and cunning.

"Virgil," he hissed, "its only normal that you'd resist a price increase, and, well…" he paused, catching his reflection in the bar mirror, and ran his hands through his hair, "and, well, become unpleasant…ah reckon…ah reckon it must be a blow to you personally, that I'm runnin' the show these days."

As Lamar rambled on, Virgil turned to mix a drink. He turned back with a beer in one of his massive paws, and the other lay flat on the bar, concealing a .38 revolver, "Have your beer and run along, sonny."

Lamar's eyes narrowed to slits. He was caught off guard. Something had changed. Normally there would be some shouting and screaming, maybe a punch or two, and usually he'd bully Virgil into an agreement. Collecting himself, Lamar retied his bandana, winked into the mirror and shifted gears. "You see how anger consumes you. Not good for your blood pressure. Let's just talk facts for a second. Fact one, there's sixty-four ounces in a gallon, which serves thirty-two, two-ounce shots of whiskey. Okeydokey? And at a dollar a shot, which is far too cheap, you make thirty-two bucks a gallon. Fact two, you buy from me at ten bucks a gallon, so that's over three hundred percent profit. So what in hell you cryin' 'bout?"

Without blinking, Virgil eased back the hammer of the .38. "Cryin'? Who's cryin'? You see any tears, son? You want to talk facts, let's talk us some facts. With a thirteen-thousand-gallon still, your finished cost per gallon of shine is around three bucks. And you been sellin' it at ten bucks a gallon; that's, say, three hundred percent profit? Okeydokey? And if you figure in the overhead it costs to run this pleasure palace, we're lucky to break even most of the time. So, run along, greedy boy. Just give me my regular order, at the regular price."

"Have it your way. We'll talk some more. Just understand, Tallapoosa is my town…and if…" Lamar paused. "And if you mess with my bike, I'll burn this shithole down."

Virgil stuck the .38 under the bar and smiled. "You can't burn cinder block stupid."

"Your right. Ah Guess I'll have to blow the sumbitch up."

Lamar shuffled back to his table, making a mental note to stop delivering to the Legion Post. By now, everyone was up and shouting as a riff from the lead guitar thundered across the porch.

da-ta-DA da-DUM
da-ta-Da da-DUM
da-ta-DA da-DUM

The band then broke into "Midnight Rider," an Allman Brothers favorite.

Lamar tapped his beer bottle on the table and sang along. "No, I'm not gonna let 'em catch the midnight rider." He was sure Virgil would come around once he ran out of moonshine for a week or two. *What the hell*, he thought, *its simple economics.* He smiled as he heard the familiar whump, whump of Billy Chitwood's Dodge Coronet roll into the lot. Lamar pulled the sleeve of his shirt up and checked the trip sheet he'd inked on his forearm. Billy would be hauling forty cases of whiskey tonight. Each case contained six one-gallon plastic jugs, a total of 240 gallons.

Clutching a long-neck beer, Billy strutted up to Lamar, wearing grease-stained overalls and a goofy smile. "Hey hey. How you?"

"Hey, Billy. I'm lovin' that hemi. You got her tuned for tonight?"

"Yeah, how'd you know?"

Lamar winked. "Shee-yet boy, I know everything that's goes on."

"I truly believe it. Yeah, that four-twenty-six hemi is so fine! Got me a second at Carrolton Speedway Sunday last. Truly fine. She's ready to roll. Billy coughed and cleared his throat. "Seriously Lamar, seriously, I'm gonna need more runs to make the payments."

Lamar gently tapped his beer bottle on the table. "Look, I busted my ass to git you a big load tonight, and I don't want any screw-ups."

"You know, it weren't..." Billy paused and seemed to collect his thoughts. "It weren't like this when Alta was runnin' things."

Lamar tapped the bottle harder. "The hell, Billy Boy, the hell. These are hard times, hills crawlin' with feds, sugar's gone high-dollar, more and more wet counties. Tonight's the last run at the old price. We been losing our ass for the last year. You're not just a bootlegger, Billy, you're a goddamn salesman, so get your ass out there and sell the new price, or it's coming out of your pocket."

Billy chugged his beer down and shouted loud enough for all to hear, "You know, this here was one sweet business when Alta was around. And you're sure-nuf screwing it up!"

"Try to remember Billy Boy, a hungry dog hunts best. Now, say goodnight."

Moments later Skeeter Tatum rumbled into the parking lot in a jacked-up '51 Ford pickup with a tarp over the back. He lumbered across the porch to Lamar's table, where Lamer spewed the same arguments and the same threats. By midnight, five more trippers came and went, and Lamar had roared off on his Harley. A surge of adrenaline flashed though him like a bolt of lightning, further masking his uncertainty. *Nooooo, they're not gonna catch the midnight rider.*

CHAPTER 4

American Legion Post, Tallapoosa, Same Day

———

IT WAS 11:30 P.M. WHEN Mandy finally signed out of ER. Running late, she rushed down the hall, skirted ventilators and CPR carts, and sprinted for her Plymouth Fury. It was a twenty-minute ride to the Legion Post. She tried to focus on the road, but her mind kept slipping back to her childhood, searching for answers.

When she was twelve, her after-school time was split between farm chores and devouring copies of *Ardent Love*. By fifteen, she had blossomed into a pretty young miss, a born pleaser. She was a big girl, just over five foot ten with an angelic face and a striking body, sometimes the Doris Day princess, sometimes the Debbie Reynold's charmer. Adolescence wasn't easy. At first, she swooned over privileged southern gents—the Ashley Wilkes types. Suffering through a string of heartbreaks, she switched direction and fell hard for the dangerous Rhett Butler types. Fortunately, a high school counselor got her into girls' basketball. She became the starting forward at West Haralson High, and went on to become a conference all-star at West Georgia College.

The only ring she had these days was her college conference championship ring, which swung on a chain from the rearview mirror. She'd never forgotten the time her coach pulled her aside after the final game and asked her how she felt about her play. She shrugged uncomfortably and asked the coach if he was pleased.

"Mandy," he said, "it's not about pleasing me. You had a great game and a great season. As you go forward, you have to decide what you want out of life. You decide what pleases you. Set your goals and go for it."

Her mind snapped back into focus as she rattled across the railroad tracks coming into town. She gripped the steering wheel at the stop sign and sighed. *Those were the glory days.*

Glory days, all right, and poor romantic choices. Her worst choice was running off with Lamar Tate, the self-proclaimed playboy of Tallapoosa. Lamar was both handsome and dangerous, part dreamer part schemer. He loved fast cars, fast women and Southern Comfort. When he wasn't running whiskey for Alta he was scheming against him. Over the years he'd been in and out of prison, always on the same charge: conspiring to violate federal liquor laws.

Mandy fell hard for Lamar, yet was sure she could tame him, and she did for a while. Somehow, she'd earned a nursing degree as she battled through an abusive marriage. With Lamar it was feast or famine. There were always money problems, and they sunk deeper and deeper in debt. When he scored big on some shady deal, he'd buy a new car and soup it up for the dirt track racing and running moonshine. Lately, he was into Harleys.

They'd separated two years back, then filed for divorce, and then endured several painful attempts to reconcile. The divorce was finalized last year, along with a court order for alimony.

Just before midnight, Mandy skidded to a stop at the Legion Post and shot inside. Pushing through the crowd, she spotted Virgil Pettimore sprawled out at a table in the corner, clutching a Pabst Blue Ribbon. He'd finished pouring for the night, and now seemed intent on drinking. He pulled himself up and gave her a hug. "Hey, shugah, how you doin'?"

Mandy glanced around the room. "Looks like I missed him again?"

Virgil frowned. "Not by much. He just roared off."

She dropped into a chair. "Darn."

"Soooo, how's basketball going?"

She smiled. "Haralson County women's team is having another good year. We beat Carroll County last week. We play Polk County this week."

"And you?"

"Had a triple double against Carroll County."

"Damn girl, you still got it. And how's ER?"

She shrugged. "Car wrecks, domestic violence, some shooting's, drunks. Same old problems. Y'know what? I really gotta run."

Mandy, paused, then threw her head back and laughed. "Say, Virgil, you know Inez Folsom?"

He sighed and shook his head. "Inez, sweet lady, comes in now and then, usually a little banged up."

"So, here's the story. Inez finally gets fed up with Tommy Lee, her no-good, wife-beating husband, and signs up for a self-defense class."

"And?"

"Tommy Lee limps into the ER tonight, looking like he'd been run through a wood chopper. A towel wrapped around his head, blood every-where. Needed a lot of stitchin'."

"Now that's a damn shame." Virgil chuckled. "Speaking of husbands, I know it's a touchy subject, but how you and Lamar doin'?"

Mandy crumpled back down. "Lousy. I know, I know, I'm part of the problem, and I really wanted to fix it, but it's over. I don't know where he's get-tin' all the money he's flashin' around every honky-tonk in Haralson County, but I'm damn sick of chasing him for alimony."

Virgil got up, reached around the bar, and opened a Coca-Cola. "Have a drink. I believe Lamar knows about you and Alta?"

"Maybe." She sighed and sipped the coke. "And maybe not. Maybe he's taking it out on the whiskey business."

"That too, but come on, he knows. Hell, Mandy, you're the talk of the town."

"Like I said, I'm part of the problem. I'm a born pleaser. I was just a kid when I ran off with Lamar. Sure, Alta's older and all, but he's helped me out a lot when Lamar was in prison, but it's not about the money."

Virgil masked a smile with his hand. "You know what Mandy it's not all about the money. Alta's a lovable guy, a gentleman, and, well, yes, one hell of a wealthy fellow. It's got to be, what do you call it, in-tox-i-cat-ing."

Mandy shrugged, not sure how she felt about it all. "You think Alta knows that Lamar's skimmin'?"

"Alta's awful good with them numbers." Virgil grinned. "He may be bai-tin' the hook."

"Maybe." Mandy shrugged. "He claims he's going straight this time. He knows I'm gone if he don't."

Virgil grinned and gave her the evil eye. "You know he's out of prison next week?"

"What!"

CHAPTER 5

Atlanta Federal Prison, Days Later

———

JUST BEFORE LIGHTS OUT, A library cart rattled down the cellblock. Raylee was not only Alta's right-hand man, he was a trustee in the prison library. He stopped at Alta's cell. "Got a book for you," he snickered. "From the…from the Warden."

Alta smiled as he saw the title, *Getting Out, and Staying Out of Prison.* He opened the cover, withdrew a small slip hidden in the due-date envelope, and quickly scanned the whiskey numbers.

"Volume's down," he murmured. "That's to be expected, but the cost of goods stayed the same. This ain't right. Either Lamar's stockpilin' or skimmin'."

"He ain't smart nuf…smart nuf… to stockpile; he's skimmin'."

"Can you get a phone call out to Virgil when you get back to the library?"

Raylee put a hand to his jaw to hold it still. "I reckon, but don't you… don't you see…the Lawd's talkin' to you. You gotta get out of the business now."

"I'm tryin'. Call Virgil, tell him I want him to check into this."

"Virgil? I got the damn numbers from Virgil. Don't you see…he's not a numbers man, and he's lazy…lazy to boot. Alta, you gotta give it up and get right with de Lawd."

"Listen up, Raylee. The Lawd can't help me on this one. Call Virgil and tell him to check things out in the moanin'' and then get his fat ass over here in the afternoon with some answers. You got that?"

"I got that, and you know what else? You're goin' to hell."

"I'll save a seat for you." Alta grinned.

Raylee wedged his face between the bars. His eyes swung back and forth like searchlights. Stepping back, he clutched a crucifix in his withered hands. "Look at you grinnin' like a damn cay-o-te...you got to repent to be saved... walk away from...from your life of sin."

"Damn, Raylee, I'm all prayed-up," Alta whispered. "A lot of folks gonna get hurt if I just walk away. It ain't that easy."

Since his religious conversion, Raylee's sermons had become a nightly occurrence. A black rhymer several cells down had heard it all before and started chanting, "Hey boss man, hey boss man, way too late, way too late for goin' straight, just as well, just as well, you burn in hell."

Banging tin cups against iron bars, the whole cellblock joined in.

The PA system switched on. Harsh static. "Hold it down," the head bull roared, "or you'll be standin' tall for a strip search."

Alta wiped his brow as Raylee shuffled off. It was nine o'clock and still over ninety degrees. He felt his heart loping in his chest. Slumping back on his cot, he reached for his pills. Raylee was right; he needed to get out of the business. He drifted off as the cellblock dimmed.

His brain purred like a mainframe as he drifted in and out of sleep. It churned through a vast honeycomb of data, running endless scenarios. The numbers that Raylee delivered were slotted into a virtual spreadsheet for his moonshine business, an empire that took in four states, hundreds of whiskey stills, and an army of bootleggers in souped-up cars, serving thousands of honky-tonks and juke joints across the South.

As Alta sorted through the numbers, images of his childhood flooded back. His father, a cantankerous mountain man, had been a looming presence in his life. A strong-willed Baptist with deep Scot-Irish roots, who'd never bent a knee to authority—not to big government, not to big business. Charlie Dryden was bathed in the holy water of Jeffersonian Democracy and passionately believed in private property and equal rights for all men. He preached a simple sermon to his son: abide by God's commandments and the Bill of Rights, and do what you damn well please on your own land.

Alta tossed and turned on his cot. The golden years of prohibition were clearly over. It was high time he got out of the whiskey business: the cost of sugar had skyrocketed, federal tax agents now swarmed every hill and hollow, and bonded liquor was now legal. Add to that, more and more dry counties in the south, teetotalers that had never approved of alcohol consumption, had voted to go wet, had voted to allow both the sale and consumption of alcohol. Alta chuckled.

The Bible belt will burn in hell.

Dry counties had always been prime markets for moonshiners. Alta ran the whiskey numbers through his head again. In spite of a declining moonshine market, his profits had declined even more. Lamar was up to something.

From time to time, he sat up and massaged his chest. He was torn by a decision he knew he had to make. Seeking affirmation, he turned to the framed photographs on the shelf: to the left, a picture of "Lightning" Lloyd Seay on the hood of his '39 Ford coupe. Lloyd, an old family friend, was a moonshine legend from Dawsonville who'd driven to stock-car fame.

"Go, Lloyd, go," Alta murmured.

In the middle was a portrait of his beloved wife, Shelby. After ten years of marriage, she finally left him. She announced she was tired of living with a man who spent half his life in prison. To the right was a picture of Mandy Tate at her graduation from nursing school. He'd come to know Mandy a few years back, when her husband, Lamar Tate, one of Alta bootleggers, was in prison for hauling whiskey. Alta, as always, made a point of taking care of his bootleggers and their families, especially when they were sent off.

He admired all three pictures and then returned to Shelby and made a decision he should have made long ago. "You'll see Shelby, you'll see," he vowed. "I'm comin' home. I'm comin' clean. I'll make you proud."

By four a.m., he was back up, pacing his cell with a sly glimmer in his eyes. The gas-tapping scheme, his most outlandish venture, spun through his head like the reels of a slot machine. He was already in for sixty thousand dollars.

The Plantation Pipeline Company pumped up to seven hundred thousand barrels of gasoline a day through a twenty-six-inch pipe that ran from refineries in Texas across the southeast, skirting Tallapoosa, and on up the East Coast. In addition to the pipeline, the last stretch of Interstate 20, from Texas to South Carolina, was under construction and would run alongside Tallapoosa. Fortunes would be made along the interstate. All he wanted was a piece of the gas business. Alta was, after all, a concerned citizen, a native son trying to support the local economy. He trembled with excitement. He understood the scale-economy game. He understood the grinding, impersonal logic of big companies with big money, driving off honest, independent competitors. He had no illusions about the corporate vultures that would line Interstate 20 with franchised service stations, restaurants, and motels, making graveyards out of every small town they passed, just as William Tecumseh Sherman, the miserable Yankee scoundrel, had done.

It seemed fair to Alta that local Georgians, states' rights and all, should have a share in the bonanza that ran through their state. And so it was that he got entangled in a scheme to tap the interstate gas line. A more foolproof moneymaker wouldn't have interested him. It was the audacity of it that piqued his interest. And, of course, he'd be protecting the homeland. A narrow smile crossed his face.

Yessir, goin' straight's gonna be tricky.

CHAPTER 6

Alabama Backwoods, Next Day

———

Up before dawn, Virgil Pettimore, rumbled down Main Street in his vintage Chevy truck while Tallapoosa slept. He vanished into darkness and reappeared in pools of light cast by street lamps. As he pulled in front of the police station and saw his truck's reflection in the window, he snickered, "Gud-damn, look at me, and look at my rig."

Shifting into neutral, he goosed the gas, backed off, and goosed it again. The front end lurched wildly. An angry beast snarled under the hood as exhaust fumes burst above the twin stacks. The front end, slathered in chrome, sent shards of light in all directions. Adding to the menace, spiked wheel hubs with clusters of jutting knife blades extended five inches beyond the rims. Virgil, a proud gladiator in a proud chariot, was ready to roll.

"Catch me if you can," he hollered and roared out of town. This sort of foolishness was a welcome diversion for a man who was on the hot seat. Crossing the Tallapoosa River, he rumbled into Alabama, heading for Muscatime. You're damn right, he'd check into things as he'd promised Raylee over the phone. Later that afternoon, he'd report to Alta on the moonshine business and the gas-tapping business.

Several months earlier, Virgil had hired a land agent to scout for abandoned farms along the Plantation Pipeline. He'd quietly leased three properties using fictitious names. It had taken weeks to get the electricity switched on. They were way behind schedule.

Turning onto a dirt road, he wound through several miles of woodlands and stopped on a hilltop. A weathered house stood below, at the end of a hollow. Yeah, he'd let things go, and Alta was on him. The cords in his neck flared as he felt a tremor in his right hand. He needed to step it up. He needed to take care of business. He shoved his hand against the dash. It wasn't fear that gripped him; maybe it was pride. He wouldn't be laughed at.

Dammed if I'll be a porch dog.

The tremor triggered memories of his boyhood. In grade school, he'd been the biggest kid in class and a self-confessed bully. Even his mother said he had a nasty disposition. He stopped growing in the seventh grade; and quickly became the one who limped home bruised and beaten. Though he held on to his nasty disposition, his reign of terror was over. These days, he chose his fights carefully and carried an equalizer.

He coasted down the hill to a sagging barn, held up by kudzu vines. Sliding a snub-nosed .38 in his pocket, he pulled on his Alabama ball cap. Lonny James, who he'd come to check on, was a rabid Auburn fan. No rivalry in college football was nastier than the one between Auburn and Alabama. The Battle of Shiloh, the South's last best chance to beat the Union, paled by comparison.

As the sky lightened, Virgil stepped from his truck and studied the clearing. Two hundred feet below the barn, the twenty-six-inch Plantation Pipeline ran across the clearing. It started at the refineries in Houston and stretched out over five thousand miles, twisting through the heartland of the South like a giant anaconda, slithering on up to the industrial centers of the North. Most southerners felt they were entitled to a share of the bonanza.

Caustic fumes stung Virgil's eyes as he sauntered up to the barn. An arc welder droned inside. Blue and orange light flashed between broken sidings. Pushing open the heavy door, he shouted, "Don't shoot, Lonny. Virgil here."

A red, battered truck sat near the back door. A two-thousand-gallon tank was chained to the bed. Lonny was welding a steel collar around a short section of pipe that looked a lot like the Plantation Pipeline. His deer rifle, a faded Auburn cap, and a pouch of Red Man lay on a bench nearby.

For years, Lonny had welded for Plantation Pipeline. Lately, he ran a few head of cattle and farmed twenty acres of cotton. He got by and pretty much did as he pleased— a smart fellow well into his sixties with a thick neck, broad shoulders, and a foul mouth.

He pushed up his welding helmet and grinned. "Hello, Virgil, what's that piece of she-yett on the front of your cap? Oh, sorry, that's an Alabama A, ain't it?"

Virgil chuckled. "Roll damn tide! We beat your ass bad last year, didn't we?"

"It has been a long year, but we'll get you in the Iron Bowl."

"Hell, Lonny, Auburn's a cow college. You boys need to forget about playing' football and tend to your cows!"

Lonny pulled on his ball cap. "Well, you see, Virgil, down in Auburn we keep our cows in the pasture and our players out of jail."

"Now, now, Lonny, everybody knows, you can't have a high tide without a low tide. So, how you comin'?"

Lonny hammered on a beaded seam. "It's a test weld. Looks like she'll hold."

Virgil felt his right hand starting to tremble and slipped it in his coat pocket. "It damn well better."

"Yeah, well, this here collar is a gas tap. It has an on-off valve and cutter inside. Once it's welded to the pipeline, we cut through the shell of the pipe. Gas won't come out til you open the hose valve."

"She'll work, then, will she?"

Lonny shrugged and sent a stream of Red Man on the straw floor. "That's why we're testing it, dumb shee-yet."

Virgil smiled, ignoring the barb. "So it passed the test; let's get on with it."

"It's more than weldin' a test tap on a test pipe. The pipeline out there pumps up to fifty thousand barrels of petroleum an hour. And this electrode I got in my hands gets up to sixty-five hundred degrees Fahrenheit. No sir, you can't be welding a gas tap on a real pipeline, not when she's pumping. Even a country boy knows that."

Virgil eyes narrowed. He'd heard all this before but never understood it. He'd never made much of an effort to understand it. *Hell, I'm a moonshiner, not a gas tapper*, he thought.

He frowned at Lonny. "So, when do they stop pumping?"

"Gawd damn, Virgil, you think they put that shee-yet out in the evening news? When I was workin' for 'em, we never knew where we'd be from day to day. They're smart sumbitches, y'know."

Virgil scratched his head. "OK, fine, so we gotta get to someone on the inside. Hell, Lonny, that's simple enough. Half of Musca-time's on our payroll already. You got any buddies left on the maintenance crew?"

Ignoring the comment, Lonny grabbed a long-handled spanner and started turning the cutter. "Now that she's welded on, let's see if she'll cut through the pipe."

Moments later, he finished tapping the test pipe and wiped his hands on his overalls.

Virgil stepped closer. "Come on, Lonny, this is pretty simple; let's get it done."

Lonny bowed his neck back like a snake fixing to strike. "Oh yeah, this is pretty simple. All you gotta do is weld this here tapping collar around *the real* pipeline, at a time when it's not pumping, and no one's looking; next you tap a hole in the pipe, back it out, and connect the hose, which we ain't got. Then, you open the valve, and fill the tank on that sad-ass truck over there." He paused and launched another stream of Red Man onto the straw floor. "And finally, you get some fool to drive it to a gas station in the dead of night and pump two thousand gallons of, Gawd knows what, into their storage tank. Oh, hell yes Virgil, this is pretty simple shee-yet."

Virgil stomped out of the barn, threw his arms in the air, and cursed at the rising sun. *Gawd damn you, Alta, you got me into this half-assed business, and now you're talkin' about goin' straight. How's that gonna work?*

He pulled out his Camels, lit up, and schemed. After several draws, he pinched off the hot end. A smile crossed his face. "The key here is to keep Alta in the game. He's got the deep pockets."

He strolled back into the barn, a man with a plan. "OK, Lonny, you're right. Just gimme the name of someone at Plantation that'll work with us, someone who can tell us when they're pumping and when they ain't."

Lonny grabbed a hammer and banged it on the test pipe. "Virgil," he said with a smile, "you are one ignorant sumbitch. Ain't nobody on the maintenance crew gonna give you what you want; you gotta find yourself a high level snitch at the head office in At-lan-ta."

Virgil's face was an angry red. "That's bullshit. Somebody here, locally, must know when the pipeline is shut down."

Lonny continued to bang on the pipe. "It's way more than that. How many times I gotta tell you, they run lots of stuff though that line—diesel, jet fuel, kerosene, low-sulfur gas, high-level sulfur gas, you name it. You best get your wallet out, big daddy, and be damn careful getting yourself a high-level snitch that can tell you *what* they're pumpin' and *when* they're pumpin' it."

Virgil paced back and forth across the barn, head down, jaw locked tight. Then he moved between Lonny and his deer rifle. "Lonny, Lonny, Lonny... try to remember, I hold a note on your farm."

Lonny glanced over at his rifle and thought better of it. "Get me the pumpin' schedule, and I'll get her done."

Virgil peeled five big bills from his wad. "Just be ready to go when ah land a snitch. Here, stick this in your pocket."

———

Lost and in a hurry, Virgil rolled down County Road 37, throwing off a red column of dust, searching for the turnoff to the Muscadine Still—one of many Dryden stills operating in Alabama. He had to see firsthand what Lamar was up to before visiting Alta in the Atlanta Prison.

"I'll say this for Cleburne County," Virgil fussed, "it's got clean creeks, good protective cover, and no road signs. Good place to get lost, good place for makin' likker."

Farther on, he pulled over at a crossroads. Cupping his hands to his ears, he walked around his truck, listening for the drone of gas burners, a drone that might come from a liquor still. A faint rumble came from the west. He drove off in that direction on what became a rutted dirt path. He was pleased the burners led him to the still, but he knew it was a bad sign. Only greedy operators like Lamar would run burners in the daytime, when the law was out and about.

He twisted through miles of marsh and vines beneath a darkened canopy, veering off the road occasionally to clip down creepers and seedlings with his spike-rimmed hubs. *Who said bushwhackin' ain't fun.*

After mowing down swaths of undergrowth, Virgil came to a long, narrow building with a rusted tin roof. Gas burners roared inside. The clapboard siding trembled as he stepped inside. It was dark and muggy and smelled of sweet mash. The fermentation area was filled with wooden mash barrels, three clusters of twenty barrels. As his eyes adjusted to the dark, he glanced around. Virgil noticed a thick foam cap floating on the surface of one cluster of barrels. Dipping his finger in the cap, he tasted it. *Too sweet to run*, he thought; then he edged his way down to the still room. Beneath a huge, upright boiler, the burners roared. A veil of steam filled the room.

Ka-plunk! His head slammed against the steaming boiler.

Junior DeMint, the loan still hand, pinned him against the boiler with his rifle.

"Who in hell are you?" he screamed.

"It's me, Virgil, Virgil Pettimore, your gawd-damn uncle."

Junior dropped the gun and stumbled back. "Sorry, Uncle Virgil. I thought you was the law. I'm plain sorry."

Hands and arms flashed in the half-light; then came the crunch of a fist on flesh, a scream, a moan. When things settled, Junior was jammed against the steaming boiler. Virgil had one hand around his neck; the other poked a .38 in his cheek.

"Don't you ever, ever, ever, pull a gun on me, son, or I'll stuff you in one of them stinkin' mash barrels."

Junior folded like an accordion as Virgil let go. "Now, where the hell d'ya keep your stores?"

"In the barn, out back."

Virgil pulled him to his feet. "Come on son, you'll live."

Stomping around in the barn, Virgil did a quick count, scratching figures in his pad. Five to six hundred bags of sugar were stacked to the right of the nave. Pallets of wheat bran and yeast were piled to the left. Several hundred cases of glass jars and paraffin cans were jammed into the loft. A hoist hung from the widow's peak of the barn, for storing pallet loads up in the loft.

Virgil's head snapped 'round as a GMC rig with a box trailer rumbled up to the barn. His eyes narrowed as he turned to Junior.

"It's a back road," Junior stammered. "Lamar put it in."

"It's a goddamn freeway."

Virgil's jaw tightened as the GMC rig, a contract sugar hauler from Savannah, pulled in front of the barn. It carried ten to fifteen tons of sugar. Moments later two empty flatbed trucks rolled up the same road and swung behind the barn. Virgil shook with anger. *What the hell's going on?*

Then it came to him. Lamar had been ordering way more sugar than needed and selling off the extra to them boys in the flatbeds, who looked to be moonshiners, looked to be competitors. *And all this is happenin' on my watch.*

"Sumbitch!"

Flashing his .38 in the air, Virgil raced behind the barn. Two hulking boys in bib overalls leaned against the fender of the first truck. They snapped up as Virgil appeared.

"You boys," Virgil gasped, "you boys better go on...git!"

"Come on, Virgil, we've met," Darnel, the taller of the two, replied. "We're from Anniston. We're in the business, too."

"I know you fellas, I do, and I know where you live. But you're gonna have to get your own sugar from now on."

Darnel eased his hand behind his back.

Whap! Whap!

Virgil fired two shots into the ground, throwing up a cloud of dust. "I hope you weren't goin' for your gun there, Darnel?"

The boys scrambled back into their trucks. Darnel growled, "You'll pay for this."

"Sometimes fear's better than love," Virgil snickered. "Here's the thing: you snitch on our little operation, and we'll burn your house down; and if that ain't a-nuf, we kill you off, real quiet like, one by one...now git!"

As they drove off, Virgil marched back into the barn. "All right, Junior, let's go to school. How many bags of sugar you need to run a batch?"

Junior perked up; he knew his makings. "Well, you see, we run on a three-batch cycle, twenty mash barrels to a batch." Junior's eyes glistened as he lost himself in his calculations. "We got two-hundred-gallon barrels, so they want two one-hundred pound bags of sugar each, one pound of sugar for every gallon of water...so that's forty bags per batch...for three batches, that's one hundred and twenty bags. You can see that, can't you, Virgil?"

"Jest keep it simple, Junior. How many bags of sugar you need a week?"

"You're right, keep it simple...well if, eva-thang falls into place...you understand it takes three days for each batch to ferment...and if we get the rotation right...I'd say five batches a week...so that'd be...'bout two hundred bags of sugar a week...'bout ten tons."

"You're sure of them numbers?"

"Damn, I ought to know; it's my job. Say Uncle Virgil, can I ask you somethin'?"

"No, hell no!" Virgil grabbed him by the collar and dragged him over to the sugar stores. "How many bags we got on the floor?"

Junior swallowed hard. "Maybe five, say six hundred bags."

"Help me with the numbers...six hundred one-hundred pound bags of sugar...comes to sixty thousand pounds...or thirty tons. So tell me, mister smart ass, who's orderin' the sugar?"

Junior froze. "I run the still house. I got nothin' to do with the stores."

"Junnniooooorrrr?" Virgil tapped his chest.

"Well, lately, Lamar has. He don't allow me in the barn."

Virgil's face tightened. "You got sugar comin' in the front door and goin' out the back door to them...to them other sumbitches, who are damn well makin' likker, and damn well competing against us."

"I'm a lowly still hand. I make whiskey. I don't keep the books. And, and..."

"And what?"

"And lately, you ain't been around here much." Junior glared through his hurt.

"From now on, what comes in here stays in here. And you'd better get smart about when you're cookin' mash; you can hear them gas burners for miles. County's crawling with lawmen."

"Yes sir, Mr. Virgil. Yes sir." Junior trembled as he spoke. "Am I gonna get in trouble with Mr. Alta?"

Virgil grinned and hugged him. "You're family, son; just keep your mouth shut and watch out for Lamar. His days are numbered."

"Yesssir."

"One more thing: I want you to stop what your doin' right now. Take that chainsaw over there and start droppin' trees on that superhighway Lamar built. Start at the other end and work your way back; drop a tree every fifty yards or so. You got that?"

Junior's head flopped up and down. "I'm on it."

Virgil lumbered back to his truck and climbed in. Reaching under the seat, he came back with a jar of Dryden's Kickass moonshine and took a long pull. Then he paged through his notepad. Atlanta was the big market for the Drydens. It guzzled more moonshine than any city in the south, but the ATF had gone after the moonshiners. They'd seized over twenty thousand stills a year around the country and over a thousand in Alabama last year. They didn't fuss much with the pint bootleggers; they mostly went after the big boys, like the Drydens.

He stuck his notepad in his pocket, switched on the ignition, and headed for Atlanta—no goosing the gas, no wrapping the chrome stacks, no throwing dirt. He'd lost his swagger. Gas tapping was full of problems, and the shine had surely gone out of moonshine.

———

Virgil screeched to a stop in the prison lot, thirty minutes late. Extending his left thumb, he spun the lid off the liquor jar, sending it sailing out the window. Smiling broadly, he drained the jar and slumped back in the seat, counting bugs splats on the windshield. His eyes drifted to the far lawn where a work crew of five trustees in leg-irons cut and trimmed. Then they doubled to ten. He squinted hard, and they were back to five.

Spikes of pain cut through the fog of the whiskey. He winced and slipped the .38 under the seat. He knew he'd screwed up bad; he knew it; and Alta damn well knew it. He wiped his brow and tried to smile.

He hooked his thumbs under his red braces, stretched them to the limit, and let them snap as they disappeared into his bulging gut. Six of the last ten years, he'd been locked inside for, as they say, conspiring to violate federal liquor laws, most of them along with Alta.

He mellowed as he reflected on the golden days of the liquor business. "Down deep I believe Alta likes me." Virgil sighed. "Not for what I am, but for what I bring to the fight. Mostly...I guess, 'cause ah don't give a shee-yet. That's gotta be useful."

Stumbling out of the truck, he braced himself on the hood and gazed up at the prison facade.

"From the outside, ladies and gentlemen," he bellowed, "you'd never guess what goes on inside."

The work crew looked over and smiled.

Having memorized the prison brochure, and pleased to have an audience, Virgil launched forth. "When completed in 1902, the twenty-three-acre compound was the largest concrete structure in the world, an imposing neoclassical design, of high-rise block marble, similar to the U.S. Capitol. A grand pediment rests above the entrance, crowned by a cupola...which..." he smirked as he adlibbed, "which doubles as a gun tower during riots. And please note, the doors, the windows, and the entire roof line are trimmed in razor wire."

CHAPTER 7

Atlanta Federal Prison, Same Day

———

HEAD DOWN, PENCIL IN HAND, Alta scanned the *Atlanta Journal* discount page. Treasure Island, a hardware discount chain, had a truckload sale on box fans and space heaters.

Hardware's the thing, I'm through with perishables.

Squeezed into a tiny cubicle, he slumped down on an iron stool with his back against the wall, the only con in the room with a starched orange jumper. Now and then he set the pencil on the counter and smoothed back his gray hair, pulled his gold-rimmed bifocals to the end of his nose and glanced toward the entrance door.

A row of cubicles ran down the middle of the room. Each was divided by a thick pane of glass with a louvered screen. A harsh ammonia odor drifted back and forth through the screen. Convicts in rumpled orange jumpers laughed and fought with family, girlfriends, or co-conspirators. Only Alta sat alone.

The PA system crackled and then blared, "Let's finish up. Ten minutes till lockup."

Alta continued leafing thought the paper as an electronic locking bolt screeched. Massive iron doors rumbled open as arriving guards marched in one side of the room and departing guards marched out the other.

He smelled Sargent Doyle before he got there, a harsh blend of raw whiskey and cheap mouthwash; then a club came to rest on his shoulder. Doyle was a *hack*, a name Alta still found amusing. H-A-C-K was prison lingo for "horse's ass carrying keys." He was also one of Alta's main inside guys.

"Hey, short-timer."

"Hey, Sarge."

"Your boy Virgil's on the way."

"What else you got?"

"Now, that'd be snitchin'."

"You get yours?"

"Aye, captain, aye."

"Oh, by the way," Alta grimaced, "today is November fourteen. Do you recall what happened on November fifteen 1864?"

Doyle sighed. "Damn Yankees! Sherman started his march to the sea."

———

At ten minutes to four, Virgil burst into the room, skidded onto the stool across from Alta, and seized the phone. "Sorry, boss…been a long day."

Alta caught a frown moving across his face and flipped it into a smile. Doc Dorothy would be pleased. Those on both sides of the glass took in Virgil's arrival and nodded amiably. As he arrived, those on his side of the glass winced and turned their heads.

Alta studied Virgil. His wide suspenders were stretched to ribbons as they cut across his T-shirt, his eyes twitched uncontrollably, and, of course, he reeked. In spite of it all, Alta was confident—not pleased, but confident—he could stop this train wreck.

"Virgil," he whispered into the phone, "you're lookin' at the new me."

The twitching subsided as Virgil pried his eyelids open with his fingers.

"I'm lookin' at what?"

"You're lookin' at the new me."

"You think, there's a new you inside of you?"

"I do."

What does Doc Dorothy think?"

"She gave me some tests, asked me some questions, and said—you know how they talk—she said, 'You're a psych-o-path with a sunny disposition.'"

Virgil chuckled. "She's got your number."

"After more testin' and some ther-o-py, she said I'm more of a so-ci-o-path, a charming so-ci-o-path."

The PA system blared, "Visitin' hours are over in five minutes."

Virgil's eyes narrowed to red slits as he jumped up and pounded on the pane. "Well, that's what you are. Smooth as silk on the outside and nasty as a snake on the inside."

No one missed the outburst. Guards appeared and slammed Virgil down on his iron stool. Alta's jaw tightened. "Pipe down and use the damn phone," he hissed. "What you got on the likker business?"

Virgil shrugged and grabbed the phone. "Lamar, that sneaky sumbitch," he wheezed. "He'd better pick him a gravestone, 'cause he's a dead man."

"Huh?"

"Got himself into the shoo-gar business. Buyin' tons of it; sellin' a good bit out the back door to some assholes from Anniston."

"How'd he slip that by you?"

Virgil's eyes twitched uncontrollably as his head dropped like a scolded hound.

Alta glanced around the room. Everyone seemed to be holding their breath.

Virgil slowly raised his head. "I've been awful busy at the Legion Post, tryin' to take care of business...here and there."

"That's not what I'm hearin'," Alta fumed. "You look like roadkill...and you stink of whiskey."

Virgil straightened up and made one pass at tucking in his T-shirt. "Well, sure, I know, I let things go."

Alta paused, trying to compose himself. The words came out hot and harsh. "Ah can't have this, Virgil. I aim to make big changes in my life, and I hoped you could help me." Alta shrugged. "Maybe? Maybe not."

Virgil slumped back. His rare attempt at candor had failed. "You're right, boss. I just ain't as good when you ain't around. But together, together we do good work. I'm back, believe me, boss, I'm back in the game."

"Back in the game, we'll see. Now, concernin' the moonshine business, here's what you do. Fly down to Thibodaux and meet up with Billy Boudreaux.

He runs the Cajun mafia in Louisiana…moonshine, shrimpin,' and what-all. See what he'll give you for the business, lock, stock, and barrel. Don't say a word to Lamar; just find a buyer and close the deal. You can shoot Lamar later," he chuckled, "if Billy don't beat you to it."

"You wanta hold on to any of the likker business?"

"No, I am out. Clean."

"Shelby's gonna like that, boss. She's not well, y'know. She asks about you."

"I know, I know." Alta ran his hands back over his hair. "I hope she'll have me back. Either way, I'm clean. Now, what you got on the gas tappin'?"

"Well it's moving along…moving along…I leased some land along the pipeline, bought some gas trucks; lots of independent gas stations want in on the deal, but," he mumbled as his hand started to tremble, "but here's the thing…we've had some problems weldin' taps onto the pipeline…" his voice trailed off, "when it's pumpin'."

Alta rocked forward on his stool and glared at Virgil. "When it's pumpin'? I never ever heard nothin' 'bout weldin' a tap on a pipeline while it's pumpin'! You said this was a done deal!"

Heads snapped up. Phone conversations stopped.

"Here I am, tryin' to be a better person." Alta sighed.

"What d'ya mean, better?"

"Like bein' more self-aware."

"Woo-we, spooky!" Virgil said and chuckled. "You think you're someone else?"

"No, stupid, I know I'm me, but I don't always know what I'm doin'."

"Well hello, Alta, when did that come to you?"

"Watch your mouth there, Virgil, watch it."

Virgil dropped the phone and grinned broadly, sensing he had gained ground. "You wantta do right, don't you? Clear the land and drain the swamp. And what d' you think you'll find at the bottom of the swamp?"

"I don't know."

"Hot cars and dead bodies that you put there."

"Let's be clear: I want out. Just help me do that."

The PA system crackled. Static. "Time's up; let's move it."

Locking bolts screeched as the iron doors rumbled open.

Virgil smacked his lips and thought. "Well, here's the thing: we need to git us an inside guy, a haw-level snitch at Plantation Pipeline. And for sure, I ain't got that kinda money or connections."

Alta eyes snapped shut as he tried to tamp down the pounding in his chest. An avalanche of problems blocked the high road to redemption. He crossed his arms and thought. "Have a word with my brother, Fred; he's well connected in Atlanta. Tell him to find a high-level snitch at the pipeline. Hell, he takes them boys to the Masters every year. Tell him I'll cover it. But Virgil, this is it. If gas tappin' is such a gawd dammed goldmine, find someone to buy me out."

"No sir, no sir, Alta—we need you."

"I ain't leavin' town; I'm just goin' straight."

Virgil stood to go.

"Say, Virgil," Alta paused. "Is Mandy getting any alimony from Lamar?"

"Not a dime."

"Do this for me. Write her a check on my account for groceries and thangs, a couple hundred dollars."

Virgil limped off. "I will…and boss I'll get this whole business right."

Alta's head churned like a mainframe as he ran a cost-benefits analysis.

Maybe the cards are stacked against my return to Tallapoosa. Going home to start over, don't seem so smart anymore.

CHAPTER 8

Dryden Still, Alabama, Days Later

———

A STREAK OF LIGHT FLASHED in the oak branches above the still house. Junior DeMint stopped and carefully set down a wheelbarrow loaded with bags of cornmeal and sugar. A moonlit night shone above the ragged canopy. He drew a breath and checked his pocket watch: four a.m.

Maybe a passing plane, a shooting star, or maybe the headlights of the law.

He crouched low like a fox on the prowl. His eyes shifted down to the still house, an abandoned chicken coop. Morning mist, heavy with the smell of sour mash, rolled up the hill. Earlier, he had pumped sixty barrels of fermented mash into a thousand-gallon still. Propane burners roared under the still as the mash cooked off.

He waited. Nothing. He turned slowly, straining to see or hear anything different. Then shoved a creaky heavily laden wheelbarrow into the still house, and loaded cornmeal and sugar into the mash barrels for another batch.

As he pushed the wheelbarrow back to the barn for more makings, he heard a muffled thump. He froze. Could be a falling limb. Could be a deer caught in barbed wire. Could be a car door closing, or maybe not. He hadn't slept in three days and his senses were shredded.

Gawd damn, somethin's wrong, somethin's out there.

He slipped into the barn and grabbed his two-way radio.

———

Lamar sat in a sleepless trance next to his bed as his two-way radio started beeping. "Yeah, Junior."

"Hey, Lamar, yeah, it's me," Junior whispered, his voice breaking. "Yeah, everything's fine."

"You know, it's four-thirty in the moan-in'."

Junior sighed. "I know…yeah, everything's fine. Got us a cap-arm leak, nothing serious. Just checking in."

"Well, patch it up; I'll send another one up next week."

Switching off the radio, Lamar went into full wild-dog alert. Throwing on his clothes, he grabbed his guns and blasted off on his Harley. The cap arm ran from the still to the thump keg. *Cap-arm leak* was code for "come quick, come armed, and come the back way." Ever since the ATF started tapping phones and radios, you needed a code.

Cap-arm leak, hmm? Lamar wondered. Could mean a dumb shit squirrel hunter had wandered onto the still. Could mean the ATF, armed with axes and dynamite, were closing in for the kill. Kind of early for either. Strange.

———

Twenty minutes later, Lamar pulled off the blacktop onto a dirt path that ran up behind the still. The weather was closing in. Thunder rolled down from the high hills. Lightning followed, piercing through the darkness. He took it slow, coasting over open fields and crawling slowly up the wooded hills to the summit. He parked his Harley near the top and settled behind a boulder. The lights were on in the still house, and the roar of gas burners boomed up the hillside.

As the dawn broke, the rain started. Lamar pulled on his rain gear and opened the cylinder of his 357 Magnum and checked the load; then he pulled his Winchester from its sheath and loaded it. He was ready but strangely on edge. Maybe Junior was right, maybe someone was out there; or maybe something was going on inside his head. Lamar had been trying to kick his whiskey habit for the last couple of weeks and hadn't slept in days.

The rain continued with the morning light. Below, in the hollow, shafts of light cut through the canopy and flickered on the still house. He'd give it five minutes, no more.

Suddenly, Lamar was trembling uncontrollably. His nerves were on fire. He clutched his head in both hands, pressing his fingers into his skull. His vision blurred. The roar of the burners became distorted.

Snapshots from the past flashed in and out of view: goofy baby pictures, a prom picture in his first bowtie; a triumphant pose at home plate, arms raised to the sky, after scoring the winning run in American Legion baseball. The good years, the happy years.

Then a ghostly chant…*Who are you, Lamar? Who are you?*

Then more images after he'd gone bad: sitting on the hood of his first car, a Plymouth Fury; a mugshot from his first trip to juvenile hall.

Then more chanting. *Who are you, Lamar? A whiskey runner? A bar-room brawler? An ass-bandit? A cheating husband? A clever snitch? Are you a bad boy…or a frightened boy?*

He covered his ears and squeezed his eyes shut. The images and chanting left as quickly as they had arrived.

The fits came and went. He usually moved on once they had passed, yet that day Lamar was shaken. He wondered, *am I just another flawed sumbitch dealing with his demons? Or am I drunk caught in the clutches of a delirium? Or, what the hell, maybe I'm just losin' my mind?*

The still house snapped back into focus. The roar of the burners returned. He quickly dismissed his latest seizure. He was, after all, an errant knight, a benevolent outlaw. Lately the guise of an apex predator, the avenging angel in a crumbling universe, served his purpose.

Lamar scanned the hollow with his field glasses. A midnight-blue Pontiac with racing numbers on the door stood below the still house. Not that un-usual. Could be Junior's; he drove stock cars on the weekend. Moving closer, the tail end of another car came into view: a '51 Lincoln Cosmopolitan, a pimp car that did well on the dirt-track circuit. Edging even closer, he saw it had Louisiana plates and a Coon-Ass-Nation bumper sticker.

Whack!

A crushing blow to the back of his head sent him flying. He screamed as he blacked out.

———

Before he understood, Lamar felt the sting of hot liquid washing over him, accompanied by the pungent smell of mash. He was caught in a fog of light and dark, alive, yet out there somewhere, on the borderline. It came again…the hot liquid, the smell of mash…burning-hot sour mash. He lay in a pool of blood and slop that soaked his clothing and long, blond hair. A glow came and went in the darkness. He blinked away the scum in his eyes. The glow remained, a naked light bulb dangled from the rafter. The rest was a smoky haze.

"What the hell?" he moaned.

Three men towered over him in the dim light. The fourth, an enormous fellow, well over three hundred pounds, sat on an oak barrel, shaking with laughter. "Bwahaha! Bwahaha!"

Lamar blinked again and saw they were dressed in cone-shaped hats, skull masks, and black skeleton robes.

"Who dat? Who dat?" they chanted.

The big boy on the barrel chuckled. "That be La-mar."

The cone heads were off dancing and singing.

"Hey La-mar, do you know?
Our Cajun Captain, Billy Boudreaux.
Billy, Billy, Billy Boudreaux,
The moonshine boss of Thibodaux."

In spite of his throbbing head, Lamar did find the skit amusing—clearly a Mardi Gras special they'd worked on.

They dragged him across the dirt floor and tied him to a post. The bloated fellow on the barrel must be Captain Billy. Off to the right, Junior DeMint was bound and gagged, dangling by his heels over the open vat, inches above the steaming brew. A heavy chain had been wrapped around his waist.

Lamar's mind continued to spin as he dropped his head back in the slop. "Ah, shee-yet."

He quickly filled in the missing pieces. The rumors must be true. Captain Billy, a big-time shrimper out of Bayou La Farouche, had bought out the Dryden Stills. Virgil Pettimore, that sumbitch, was behind it.

"So, golden boy, your still hand there, Junior, ratted you out. Said you'd be coming in the back way."

"Let's talk, Captain Billy," Lamar rallied. "There's a lotta stuff Virgil didn't tell you."

"You somethin'," said Billy. "You come up here to my still, toting them guns like some badass warrior. No, Mister. Moonshine, you ain't no warrior," he paused, searching for a cutting remark. "You be a vulture, pecking around in the garbage, feedin' on the dead and the dyin'."

Lamar forced a smile. If this was it, if this was how he would go out, he was damned if he was going quietly. "Well, Captain Billy, if you're in the garbage business…you damn sure need a vulture."

Billy shrugged indifferently and nodded to his boys. In a flash, they were on him. After a brief tussle, he hung next to Junior inches above the steaming brew. The Cajuns danced around the vat and broke into a verse of Jambalaya:

"Jambalaya, a-crawfish pie and-a fillet gumbo
Cause tonight I'm gonna see my machez a mio
Pick guitar, fill fruit jar, and be gay-oh
Son of a gun, we'll have big fun on the bayou."

Billy leaned over the vat and grinned. "Now what you think Mister. Moonshine? Now you be gay-oh?"

With the spunk of a dying man, Lamar shot back, "Okay, okay, so maybe I can't hurt you. But I can damn sure help you; I got a lotta of connections."

"C'est la vie," Billy jested as he nodded to his boys. Lamar disappeared into the hot mash.

He spit and coughed as he was hoisted up, yet he was pleasantly light-headed. What was it? He'd started as a still hand and knew the alcohol content of fermented mash could get up to 15 percent, and then…and then, it all came back to him…and then it gets stronger and stronger as it is distilled. He inhaled deeply. *Maybe this is how dying goes?*

"Connections!" Billy revved up. "I got more connections than Ma Bell. I run the Cajun mafia, and I'm well connected with the Dixie mafia, not to mention that I'm old friends with the governor of Alabama. No, Mister. Moonshine, I don't need much help from you."

Lamar gave it his final shot. "It ain't the big shots and high rollers that'll get you dead around here, it's the po' folks. And most of 'em are beholden to Mr. Alta Dryden."

Billy nodded to the cone heads, and Lamar disappeared again. When they yanked him up, his forehead and cheeks had started to blister and peel. Somehow the alcohol had neutralized the pain. He snorted, spit, and then licked his lips. "Lemme say a final word 'bout Alta."

Lamar jackknifed at the waist, pulled his head and shoulders up to his hips, and smiled. "Alta Dryden has been a savior to this community. When times are bad, he's there to pick you up; if you're doin' hard time in prison, he's there to help your family; if there's a school that needs building or a church that needs a new roof, he's there. People in these parts adore Alta, and they're beholden."

Lamar strained to hold the jackknife; inhaled deeply, knowing it was probably his last; and said, "Now when an outsider comes around here, a different kinda fella, say a big, fat-ass Cajun fella, then people say, 'Who he? He ain't much. He ain't our'n.'"

Gasping and choking, he tumbled to the bottom of the vat. His lungs filled with hot mash; his legs were caught up in the rope. The chains anchored him to the bottom. It was over. He waited for the light show, for his life to pass before him.

Nothing. Well, damnation!

Then came a banging on the vat. Then, as he bid farewell to his hound and his Harley, a shock wave pulsed through the mash, a streak of light shone through the side of the tank. Then more banging and another streak of light, the blade of an ax.

CHAPTER 9

Atlanta Federal Prison, Days Later

———

THE CLANG OF METAL ON metal echoed down the cellblock, as guards made their morning rounds. Alta peered through the half-light of his cell, feeling the clutches of confinement. Without thinking, he reached for his pills but then pulled back. Today was leaving day. He jumped up and let fly, "Yeeeeeeeehaaaaaaaaw! I'm free!"

Chanting like a schoolboy, he hopped around his cell. "Gettin' ready, I'm in charge, leave the whiskey with the Sarge. Startin' over, startin' now, only what de Lawd allows. Livin' right and livin' free, headin' home to sweet Shel-by."

A familiar voice shouted down the cell block, "Hey, boss man, you freed-up?"

"That you, Fa-row?"

"Speakin'."

"I'm freed-up. Say, Fa-row."

"Speakin'."

"You're the boss now. I'm out."

"I'll take care of business."

"And Fa-row, if you don't mind, work with the Sarge and Raylee?"

"Don't you worry, Mr. Alta, don't you worry. And…so long."

"So long, friend."

53

A rogue breeze whistled through the cell as the morning light played down the hall. The roar of a departing plane at Hartsfield Airport reminded Alta of the simple joy of unrestricted movement, coming and going as you please, heading out with a clear destination or just wandering, floatin', free. He chuckled to himself. The light and the breeze had probably been happening all along—tricky, this business of perception. After a final session with Doc Dorothy, he'd meet with the warden, and then he was out the door.

Alta's civilian clothes had arrived sometime during the night. A finely pressed black suit, a starched shirt, and a tie now hung on the cell door. Neatly folded socks lay across polished black shoes on the floor. Alta smiled.

Steppin' out.

As he packed his few possessions, he paused to admire the pictures of Lloyd, Shelby, and Mandy. He carefully set Shelby's picture on his lap. Surely, she'd heard he'd sold off his liquor business. Surely, she'd heard he gone legit. Surely, she'd join Virgil for the ride home.

As he emerged from his cell, he looked every inch the corporate executive heading for the boardroom. Guards cuffed him and escorted him to the psych ward. His last walk down cell block B was a gauntlet of taunts and cheers. Raylee proclaimed him saved. Then the chant began, "Hey boss man, hey boss man, way too late, way too late for going straight, just as well, just as well you burn in hell, you burn in hell."

———

Doctor Dorothy Epstein, the prison psychologist, was ready and waiting as Alta was escorted into the room. Not more than five feet tall, Dr. Epstein marched behind her desk in a starched white coat. Born in Flatbush, New York, she received her doctorate at Columbia and interned at Bellevue hospital before heading to Atlanta to save the South.

In a heavy New York accent she said, "Congratulations Alta, your record shows you are a great big success at crime and a great big failure at life. Do you have any idea why you've spent most of your life locked in a cage?"

Alta knew there was no correct answer. Nevertheless, on this auspicious day, he foolishly tried to brighten his farewell. "Well, them federal agents are gettin' younger and faster, and I'm gettin' older and slower."

"That's so damn you. When a situation gets uncomfortable, do you ever stop and ask yourself why? Noooo, you don't. You either avoid it with that Dixie-peach blather, or you attack with a velvet glove, smooth and cunning. That's the book on you."

"Sorry, Miss Dorothy. I'm tryin' to change, but I'm gonna need your help."

"My help? Fuhgeddaboudit! Help your own damn self."

Alta's head snapped back. "What was that?"

"I said, for-get-about-it, stupid!" she fumed as she stomped back and forth, stretching out her arms as if invoking Doctor Freud himself. "You cannot survive this wild-ass lifestyle. If you don't get shot, you're gonna drop dead from a heart attack. Only you can understand the demons running around in your head. Only you can harness your better angels. So, big boy, how about *you* taking re-spon-si-bil-it-y for *yourself*?"

Alta nodded contritely, afraid to even blink at the New York spitfire.

Of course she was right. Sure, he needed to become more in-tro-spec-tive. He'd come to hated that word. He was awful at it. Nobody from the piney woods of West Georgia talked that away. He inhaled deeply and pursed his lips. "OK, all right, sweet Jesus, I surrender. I was jest tryin' to be pleasant. I'm gonna miss you."

Dorothy came around her desk and extended her hand. "And you better be good to Shelby. Bless her. Somehow she finds you worth saving. You'll need her, Alta; you'll need her."

Alta's last stop was at the Warden's Office who warned. "Alta, you can't go home and start over."

Alta nodded and thought. *But, how can I make things right and stay out of sight?*

Just before noon, Virgil pulled into the parking lot in a fully loaded 1939 Ford Coupe, the very car driven by Lloyd Seay of NASCAR fame. He spun brodies in the gravel lot and then skidded to a stop below the main cellblock. Hell, it was a big day. Alta was getting out of prison. He took a sip of whiskey and got out, leaving the car running. The souped-up coupe had a V8 engine with an oversized camshaft that loped along at over six hundred revolutions per minute, a snarling tiger ready to pounce.

In the past, Alta and Virgil had sponsored their best whiskey haulers at the Dixie Speedway. Virgil secretly felt the time was right to build a dirt track in West Georgia. Surely Alta would agree. He raised the hood and went to work with a rag, polishing the chrome air filters that sat proudly on top of triple Stromberg 97 carbs. Grinning broadly, he toyed with the idle adjustment, trying to synchronize the carburetors—and wake every sleeping dog in the county. The engine screamed, reverberating across the prison yard and down every cellblock, followed by the sweet mellow wrap-wrap-wrap of the glass pack mufflers. He grinned up at the warden's window, as he shut her down. Everyone in the joint knew he'd arrived. To cap it off, he bellowed, "Yeeeeeeeehaaaaaaaaw!"

———

All trimmed and tucked, Alta strolled proudly across the rotunda in a three-piece suit escorted by armed guards. If you didn't notice the cuffed hands behind his back, you'd have thought he was the warden on a tour. Two guards un-cuffed him and released him into the waiting area by the front door.

Sergeant Doyle arrived from nowhere and extended his hand. "Good luck, Alta, good luck."

Alta nodded. "Thanks, Sarge." He paused, looked around and whispered, "You're in charge. Work with Fa-row and Raylee, will you? I'm out of the whiskey business."

Doyle nodded and patted his sidearm.

"Thanks, Sarge."

"And Alta, if you don't mind, stop by the cemetery on your way home."

"I will."

Shaking like a fly in a web, Alta waited near the prison entrance, almost a free man.

————

Several minutes later Virgil burst in. They jostled like circus bears as they walked away from the prison.

Virgil pulled out the Mason jar. "Thought you might be thirsty."

Alta smiled broadly. "Maybe later."

He fingered the pills in his pocket as they headed for the parking lot. Later, there'd be a gathering at the family home place along the Tallapoosa River. He'd be seeing the twins and his old buddies. He missed them all. But he longed for Shelby, a good wife and mother, big-hearted, high-minded, better than he deserved.

Virgil beamed as they got to the parking lot. "I got a little surprise for you. See the black car over yonder?"

Alta scanned the parking lot. "I'll be tarred," he bellowed. "That's Lloyd Seay's coupe! Where the hell did you get it?"

"I rented it for the day, from the family up in Dawsonville. Cost me a bundle. Welcome home!"

"The hell—you stole it."

Alta walked around the coupe, passing his hand over the number seven painted on the door. He tried to peer though the smoked glass windows. Hoping against hope there was more. Hoping Shelby was inside.

"Damn she's a beauty. You got any other surprises for me?"

"Well, ah…no, not right now," Virgil winced. He seemed to know the question was coming, but still wasn't ready for it.

Alta opened the door to an empty car.

"Sorry," he stammered. "Shelby couldn't make it."

"It's not that much of a drive."

"No sir, but she just wasn't up to it today. We'll see her soon enough. Come on, let's take a look at this beauty."

Virgil pulled him around to the front of the car.

"She really is sumthin',"Alta said, smiling.

He'd lived with the picture of Llody's coupe for years. Now before him was the real thing, with fully rounded fenders and menacing headlights. The hood was a knife-edge at the front that widened to a sleek V shape. Louvers, trimmed in chrome, extended back down the sides, helping the beast to breathe.

Virgil snickered like a schoolboy as he popped open the hood. "She's got a big V8 engine with more horsepower and stability than any whiskey car of its day. Of course, they added extra carburetors, heavy tires, and stronger suspension."

Alta nodded. "It made a lot of sense, ole Lloyd takin' her to the speedway."

"While we're talkin' speedways, you need to think about building one in West Georgia."

Alta was delighted but couldn't stay focused. "Say, when's this homecomin' starting?"

"About three. We got plenty of time."

"You know, I spent three years in prison this time, and beyond seein' Shelby, there's just one other thing I'm achin' to see."

"You name it, boss."

"Y' know Great-Grandpa Dryden fought and died in the Civil War, and I'd like to visit the Oakland Cemetery. It's right up the road."

"He's buried there, is he?"

"Yeah…somewhere."

Virgil eased out of the prison parking lot and geared down coming up to the first light, pleased with the full-throated roar of the glass packs. When the light changed, he hammered it, laying a patch in first gear.

Everyone recognized the car. Young hot-rodders and aging bootleggers alike smiled and waved.

Virgil chattered on. "It's the power-to-weight ratio that makes her fly. Lloyd won him races at Lakewood and Daytona in this car. Started his career runnin' whiskey down from Dawsonville."

"It's a pity," Alta scowled, "his cousin shot him dead over a moonshine bill."

"It's more than a pity, it's a damn shame."

"Pull over at the brick archway. That's the entrance to the cemetery…and bring your camera."

Virgil, hoping to do more cruising, frowned as he shut down the coupe. Alta walked him down to the Confederate Obelisk. "It's made of Stone Mountain granite. This whole section marks the graves of thirty-nine hundred confederate soldiers, all with proper headstones."

Alta wandered over to his favorite memorial, the Lion of the Confederacy, a massive piece of North Georgia marble depicting a lion resting its head on the confederate flag and guarding the field below.

"Three thousand more confederate soldiers lie in unmarked graves in this field. The lion keeps an eye on them. Most of these boys died in the Battle of Atlanta. Great-Grandpa is out there somewhere. God bless 'em all."

Alta dropped to his knee and spent several minutes praying. He glanced over at Virgil who seemed overwhelmed with emotion. "You all right, Virgil?"

Virgil wiped away tears. "Yeah, I'm fine. It's just that we had family in the war as well, and we never knew where they were buried."

"You're not alone, Virgil. And you never know, they may be right out there below the Lion."

———

They walked north up the ridge, just below the Bell Tower.

"See that flat piece of a land on up there?" Alta pointed.

"Yes sir."

"A two-story farmhouse stood there during the Civil War. It was the headquarters of the confederate commander John Bell Hood during the Battle of Atlanta."

Virgil fidgeted; he'd lost interest in the Civil War and was raring to drive Lloyd's coupe.

"Y'see, for the South, there weren't many bright spots in the war, but this was one of 'em."

"I believe we lost the Battle of Atlanta, and I'm almost certain we lost the war."

Virgil's sarcasm didn't deter Alta. "So, here comes W. T. Sherman and thousands of blue bellies. And what does General John Bell Hood do?"

"I don't recall."

"Well, right down there below us, he blows up the Atlanta Rolling Mill and eighty-one cars of confederate ammunition."

"John Bell Hood, was it? I like the man. But then, as I recall, W. T. set everything ablaze."

"More or less. So that was the old South, one hundred and ten years ago. With all its pain and suffering, it's still our tradition, and I believe we got to honor the good parts."

Alta scanned the cemetery, then turned on his heels and shouted, "Now let's take a look at the Atlanta skyline…the New South. I've done my homework on this."

"I understand," Virgil said and shrugged. "You've had some time on your hands."

They moved to the highest point on the cemetery ridge, 125 feet above downtown Atlanta.

"Spread out below us are the symbols of power," Alta proclaimed in a raspy drawl. "We'll start with the state capitol with its magnificent golden dome."

Virgil nodded patiently. "So, how high is it?"

"Glad you asked. At two hundred eighty-seven feet, it is respectfully one foot lower than the national capitol. And as you can see, it's surrounded by federal buildings keeping a watchful eye on things. All of this big government, of course, is dwarfed by corporate skyscrapers. One Park Tower, the Equitable Building. But Two Peachtree Building wins the prize, standing five hundred sixty-five feet high. So yes, the South has risen from the ashes. The phoenix flies again."

Virgil jingled the keys of the coupe. "It's good to be out of prison, ain't it?"

"Yeeeeeeeehaaaaaaaaw!"

———

Virgil pulled onto I-75 North and opened up the V8.

Alta's head snapped back as the speedometer jumped from sixty to ninety in seconds.

"Nice, the way she takes a curve."

Alta closed his eyes and tried to recall the roads he'd run as a boy, hauling whiskey down from Dawsonville. "Say, Virgil, we got time for cruisin'?"

Virgil goosed the pedal with a grin. "I planned on cruisin'."

"How 'bout we cruise up State Route 9?"

"Cruise up Thunder Road! That's what we'll do!" Virgil broke out singing, "Thunder, Thunder, Thunder Road."

A grin crossed Alta's face as boyhood memories filled his head.

Back then, it was just a red dirt road, snakin' down from Dawsonville. Tall pines, a country store, a roadside garage…peaceful, real peaceful. Come nightfall, and the crickets got to chirpin' and the tree frogs got to croakin'…and there was fine night music. Then, the moon went behind the clouds and around the bend came the roarin' thunder of bootleggers racin' down the road and the feds lurkin' in the darkness…and the chase…and the getaway. Yes sir, them were the days.

"You're grinnin', Alta. Hang on, and I'll give you a bootlegger's turn."

Virgil hammered the pedal and hit ninety in a flash. "So there I was, three in the mornin', racin' down Thunder Road with a trunk load of likker, and I see a roadblock ahead. Luck was with me, I had just passed a secret cutoff, my only getaway. A perfect bootlegger's turn was called for."

Virgil found a steep stretch of road heading north. The high side full of pines and laurels, the low side a cliff with a grand view of South Georgia. He heaved back on the hand brake and cut the wheel to the left. Tires screeched as the tail end of Lloyd's coupe swung violently sideways. Midway around the turn, they skidded toward the cliff. Alta jammed his feet against the floor-board, closed his eyes, and grinned through it all. As they teetered on the edge, Virgil cranked the wheel an inch or so harder to the left, released the handbrake, and straightened out the tires. The tail end snapped back onto the blacktop. Virgil roared with laughter as he shifted into low and headed south.

"Thunder, Thunder, Thunder Road," he sang.

Alta gasped, "You got a lot of boy in you, Virgil."

———

After rounding the Cummings Courthouse, they headed home.

"How's she lookin'?" Alta asked.

"What's that?"

Alta grimaced. "I said, how's she lookin'?"

"Shelby? Not good."

They drove on in silence. As they passed through Villa Rica, Virgil glanced over at Alta. "So, what were the warden's parting words?"

"Alta shrugged. "He said 'going home is not the best place to start over'."

"Hmm? So, why you goin' home?"

"Cause I got sumthin' to prove, stupid."

Virgil shrunk back in silence, and they cruised along Highway 78. As they came into Bremen, Alta's face lit up. "Say, Virgil."

"Yeah, boss."

"You mind stoppin' for a bit at the depot?"

"No, but make it quick."

Alta jumped out as Virgil pulled next to the train platform. "This'll only take a minute."

Alta hurried over and sat on a park bench, facing the tracks. His eyes glazed over, as he drifted back in time. In the early '30s when he and his brother Fred were kids, Grandpa Dryden had taken them to the Bremen train depot on Saturday mornings. They watched the train come and go as Grandpa quizzed them. He'd been a conductor for the Georgia Pacific Line and was an expert on trains, train songs, and all things having to do with local transportation.

———

As he and Fred sat on the bench watching the train pull into the station, Grandpa burst into song:

Oh listen to the jingle
The rumble and the roar
As she glides along the woodlands
Through the hills and by the shore

Fred and Alta grinned as Grandpa sang and went into his train quiz. "So, Fred, do you know how this train line was first used?"

"Shucks, that's easy. It was called Old Alabama Road, a stagecoach line for transporting settlers."

A sly smile crossed Alta's face. He felt he was better at trains and transportation than his brother. "Fred left some stuff out," Alta chided and strutted in front of Grandpa and Fred. "Long before Old Alabama Road was a stagecoach line, it was an Indian trail. And then, in 1828, gold was discovered in Georgia. Seems the Tallapoosa River had been washing gold nuggets down the Appalachian Mountains forever. Tallapoosa was said to mean 'golden water' in the Creek language."

Grandpa pulled on his chin. "You ain't showin' off there, are you, Alta?"

"Oh, no sir, Alta said with a sigh. "But then in August of 1864, Sherman and his yellow-bellied army marched down Old Alabama Road to the siege of Atlanta. Alta shook his head, then suddenly brightened. "But you know, the road runs both ways. It don't seem to care."

Fred jumped up and pushed Alta aside. "By 1882 the Georgia-Pacific line ran east to west from Atlanta through Bremen to Birmingham," Fred said, smiling with pride.

Grandpa gushed. "That's real good Fred. You boys know your roads and rails."

Just then the station master hurried out of the depot and shouted, "The Birmingham train is coming down the track."

They all cheered and broke into song:

Well she came down from Birmingham one cold December day
As she pulled into the station you could hear all the people say
She's from Tennessee she's long and she's tall
She come down from Birmingham on the Wabash Cannonball.

———

"Come on, Alta, we're gonna be late," Virgil hollered from the front fender of Lloyd Seay's Ford Coupe.

As they continued west on 78, Alta noticed the pipeline easement that ran along the highway. His eyes lit up. Oh yeah! He knew a thing or two about the gas pipeline. For the first time in December 1964, the Plantation Pipeline Company transported 636,553 barrels of fuel from the Gulf Coast of Texas across the heartland of the South and on up to Baltimore, Maryland. At the time, it was the largest single, privately financed construction project in the U.S.

Big oil, Alta chuckled to himself, mighty big oil, mighty "big pockets" and mighty big profits. And yet, "small pockets," he reckoned, could make a decent profit as well. Virgil looked over at Alta. "You're grinnin' again, boss. It's good to have you back."

Alta nodded. "It's good to be back. Three years in the pokey, and lots of change out here. Y'know I'm goin' straight. Jest lookin' for legal deals nowadays."

Virgil smiled impishly. "Legal deals. I like the sound of it. And if you're likin' this car, you're gonna love your own motor speedway out here in West Georgia."

"Yeah? We'll see. Maybe."

Virgil turned off Route 78 and headed south toward the Interstate. "Talkin' about speed, let me show you a new section of I-20."

Alta had read about the construction but had never seen it. Most of it had opened in the last few years. It stretched between Texas and South Carolina, running across Louisiana, Mississippi, Alabama, and Georgia. Virgil drove to the exit near Tallapoosa, and they gazed at the new construction. The six-lane freeway throbbed with long-haul trucks and locals heading east and west.

"Woo-wee! What we got here?" Alta hollered, yet his heart sank at the same time. In spite of the opportunities, the Interstate meant money leavin' town.

"It's a gawd-damn bonanza," Virgil howled. "Every exit's like this: gas stations, motels, fast-food joints, and the strip malls are on the way. Most of 'em are thievin' Yankee bastards."

"Y'know, I get it. The big boys are making money; why not us?"

"It's our time, ain't it?"

"You know, Virgil, I been thinkin' about two or three OTASCO stores, auto parts and such. There could be some nice niches between country stores and the big-box boys."

"Where would you'd put 'em?"

Alta shook his head impatiently. "Hell, I don't know. I don't know. Let's get on home. I'm worried about Shelby."

CHAPTER 10

Dryden Home Place, Tallapoosa, Same Day

IT WAS EARLY AFTERNOON WHEN Virgil turned onto the red dirt road that led to the Dryden place. Alta fiddled nervously with his glasses. They came to a stop at a heavily wooded area near Walker Creek, the first of two locked gates. The farm, what there was of it, lay fallow—a good place to hunt and get away. Alta's family, Shelby and the twins, lived on Broad Street in town. That was home. This place was their retreat.

As Alta unlocked the gate, the light bar on a parked police car flashed red. Police Chief Sonny Hoyt, a wide load in a blue uniform, lumbered down to the gate. He'd put Alta away several times and was itching to catch him on a big bust—just the thing to push his career ahead.

Sonny extended his hand. "Welcome home, old-timer."

Without missing a beat, Alta shook hands. "Well, lookie here, Chief Hoyt, awful nice of you to drop by. Come on in and have yourself some ribs."

"Another time, Mr. Alta, another time. Just wanted to let you know I'm out and about, keeping the free world safe."

"I'll sure give you a call if I'm in any danger."

"And I'll sure enough keep an eye out for you."

"You do that, Sonny."

Sonny headed for his car, turned back, and smiled. "And by the way, if I was gonna get out of the whiskey business, I damn sure wouldn't come roarin' back into town in some famous bootlegger's car."

Virgil smiled sheepishly. "Sorry, boss. I never thought of it that way."

In another mile, they reached the farmhouse. Only twenty-three acres of the original farm were still in the family. Some was good bottomland. Most of it was rolling hills and woodlands covered with loblolly pines and scrub oak. The Tallapoosa River meandered through the southeast corner.

In the early days, sections of flatland had been cleared for cotton and always a patch of corn and a field of rye. It was all a tangle these days. However, if you knew where to look, an ancient water-powered tub mill could be found up Walker Creek. Corn and rye had been ground there for years, both for flour and moonshine. When the creek was running high, two or three bushels of corn could be ground in a day.

Virgil slowed to a stop at the second gate, just below the farmhouse.

Alta braced his hands against the dashboard and inhaled deeply. "Virgil, you sure I'm out of the whiskey business?"

"Gawddamn it, Alta, I told you. I got a bag of money in the trunk, eighty thousand dollars. The stills and all are now in the hands of Billy Boudreaux, that voodoo pile of shee-yet from Thibodaux."

Alta frowned, "They better be...and what about the tapping?"

"Gotta contract on a land swap; a fella from Villa Rica wants in on the deal. I'm doin' a title search on the land," Virgil lied. "Should go through next week. You're clean, boss, you're clean."

The woodlands opened up as they pulled through the gate. Down below, withered corn stalks swayed in the breeze. A neglected farmhouse with a wraparound porch angled to the right. Rebel flags hung from the railings. The sweet smell of barbecued ribs drifted down the hill.

A gathering of old friends, righteous citizens, and co-conspirators milled about the yard, enjoying the ribs and sweet tea. A string band struck up an improvised welcome home song as Alta appeared down at the gate. Everyone joined in.

Hello Howdy, let's get rowdy
Alta's back to lead the pack
Three years in a prison cell

Now he's out and lookin' swell
So let's all sing and hoot and holler
Grab a jar and have a swaller
Oh, there's been hard times
Since you been gone
Too much money leavin' town
We ain't lookin' fer no char-ity
Just a helping of pros-perity

Alta smiled broadly. "Well, well, how 'bout that? Let's git on up there."

"Hold on there, boss. Shelby says the two of you need to talk. Wait here, I'll get her."

Alta stepped out. Virgil rumbled up the road in the famous coupe, which immediately snapped the heads of old men and young boys alike.

———

Bracing heavily on a cane, Shelby hobbled carefully down the hill. A black wig shifted from side to side as she approached. Her face was gaunt, her expression stern. In the last two months, she'd begun chemotherapy treatments. Shelby stopped short, struggled to clear her throat, and then gasped, "Well, hello stranger."

Alta shifted awkwardly. Showing emotion was a big mistake in prison. Shelby had been the rock he leaned on: trim, well-dressed, fashionable. Today she wore a frayed flannel robe, and her lipstick wandered.

He nodded politely, masking his shock.

"Good lord, Shelby, I thought you were…were doin' better."

She stood her ground, pinching a smile. "Well, it's back. I'm puttin' things in order."

"You'll see, I've changed," he said, extending his hands openly. "What kin I do for you?"

"Just get yourself straight and come by now and again."

"I sold my liquor business—I'm out."

Shelby tried to laugh and gave up. "It took you what, a total of nine years in prison to figure that one out?"

"And I'm gettin' out of the rest of it. Goin' straight. You'll see, I promise."

"Do tell, and if promises were diamonds, I'd be Liz-a-beth Taylor."

"You'll see."

"Go on, get up there and say hello to your friends. I cleaned out your things at home, dumped them up there at the farmhouse." Leaning heavily on her cane, she paused, caught her breath, and rasped on, "Alta, you ain't coming home with me; you ain't welcome no more. I got all I can do to make it through the day. Now go on, git."

Alta froze, crushed by the rejection. They stared at each other for the longest time.

"Alta," Shelby fumed, "You got to git to be gone."

She turned and hobbled back up the road. Jack, one of their twin sons, helped her into the long black Buick, and they drove off. The gathering fell silent as the car disappeared. No one missed the drama.

Alta steadied himself on a fence post. For all those years in prison, he had hoped beyond hope that his going straight would trigger a change, a renewal, the beginning of a better life with Shelby. His hopes were now shattered like a Mason jar on a hard rock. His heart raced full throttle as he fingered the vial of nitroglycerin pills in his pocket. Inhaling deeply, he tried to calm himself; then he placed a pill under his tongue. Some homecoming.

The band attempted another verse and folded. Women scurried into small coveys and chatted; most sided with Shelby. Men huddled around the Ford Coupe as Virgil rapped the twin Stromberg carburetors. Despite the awkwardness, no one was leaving, not without paying their respects to Alta. They were drawn to him like a fish to a lure. In one way or another, they were all beholden. He made his way through the gathering, shaking hands and reconnecting.

Before they departed, Alta turned to Virgil and sighed. "We need to get that money down in the root cellar. How about you pull Lloyd's Coupe to the back of the house?" Alta unlocked the cellar door, and the two men disappeared down a ladder. A rusted-out, refrigerator stood in the corner of the cellar, bound in tow chains. Alta spun the combination lock and pulled the refrigerator door open.

"Virgil, how about you count the cash?"

Virgil emptied the bag on a workbench. "It's all in hundreds."

Alta's eyes flashed as he booted-up his brain. "Eighty thousand in hundreds."

Rolls of bills were crammed on every shelf.

"I guess we should be drawing interest on this, but one way or another, Uncle Sam would get wind of it."

Alta kept two of the rolls and shoved the rest into the vegetable drawer. He handed one to Virgil. "Here you go, buddy; take it. Thanks for all your help."

"You ain't worried that someone will rob you?"

"The twins got more guns than an armory upstairs. No, I ain't worried; I got a couple more fridges like this stashed around the county." Alta leaned up against the ladder and then slumped on a rung. "Say, Virgil, 'member how we was talkin' about buyin' an OTASCO store or two?"

"Sure enough; we'll take it up tomorrow."

"No, let's put it on hold. I ain't doin' nothin' til I get Shelby well."

Virgil shuffled awkwardly back and forth. "Sorry I didn't tell you about her condition. She made me promise."

"I understand. I guess I'm goin' to live here for now. You take care of things for a bit. And unhitch me from that damn tapping business. Understood?"

"You bet." Virgil nodded, looking a little taken a back.

"I got to care for Shelby, and I got some thinkin' to do."

"You're doin' the right thing; I'll take care of things." Virgil hesitated. "Say, Alta, Mandy Tate, Lamar's ex, is down at the boathouse. She came the back way."

Both flattered and annoyed, Alta rolled his eyes. "I don't think so, Virgil; another time."

"She didn't come to visit. She's real upset."

Alta hesitated, shook his head from side to side, and headed for the river.

Mandy sat on a bench behind the boathouse, smoking nervously. She'd come directly from the hospital, still wearing her uniform. Nearing forty, she was still a beautiful woman with natural black hair turning gray. She stood up as Alta appeared, wiping away mascara that ran down her cheek. They hugged briefly.

"Hey, old friend," Mandy said as she stepped back. "Not much of a homecoming?"

"Not so much, no. You been crying?"

"Yeah, well, I'm an emotional girl."

"You're a fine woman."

"Let's leave that one alone. I wanted to thank you for all you've done for me. I couldn't have made it without you."

"I hear Lamar's runnin' wild."

"We've split for good. Look, Alta, I know you got a score to settle with him, but…"

"But?"

"But he's pretty beat up now. Them Cajun boys damn near killed him. Limped into the ER with his face all messed up, patches of skull hair was burnt off and third-degree burns on his head. I'd keep an eye on your boy Virgil as well; not sure what he's up to these days."

Alta's jaw dropped. This was new information. "I'll keep it in mind."

"There's more. Lamar…" Mandy hesitated. "Lamar's out to kill you and Virgil. Says you put Billy Boudreaux on him."

"Was he drinkin'?"

"Of course."

Mandy ground out her cigarette and tossed her head back with a smile. "You take care of Shelby, you hear? See you around."

Alta was fuming as he walked back to the house. Three shots rang out— pop, pop, pop—followed by another three-shot volley. Virgil was sitting in a rocking chair at the back of the porch, reloading his .38 pistol as Alta arrived. Some tin cans were on the fence post; some were on the ground.

"Put that damn thing away," Alta growled.

Virgil knew he was in trouble but wouldn't shut up. "Gotta stay battle ready!"

"You know anything about Lamar gettin' smacked up by them Cajun boys?"

"I didn't tell 'em to smack him up," he sputtered. "Hell, I didn't know Lamar would be at the still when they came."

Alta glared at Virgil. "You made a mess out of somethin' that should've been handled smoothly. He was at the still because outsiders were on the property. That's the way it's supposed to work."

"Come on, Alta, they bought the business. They can do whatever they damn well please. We got the money. It's clean."

"With Lamar, we got an angry, wounded snitch. You call that clean? He's got the motivation; all he needs is the opportunity. Don't you remember any of the crime theory we got in prison?"

Virgil pulled out his .38. "Well, I'll show you motivation. I'll take his ass out."

"The hell. Did you forget I just got outta jail today?" Alta rubbed his temples and thought.

"You got a meeting set up with Lamar for tomorrow, am I right?"

Virgil's jaw went slack as he slumped back in the rocking chair. In Alta's absence, he'd done as he pleased. "Meetin', yeah, tomorrow. I hear he's gunnin' fer us. May have to take the boy out first."

In a flash Alta grabbed Virgil's pistol and whipped it across his forehead. "Shut the hell up!"

Virgil screamed and crumpled to the ground. Blood gushed from a gash across his forehead.

Alta winced, knowing he had failed Doc Dorothy's self-awareness test. Pulling Virgil up on his feet, he shrugged. "Sorry, Virg. Clean up and go home."

Alta stomped into the house and wrote a note to Lamar. He wanted to delay their meeting until Shelby was better. He'd have his son Buck deliver the note. So, for now, Lamar was off the hook, but not for long.

He'd snitched and skimmed. That would never be forgotten, never be forgiven.

CHAPTER 11

Lucky Star Trailer Park, Bremen, Days Later

————

LAMAR BURIED HIS HEAD IN a pillow—too much whiskey, too little sleep. Freightliners from the Sewell Mill roared by, buffeting his single-wide. At three a.m., he staggered to the ice box, chugged a quart of milk, belched, farted, and collapsed on the couch, still mostly drunk. An acrylic painting of an African wild dog hung over the bed. It flashed into view and then disappeared as the lights of passing cars flared through the blinds. Sensing danger, the ears of the wild dog stood tall as blood dripped from its fangs. Caught in the grip of alcohol and his own robust fantasies, Lamar swung into full wild-dog mode.

He'd been pulling stitches and scabs from his head since Billy Boudreaux and the Cajun pranksters dunked him in the mash vat. An angry scar ran from his forehead and up across his skull. In ER, they'd shaved several inches around the ragged gash, leaving a white stripe down the middle of his golden locks. He wore a baseball cap when he went out these days.

As he dozed, a truck roared outside his trailer and slammed to a halt. Doors popped opened, men laughed, and someone shouted, "Hel-lo Lam-ar, dar-lin'!"

"Fuckin' lowlife!" Lamar growled.

Caaa-shearrrr-uuuo! Caaa-shearrrr-uuuo! Then…Thump! Thump! The shells rocked the trailer on its cinder-block frame and tore into the tin siding.

A spray of shot shattered a window and sent buckshot rattling around the trailer like gravel in a tin can.

Lamar hit the floor and rolled over to the window as a white Chevy pick-up roared off. It looked a lot like Virgil's pickup.

"Sumbitch!" Lamar hollered. *This ain't the way it's supposed to work. They whack me; then I whack them. They shoot at me; I shoot at them. Gawd damn, it was my turn to do the shootin'.*

Tiptoeing around glass splinters, Lamar swept up and taped a towel over the window. Alta was clearly back in town. He'd sicced the Cajun boys on him and wanted to meet with him at the ballpark today. Then there was Mandy. She was awful needy, and Alta was helpin' her out. That didn't sit well. Then Virgil, damn Virgil, shot up his trailer. *Oh yeah*, he'd meet with Alta, but he'd bring a posse and ambush 'em. He smiled as he drifted off.

He was at peace when he woke up an hour later. Gone were the doubts that haunted him; gone was the gallery of bad-boy masks he had worn over the years—the street fighter, the ass-bandit, the great pretender, the unfaithful husband, the whiskey runner, the snitch. Yet again, he was reborn as an avenging angel.

Still in his underwear, and only marginally sober, Lamar shuffled over to the kitchen table. Beyond hunting magazines, his main reading was a biology textbook from high school. He flipped to a dog-eared page that had first put him onto the concept of an apex predator. He read out loud, as if from scripture, "In an ecologically unstable relationship, where two species are competing for an ecosystem, the apex predator preys upon both and tends to create stability."

He pulled on his boots and paced the trailer like a trial lawyer in front of a jury box. "Ladies and gentleman, that's what we got here in West Georgia. We got carpetbaggers and rebels; we got moonshiners and feds. We got the lawful and the lawless all competing, all creating instability in the ecosystem. Now, we just can't have that. Can we?"

He flipped to another passage. "The African wild dog, a classic apex predator, combines the traits of a large carnivore with wolf-pack instinct that allows it to rival lions and hyenas."

He howled his best wild-dog howl: "Aaaaah-ooooooooooooooh… Aaaaah-ooooooooooooooh!…*AAAAAH-OOOOOOOOOOOH!*

As Lamar danced across the kitchen, his clock radio switched on. "Good mornin', good mornin', and a special good mornin' to all the still hands out there in moonshine land. This is Rhubarb Jones coming at you from WSKY up in Asheville, North Carolina. We're gonna kick it off with a little wake-up song by George Jones called "White Lightenin'."

Lamar danced around the trailer keeping time with the music. Makin' whiskey was great fun and runnin' from the law was even more fun. As he scooted by the trailer door, he noticed an envelope stuck underneath. Inside he found five one-hundred-dollar bills and a note from Alta.

Dear Lamar,

Please forgive me, but I have no mind for business these days. My wife, Shelby, is seriously ill and needs my full attention.

We do need to work things out. In due time, I want to do just that. I am sorry to hear that Mr. Boudreaux and his boys roughed you up. That was not my intention.

Please use the cash to put against any medical bills. Once Shelby is back on her feet, I will contact you and arrange a meeting.

Thank you for your patience in this matter.

Respectfully,

Sam Alta Dryden

Though Alta was probably sincere, Lamar felt he'd been out maneuvered. He was ready for combat. There was nothing noble about waiting. The ecosystem, after all, was rife with instability. *We need a killing.* Virgil needed to die; Alta needed to suffer.

"Kill the head, and the body will die, then we can all say good-bye."

Yet, he knew not to hurry Alta Dryden, not in Tallapoosa. He loaded and unloaded his latest weapon, a 357 Magnum pistol and conspired.

The rest of the morning, Lamar made detailed notes on a yellow pad, not really sure what he would do with them. He set down everything he could recall about Alta's vast moonshine operation that he sold off to Billy Boudreaux. He named names and locations of stills, stash houses, raw material suppliers, and whiskey wholesalers. Everything the feds would need to shut Billy Boy down. His lips curled into an evil grin as he repeated the words of the George Jones song, "Well the G-men, T-men, revenuers too, searchin' for the place where he made his brew."

Neatly folding the page of notes, he thought, *I say we give them revenuers a hand.*

Lamar had also heard that Alta and Virgil were up to something new, something big, really big. Again, he made detailed notes of the bits and pieces whispered about town. In spite of the outlaw's code of silence, little stayed secret very long in Tallapoosa. It was rumored that Virgil was leasing land along the Plantation Pipe line.

What the hell is that all about?

And last night at the High Hat Bar, over way too many drinks, Lonny James had mention that he was doing some welding on a pipe, or some such, for Virgil. Whatever it was, Alta had the brains and deep pockets. Virgil did the dirty work. He'd stay on it. If it was illegal, which it probably was, Lamar would have an edge. He carefully sealed the notes in an envelope. He'd keep them somewhere safe until he needed them—good ammo. He popped a cold beer and let go with his best wild dog howl:

"Aaaaah-ooooooooooooooh…Aaaaah-ooooooooooooooh!..
AAAAAH-OOOOOOOOOOOH!

Strangely, that night he dreamed a good dream. He became an upstanding citizen of Tallapoosa, president of the Kiwanis, a deacon of the church, a loving husband, a wonderful parent. He'd forsaken the good life but still dreamed of it. Part of him wanted it back.

CHAPTER 12

Dryden Home Place, Tallapoosa, A Month Later

———

ALTA PUSHED HIMSELF UP FROM bed at 7 a.m., searched for the first light of day, and then flopped back down. His mouth was dry and his head was pounding. Another night of bad dreams. A month had passed since he got out of prison. He'd closed himself off from everything but helping Shelby. Once a week to Carrolton for chemo, and the horrible sickness in between.

What had happened to his high-minded airs? He wasn't lonely, but he felt alone. There was a darkness about it, a fading away, a passing. Perhaps the darkness between the light? He'd always willed his way through every setback. Now he was empty. The fire burned low. The solitude was cleansing; the idleness was strange. Perhaps the rousing drumbeat of redemption would return? Yet, that wasn't all of it. He also felt better about himself, better than he had for a good long time. That was the lone flicker of light in a pall of darkness. But nothing, not even a legitimate business opportunity, nothing was more important than getting Shelby back on her feet. On her good days, she'd be off for a ride to the top of Mount Tally with one of her sons. On her bad days, she couldn't crawl out of bed.

At eight sharp Virgil rumbled up the hill in his '48 Chevy pickup, yelping and honking. He raced in circles, cutting a furrow in the green pasture, peeling up hunks of turf along the way, and then skidded sidelong on the gravel road to the porch. He flashed an evil grin and goosed the pedal. A red plume of dust drifted south. The fully loaded V8 shrieked wildly. Yard chickens squawked, flapped their wings, and tried to fly. Fang, Alta's hound set to howling and disappeared under the porch. Virgil considered this morning fanfare good fun. He'd gone into the Legion Post early, cleaned up, and brought his breakfast with him. He hustled up the porch steps, a bag of boiled peanuts in one hand and a can of Pabst Blue Ribbon in the other.

Surrounded by moldy fishing gear, Alta deliberately kept his head down as he tinkered with a tangled fishing reel. Virgil was running wild these day; Alta needed to set him straight.

"We gotta get a move on," Virgil bellowed as he stomped across the porch. "Lots to do…like gettin' out of the gas-tappin' business, like puttin' Lamar away for good, like gettin' into some le-git-i-mate business. Like you promised, Alta, like you promised."

Alta cleared a knot and unspooled the rest of the line. He looked off in the distance. "Gonna take Buck's kids fishin'."

He tied off the end of the line to the sprocket and reeled in the rest. "We limed the pond and stocked it with bluegill."

Virgil exhaled as he dropped onto a bench. "Where's your fire, Alta? Where'd it go?" His eyes narrowed as he set the beer and peanuts on the railing. "Everyone's waitin' for you to make a move. They don't want to cross you. They want to get onboard."

Alta shrugged. Though scarcely aware of it, he had mastered the art of grim silence in prison. His lips thinned and flickered from a smile to a frown. He carefully pieced the spinning reel together and attached it to a pole.

Virgil's shoulders sagged, as a flock of crows landed on the roof and edged closer. Suddenly they swooped on the boiled peanuts. Amid the screeching and flapping of wings, the bag burst and peanuts scattered.

Alta head snapped back with a grin. "Even them crows are onto you, Virgil."

Again and again, the crows swooped in tight sorties, stealing away the rest of the peanuts.

Grabbing a broom, Virgil swung wildly. "Sumbitches!"

Again it fell silent. Virgil settled back on the bench, breathing heavily. His beer was kicked off the porch and drained on the ground.

Alta knew swooping crows were not to be taken lightly. He believed it to be biblical payback, Armageddon of some sort. He composed a parable on the spot but then though better of it. Swooping was nothing to fool with.

Alta rose and paced back and forth. "I'm stuck here; there's some sadness in it, but I aim to do right by Shelby, and that," he turned to Virgil, "that feels good."

Virgil hunched forward without sitting up, lookin' as guilty as a runaway hound. "You're sure enough stuck. You ain't doin' right, and you ain't doin' wrong. Lately, you ain't doin' nothin'."

"I'm takin' my time, tryin' to put things together properly," Alta admitted. "And you, Mr. Pettimore, you sure as hell are stirrin' the shee-yet. I hear you shot some more holes in Lamar's trailer. How we gonna do right with you and your violence? Even I know, violence begets violence."

Virgil perked up. "No, no, no. Violence is like gasoline; it spreads around your enemy's home…you light it off, and your problems go up in smoke."

Alta turned his palms to the sky and balanced them like a scale. "You burn a man's home? He burns yours? You're both homeless."

Alta took his time threading the fishing line through the eyelets of the pole. The silence got to Virgil, who slumped against the banister as his legs started pumping. Tying a practice plug to the line, Alta aimed at the front door and cast. Plunk! The plug hit the door and dropped to the deck. Thud!

"Well…how 'bout that?"

The crows circled back on cleanup patrol, saw no more peanuts, and returned to their roost.

Alta knew Virgil responded poorly to prodding and preaching, yet he pushed on, "Lemme be clear. There's a difference between anger and fear. When you're angry, you get violent. That's you're thing. You seem to enjoy it. Then that violence begets more violence. That's my point."

"You already said that. I ain't buyin' it."

Alta remained grim-faced. "Okay, here goes; lemme get down to your level. Here's the point you're missin'; when you're angry, you ain't thinkin', you're emotional, and that's your problem."

Virgil shrugged and rolled his eyes.

Alta shook his head. "I'm gonna break it down some more. So, this guy's got you down, and he's stompin' on you. What's gonna stop him?"

"I'd shoot the bastard."

"No, no, he's got your gun. What's stoppin' him?"

"Nothin'. If I was him, I'd shot me."

"And you'd be dead, stupid. Now, what if you'd put a sharp rock in his shoe, so every time he stomped on you, a pain shot up his backside? Y'see, fear's a lot different than anger. Fear's a good thing. Anger makes you charge ahead; fear makes you stop and think."

Virgil scratched his head. "How'd you get the rock in his shoe?"

Alta cast the plug at the door and grinned. *Plunk! Thud!*

"You seeVirgil, *if* someone threatens you, *then* you tell'um what you're gonna do in return. It's a simple *if-then proposition*. That there is puttin' the rock in their shoe."

Virgil shrugged and tied his bootstrings tight.

Alta looked up. "Now, Virgil, I'd like to move on to the gas-tappin' business. The last time we talked, you said you had a land swap arranged with a fella from Villa Rica. I get the land, he gets the tappin' business. How's that goin'?"

Virgil shrugged. "Like I said, the title search is underway. We should be hearing somethin' any day now. If you're happy with the deal, you sign the papers, and you're free and clear and an honest man."

Alta frowned. "Would you say we're a week away?"

"You never know, but that sounds about right."

"Well, let's go back to the *if-then* business. *If* this don't go through pretty soon, *then* you and I ain't doin' no honest business together."

Virgil frowned. "You put a rock in my shoe, right?"

"You got it. No anger, no violence; it's all in your hands. You decide what you want to do. Now git."

Virgil shuffled off, not sure what had hit him. Alta headed for the kitchen, where he fried up some bacon and eggs and put on a fresh pot of coffee. Each day, after breakfast, he took long walks about the home place, bushwhacking through overgrown trails. Then he was off to care for Shelby. He cooked, cleaned, and sat quietly beside her as she slept. Around five in the afternoon, he'd say his goodbyes and head back to the farm and in for the night. He was strangely at peace with his monastic life. His heart had throttled back. He hadn't taken a pill in weeks.

———————

That afternoon, when he got back to the home place, his mailbox was full. Everyone in Tallapoosa, it seemed, wanted to meet with him. Everyone had a get-rich scheme that needed his backing. You'd think he'd won the lottery. At the bottom of the pile, he found a small pink envelope from Shelby. So like her—they visited daily, yet she chose to deliver a note. She wanted to meet him at the Mount Zion Baptist Church at five thirty.

He arrived at the church early and waited peacefully on a bench outside. His hands formed a steeple; his thumbs chased each other in circles. He breathed slowly and deeply: three beats in, three beats out, just like Doctor Dorothy had taught him in prison. He smiled.

Sure enough, he'd changed, *a repentant moonshiner doing yoga.*

The Buick rolled up at five thirty. Jack, their son, was driving. Shelby sat rigidly in the backseat behind a long black veil. Rolling down the window, she whispered faintly, "Hello, Alta."

Alta squinted as he looked inside. "Hello, Shelby, hello, Jack."

"Get in, stranger."

Jack got out and strolled over to the cemetery for a smoke as Alta stepped inside. He winced slightly as Shelby pulled up the veil. Though he saw her daily, he hadn't notice how frail she'd become. Her words came slowly and painfully.

"I've been doin' some hard thinkin'…here of late…and I believe we need to talk," she hissed in a dry, raspy voice.

"Well yes, of course, you look…ah…" Alta searched for the right word. "You look rested."

She smiled grimly. She seemed to enjoy his discomfort. "Yes, I guess I'm rested…I hear you're holed up at the home place…like a damn hermit. Well, let me tell you…"

"Shelby, just let me say one thing," Alta broke in, pressing his hands to-gether as if in prayer. "This may not come out just right, but here goes. I truly have changed, deep down. And yes, I've said it before and fallen short. So, I ain't makin' no promises, and I ain't askin' for forgiveness. It's up to me, I've gotta earn it."

"Well now, don't that sound noble..."

Fearing the worst, Alta pushed on. "There is sumthun' else I'd like to say...if you don't mind?"

Shelby pursed her lips and nodded.

Alta reached over and folded her hands into his. "Now I ain't never been a romantic fella, and I ain't never really said how special you are to me, but, Shelby, darlin', I'm sayin' it now. You're the best thing, the absolute best thing that ever happened to me."

Shelby turned away, gathered herself, and turned back. "Now, if you don't mind, I'd like to say what I got to say."

Alta beamed, sensing he had done something right. "I been workin' on them words for quite a spell."

"Well, first off, Alta, darlin', don't you ever, ever use that word darlin' to me...it's a phony Southern word. Now, getting' back to...your thinkin' I'm special and all...even if you mean it, it don't count...not unless you keep your sorry ass out of jail. That's key, don't cha reckon?"

"Yes ma'am. That's exactly what I'm gonna do. Stay out of jail and help you get back on your feet."

"Well, hal-le-lu-jah! We agree. And one more thing, Alta, I've decided your coming home. I don't want no more of this hermit business. You need to get on home. Then get on with makin' an honest living. Did I say honest?"

"You did."

Alta started to grin but Shelby shot him a look that said "shut up if you know what's good for you," and Alta nodded.

Part 2

CHAPTER 13

Bremen, Next Day

THE NIGHT WAS GOOD FOR rocking. A rising moon threw light in dark places. A cleansing wind blew through the pines. Alone with his thoughts, Alta gently rocked on the back porch. Seven days had passed since Shelby had called him home.

It had been a fine day. They reminisced for hours, telling and retelling stories of their courtship, their first home, raising the twins. Treasured moments flooded back. Shelby laughed in spite of her pain, her spirits were high. She slept peacefully now. Later in the week, they would drive to Atlanta to meet another oncologist, to explore another treatment.

It was also a good night for reflection. As the clouds drifted by, the moonlight came and went. Alta's therapy sessions in prison had been difficult yet helpful. Doc Dorothy had prodded him down the dark roads of his mind. He now knew more about himself, why he did what he did, and how to see storm clouds rolling in. Rocking peacefully, he considered his progress. He was definitely on the move, small, tentative steps forward. He was more introspective—Lord, how he hated that word. His heart had settled down. He hadn't had the big one, the myocardial infarction that was predicted.

He'd combed through the trade papers, researched the local market, and had a couple of legitimate business opportunities in mind. After all, the rules of commerce operated pretty much the same whether your business was legal or illegal. He'd make it work. As the moon cleared a passing cloud and illuminated his face, he nodded his assent. He was on the move, leaving behind the night crimes, the dark hollows, the midnight runs, pushing forward, headed for higher ground. Yet he knew a lifetime of crime and cunning, like gravity, was always operating at some level, tugging at him, pulling him back. Redemption, he concluded, was a narrow path up a slippery slope.

Yes, there would be trouble ahead. Lamar was as loony as he was violent. He'd skimmed thousands of dollars from Alta's moonshine business, had a reputation of snitching to the feds, and desperately wanted revenge for the beating that Billy Boudreaux and the Cajun mafia had put on him. Clearly, Lamar, the slick, blond pretty boy, was trouble.

Then there was Virgil, his oldest business partner. Virgil, had declared war on Lamar. Alta had never completely trusted Virgil. He was a good enforcer but always working his own deals, most of them crooked. On top of that, the feds were closely monitoring Alta's every move, the tax boys, the ATF. Hell, no one believed he was going straight.

By God, I'll fool 'em; I'm movin' on.

Without warning, dark clouds swept in a windy downpour. He considered going inside, shrugged, and rocked on through it. Pounded by the storm, he was penitent. It was cleansing.

———

Alta smiled confidently in the mirror as he straightened his tie. Today was big. He looked every inch the banker in a dark suit, wingtips, and a gray fedora. This was the day he would scout for legitimate business.

Before leaving, he looked in on Shelby. The room smelled of camphor. Fluids had accumulated in her chest, and her breathing had gone from a labored wheeze to a faint rattle, and she was having trouble swallowing. Alta desperately wanted to show Shelby that he had found a legitimate business. He kissed her forehead and was off. His sons, Jack and Buck, would tend to her while he was gone.

He had arranged a secret meeting with Chester T. Pope III, an old family friend and the president of the First Federal Bank in Bremen, ten miles east of Tallapoosa. As Alta pulled the Buick out of the garage and onto Bowden Street, he noticed a police car parked beside the road. He tipped his hat to

Sonny Hoyt, the Tallapoosa police chief. Radio in hand, Sonny returned the gesture and fell in behind him.

Damn, Alta though, *Sonny will call his wife, Irene, the police dispatcher, and she'll call her sister Mabel at the restaurant on the Bremen Square, and she'll tell everyone in town.* He quickly changed his route, taking the back road to Bremen. The Buick rattled over countless railroad crossings, as did the patrol car. You just couldn't get to Bremen without passing over a maze of spurs and sidings. Railroad towns were like that.

Bremen, much like Tallapoosa, had a checkered past. At the turn of the century, cotton poured into town from the Mississippi Delta, first by wagon and then by rail. The cotton was loaded into huge warehouses that lined the tracks; then on to cotton mills, then and on to mammoth textile mills like Sewell's and Hubbard's. Bremen became known as the "Clothing Manufacturer of the South." Tom Murphy was the town's other claim to fame. He grew up in Bremen and still practiced law there. He went on to become Georgia's most powerful politician, currently serving as the Speaker in the Georgia House of Representatives. A notch or two down was Chester Pope III, spinning his magic.

Alta slipped into the town square, hoping to avoid detection, though Sonny Hoyt was still tailing him. He stole a glance at the Murphy Law Office as he drove by. Everyone stood at the window, waving at him. He continued around the square, passing Mabel's Country Kitchen, a local favorite. Virgil Pettimore sat on the hood of his Chevy pickup, sipping coffee and grinning. Alta pulled down his fedora and looked away. He parked at the rear of the First Federal Bank. As he walked in the back door, Verlene, Chester Pope's secretary, smiled and whispered into the phone, "Gotta go, he just walked in."

Chester shook hands vigorously and whisked Alta into his vast office, all mahogany and brass, and seated him in front of a Haralson County lot map. "Sorry for the fanfare. You're quite the notorious fellow around here."

"That, Mr. Pope, is a thing of the past."

Well over six feet tall and in his eighties, Chester paced the floor in front of Alta, shoulders stooped, hands clasped behind his back. A receding chin beneath a prominent nose gave him a hawk like profile. The sharp edges were softened by a glen plaid suit, penny loafers, and a worn alligator belt with an engraved silver buckle. All in all, Chester had a suspicious air of propriety.

"That's what's bothering me," Chester replied in a raspy baritone. "Let me be clear from the get-go: this bank will not be a party to any criminal ventures."

Alta smiled inwardly. He knew what was coming: first the righteous foreplay, then the legal finagling, and then, after further mock anguish, the deal. He sat back in his chair, admiring the diplomas and plaques that hung like chum bait on Chester's wall: BA, Vanderbilt; MBA, Duke University; Doctorate of Jurisprudence, University of Georgia; past president of the Rotary in Bremen, Buchanan, and Tallapoosa; chairman of the Bremen Board of Education; past chairman of the Haralson County Planning Commission. Chester cultivated relationships with high rollers like Vidalia farmers cultivated onions: big front end investment and then epic harvest. He'd made big money in Atlanta land development, and in strip malls and casinos in Phenix City, Alabama. Then moved back to Bremen to be near his grandchildren. His bank was strategically located on the town square, facing the courthouse, two doors down from the Murphy's Law office.

Alta nestled deep in the tufted leather couch. A skilled negotiator, he wore a poker as he sifted through his assessment of Chester. To his credit, Chester was indeed a polished, impeccably dressed man of commerce with fine credentials—and a world-class conniver.

Chester blinked ever so slightly. "So, Mr. Dryden, what brings you here this fine day?"

"Well, Mr. Pope, I'm thinkin' about buildin' some spec-homes."

"Lawfully?"

"Hell yes, lawfully."

"Alta, there's no money in real estate. Folks are just gettin' back on their feet from the downturn."

Alta paused. Pulling his arms up, he cradled his head in his hands and mentally rehearsed his plan. As it fell into place, his head popped up, and he flashed an impish grin. "Well, you see, Mr. Pope, I've spent some time down at the courthouse here lately. There's a slew of folks living in small, two-bedroom homes that have been handed down over the years. Most of 'em are paid off. Their families are growing, and they're lookin' to move up.

"Most of 'em couldn't qualify for a loan."

"Indeed, that's my point. But, *what if I* bought their homes for, say, twenty-five thousand dollars which is fair market value. And then, *what if they* applied that to a down payment on a fifty-thousand-dollar home, a home that I built?"

Chester's eyes narrowed. "I never liked two *what-ifs* in the same sentence. Where's all the money comin' from?"

Alta chuckled. "It's hard-earned whiskey money."

"My ass, its dirty whiskey money."

Chester stumped back and forth on his cane. "It don't sound good. The feds will want to know where you got the loot."

"I know, I know, there's some risk in it. Try and remember, I'm tryin' to do-right here."

Chester's head spooled in circles like a prospector panning for gold. "I see a lot of risk, and not much reward."

"But, what if we do this," Alta's eyes lit up as he spoke, "what if you're their banker? They'd put down the twenty-five thousand from the first house, and you'd give 'em a mortgage for twenty-five thousand on the new one, and you're holdin' the note. That don't seem too risky."

Chester puckered his lips, seeming to reconsider. "Well, from a strictly legal point of view, it'd be risky, damn risky."

Alta paused. *I'll probably have to sweeten the deal to get him onboard, but I'll lead with a barb.*

"Well, let me ask you this, Mr. High and Mighty. Why is it that you always seem to own every piece of land around here that gets condemned for a school or a hospital?"

Throwing his head up and arching his back, Chester replied, "Now that, sir, that is pure goddamn genius. Hell, I never spent a day in jail."

"Look, you old gasbag, I ain't no saint, but I want to do right. So, if I was to start with, say, a forty-acre parcel, and build, say fifty or maybe sixty homes…would that be legal?"

Chester's eyes lit up. He ran a long, arthritic finger over the map. "Now *that, that* very well could be legal. I've got a couple of choice parcels we could look at."

"Well, maybe," Alta hedged. "Don't you see, the whole idea is to provide good value to the buyer and to the community at large?"

Chester pulled on his chin, "I see where you're headin' with this. I think we can work somethin' out. It won't be cheap. But you're right, we'd be providing good value to the community, and don't you think they'd be beholden?"

Alta winked. "I believe they would."

A deafening roar came up from the town square, setting the windows to rattling. As they looked out, a Harley roared around the side of the courthouse and screeched to a stop in front of the bank. Lamar Tate hopped off his bike and leered up at Alta and Chester, giving them an "I-can-see-you" gesture, and then he let go with his best wild-dog howl:

"Aaaaah-ooooooooooooooh…Aaaaah-ooooooooooooooh!
…*AAAAAH-OOOOOOOOOOOH!*

Chester groaned. "He's a dog now?"

"According to Virgil, he's a wild dog out to save the planet."

"Good Lord. Like I said, Alta, this won't be cheap."

As they finished up, Alta added, "I'm gonna need some help on one more thing. I'd like to buy two OTASCO franchises, auto parts and such. One for here in Bremen and one for Tallapoosa. Could you look into it?"

Chester smiled. "Can you tell me more?"

"Not now. I gotta go. So, we got a deal on the real estate?"

Chester rolled up the map of Haralson County. "Take this with you. I'll draw up the papers. We'll work it out."

"Good, good, good. I gotta go."

"Hang on, Alta. I got a favor to ask you."

"How'd I know this was comin'?"

"No, no, it's not about me. I'd like to put your name up for the Tallapoosa Town Council. We got an opening."

"So long, Chester."

Alta smiled as he hustled back to the Buick. I hope' Shelby will be pleased.

CHAPTER 14

Mount Zion Baptist Church, Tallapoosa, Same Day

———

ALTA WAS BEAMING AS HE drove home from the bank. The land deal with Chester Pope was far from done, but he was sure it would happen. Helping poor folks move to better homes, to a better life, that's got to be legal. A first step up the slippery slope of redemption. He hoped Shelby would be pleased.

When he was almost home, he turned around and headed back the other way. He drove to the east side of Tallapoosa, searching for the proposed property. After several false starts, he found the forty-acre plot, posted with a "For Sale" sign.

He swung the car door open and then sat back. He needed to get back to Shelby, but something was pulling the other way. He struggled to understand it, to control it.

When it came to making money, Alta could see around corners. He simply divined the future. The left side of his brain glowed as he ran the financials. Numbers flew through his head, slotted into equations, and fell into tidy columns—profit, loss, and return on investment. Yet, it was more than working the numbers. It was the thrill of the hunt, the head game, outwitting the competition, outwitting the system, the jolt of power that came with winning. He walked around the property for more than an hour, lost in his deliberations.

A switch flipped in his head as a train rumbled through town. The numbers faded. He checked his watch and groaned. "What in hell am I doin'?"

Doctor Williams and Alta's son, Jack were huddled on the front porch as he drove up.

Jack's eyes narrowed as he asked, "Where you been?"

Not waiting for an answer, Jack continued, "You better get in there. She's been asking for you."

Avoiding Jack's glare, Alta turned to the doctor. "How bad is it?"

"She's failin', Alta."

A single shaft of sunlight cut through the darkened room. Shelby slept upright, propped up with pillows. The faint rattle of her breathing broke the silence. Alta sat quietly next to the bed, uncertain how to proceed. He mopped sweat from his brow and looked on. Eventually she sensed his presence. Smiling weakly, she tried to speak, gave it up, and pointed to the water glass on the night table. He fumbled with the glass, recovered, and handed it to her. After an awkward pause, he mumbled, "Sorry."

Shelby worked her mouth up and down, trying to speak. A dry hissing sound followed, and then words, short broken fragments. "Alta...I'm scared... my dreams...my dreams are empty."

"I'm here, Shelby, I'm here for you."

A bitter smile darted across her face. "Yes...you're here...finally."

Alta tipped his chair back nervously and mopped his brow again. He was good at making deals; he wasn't much good in the ways of the heart.

"My dreams are empty," she whispered. "The color's gone...the music's gone."

Alta looked on helplessly. After a moment, not sure what he was saying, he replied, "You gotta let go of your dreams; hold on to your memories."

"Damn, Alta...is that the best you can do?"

Trying to fill the hole he'd dug, Alta stumbled on, "Dreams may come, and dreams may go, but memories are forever."

Shelby shook her head. "Alta, that don't help much either."

"I know."

"Take me to the church on the river?"

"Yes ma'am, if it's okay with the doctor."

"Just get me there."

———

Twenty minutes later, Shelby, a fragile porcelain doll wrapped in a quilt, sat on a bench in front of the Mount Zion Baptist Church. The sun was starting to set. The river wandered below, a ribbon of gold in reflected light. Shelby moved slowly back and forth, in a trance, as if she was keeping time.

Alta disappeared for a moment and then was back with the property map. "Now, Shelby, you remember what you told me last time we was here?"

"I'll let you do the talkin'," her voice cracked.

"You said I needed to get on home, get on with makin' an honest living."

"That's a fact."

He unrolled the map. "Well, let me show you sumthin'. See that parcel there, circled in red? I'm gonna buy it. I talked with Chester Pope down at the bank. It's pretty much a done deal. Then, I'm buildin' homes, homes for po' folk."

"Honest, is it?"

"It is, and good for the town."

"No, I mean, the way you're goin' to do it?"

"Well, hell yes, pretty much."

Shelby's eyes sparkled as a smile spread across her withered face. "Well, good for you, Alta, gud for you. I'm proud of you."

They sat quietly, hand in hand, watching the sun go down, passing from an auburn spray to a salmon colored veil as the fading light glanced off the passing clouds.

Alta fixed on Shelby's eyes: pale jewels on dark velvet, a fading incandescence, and then dark drifting clouds. She seemed at peace.

Her hand flew out to his side. "Are you there, Alta? I can see colors now."

"In your memories?"

"In my dreams...in my memories...everywhere."

"And the music?"
"I can hear the music, too."
"Sing it, Shelby, sing it."
She sang in a low, crackling voice,

"Darling I am growing old,
Silver threads among the gold
Shine upon my brow today
Life is fading fast away."

She slumped against him. "Are you still there, Alta?"
He felt her hands go cold. Lost in a flood of emotions, he murmured, "I'm here, Shelby, I'm here."
"Sing for me, Alta, sing for me."
He sang as she faded.

"But, my darling you will be,
Always young and fair to me
Yes, my darling, you will be,
Always young and fair to me."

CHAPTER 15

Tallapoosa, Days Later

LAMAR SAT ON THE EDGE of the catwalk that ran around the Tallapoosa water tank. His feet dangled over the edge. The town spread out below, peaceful, malleable, his to save, his to control. Yet he was miserable. He'd run out of patience and money. The golden days of skimming big bucks off the Dryden's' moonshine empire were over. Billy Boudreaux had nearly killed him. He needed to settle the score. Vengeance burned through him. Surely Alta was behind it, but Virgil Pettimore, that twisted sumbitch, had set it all in motion. Growing up, Virgil had constantly harassed Lamar. Their families had feuded for years.

Lamar pulled himself up on the catwalk, weighing his options. Maybe he'd kill them both. Maybe not. Maybe just Virgil. He was open to any solution that would bring a full measure of revenge while putting some serious money back in his pocket. But hang on, it was Alta who had postponed the showdown, asking for time to care for his ailing wife. Maybe they were just buying time. Lamar had honored the deal but now sensed they were up to something big. Figuring it out would give Lamar an edge. He smiled wickedly and hurried down the ladder. He had a plan.

Like most predators, Lamar began the hunt with the prowl. That night he hung out at the High Hat, the roughest joint in town. As he entered, he pulled his ball cap down, the one with the wild-dog patch on it. He sat in a dark corner, eyes peeled, ears perked, listening.

Sure he knew most of them had marked him coming in the door. They knew of the long-running feud between him and Virgil, and that Alta was a part of it. They also knew that feuds never died, not in the South. They might simmer quietly for a while, sometimes for a generation, but then they'd boil up again. Once sullied, family honor had to be put right. They all got that, and they understood there might be some shooting and maybe some killing.

After a few nights of prowling, Lamar had heard it all: happy drunks talking nonsense; the high school coach with a losing record, planning a comeback; aging cowgirls searching for their tall, dark stranger; young studs lying about their sex lives; and lint heads from the mills complaining about working conditions. Finally one night he heard some of Virgil's boys, mostly welders, letting slip something about the Plantation Pipeline. That was all it took for Lamar to shift from prowling to stalking.

Night after night, he parked down the street from Virgil's house waiting and watching with a thermos of coffee. At 4 a.m. on Friday, Virgil pulled out of his garage and headed east on Highway 78. Lamar lost him near Villa Rica. The next morning, Lamar was at it again. After miles of turns and crossings, Virgil came to a stop at a weathered barn on an abandoned farm, somewhere east of Villa Rica.

Lamar followed at a distance, turning off into a shrub oak thicket above the barn. Grabbing his binoculars, he scrambled down to the back of the barn, coming to rest behind a rusted-out tractor. A light was on inside the barn, and he heard voices. He focused the binoculars and saw Virgil standing next to Lonny James, the welder.

What in hell are they up to?

He scrambled back up the hillside and waited. As it got light, he scanned the barn and the fields below.

"I'll be damned," he gasped. The Plantation Pipeline ran directly behind the barn, no more than twenty yards away. A narrow trench ran from the barn to the pipeline. He balled his fists. His eyes narrowed to slits as his lips thinned and curled slightly back into what looked like a snarl.

Done stalking; time to kill.

Lamar got to the farm at 3 a.m. the next morning well before Virgil. Things had changed. Shelby Dryden had passed. As far as Lamar was concerned, the cease-fire was over. He brought along his model 92 Winchester carbine, the one John Wayne had used to save the West. He also brought along an eight-foot plank with six-inch spikes driven up through it. Once Virgil and Lonny arrived, he would place it on the road that ran back from the barn and cover it in dirt. It would slow them down if he misfired.

He loaded the rifle as he waited. He'd seen most of John Wayne's movies and knew every gunfight by heart, every Western town saved from outlaws. He set his rifle on a rock, pointed down at the barn, and waited.

––––––––

When Virgil pulled out of his garage at four a.m., the bed of his pickup was loaded: a hot tap, sections of two-inch steel pipe, and a box of fittings. The tap had a steel collar that would be welded around the pipeline. The top of the tap had a valve with a cutting edge that could cut through the shell of the pipeline. The gas was tapped by opening the valve to a hose that ran into the barn. Virgil arrived at the farm without incident in the late afternoon.

Lonny had set up shop at the back door of the barn. He was cutting threads on a section of two-inch pipe clamped in a tripod vice. His rifle and a pouch of Red Man tobacco lay on a bench nearby. As usual, Virgil pulled on his tattered Alabama ball cap before entering "Roll damn tide!" he taunted. "I got sum goodies for you."

Not about to let work get ahead of football, Lonny tipped his ragged Auburn cap and smiled broadly. "Roll tide, my ass," he chuckled and shot a stream of Red Man into the straw. "You gonna lay down a bet or jack your jaw?"

"You got it. Twenty-five dollars on Alabama, straight up."

"Damn, you're favored. I'm gonna need some points."

"I'll give you three points, take it or leave it."

"I'll take it. Now, what's that you got for me?" as he shot another stream of Red Man into the straw.

"Got the pipe and the hose." Virgil hesitated. "And the hot tap."

The muscles in Lonny's neck flared out and his eyes burned red. "How many times I gotta tell you, cow turd, I ain't weldin' no gawd damn hot tap to no gawd damn pipeline while gas is a-runnin' through it."

Virgil crowded him. "Shut up and listen."

Lonny exploded, grabbing Virgil by the collar. "No, I ain't doin' it, not unless your fat ass is straddled over the pipeline while I'm doin' it."

Virgil yanked Lonny to the ground. The two men rolled in the dirt, locked in each other's arms. When the dust settled, Virgil had the bib of Lonny's overalls in one hand and a knife at his throat in the other.

"Settle down now, Lonny dar-lin'," he said as he gasped. "Listen to me. Listen carefully! Fred Dryden, Alta's brother, got ahold of the pumping schedule from a high-level snitch at Plantation's head office in Atlanta. Cost him a fortune. Alta don't know about it yet. We gotta get this sumbitch up and runnin' and sell some gas 'fore he does."

Lonny let go of Virgil's collar. They stood and dusted themselves off.

"All right, cow turd," Lonny gasped. "When do they stop pumpin'?"

"Today from three to five," Virgil wheezed, returning his buck knife to an ankle sheath.

Lamar had Lonny in his sights first, but was partial to Auburn, so he moved on. He had Virgil in his sights next and desperately wanted to kill him. But then he had a flash of pure genius.

I don't need to kill anyone. I just need to let them know that I know what they're up to. I'll just leave my calling card.

Before firing, he whispered, "Bang, bang, shoot 'em up. Grab your gun. Bang, bang, shoot 'em up. Here I come."

Craaaaack-boooooom! The Red Man pouch exploded. Both men hit the dirt. Shreds of chewing tobacco rained down on them as the bullet rattled off the blade of a stock plow. A wild dog howl echoed down the hillside. Seconds later, Lamar was back in his car, racing down the road, first snickering, then howling, and then snickering, savoring the moment.

———

It took Virgil a short while to fix a flat tire and get over to the Lucky Star trailer park. It was eight a.m. when he parked just down the street from Lamar's single-wide and calmly loaded three shells in his ten-gauge. He pulled to the side of Lamar's trailer in broad daylight…*Kaaashuuww! Kaaashuuww! Kaaahshuuww!*

Now it was Virgil who snickered as he drove off. Most of the buckshot had rattled off the metal siding, but he'd damn well left his calling card, tit for tat.

"Thank your lucky stars, Wild Dog! Thank your lucky stars that I ain't in a killin' mood!"

CHAPTER 16

Funeral Home, Tallapoosa, Next Day

———

BITTER WIND AND RAIN BLEW through Tallapoosa as Alta and Jack Dryden waited patiently in the Buick outside the funeral home. Shelby would be buried in three days, and they'd come early for their meeting with the funeral director. Alta fumbled with his note pad. Jack fidgeted with a new pocketknife. They waited in awkward silence.

Alta eventually looked up from his note pad. "So Jack, I'd like you and Buck to say a few words at the graveside. How would that be?"

Jack was tall, lean, and nineteen, smart as hell, responsible, but definitely on the wild side.

"Sure," he replied flatly.

"I'd like it to be a proper funeral. Your mother would want that."

"Yes sir."

"I was thinking, maybe we'd have a few close friends, private like, out to the home place afterward. How's that sound?"

A faint glimmer came into Jack's eyes. "Close friends, out to the home place? Sure, let me handle it."

"Small and private, you understand?"

Alta laid his hand on Jack's shoulder and smiled. Both the twins were devoted sons. For years, they'd joined their mother on the weekly visits to the Atlanta Federal Prison. When Alta was out of prison and back to moonshining, Jack often drove as they traveled the back roads of Georgia and Alabama,

101

from small country stores to honky-tonks to big wholesalers. They called on new customers, collected overdue accounts, and waved the flag. Jack learned fast.

With a twinkle in his eyes, Alta asked, "y'know what I'm thinkin'? Sittin' here in front of this funeral home?"

"Are you thinkin' about the funeral home you own in Rayburn, Alabama?"

"Wasn't that a honey? Good money in funerals, better money in moonshine. Sold it last year."

"Did you?"

"The Marshall County sheriff finally figured out that them new caskets comin' in the back door were loaded with moonshine from our Musca-time Still. You know, a fella needs a drink, especially when he's grieving'. That little ole funeral home served pint bootleggers all over Marshall County."

"Now that's a fact, Daddy, that's a fact." Jack pulled a jar of moonshine from the glove box and had a sip.

Alta checked his watch. "The folks ahead of us are runnin' late. I hope he knows we're waitin'?"

They lapsed again into silence as Alta flipped through his note pad. Then he glanced over at Jack, who was cracking his knuckles, first on the left hand and then on the right. He looked uncomfortable, as if he had something to say.

Finally Jack spoke. "So?"

"Yes, son?"

"So, how you feelin'?"

"Well..." pausing, gathering his thoughts, "I'm saddened...that'll never pass...but more than ever...I'm committed...no, I'm dedicated to movin' ahead with...with legitimate business."

"We're all mighty pleased about that, but I was just wondering. How are you feelin'...about?"

Alta turned away and cringed. The Drydens didn't talk much about feelings. Shelby never talked about her sickness. Alta never talked about doing hard time.

Jack continued, "How you were feelin' about all this?"

"I…well now…" Alta stumbled, running a hand through his hair. "I'd say I was feelin' like I'm crossin' a river, movin' to higher ground."

"That's good, Daddy, that's good. No more backslidin'. So, who all is comin' to the funeral?"

Alta turned a page in his note pad. "We got a few politicians and dignitaries: Tom Murphy, Speaker of the House; Nathan Dean, our State Senator from Cedartown; the Mayor of Tallapoosa, the Howes, the Popes, and a few other high rollers from Atlanta."

"They knew mama, did they?"

"I reckon." Alta moved on. "Guess who called me this mornin'?"

"No tellin'."

"Remember that mean old Billy goat from Phenix City, Alabama?"

"Head Rebel?"

"That's him, Head Rebel, our best customer in that city of sin."

Alta smiled as he reflected on the "good ole days." "Every weekend, thousands of soldier boys from Fort Benning, Georgia, poured across the bridge to drink and gamble in Phenix City."

"So Daddy, is it true that General George Patton drove tanks across the bridge to clean up Phenix City?"

"Well now, General George was in charge of Fort Benning in those days. That's a fact. I'd like to think that it happened. It'd make a fine movie. Anyway, Head Rebel wants to come to the funeral."

"Bless him, he was one lyin', cheatin' sumbitch."

"That he was. Then there'll be family, and all your mother's friends. And you know, I'd better invite Doctor Dorothy from the Atlanta Federal Prison. She's a ball of fire, helped me a lot."

"How about other folks in town?"

"I'd rather not. I want to keep it small and proper."

Jack nodded with a mischievous smile. "Small and proper. Absolutely."

The front door of the funeral home swung open, and they were beckoned inside.

Jack took a slug of moonshine and climbed out of the car. He paused as he got to the top of the steps. "By the way, Daddy, didya hear, someone shot up Lamar's trailer?"

"I heard."

"He's okay. Police don't know who did it."

Alta nodded calmly. On the inside he was troubled. Lamar had snitched on a lot of moonshiners. A lot of people wanted him dead. But he knew it must have been Virgil. Alta hoped Virgil could help him sell off the tappin' business. After that, he had to go.

CHAPTER 17

Mount Zion Baptist Church, Tallapoosa, Next Day

MORNING CAME QUICKLY, A FAINT glow, a gentle breeze, and then daylight and a howling wind. It gusted wildly as close friends arrived for the funeral. Running late, the Drydens rolled up in two black limousines. The Mount Zion Baptist Church, a modest clapboard structure, was anchored to the hillside. Graceful lancet windows ran along the sides. A cupola sat above the peaked roof, narrowing to a simple cross that swayed in the wind. The muted notes of the hymn "Built on a Rock" came from the organ inside.

Bracing against the wind, the Drydens hurried up the steps and into the church. Alta paused as he reached the wooden bench at the entrance and turned back toward the river. Gray-flecked whitecaps formed, peaked, and started over as the wind moaned along the river. Shelby had died in his arms a week earlier as they sat together on the bench, gazing out at the river. Alta bit his lip and glanced over at the parking lot. It was full, but not packed. Shelby would like that—a small, proper funeral.

He waited at the back of the church as the family crept up the main aisle, saying their goodbyes at the open casket. A plain wooden cross hung above the pulpit. Just below, the casket seemed to float in a sea of flowers. A spray of red and white roses stood to the right. Bouquets of white lilies and yellow kalanchoes spread beneath it, and a spray of pink carnations stood to the left.

Every flower shop this side of Atlanta must have worked through the night to pull this off. At the door, Cecil Waters, an aging bootlegger who helped out at funerals, slipped Alta a small envelope as the organ struck up another verse of "Built on a Rock." Alta ambled down the aisle, nodding gravely to friends and dignitaries: The Speaker of the House, the State Senator, and his banker, Chester Pope III. To his surprise, Doctor Dorothy Epstein, all five foot three of her, had come over from Atlanta. A tight white perm, makeup, and a frock coat did little to hide her petulant side, a born street fighter from New York City. Mandy Tate, towered above Dr. Epstein. When off work, Mandy wore flannel shirts and faded jeans and braided her hair in a pigtail. That morning her hair fell to her shoulders. A black sheath dress revealed a striking figure. Alta arched his brow discreetly.

As Alta reached the casket, he took in the scents and shades of the flowers. Bending quickly, he kissed Shelby's forehead and stepped back. Every eye in the church was on him. Though outwardly composed, he was crumbling inside. His head hammered, and his heart galloped. He willed himself back. He'd learned to tamp down his feelings and carry on in prison. Shelby had forgiven him when he was past forgiveness. Though her light had dimmed, she would lead the way.

His eyes moved to a huge spray of roses on the end of the casket. "Deepest Sympathies, Captain Billy" proclaimed a banner that ran across the spray. Captain Billy, the head of the Cajun mafia, now owned Alta's moonshine business. Billy and his thugs had nearly killed Lamar in the changeover. A thin smile danced across Alta lips. He slipped the small sympathy envelope in his pocket.

As the deacon closed the casket, the pastor came to the pulpit and everyone stood. After a hearty welcome, and a proper eulogy to Shelby, the pastor read Psalm 18:28, "Oh Lord, you light a lamp for me…" Then they all sang "There Is a Green Hill Far Away."

Between scriptures, Alta opened the envelope that Cecil Withers had handed him earlier. Inside he found a phone message from the funeral home.

Alta, Dearest,
  All my love and sympathy. I am driving over from Selma. Had some car trouble. I'll be there, but I'll be late.
Fondly, Thelma.

Alta squeezed the note into a ball and stuffed it in his pocket. Good Lawd, Thelma from Selma: a distant cousin, aging spinster, and a collector of family heirlooms. We'll have to padlock the china cabinet.

The note from the second envelope read:

Bonjour Mon Ami,
  Can't make the funeral. But please thank Jack for inviting us to the big hoedown. We'll definitely be there. We'll bring plenty of crawfish pie.
Au Revoir, Captain Billy

Alta shuddered. He slipped it to Jack, who sat next to him. A sheepish grin appeared on Jack's face as he read it.

Alta shook his head and whispered, "The big hoedown?"

Jack mouthed the word, "Sorry."

Alta moped his brow and sighed. The remainder of the service went off as planned, proper and respectful. They ended with a rousing spiritual.

Will there be any stars, any stars in my crown,
When at evening the sun goeth down?
When I wake with the blest in the mansions of rest,
Will there be any stars in my crown?

CHAPTER 18

Dryden Home Place, December 1975

———

As ALTA HAD REQUESTED, THE burial was a small, private gathering of invited guests. The wind howled through the oak trees that skirted the cemetery. Though the clouds darkened, it didn't rain. When the service ended, the Drydens climbed into the limousines and headed down Old Highway 100 for the home place.

Alta sat quietly in the back seat of the car, his eyes closed and his head back. His heart was in overdrive. He inhaled slowly through his mouth, to the count of three, and exhaled slowly through his nose, to the count of three, just as Doc Dorothy had taught him, and slipped a nitroglycerin from his pill case under his tongue. Unlike his heart, his head was stuck at a crossroads somewhere between relief and anxiety.

The limousine slowed as they reached the Walker Creek turnoff, the first locked gate to the farm. Alta shook his head and tried to focus. Several dozen battered cars and trucks were parked along the road. Strung out behind him, a procession of twenty or so luxury cars, Cadillacs, Buicks and Lincolns, had come to a halt. Alta's head swung back to the parked cars. "Who are these folks?"

Jack grinned broadly. "They're comin' to Mama's hoedown."

"Like hell they are. Damn, Jack, I told you to keep it small and private."

Jack threw up his hands in defense. "Hold on, Daddy; remember when I was growin' up, you used to say, 'never stop thinkin'?"

Alta shrugged. "I reckon."

"Well, here's the thing, I heard about you buildin' them fifty-thousand-dollar homes," Jack paused with a grin. "And then buyin' up a bunch of twenty-five-thousand-dollar homes and gettin' them folks to trade up to the new ones. Hell, Daddy, that's pure genius."

Alta's eyes lit up. "Why, thank you, son. But how'd you hear about that?"

"Come on, this is Tallapoosa; everybody knows everything about everybody."

"I suppose. What's your point?"

"Well, I got to thinkin', like you taught me. I'm thinkin', what's Daddy gonna do with them twenty-five-thousand-dollar homes?"

"Well...what'd you come up with?"

"Well, I poked around a bit and got to talkin' with folks that are livin' in trailer parks. A lot of them are lookin' for sumthin' bigger than a double-wide."

"The hell?"

Clive Barnes, the limo driver, jumped in. "The boy's got a point, Alta. Most of them folks are back to work at the mills and whatnot. Business seems to be pickin' up."

Pulling on his chin, Alta looked at the funeral procession behind him and then over at the jalopies parked along the road. "So them folks there, them po' folks, are from trailer parks?"

"That's right, Daddy. I invited 'em. From all over the county."

Alta held a frown for the longest time; then he chuckled. "Well, Jack, that's some damn fine thinkin'."

Jack beamed. "Thank you, Daddy."

"You got the key, son. You better let 'em in."

"There may be more."

"I never doubted it."

The motley procession of high-end sedans and battered coupes followed the Dryden limos through the scattered woodlands and up to the weathered farmhouse. The porch wrapped around the house and was lined with card tables. Smoke drifted from the chimney and spread along the tree line, searching for a hole in the overcast sky. Several acres of yard and pasture surrounded the house and ran up to the barn; beyond that was a thicket of scrub oak and Georgia pine.

Earlier in the week, Jack and his brother Buck had brought a work party out to the home place to set things up. They'd cleaned out the barn and swept up the part with the wood flooring. There might be some dancing. A bluegrass band from Dawsonville unpacked their instruments as two boys from the volunteer fire department in white aprons tended the barbecue grill. The sweet smell of pork ribs drifted down the hill. Alta took it all in, amazed and apprehensive.

He and his sons went inside as the funeral procession poured into the yard. Women scurried to the porch with their favorite dishes. Men gathered in small groups and smoked. The trailer-park folks parked in the lower pasture. Their children and dogs spilled out as the parents looked on, not sure how to proceed. Slowly they made their way to the front of their cars, leaned against the fenders, and patiently waited their chance to have a word with Mr. Alta.

The food was quickly laid out, buffet style, around the porch—tea sandwiches, green salads and a variety of pasta casseroles. Trays of glazed ham and pulled pork, along with baskets of fried chicken and cornbread, came next. A dozen pitchers of sweet tea were lined up after that. Finally the desserts— seven-layer chocolate cake, ambrosia, pecan pie, and banana pudding—were spread across the last couple of card tables. No one would go hungry.

Once the food was set out, the women joined their husbands in the receiving line that stretched out the front door and around the side of the house. Inside, Alta and the twins stood in front of the fireplace, greeting guests. Mr. Clem Robinson, the mayor of Tallapoosa, followed the first wave of dignitaries. "All our sympathies, Alta. Shelby was a fine woman."

"Well, thank you, Clem."

Clem bent close to Alta's ear and whispered, "I hear you may throw your hat in the ring for councilman. I'll support you on that."

"Thanks, Clem; I haven't ruled it out."

"Good, good, just so you know, I'm steppin' down real soon. There'll be several openin's comin' up soon."

"Thanks again. Go get you some food."

Chester Pope and his wife Mattie, a proper Southern lady, came next. Mattie reached for Alta's hand and enclosed it in hers. "Your Shelby brought so many gifts to our life. We will never forget her."

"Thanks, Mattie, thanks, Chester. She loved you both."

Mattie nodded and moved on. Chester, lingered. "We need to talk on Monday."

Though he tried to whisper, his voice boomed across the room. "We'll close on the land deal next week. The Planning Commission is ready to approve your building permit. It's all teed up."

Alta put his arm around Chester's shoulder and tried to move him along. "That's fine, Chester, that's fine. I'll call you on Monday."

Chester dug in his heels. "Hang on a second, there's something else. The word's out on your plans to build them homes. Bud Meeker, the big homebuilder, is furious. He'll try to block you, one way or the other. We'll talk Monday. And one more thing. Who the hell are all them poor folks parked at the bottom of the pasture?"

"Damnit, Chester," Alta whispered. "We got a lot of folks waitin' behind you. Go on. There's some good whiskey in the barn."

Jack joined his father at the window. "How you doin'?"

"Damn, son, this could get out of hand. How d'you plan to handle the folks from the trailer park?"

"They want to talk to you. I'll arrange it."

"You damn well better."

Out in the yard, Alta also noticed Doc Dorothy talking with Mandy Tate, Virgil Pettimore, and Head Rebel. She'd have their numbers in a minute or two.

A cloud of dust rose from down below; then a mud-spattered Chevy sedan roared up the hill with its horn blaring away. An arm waved from driver's side. Alta noticed the Alabama license plate as it lurched to a stop on the front lawn.

"Good Lord, Jack," Alta hissed.

Out popped Thelma. Clad in yards of red gingham and topped with a matching pillbox hat, Thelma cackled like a hen. After announcing her family connection, she made a beeline for the china cabinet.

Jack swallowed a grin as Alta grabbed his arm and said, "Ask Mattie Pope to keep an eye on your dear Aunty Thelma, or she'll carry the house away."

Alta returned to the reception line and found Doc Dorothy waiting. They shook hands and she held on. She placed her free hand on his wrist. "Hello, Alta. I've missed you; give me a hug."

Alta forced a smile as they embraced. "Thanks for coming. It's quite a drive from Atlanta."

Continuing to hold on, she fired back, "I came for Shelby. She was more wife than you deserved."

"I know, I know."

"Are you taking your meds?"

"Yes ma'am, every day…sometimes."

"I just took your pulse. It's one hundred and eighty."

"Well, it's a big day."

"And it may be your last. We need to talk, later."

"Yes ma'am, later."

Alta stepped back from the receiving line and slowly ran his hand down the front of his jacket, as if to brush off lint. He felt the hammer blows of his heart and fumbled in his pocket for his silver pill case. It was empty.

Jack looked on. "You OK?"

"Shelby would have remembered to bring extra pills," he mumbled to himself.

Jack moved to Alta's side and whispered, "You better sit."

"Like hell."

Head Rebel, one of Alta's oldest moonshine customers, suddenly stumbled in the front door; grinning from ear to ear. He was decked out in a white linen suit and a tattered plantation hat. The suit, though well pressed, was soiled. Beyond that he looked dashing, with a shoulder-length gray ponytail and a Van Dyke beard. He seemed to be going for a Colonel Sanders look.

Head Rebel shuffled across the room, tripping over an end table and somehow recovering. "Hello, where the hell's Alta? Oops! Oh, there he is!"

Alta lit up and seemed to recover. "I'll be, it's Head Rebel. Thank you for comin'."

Head Rebel dropped into an easy chair near the fire. "Sorry, Alta; I've been drinkin'. Lost my wife, Tammy, a month ago. I know you're hurtin'; sorry."

"Thank you. There was an awkward pause until Alta finally asked, "So, what are you up to these days?"

"I'm out of the whiskey business. Got me a proper antique shop, sterling silver, plantation stuff, knock-offs from Asia, the works."

Alta stifled a grin. Was this providence? Had the Lord intervened to help him deal with his curse? *Head Rebel has an antique shop? Hot damn!* Alta pulled a roll of money from his pocket and peeled off two one-hundred-dollar bills. "You got me thinkin'. Maybe you could do me a real big favor?"

Head Rebel blinked through bloodshot eyes. "I'll do what I can."

"Thelma, Shelby's distant cousin from Selma, Alabama, just arrived. She's a big collector of plantation silver. As we speak, she's lootin' the house, lookin' to enlarge her collection."

"Thelma from Selma! That's her name? Is she pretty?"

"Oh, hell yes, in her own way. How about you do this? How about you invite Cousin Thelma down to your shop in Phenix City?" Alta slipped him the hundred-dollar bills, "And gift her a few heirlooms."

"Consider it done."

By noon Lamar was set up behind a rocky crag above the Dryden barn. He'd rode his Harley three miles on a game trail and hiked the last half mile, lugging his Winchester rifle and his 357 Magnum. Four days had passed since he'd tracked Virgil to the farm in Villa Rica along the Plantation pipeline and fired a shot into Lonny's Red Man tobacco pouch, leaving his calling card. Later, Virgil had fired three shotgun blasts into his trailer, leaving his calling card. It was time to get serious.

Lamar had Virgil in his sights earlier, while Virgil was in the reception line, but thought better of it. Now Lamar slipped down to the back of the barn. Virgil sat alone on a bale of hay in a cattle stall, sipping from a jar of moonshine. A bluegrass group was raising a ruckus in the front of the barn.

Lamar slipped inside and eased up behind Virgil, jamming the barrel of the 357 Magnum to his head. "Say a word and you're dead."

Virgil bolted upright, recognized Lamar's voice, and slumped back on a hay bale.

Lamar snickered hysterically. "Before I blow your fat ass to kingdom come, I want to know who's behind the gas tapping?"

"Well, blow me away, piss-ant."

Lamar's face broke into a twisted smile. He pulled the hammer back and shoved the barrel under Virgil's chin. "I'm countin' one...two..."

"All right, all right... Alta funded it while he was in jail...but here's the thing...he thinks we sold the business to them Dixie mafia boys from Biloxi, Mississippi."

"So Alta don't know you didn't sell?" Lamar clucked. "Damn, this is good. Well, here's my deal: ah want in, or I'll take this whole twisted mess to the sheriff."

Virgil grinned. "Shee-itt, he's in our pocket. Look, the only way this is goin' work is if we can get some money comin' in. Tap some gas and sell it. Then we can buy Alta out, if he wants out."

"So, I'm in?"

"You're in; just keep your mouth shut. I'll get back to you."

———

The hoedown was over and the guests were leaving as a rawboned fellow in bib overalls and a dusty fedora came up to Alta.

"Mr. Dryden, sir, my name is Withers, Tommy Withers. Can we talk? My folks are at the bottom of the pasture."

Alta shook his hand. "Glad to meet you, Mr. Withers. Let's talk."

They walked down the pasture to the gathering.

"Well Mr. Dryden, sir, your Jack, there, said you might be up to sellin' or rentin' some homes that we might could afford."

"Sure enough." Alta squatted on his haunches and grabbed a stick.

"Here's the thing," Alta said, "the deal ain't been struck. Nothing's for sure. Y'all know that I-20 is about to open up?"

They all nodded as Alta drew an east-west line in the dirt. "Now, most folks will tell you that them big interstate highways will destroy the small towns along the way. That's money leavin' town. Am I right?"

The men looked at each other and nodded.

"Now, we don't want that, do we?"

They all shook their heads.

"So, we gotta protect our community, right? So yes, I will have some affordable homes for sale. If you got a steady job, you might get in with five percent down on a twenty-five-thousand-dollar home."

He scratched the numbers 1,250 in the dirt. "Most of you just got your Christmas bonus, and if you sell your trailer, by golly, you're into an affordable home for one thousand two hundred and fifty dollars. How's that sound?"

Tommy Withers looked around. There was some head shaking and some approving nods. "What's the monthly payment come to?"

"That'd be two hundred dollars to buy, two hundred fifty to rent."

"I don't know." Tommy frowned. "That's still a lot of money."

"That's a fact, and I don't want any of you to rush into it, but I do have a one-time killer deal, if you're interested."

Tommy looked around at the others.

"What you got for us, Mr. Dryden?"

Alta stood and extended his arms. "Let's say you decide to rent for the first year…see if it works for you, and then you decide you want to buy, well, here comes the killer deal…I'm gonna let you apply all that rent money, that's three thousand dollars, against the purchase price. That's the deal: apply the rent to the purchase price."

They group fell silent.

As they considered, Alta's head turned. He heard a police siren in the distance; then he continued, "Good, good, but here's the thing," slowly reeling them in, like a barker at a carnival. "You got to keep up them homes, right?"

The group looked around at each other and nodded more cautiously.

"Good, good. So, let me ask you...wouldn't you want to keep that new home shipshape, so it held its resale value? 'Cause, who knows, in a few years, you could move up to, say, a bigger home."

The wives, who spent most of their day's shut-in stifling trailers with too many dogs and kids, chimed in unison, "Amen!"

"So, if I was to buy two OTASCO stores, which I'm aiming to do, one here in Tallapoosa and another in Bremen—y'know, hardware, auto parts, and home repairs—in order to, if you will, keep money from leaving town...I was just wonderin' if I could count on your business down at them stores."

Jack beamed from up on the hill as he heard his father spin his web.

The trailer folks shook their heads in amazement and then broke into applause.

Jack watched his father work the crowd, then he guided him back up the hill. "You're awful good. Applying the rent to the purchase price, that's real good."

"Thank you, son, it just came to me."

"I found your medicine, if you needed it."

"Nah, I'm feelin' like a racehorse right now. Say, did I hear a police siren earlier?"

Jack blanched. "The ATF arrested Captain Billy and his gang at the first gate."

"What for?"

"It was Lamar again. He told 'em that Billy was the new owner of your moonshine business."

"Good Lord, how do I crawl out of the mud?"

"Keep a climbin', Daddy; you got to be strong. Anyway, Doctor Dorothy wants to say good-bye. She's waitin' on the back porch."

Dorothy saw him coming and hollered, "I wanted to wish you well before I go."

They hugged. Then Alta held her at arm's length. "Honestly, how do you think I'm doin'?"

"Well, Alta, how do *you* think you're doing?"

"If I was to speak on my own behalf, I'd say, I'm engaged in the legal business of building moderately priced homes for the good citizens of Tallapoosa, and I'm completely out of the illegal moonshine business."

Dorothy sighed. "I've met Mr. Chester Pope and Mr. Virgil Pettimore, your business partners, I believe. Chester's an educated outlaw, slippery as a snake, and Virgil is a redneck outlaw and a damn bully. No, Alta, it does not look good."

He paced back and forth in front of Dorothy. "You still think I'm a so-ci-o-path?"

"I have come to realize it's deeper than that. You got two broken parts, your heart and your head. I believe you can fix your heart. Your head, that's another story."

Alta took Dorothy's arm, and they walked back out into the orchard. "Let me get this straight," he said. "You're sayin' my heart and my head are broken. But if I use my head, I can fix my heart? So, how am I gonna do that?"

Dorothy frowned. "I think you have some sociopathic tendencies in you, but it goes deeper than that. You see, there are some things that can't be explained by psychology. I overheard you talking to those trailer-park folks, and I know you have some wonderful qualities."

"You know I'm tryin'."

Dorothy cocked her head to the side, searching for an explanation. "Do you know much about witchcraft?"

"Not a lot."

She led him to a bench beside the orchard. "Sit down, Alta; this is serious. See, I think you've got a curse."

Alta looked horrified. "That's bad!"

Dorothy went on. "The good part is, you are a genius. The bad part is, you spend most of your time trying to prove it. And when you are at your best proving it, you're morally blind. You can't tell the good from the bad, the legal from the illegal. It will eventually consume you, unless your head starts to obey your heart. Otherwise, your heart's gonna seize up—maybe a full blown heart attack."

Alta collapsed on the bench, suddenly feeling dizzy. He smiled contritely at Doctor Dorothy. "So if I can't think my way out of the curse, what's left?"

Dorothy patted his knee and spoke gently. "Holy men have taught us from the dawn of time that only your heart can defeat the demons in your head."

"I'm not lookin' to be no saint, but I'd like to break the curse."

"Then you got to find something to love that's more important than being the smartest man in West Georgia."

CHAPTER 19

OTASCO Store, Tallapoosa, Days Later

IT WAS DARK AND WINDY when Alta arrived at the store that morning. The thermometer outside read twenty-nine degrees. It wasn't much warmer inside. He scurried about, making coffee and building a fire in the wood stove. The Great Storm of 1975, as the weatherman called it, roared out of the Rocky Mountains and swept across the Midwest. Gathering all its fury, it slammed into the Southeast, producing forty-five tornadoes and twelve fatalities. Tallapoosa missed the brunt of it, yet seventy-mile-an-hour winds lashed through town, toppling trees, ripping down signs, and pushing trailers off their blocks. Between the storms, Alta and the twins stayed busy clearing debris from the streets. And now a damn cold snap.

He poured coffee and folded into a stuffed chair beside the stove. He savored the smell of coffee and the scent of pine logs crackling in the stove.

Alta was now, heavily invested in legitimate business ventures, what with opening the OTASCO stores and building affordable homes for working people. He was committed to developing a decent community in Haralson County, and he was committed to beating the curse. Even Chester agreed that he was a man on a mission.

The Tallapoosa OTASCO store, a stout two-story bunker in the heart of town, anchored to the corner of Alewine and Main Streets. Amid the calm and the storm, Alta and his boys had lugged boxes of home appliances and auto parts into the store. Lawn mowers, bicycles, motor oil, and tires were strewn up and down the aisles. Out front, a white metal awning extended over the sidewalk. Two-foot red letters spelled out OTASCO on the sign above the awning. In 1918, Sam and Herman Sanditen, Jewish Lithuanian brothers, opened the first Oklahoma Tire and Supply Company in Okmulgee, Oklahoma. By 1968, OTASCO's fiftieth anniversary, the chain had 455 units in twelve states. Alta would make it work.

The back door slammed, and young Jack Dryden waltzed in. "Good morning Daddy; you're early."

"Hey, son, you're late."

Jack grabbed the binoculars and headed to the front of the store. "Well, lookie, lookie. Daddy, I got somethin' to show you."

"What's that?"

"It's Mr. High Pockets Hitchcock across the street at Western Auto."

"What's he up to?"

Jack handed him the binoculars. "Take a look, but stay behind the display case."

"I'll be damned, he's watchin' us, and we're watchin' him."

"He's spying. Y'see, his binoculars are set up on that tripod. I been watchin' him for a day or so. Every time we put a pricing poster on the shelf, he's watchin' us and writin' somethin' down."

Alta shook his head. For years, Ray Hitchcock, who owned the Western Auto, had a near monopoly in the home and auto business. He was premium priced and held exclusive franchise agreements with the big-branded manufacturers. "I forgot, this is how legitimate, do-right commerce works."

"It's an open market, Daddy."

"Yes, it is."

Alta chuckled slyly, and went to work on his own surveillance system. Binoculars were duct taped to a ladder hidden near the front window. Alta kept an eye on Ray and considered what he would promote at OTASCO's grand opening.

Later that day, Tallapoosa, still in the clutches of a cold spell, was notified that its natural gas allotment had been severely cut. The schools were closed, the factories ran three-day weeks, and everyone was told to keep their thermostats no higher than forty degrees.

Like a hound on a possum, Alta made a quick phone call to an old prison cellmate in Southern California, which happened to be weathering a hot spell. He was referred to Chino State Prison, where they reconditioned box heaters. He immediately bought a freight carload for a sinful discount. In three days, he would launch his first assault on Western Auto. He paused and rubbed his temples after hanging up.

Was the curse of genius at work here? Surely not. He was simply seizing a fleeting opportunity. In sales, whether it was moonshine or box heaters, you were either a hunter or a trapper. Selling was a hunter's game, anticipating needs and delivering value. Genius? No way. He was just a street-smart merchant.

After locking the store at the end of the day, Alta shuffled across Main Street and lingered in front of the Western Auto. The merchandise in the window was definitely first class. The industrial smells of tires and motor oil were masked by the pleasing aroma of Pine-Sol. He made a mental note to get some Pine-Sol.

Stepping inside, he shouted, "Hey Ray, Alta here!"

Ray emerged from the backroom wiping his hands on a rag. "Why, hello, Alta. How are you?"

"I'm hoping to open next week."

Ray extended his hand. "Good for you. Town's kind of empty these days, what with the weather and all."

Alta noticed the price on the huge end-aisle display of space heaters. "I think folks are ready to buy. We just gotta get 'em out on the street."

Ray swallowed hard. "Say, Alta, I hope we can get along now that we're..." he faltered, "now that we're, so to speak, competitors."

"Let's do that, Ray. Let's get along and do what's right for the community," Alta replied, not sure what that meant.

"Well, on that note," Ray added as he walked over to his end-aisle display of lawn mowers, "not to upset you, but I couldn't help notice you're displaying Toro lawnmowers."

Alta stared pointedly at Ray's binocular set-up behind the counter, and grinned. "I guess you would know."

Ray flushed red. "Here's the thing, y'see…I have the exclusive franchise for Toro in West Georgia. So…you see, legally, you can't be doin' that."

"Hmm? Well, thanks for pointin' that out there, Ray. I want to run an honest business, honest competition and all."

Alta tipped his hat and sauntered out the door and on down the block to the city hall. Since Shelby's funeral, he'd decided to run for city council, and he had been appointed on the spot. He reckoned the town needed help. Lately, he'd been spending time in the evenings reviewing public records.

Though Tallapoosa was still in the doldrums of the recession and battered by winter storms, Alta was confident that better times were ahead. He'd checked the business license ledger first. One hundred twenty-four licenses had been issued to date, 15 percent more than the previous year. The economy was coming back, though no one believed it. Some of that business would be done out on the interstate.

"Money leavin' town," he growled.

The more he dug into local issues, the more problems he uncovered. In the 1960s, a state judicial panel had declared the County Unit System invalid. The system allotted votes by county rather than by population. Nowadays, 76 percent of Georgia's 159 counties were rural and sparsely populated. Eliminating the County Unit System triggered the decline of rural power and largesse in Georgia. Tallapoosa was like an aging prom queen who had let herself go. Downtown had run-down, empty storefronts, broken sidewalks, and weeds popping out of every crack. The sewer taxes were too high, the roads needed paving, and old-timers on the poverty line needed a nutrition program. Add to that, they needed to attract more industry and prepare for the bicentennial celebration.

Alta was fast asleep with his head resting on a tax ledger when he heard the knocking. He blinked up at the clock as he shuffled to the front door.

Chester Pope rapped on the door with his cane and burst inside once it was unlocked.

"Dad-gum-it, Alta, you're a hard man to find."

"Come in, come in," Alta yawned. "What's wrong?"

"I told you Bud Meeker, the big homebuilder in town, might be trouble. Well, his ass-hole lawyer just called."

"It's a little late for that, ain't it?" Alta shrugged. "The homes are all framed up."

"It's a lawsuit," Chester barked. "He don't want your homes. He wants your money."

"How's he do that?"

"I've had problems with him before. He had an option on the property I sold you. He says I defaulted on the deal."

Alta rolled his eyes. "Surely, counselor, you did the right thing?"

Knowing not to blink, Chester stared directly into Alta's eyes. "Hell yes; mistakes were made. Kind of a gray area."

"That one, counselor, is on you."

"There's also a problem with the building permit. Bud's lawyer, the ass-hole—actually, they're both ass-holes—questioned where the money came from."

Alta eyes suddenly sparkled. He'd had a comic insight. He had sworn to do right and deal with the darn curse, and he damn well meant it. Yet, the boy in him loved a prank. He loved to pull the tail of big business, or big government, or a competitor.

"Say, Chester, doesn't Meeker own that ranch-style mansion up on the hill near Buchanan?"

"That he does. Out on Highway 120."

"Good; here's what you do. Take a full-page ad in the *Tallapoosa-Beacon*, call it a fire sale, whatever. List it at two hundred thousand dollars. No phone numbers, just the address. And put something in there about how any offer will be considered. That ought to set the dogs a-barkin'."

"Alta, as your banker, I gotta tell you, that ain't funny."

"The hell it ain't."

CHAPTER 20

Tallapoosa, Days Later

THE TEMPERATURE DROPPED TO ZERO as gale-force winds whipped through town. Alta, his sons, and a forklift crew from the depot met the morning train with a railcar full of space heaters from California. The railcar was shunted onto the siding across from the store, and they worked through the night, moving pallets across the street and into the basement of the store.

The next morning, as the weather permitted, Alta and the boys built displays for the opening day promotion. The heaters were priced 40 percent below Western Auto's price. Jack booked ads with the radio station and with all the Haralson County papers. As the wind died down, he posted signs on every telephone pole in town that read:

OTASCO's Grand Opening!
Come to the Lollapalooza in Tallapoosa.
Huge Discounts on Reconditioned Space Heaters

This was the jolt Tallapoosa needed to kick-start the local economy, to put OTASCO on the map. The store was sparkling and chock-full of bargains. Alta's only regret was he hadn't had time to open his other OTASCO store in Bremen.

Before leaving that afternoon, he eased over to the ladder with the binoculars strapped to the side and focused in on Western Auto. Ray Hitchcock stood behind his binoculars, glaring back at him. Alta stepped away and laughed, then headed for his pickup. He laid an arrangement of roses and a ceramic vase on the front seat and drove west on Highway 78 to the cemetery. He had a lot to share with Shelby.

You'll see, darlin', it's all legal, and it's all on account of you.

He lugged a folding chair, the flowers and the vase down the hill to her grave. Once he'd arranged the flowers by the headstone, he settled into the chair. Looking out on the white-capped river, he sang Shelby's favorite hymn:

"Shall we gather at the river?
Where bright angel feet have trod,
With its crystal tide forever
Flowing by the throne of God?"

Rattling along like an auctioneer at a steer sale, Alta shared his progress with Shelby. "You're gonna like this one. Remember that tinhorn builder, Bud Meeker? Well, he's tryin' to block my subdivision. Sooooo…I put his house on the market, that mansion out on Highway 120, for peanuts…and I been appointed to the city council. We got to be ready for the bicentennial, and here's the main thing: it is all leee-gitt."

Alta caught his breath as the sun set over Alabama. "And finally, Shelby darlin', I truly miss you."

As the light held, he pulled out the *Atlanta Journal* and pored through the ads section for used Toro lawnmowers.

———

Mandy had finished her shift in the ER and was changing out of her scrubs when she got the call. "Hello, Nurse Tate here."

"Hello Mandy, I'm calling from the Atlanta Federal Prison. Can we talk?"

Mandy immediately knew who was calling. The strong New York accent gave it away. "Oh hello, Doctor Epstein."

"Call me Dorothy. We need to talk about Alta. I'm concerned."

Mandy buttoned her blouse and sat down, "Really? I haven't seen him since the funeral."

"He's grieving something awful for Shelby. He talks about doin' right, and I know he's busy with the store and his building business, but I worry about him."

"I won't lie," Mandy replied as her smile became a frown. "I have feelings for Alta, but it's not normal for me to be calling on him. Shelby hasn't been gone now but a month."

"Usually I'd agree, but Alta's never been normal. He's got plenty of chutzpah, but he's a scoundrel. Very smart, but he's got demons running around in his head like he's cursed."

"So true."

"I'm thinking you should pay him a visit. Don't phone or anything. Just drop by."

"Just drop by?"

"That's it. He doesn't know it, but he needs a friend. And…there's one more thing…he's got a serious heart condition."

"How serious?"

"Look, Mandy, you're a nurse, and I'm a doctor; this is confidential, OK?"

"OK."

"Its coronary artery disease," said Dorothy.

"Doesn't surprise me." Mandy shook her head. "He carries a lot of stress. He complained of chest pains at the wake. Claimed it was indigestion, too many ribs."

"He's cagey that way, Mandy. The risk factors are all there: overweight, overstressed, and classic denial. In prison, he popped nitroglycerin pills like jelly beans."

"Can he control his heart?"

"Can he? Hell yes. Will he? Probably not." She paused and cleared her throat. "Alta's already had several heart attacks that he's kept to himself."

"Thank you for telling me all this, but," Mandy stood up and paced back and forth, "you need to know this. There's no future for Alta in my life, unless…unless he stays out of prison."

"That's perfect! That's what he needs to hear. By the way, he visits Shelby's grave every day, right about now."

Mandy laughed. "I'll go."

Alta recognized the fragrance of the perfume as it drifted by and narrowed it down to Mandy as she burst from behind a tree.

"Hello, stranger!" she hollered.

Alta beamed and popped up. "Mandy! My goodness, what a treat."

He'd forgotten how striking she was: tall, broad-shouldered, yet alluring. Long dark hair streaked with silver gray hung over a well-fitted white uniform. She'd been a high-scoring forward on the West Georgia College basketball team and still played in the women's league.

"How'd you know I was here?" asked Alta.

"A little bird told me."

Alta stepped forward and gave her a hug. "This is real nice."

Mandy broke it off. "Doc Dorothy asked me to drop by, and here I am."

Alta's face glowed like a new moon, then he shrank back, a chastened schoolboy. "I didn't mean to suggest…"

Mandy blushed as she shrugged contritely. They both laughed at their awkwardness.

"Let's start over. It *is* good to see you Alta," she said, beaming.

Alta handed her the folding chair and sat on his coat. "And *it is* good to see you."

After a long pause, they both started to talk at once and then stopped.

Alta pointed to her. "Sorry, you first. How're you doin'?"

"Well I'm getting' along," she said and smiled dismissively.

"Is Lamar making alimony payments?"

"Not a lick."

"You're still workin' in the ER?"

"Senior nurse working for the blessed Bridget Mulligan."

"Gud, gud, and you're getting by financially and all?"

Mandy paused and looked away. "Not really. Lamar and I still have a joint account and what with his new Harley and all his other boy-toys were way behind. They're lookin' to garnish my wages."

Alta shook his head. "No sir, that ain't gud. Can I help out in any way?"

Mandy snapped around and glared at Alta. "I ain't here to talk about my problems. How are your boy's doin'?"

Alta flinched at her response and made a mental note to look into it. "They're good boys. They been helpin' out, setting up the store. Buck, he don't talk much, and Jack, he never stops talkin'. Buck is working full time at Stoffel Seal. On the weekend, he's out with his kids hunting and fishing. Jack is a volunteer fireman and works full time for me at the store. They both miss their mama somethin' awful."

"They're not alone. You know Shelby did my hair for the last three years while you were in prison."

"No way, she never said a word."

"She wouldn't."

Alta stood up and stretched. "You want to take a ride?"

"Where to?"

"To Bremen. I want to show you sumpthin'."

"No funny business?"

"Are you kidding? I'm on the city council."

"That's not what I mean."

———

Mandy smiled politely, wondering what she'd got herself into, as Alta parked across from a row of storefronts in Bremen. They got out and walked around. Mandy knew all about Bremen. Her father, Vassar had worked off and on in the mills. The Sewell Mill stood right down the street, still one of the biggest clothing manufacturers in the South. The street lights came on as they crossed the road. A freshly painted OTASCO sign hung above the middle storefront.

Alta unlocked the door and shoved it open. "Here she be."

Cobwebs hung from the rafters and swayed in the breeze that blew in the door. The long, narrow room was empty, except for a blanket of dust covering the floor. Mandy sneezed, pulled a handkerchief from her purse, and sneezed again.

They stepped back outside and sat on a bench.

"You got a lot of work ahead of you, Mr. Dryden."

"I'm thriving on it right now. The subdivision is moving along, the Tallapoosa store is having its grand opening tomorrow, and I hope to get this store up and running real soon."

Mandy nodded and looked curiously at him. "And you're feelin' good about all this?"

"I am, but I really want to know how you're doing."

She looked away. "I'm a big girl," she faltered, "I'm gettin' by."

Marriage had been a disaster for Mandy. She had a fatal attraction for dangerous men, "bad boys" like Lamar. After the divorce, she'd gone from man to man, still obsessed with dangerous men. Out there on the weekends, on the prowl, she enjoyed herself, yet, she was torn, addicted to the excitement, frightened by the danger. Lately, she'd reined in her lifestyle. She no longer played the field; she stayed home, stood her ground, and tried to take control of her life.

Alta locked his hands behind his head and stretched his legs out on the sidewalk. "It's none of my business, but I'd like to help if I can."

"You been more than generous over the years, both to me and to every other down-and-outer around here."

Alta rolled his eyes modestly. "That's probably my best side."

She ran her fingers through her hair. She was stuck on Alta's earlier question. "How are you doing?"

I no longer ask myself that question. I guess I have lost my innocence.

She looked up blankly. "Sorry, what did you say?"

As they talked, Sonny Hoyt, the Tallapoosa police chief, cruised by in a patrol car. Alta smiled and waved at Hoyt, who looked away. "He follows me wherever I go. Thinks he's a super cop."

Mandy shook her head in amazement. "Are you kidding? Every cop in the state wants to bust you, and when they do, you'll never go to trial in Haralson County. They're just toyin' with you."

"I'm bein' lawful."

Mandy pulled her championship ring from her pocket and clutched it in her hand. "How do you keep it together?" she fumed. "Your bein' lawful?…with Virgil and Lamar, your main men in a rollin' gunfight across West Georgia, and good Lawd, I met Head Rebel and Billy Boudreaux at Shelby's wake—they're a nasty pair. How do you keep it together? What's your secret?"

Alta smiled. "It's nothin' special. I just block it out and move ahead."

"Yeah, there's that," Mandy frowned. "Or maybe you're just a dumb-ass honey bear with a failing heart and no conscience."

Alta wiped his forehead, stared at Mandy's ring, and tried to change the subject. "I've never seen that ring before."

"Back when, y'know, I played for the West Gerogia Lady-Braves, and we won the Conference Basketball Chanpionship. It's my lucky charm. Anyway, you'd better get me back to my car. I gotta go."

Alta shook his head as he dug in his pocket for his car keys. "How's the lucky charm work for you?"

Mandy grimaced. "It keeps me from trying to please dangerous men."

They drove back to the cemetery in awkward silence.

Alta parked next to her pickup and blurted, "I'd like to help you out. I'd like you to manage the Bremen store."

Mandy's hand dissappeared into her pocket and clutched the basketball. She tossed her head from side to side. "No way."

CHAPTER 21

Tallapoosa, Days Later

LAMAR'S EYES GLAZED OVER AS he watched the sun sink behind the Talladega Mountains. He crouched on the narrow catwalk that ran around the water tank high above town. His mind drifted from the backwoods of Haralson County to the savannahs of North Africa. In a blink, his ears perked up, and his lips curled above jagged teeth. He was in full wild-dog mode, an apex predator poised for the hunt.

The "wild dog thing," as his friends called it, began as an innocent diversion, a touch of whimsy. He'd grown up on John Wayne movies and moved from the local sheriff phase to the global vigilante phase, and finally he'd morphed into an apex predator—the wild dog, the peace-keeper of the ecosystem.

As a teenager, he'd run moonshine into Atlanta for a hundred bucks a night. That was the mother lode for a poor boy from the South. Soon enough, he was awash in fast bikes, fast girls, and Southern Comfort. He was vaguely aware of the two Lamars, the bad-boy biker and the wild dog, but had little control over who might appear. His waking dreams were filled with images of both: the flashing lights and wailing sirens as the law raided their liquor still; the howl of African wild dogs bringing down an aging lion; the smell of burning flesh as he was cooked in a steaming mash vat; a shotgun blast and the rattle of buckshot inside his single-wide.

He seized the railing of the catwalk and shook his head, trying to drive off the images. Honking horns broke the silence. His head cleared. A Grand Opening searchlight swept across the sky, as Main Street snapped clearly into focus below. All roads into town were jammed. Headlights lined Highway 78 coming in from Alabama. Cars and trucks double parked along Alewine Street as shoppers hurried into OTASCO. Red balloons danced above the store while the searchlight continued to sweep across the sky. Alta's space heater promotion seemed to be a huge success. Yet, this could be good or bad. Good for the town. But it could destabilize the ecosystem if Alta gained too much power.

Lamar pulled out his bike keys and rubbed a voodo charm on his pant leg. He'd heard Doc Dorothy believed Alta had a curse, and he knew a thing or two about a curse. He gripped the railing and pontifiated.

Whether you call it original sin or bad luck, we all have a measure of good and evil coursing through us. Sure, there are lots of terms for it. Personally, I agree with the Doctor. I call it a curse, and everybody knows there's only two kinds of curses: a middling-curse and a damnable curse.

His head snapped back as he chanted. "With a middling-curse, the forces of good outweigh the forces of evil. Life is a struggle, but most folks break the curse and are stronger for it. But, with a damnable-curse, the forces of good and evil are equally balanced. Life is one hell of a ride, but the curse breaks them in the end. Kind of a nasty trick wouldn't you say?"

He held his charm up to the sun and continued. "The other tricky part about a curse is ya never know what kind ya got. So, here's ole Alta struggling to break his curse and not knowing what he's up against. Now me and Alta don't always get along, but I'd like to see him break the curse and land a few blows on the devil back. You never know, it could be good for business."

Two weeks had passed since Lamar had jammed a 357 Magnum under Virgil's chin and threatened to blow his head off. But now, he understood the big picture. He understood that Virgil had lied to Alta, had told him that he'd sold his tapping business to the Dixie mafia. Alta, who was bent on going straight, was caught in a tangled web. Add to that, the FBI and the ATF were lurking around, bent on putting Alta behind bars for good. And then there was Fred Dryden, Alta's brother, who, unlike Alta, was humorless and not at all concerned with going straight. Lamar thought perhaps he could benefit financially from a cut of the gas tapping—and have the satisfaction of ruining Alta as he stabilized the planet.

"Hell," he chuckled. "I got more choices than a sailor on shore leave."

The lights of town flickered in the darkness as he crept along the catwalk. Time to do some prowling. He climbed down from the water tank and felt his way around the cyclone fence to his Harley.

Moments earlier, Fred Dryden, Alta's older brother, spotted Lamar on the water tank. He dimmed the lights and eased his Ford van to the base of the tank. Fred and Boo Thrower, a lumbering giant in Big and Tall bib overalls, watched as Lamar fumbled with his Harley keys. Boo slipped behind him and wrapped his arm around Lamar's neck. Lamar's head snapped back, and then he went limp. With the paws of a gorilla, Boo dragged him to the van, stuffed a rag in his mouth, bound his hands and feet, and crammed him into the back.

Fred grinned broadly, pleased with Boo's execution. Though Boo had never learned to read or write, he could pull a tractor through a mud park. He wore filthy overalls and smelled of the barnyard. Fred quietly shut the rear door and slipped into the driver's seat. Flipping on the running lights, he eased the van down to East Alabama Street and stopped. It was dark at this end of town. Several blocks away, it looked like the circus was in town. The searchlight in front of OTASCO still swept across the sky. Though the temperature had dropped into the forties, the town was packed. Bundled up, they ambled along the sidewalk, shopping, visiting, laughing, glad to be out. Most toted a space heater under their arms.

Fred drove east on the Highway 78, pulled into the American Legion Park, and wound his way through vintage World War II tanks and planes, coming to a stop down by the lake. The parking lot was full, and the bar was jumping. A Hank Williams love song boomed from the jukebox as under-age couples danced on the back porch. The OTASCO sale seemed to have sparked a party mood.

Fred switched off the motor, took a hard pull on a jar of moonshine, and looked into the back. Boo squatted next to Lamar, whose pupils had rolled inside his head. Boo gently tapped his forehead, and the pupils returned for a moment. Boo smiled.

Fred smiled back. "How's our boy?"

Boo tried to clear his ragged voice. "Comin' rou-nd."

"Whack him a good one, if he tries anything."

As a boy, Boo had broken his jaw falling off a hay truck. They'd never got it set right. The lower jaw jutted to the right of the upper jaw. Words tumbled around in his mouth and sloshed out. He carried a drool rag.

Fred got out and lit a cigarette. Unlike Boo, who wore bibs, Fred wore an extra-large suit off the rack at J.C. Penney. Chuckling in eagerness, he tightened the knot of his hand-painted tie, pulled his dropping trousers well above his paunch, and took up the belt a notch. For years, he and Virgil had headed up Alta's moonshine empire. Alta was the boss but never had full control of either of them.

At five to nine, he got back into the van. Among other things, Virgil ran the American Legion Hall. Earlier in the day, Fred had arranged to meet him down by the lake at nine. As he waited, Fred pulled out his new Colt 45 pistol, loaded a seven round magazine into the walnut gripped handle, and racked a round into the chamber. He carefully placed the pistol back in its holster and slid it under the front seat. He glanced back at Boo, who had become fascinated with Lamar's eyes. "You ready?"

"Yaah."

"When he sits in the passenger seat, drop the choke rope over his head and hang on."

"Yaah."

As Virgil ambled down the hill, Fred flashed a crooked smile, a smile that had cut permanent fissures in his face. He reached over and swung the passenger door open as Virgil arrived. "Get in. Let's talk."

As Virgil got in, Boo slipped the choke rope over his head and pulled. Virgil's head snapped back against the seat. He sputtered but couldn't get a word out.

"OK, Boo, tie him off, but don't choke him to death."

Virgil lurched forward, thrust his legs up and tried to kick out the front window, then went limp. He was quickly gagged and bound.

"So, Virgil, if you want to make it through the night, you need to calm down. We're going to take a ride out to the Devil's Kitchen and talk some business," snarled Fred.

Fred pulled out of Legion Park heading east. Just before the bridge on Old Ridgeway Road, he turned into a rutted dirt lane. Fog rolled in as they wound their way through heavy woodlands. Fred chuckled inwardly. *It don't git much better than this—a jar of corn whiskey, a loaded Colt 45 in my pocket, and runnin' around in a hopped-up old van with two hostages. Good lord, what more can a country boy ask for?*

Fred was convinced his brother Alta, the smart one, would be impressed with the caper. He slowed to a crawl as an overgrown graveyard came into view. Crumbling limestone markers and crosses canted in every direction. Kudzu vines choked out the rusted remains of an iron fence. He stopped in front of a large headstone with the word PEACE carved in it. Flipping on the high beams, he left the motor running, and stepped out. Pulling his gun role from under the seat, he clipped the khaki belt around his waist. The Colt 45 Manstopper was snug in a leather flap holster that hung from his right hip. Several canvas magazine pouches hung from his left hip each holding two, seven round magazines. Fred had "cocked and locked" the .45 Manstopper earlier. He'd watched his share of gangster movies and had recently moved up from a .38 to a .45 caliber, pleased with the easy reload feature of the .45. He waved the Colt back and forth looking every bit the World War II warrior, then turned to Boo, "OK Boo, one at a time, set our boys in front of the headstone."

Boo set them carefully on the ground and gently patted their heads. Fred jerked out their gags, and pointed to the headstone. "Now boys, what's that say?"

They both mumbled, "Peace."

Boo grinned broadly, like a kid at a matinee. Lamar's eyes seared with hate. Virgil was glad to be breathing.

Fred strutted back and forth like a ringmaster. "So boys, here we are in the Devil's Kitchen. They say there's been some killin' done out here. Virgil, I believe you'd know somthin' 'bout that."

"Nothing on my police record," Virgil snapped.

Fred's hand flashed to his side holster, returned with the Manstopper and shoved it against Virgil's forhead. "There might be some killing here tonight. Boo there, brought a long handled shovel. We may plant the both of you right here like calla lilies."

Lamar's eyes narrowed trying it seemed to read Fred's intent. Virgil clenched his jaw and glared at Fred.

"So, as I was sayin', I'm flat ass tired of you boys runnin' around shootin' at each other. That, by God, has gotta stop. Are you hearin' me?"

"We get that Fred," Virgil barked. "What's the deal?"

Lamar sneered back without a word.

Fred bent over and wacked Lamar with the butt of the pistol. "You got nothin' to say, you scheming little bastard? You tryin' to stay ahead of me on this? Tryin' to figure if you should hang with us or snitch to the feds?"

He turned to Virgil who was laughing and laid his head open as well with the pistol butt. "Funny, ain't it?"

Fred glared at both of them. "So listen carefully: this whole thing is a house of cards if Alta pulls out. And he will pull out if he hears about it right now. We need about three weeks to get it really going."

Fred squatted down next to Virgil. "Tell me if this sounds right. Here lately, we been running seven trucks a night, from the one tap in Fruithurst to local gas stations. That's over seven thousand gallons of gas, and at forty cents a gallon, that's two thousand eight hundred a night."

Still bound, Virgil, wiped the blood from around his eyes with his sleeve. "That's maximum; we need more trucks and more taps."

"Bingo! So what about it, Lamar? If you take over distribution, get more taps, more trucks, more customers, and manage that, you could be making, say, four hundred bucks a night. You run that out for a week or two, and it beats the hell out of snitch money."

Lamar's eyes narrowed. "Let me think about it."

Fred sunk to his knees and landed a roundhouse to the back of Lamar's head with the butt of the gun. Blood splattered across the headstone. "OK, you got a minute."

Whirling around to Virgil, Fred continued, "While pretty boy, or is it Wild Dog, makes up his mind, let me ask you: can you work with Lamar if he's in? And if he's not, can you help me dispose of him?"

"Yes to both."

"OK, Lamar, time's up. I don't want to sway your decision, but you must have figured out by now, there is no way you're leaving here…knowing what you know now, unless you join us. And even if you join us and snitch, first your father and then your mother will end up in a deep well in Alabama."

Lamar smiled through the blood. "Well, hell yes, I'm in, but who's funding this big operation?"

"Fer now, the three of us, stupid."

Boo wiped the blood off Lamar's face with his rag, set him on the floor of the van, and returned for Virgil. After they were both bound and gagged, Fred drove back to town.

They dropped Lamar off at the foot of the water tank and then pulled to the rear of the Legion Hall. Most of the crowd had gone home for the night. Fred and Boo stepped to the rear of the van.

"Boo, get on up to the back of the hall and make sure no one comes our way."

Boo nodded and was off. Fred pulled Virgil out, untied him, and removed the gag. "Sorry, Virgil, I didn't plan on whackin' you, but it had to be convincing."

Virgil winced. "Fred, you're one twisted sumbitch. You sure you know what you're doin'?"

Fred crossed his arms and rocked back and forth. "I know we ain't gettin' seven trucks out a night. And I know we don't have three weeks before Alta figures things out. That was all for Lamar's ears."

"Alta hounds me every damn day about closin' the deal with the Dixie mafia," Virgil fumed. "I truly believe he's been born again, or whatever you call it."

Fred slipped a brown envelope from his coat pocket. "Alta's got fifty thousand into the tapping deal. Right?"

"He does."

"Give him this tomorrow. It's ten thousand in cash, a twenty-percent down payment. Tell him Billy Blue-Eyes from Biloxi is in, and he's out. He'll get the rest at the end of the month."

Virgil chuckled. "You got a lot of weasel in you, Fred. Where'didya get the loot?"

"None of your damn business," he smirked. "Let's just say its family money. I know where the cash is stashed."

"And if Alta goes for this yarn, we got a month. Is that it?"

"That's right. But that ain't *it*. You and Lamar got to make this thing work. That's *it*.

CHAPTER 22

Tallapoosa/Bremen, Days Later

———

ALTA STEWED QUIETLY AS THE ceiling fan sent burnt coffee fumes and cigarette smoke into a dirty haze that hung over the council chamber. The council was mired in a consensus of caution. Growing up, they'd all been scarred by the Great Depression and were still stinging from the deep recession of the 1970s. To their credit, they'd guided the town through the hard times with layoffs, cost cutting, and general prudence, but hope had dimmed. Hunkering down was now the key to recovery.

Alta absently scribbled numbers on a legal pad, playing with the math of first and second mortgages while debating whether to resign from the council. The meeting was running late, and he had work to do at the store and didn't want to keep Chester Pope, his irritable banker, waiting. Earlier in the meeting, he'd cast the only affirmative votes on two proposals he'd initiated, one to fill potholes on Main Street and the other to develop a "Meals-on-Wheels" program to feed the elderly.

His hardware store had been a great success, and he had contracts on most of the homes he was building. Now was the time, he felt, to promote prosperity. Yet, he was still hell-bent on going straight and kick-starting the local economy, just not very good at democratic wrangling and consensus building. If this was how honest people got things done, he needed to get better at it.

Rapping his gavel, Mayor Clem Robinson concluded, "Thank you, gentlemen. It's been a good meeting."

Gathering their files, the council members nodded their approval. Alta scowled as he stood up. The room fell silent.

The mayor set his gavel down. "Alta, you got somethin' to say?"

Alta shrugged. "Boys, I guess I'm the only one in town who believes the hard times are over. I'm not sure I'm gonna be much help on the council. Anyway, I'm late for a meeting."

———

Alta hustled out of City Hall and scurried across the street. Chester pulled to the curb in his canary-yellow Coupe de Ville as Alta arrived back at the store. Flinging open the passenger door, Chester shouted. "Come on, Alta, let's take a ride."

"Make it short; I got lots to do. And…and what the hell happened to your ruby-red Lincoln?"

"Cadillacs are the future."

Moments later, Chester pulled up to the construction site. Roofs were going on most of the homes, the rest were getting a final coat of paint. Chester unrolled the blueprints and poked at it with arthritic fingers. "According to plan, they all should be finished by Friday?"

Alta hesitated. "Supposed to be…yeah. That was Friday, was it?"

"I'll take that for a yes. Gawd damn, Alta, we got buyers waitin' to move in. Their applications are in, but we'll have to come up with some mighty creative mortgages. Some of them will need second mortgages. Take Tommy Atkins, the foreman down at Sewell Mill; he's ready to move in this week, and we got a trailer-park family ready to move into Tommy's old house once he's out. There are half a dozen folks in the same situation as Tommy, and…" Chester's face turned red as he gasped for breath, "and, our builder is screaming to get paid, and we got a couple of missionaries on the planning commission snooping around. They want to know where the money's coming from for all this."

Alta pinched the bridge of his nose, checking his temper. "So what didya tell 'em?"

"Damn, Alta, I told 'em its jest dirty moonshine money that we got stuffed under a mattress."

"That ain't exactly right. The money's locked in iceboxes here and there."

"That, my friend, will not be funny in court," Chester growled.

A smile flickered at the edges of Alta's mouth. "Truly Chester, what didya tell 'em?"

"I was very professional," he said with a snicker. "I jest lied to 'em." Chester rolled up the plans. "I'm needin' some serious time with you tomorrow. The paper trail on this has got to be seamless."

Alta pulled a notepad from his shirt pocket. "How does eight sharp at the store sound?"

"I'll be there."

They were back in front of the store within minutes. Space heaters were prominently displayed in the front windows.

Chester chuckled. "How you doin' on your heaters?"

"Bought 'em cheap. Sold 'em cheaper. Put our little store on the map."

"So, you lost money?"

"Chester, for an educated man, you don't know much about retailing."

"Just to be clear, you lost money on the whole railcar of heaters?"

"It's called a loss leader; that's the way it works."

"I'm thinkin', you better get back into traditional crime. You got a knack for it."

Alta jumped into his pickup and headed for Bremen. He'd called Mandy daily for weeks, trying to meet with her. She'd refused, then postponed, then agreed, and then canceled. She'd reluctantly agreed to meet him at his Bremen store that evening.

Fog rolled down Atlantic Avenue as he pulled up to the Bremen store. Street lights shown dimly through the front windows. Boxes were stacked to the ceiling. Before unlocking the front door, he checked his watch. "Six-thirty," he sighed. "Just made it."

The room remained dark when he flipped on the light switch.

"Damn," he groaned. "We were supposed to get power today."

Returning to his truck, he turned on his headlights, which threw shafts of light between stacks of boxes. He was keen to see the refitting of the former pool hall. The long narrow room smelled of sawdust and paint fumes. The carpenters had finished the main counter and shelving. A fresh coat of orange enamel shined from the walls. He got busy sweeping up and moving cases of motor oil up on the shelf. He lifted each case over his head, straining on tiptoes to get it up to the highest ledge. After the third case, he stepped back, stumbled, and collapsed. His heart pounded wildly as he lay on the floor. He felt a sharp pain in his chest.

The room spun around as he pulled up on his knees. He rose slowly, reminded of Doc Dorothy's instructions: inhale, one thousand one, one thousand two, one thousand three; exhale, one thousand one, one thousand two, one thousand three. The doctor's advice echoed through his mind: "It's your head, stupid. Your head will lead you where your body can't follow. Listen to your body."

The burning in his chest passed as Alta rested on a long, casket-size box. He tried to listen to his body as his head went to work on the events of the day. He was unhappy with city government. He'd probably resign. His effort to provide affordable housing to a beleaguered community was under attack. And, noting it was 7:30 p.m., Mandy had stood him up.

The headlights from his truck dimmed and then died as he bemoaned his fate.

Hadn't he walked the line? Wasn't he going straight? Was redemption really out of the question? He stretched out in the dark and stared at the ceiling.

———

Bremen was lost in the fog as Mandy raced into town. She'd taken an unpaved detour around the construction on Highway 27. Her car was covered with red Georgia clay. Parking next to Alta's truck, she checked her watch. It was ten to eight, and the store was dark. She clutched the steering wheel and tried to push away the horrible images of her double shift in the ER.

As she had finished her first shift, ten cars piled up on the Interstate, blanketed in fog. Sirens screamed and red lights flashed as ambulances stacked up at the hospital's emergency entrance. The ER team scrambled in full triage mode for three hours. Stretchers and gurneys packed the hallways and waiting rooms. Some victims moaned, others howled. Most sat stoically in silence, wrapped in bloody bandages. Off-duty doctors and nurses raced back to the hospital and hurried into the ER. Mandy was relieved at seven-thirty.

She rubbed her temples, trying to ease a piercing headache. Triage, she reflected, was both humane and awful. For those not in life-threatening conditions, treatment was deferred. The idea was to maximize the number of survivors. She ran her hands through her hair and flipped on her high beams. Where the hell was Alta? She left the motor running and the lights on and scurried inside. Shoving open the door, she hollered, "Hey, Alta, you in here?"

A feeble moan came from the back of the store as Alta's head appeared in the headlights. "Hey, Mandy, is that you?"

She weaved through the boxes. "It's me, it's me; I'm runnin' late."

Alta struggled to get up. "Hey, it's me here, and I'm runnin' down."

"Damn, what happened?"

"We'll talk. If Mabel's Country Kitchen is still open, let's get somthin' to eat."

They shuffled down the street to Mabel's and found a booth in the back. Mandy took off her overcoat, noticed bloodstains on the sleeve of her uniform, and pulled her coat back on. Alta looked on quietly.

"You want to talk about it?" he asked gently.

"Bad night on the Interstate, bad night in the ER. I had to pull a second shift," she said with a sigh. "What about you? You look like hell."

"Nothing much. I got to sweepin' up and stackin' oil, and I kinda got dizzy. Probably the paint fumes; anyway, I'm glad you're here. I do need some help."

Mandy bit her bottom lip. Alta was such a damn liar. Yeah, sure, probably the paint fumes. Doc Dorothy was right.

After they ordered burgers and fries, Mandy tried again to get Alta to talk about his dizziness, which had probably been a heart attack. "Alta, you listen to me," she declared and then paused nervously. "I've got some feelings for you. But I've never been much good at pickin' friends."

Alta perked up as the color returned to his face. Mandy slid salt and pepper shakers around the table like pawns on a chessboard. "If I was to come to work for you as…I'm not sure what to call it."

Alta broke in, "Don't you worry. I'll take good care of you."

"Hush up," she shot back. "I don't want you takin' care of me. As I was sayin', I'm not sure what you call it, but I don't want a relationship, I want an arrangement."

Alta's brow shot up. "I'm listenin'."

She continued to move the salt and pepper shakers around. "I got a good job with benefits at the hospital. I'm not likin' it much anymore, but it's steady."

Alta cleared his throat. "I know I'm a bit of a lost soul, but I truly have feelin's for you."

Mandy's eyes sparkled as she slid the shakers back against the napkin holder. "Well good, good, good. Here's what I'm thinkin'. I'd like to have a go at runnin' the store, but at a fair wage, and…and I'd want a piece of the action."

Alta's head popped back. "Damn, girl, didya get yourself a lawyer?"

She grinned broadly. "The Honorable Thomas Murphy."

Alta rolled his lower lip over his upper lip in what looked like a pout. "And what percent of the action you lookin' for?"

"Mr. Tom said I should ask for a third, with an option to buy up to fifty-one percent."

Mabel heard the last of Mandy's terms as she arrived with burgers and fries. Winking at Mandy, she asked, "Can I get you anything else?"

Mandy winked back. "I think we're good here."

Alta reached across the table and shook Mandy's hand. "You got youself a deal—sorry, an arrangement. I'll have a contract drawn up in the mornin'."

"And Alta, honey, I believe we'd both like more of a relationship, but that's not happening unless," her head snapped back, and her eyes narrowed, "unless you stay the hell out of jail. You understand?"

He swallowed hard. "Fah-evah."

CHAPTER 23

Tallapoosa, Days Later

———

ALTA PARKED BEHIND THE STORE at five o'clock in the morning with a head full of problems to solve. But first he'd watch the sunrise. When coffee was done, he pulled his rocker near the front window and took to rocking as the first light of dawn peeked over the water tank. At the foot of the tank, an arc welder flashed red and blue out the bay door of Smith's Auto Service. They'd work all night when they got behind. The sweet smell of smoked pork drifted down the street from the Rib Shack. To the west of town, the doors at Lipham's Department Store swung open as Tallapoosa woke up. Alta looked up at the water tank just for fun. By now, most folks knew that Wild Dog Tate hung out on the catwalk like a bird on a wire. No sign of him yet Alta shrugged. Lamar was a midnight rider, not much of an early riser.

Doc Dorothy had told Alta to stop overloading his wagon with problems and pulling them around all day. "That," she said, "creates stress and stress raises hell with your coronary condition." In an attempt to empty his wagon, Alta turned first to his store.

I'm happy with the grand opening, and I'm confident business will grow.

Interstate 20 and the motels and strip malls that were popping up like mushrooms concerned him the most. He glanced up and down Main Street and pursed his lips. As much as he loved Tallapoosa, it needed a facelift if they hoped to keep money from leaving town. Maybe he should take a more active role in city government—see if he could kick-start the local economy. He'd look into it.

He refilled his coffee cup and continued to empty his wagon. *As far as my homebuilding business, that seems to be stuck in local politics. The planning commission is looking into my financing. That's a nasty one.* He hoped Chester had a way around it. They'd meet later that morning.

Just then, the morning train sounded its alarm: *Whoo-whee! Whoo-whee! Whoo-whee!* It rumbled through town, setting the tracks to chattering: klank-ka-ta, klank-ka-ta, klank-ka-ta! The store shook: nuts and bolts rattled in metal bins; rakes and shovels swung back and forth on wall hooks. Alta popped up with a grin and shouted, "Whoo-whee! Whoo-whee! Baby!"

As a young man during World War II, he'd sold pint jars of moonshine to soldiers passing through town on troop trains. Back then the freight train business was an important part of the local economy; nowadays, the trains didn't stop much.

Thinking about the past got Alta thinking about Shelby and her passing, and that got him thinking about Mandy, and that got him back to rocking. Both fine women, and both damn well demanded he stay out of prison. Alta, however, was finding his life of crime was a mighty big hole to climb out of. He was pleased he'd sold off his moonshine business. Getting out of the gas-tapping business was another story. Virgil's land swap deal continued to drag on. Virgil also said he was looking into selling the business to Billy Blue-Eyes from the Dixie mafia out of Biloxi.

As Alta stood up to stretch, Jack, his son, barreled up the street in his '48 Ford Coupe, jumped the curb, swerved back on the road, and skidded to a stop. Stumbling out of the car, he lurched up to the front of the store. His face was flushed, and his eyes were red-hot coals. His blood-alcohol content appeared to be off the charts.

"Good mornin', Daddy," Jack said, smiling. "You'd be proud of me. The party is still goin', but I, bein' the responsible one, left early to get to work on time."

"Good mornin', party boy," Alta said as he sat back in his rocker. "You look like hell, and you stink of whiskey. Go wash up!"

As Jack headed to the back of the store, he paused at the counter and turned on the battered Philco just in time to hear his special request.

"Goooooood moooooor-ning! This is Rhubarb Jones, comin' at you from WSKY in Asheville, North Carolina. We're gonna open with a country classic and one hell of a train song. Ya'll know it and love it, 'The Wabash Cannonball.' And it's going out to all my friends in Tallapoosa, Georgia, where I grew up—and where they know a thing or two about trains. And I want to especially thank my good buddy, Jack Dryden, for this request."

Oh listen to the jingle
The rumble and the roar
As she glides along the woodlands
Through the hills and by the shore
Hear the mighty rush of her engine
Hear that lonesome hobo's call
We're travelling through the jungles
On the Wabash Cannonball

Jack high-stepped back to the front door, trying to drive off his hangover. Alta popped up from his rocker. "Good Lawd son, turn it down."

"Yessiir."

Jack looked out the window and noticed Ray Winchester at the Western Auto pushing a Toro power mower out on the sidewalk. "Hang on, Daddy, Mr. Winchester is setting out his mowers."

Alta grinned. "See if he's got price tags on 'em."

Jack stepped over to his makeshift spy station, deer binoculars taped to a ladder, and focused in. "Hello! It's got a tag on it. Let's see, he wants a hundred and fifty dollars for the Toro Whirlwind model."

"See if you can tell where he's gettin' 'em."

"It sez, let me see, Toro Distribution Center, Talladega, Alabama."

Alta pulled out a roll of cash and peeled off three hundred-dollar bills. "Take my truck and get over to Talladega and buy two of 'em. Don't tell them where you're from."

"I'm gone."

Jack flew out the front door as Clem Robinson, Tallapoosa's mayor and the local Chevrolet dealer, walked in.

"Say, Alta," Clem whispered, though the store was empty. "Can we talk?"

Alta smiled. "Speak up, Clem."

"I'm movin' to Birmingham. I'll be resigning as mayor tomorrow."

Alta patted Clem on the back. "I wish you well."

"Look, Alta, I got no dog in the fight, but I think you ought to run for mayor."

"Thanks, Clem, but I don't believe I'm cut out for politics."

Clem headed for the door. "I gotta go, but I believe you been right about gettin' the town movin' again."

"Thanks, Clem. Good luck in Birmingham."

Settling back into his rocker, Alta pulled out his pocket watch. *Ten to eight, and I'm bushed.* Chester would be arriving soon enough with a passel of problems.

He wrapped his arms around his chest and tilted back in the rocker, counting the water stains on the ceiling. His chest was tight again, restricted. It wasn't like this in the old days.

Maybe it's just aging? There is less joy in the hunt. Shelby's gone, but there is Mandy to fuss over. Bless her.

At eight sharp, Chester arrived in his Coupe de Ville. Chester's hearing was failing slightly faster than his sight. He hunched over his cane and hobbled into the store, scorching the morning air with obscenities.

"Sumbitch! You with your high curbs, and your sidewalks full of potholes, and me with my miserable gawd damn aching joints. How's a senior citizen supposed to get his sweet ass around?"

Alta pushed back in his rocker and howled. "Chester, for an educated fella, you got yourself a foul mouth."

"Just get yourself a proper gawd damn office."

Alta pulled up another rocker as he shook Chester's hand.

Just outside of town, another train sounded its warning horn. The roar of the engine and the clanking of the wheels were deafening. Alta and Chester waited patiently in their rockers for it to settle down.

As the train passed, Alta smacked his lips. "Before we get started on my problems, please tell me what folks are sayin' about my space heater promotion."

"It was dandy," Chester said with a grin. "Folks around here have a good feelin' about you, son."

"Good feelin'." Alta winked. And how 'bout me tryin' to sell ole Bud Meeker's mansion on the hill?"

"Everybody loved it, 'cept ole Bud and his asshole attorney—who, I might add, plans to charge you with tax evasion."

"Charge me? What do I do about that?"

Chester rolled his head back and reflected. "Both our families fought in the Civil War, right?"

Alta nodded. "Long ago."

"You know anything about Nathan Bedford Forrest?"

"A hell of a Confederate general, I hear."

"And damn shrewd business man to boot. So, you're being charged, right?"

Alta brooded quietly as Chester pulled himself out of the rocker and stomped around the store, poking his cane in the air. "You know what the good general had to say about that?"

"I don't recall."

"'Well,' he said, 'never stand and take a charge...charge them back.'"

Alta eyes lit up. "A fightin' man! I do recall a dozen horses were shot out from under him."

Chester stepped in front of Alta and leaned over his cane. "A fightin' man indeed, and so are you, Alta, and so are you. You've got a lot of the general in you. In better times, there's no tellin' what you might have become."

Chester eased down into the rocker, crossed his legs, and fiddled with his cuff links. Alta got up and paced around the store. Chester watched and waited. He knew better than to rush Alta as he shuffled new information around in his head. He was awful good at analyzing things and rearranging them in clever ways...some legal and some not so much.

Alta slowly shuffled to the back of the store then swooped back like a hawk on a field mouse. "So if I was the mayor of Tallapoosa, would I have an edge with them boys on the planning commission?"

"Formally, not so much; informally, oh hell, yes."

A flicker of a grin shot across Alta's face. "Let me stew on it. Did you draw up the contract for Mandy?"

Chester rolled his eyes. "Are you in heat or somethin'?"

"She's a fine lady. She deserves a break."

Chester pulled out the contract and shrugged. "You're the boss. This gives her thirty-three percent of the store straight up. It's binding. You both need to sign it."

Up again, Chester stooped over his cane and leered at Alta. "As far as the new homes and all, I'm very upset. I'm not going down with you on this deal if it falls apart."

Nodding agreement, Alta leaned back in his rocker. He knew there was a point where even good partners turned on each other, even when they were trying to go legit, even when they were trying to do the right thing. As a boy, his father, Charlie Dryden had pounded into his head, "If you want to be a success, you gotta keep your relationships in order."

"Chester, I truly want these folks in town to get into their new homes. I'll cover all their expenses if we can't get 'em in on time, both those movin' up from the trailer park and those movin' into the new homes."

Chester flashed a smile. "Coverin' their expenses is the right thang to do, but...it's gonna cost you."

"I suppose. As for the planning commission, I got a plan. Don't worry!"

———

Virgil Pettimore skidded to a halt in his vintage Chevy truck as Chester's Coupe de Ville eased away. Stray cats ran for cover as Virgil rapped out the twin carbs and shut down the howling beast. A wide grin spread behind a bobbing toothpick as he lumbered through the front door.

Alta chuckled to himself; the boy was damn good at arrivals.

"Come on Alta, I'll drive. I got somethin' to show you."

"I'm mighty busy Virgil. What ya got?"

Virgil rubbed his palms and snickered. "A gold mine."

"Maybe later."

"Come on Alta. You gonna run with the dogs or stay on the porch?"

Alta shrugged. "Run, I reckon."

Virgil sailed down Highway78, headed west. Sonny Hoyt, the chief of police, fell in behind them as they rumbled past the High Hat bar.

Alta scowled. "We got company, hot shot."

"The hell! This is so damn legit, you'll like it."

Virgil pulled onto a dirt road near Old Town and gunned it through scattered woodlands. Brown clouds plumed above the tree line up ahead. The howl of what seemed to be a pack of wolves rang through the woods. Three boys in battered cars flashed by as Virgil burst into the clearing. Sonny Hoyt immediately flipped on his red light and siren.

Lost in a cloud of dust, the cars spun on around a dirt oval. Alta's eyes widened as the red light filled the rearview mirror. "Damn, Virgil, what you got me into?"

Virgil shot Alta a goofy grin and skidded to a halt. He hurried back and met Sonny as he got out. "Come on, Chief, we're lookin' to buy some property. That ain't against the law."

Sonny reached inside the patrol car and flipped off the siren but left the red light flashing. Crossing his arms over his ample gut, he grinned. "Anything Mr. Alta does is my business these days."

Virgil waved his arm up and down like he had a checkered flag in it. Lost in the dust and thunder, the boys took a victory lap.

Alta stepped down from Virgil's jacked-up Chevy, wiped the dust from his glasses, and shook hands with Sonny. They chatted cordially and settled on the fender of the patrol car. The three whiskey-haulin' cars skidded to a stop: Junior DeMint in grease-stained Levis and a T-shirt jumped from his Hudson Hornet; Billy Chitwood sailed feet first out the window of his '64 Dodge; and Skeeter Burns, a born gymnast, shot out the roof of his Flathead V8, completed a midair flip, and landed on his feet.

All in all, Junior, Billy, and Skeeter were solid country boys. They'd made serious money running moonshine. Lately, they were mostly caught up with dirt tracks and pole dancers.

The wind howled and kicked up a cloud of dirt that went red as it blew by the flashing patrol light. Virgil stepped into the crimson spotlight and waited for things to settle down. Despite a nasty disposition and a tendency to shoot anyone that pissed him off, especially Lamar, Virgil had his moments. He grinned broadly and was off. "Now friends, this is A-mer-ic-a, where anything is possible. Am I right?"

The boys cheered as they worked on their hair. Sonny, sensing something illegal was about to happen, flipped through his ticket book, searching for a fitting citation. Alta leaned on the front fender and chuckled.

"Lemme paint the picture," Virgil said as he stomped about in ankle-deep dirt. "Here, right here in West Georgia, anyone with a little start-up capital, a friend with a bulldozer, and a few acres of land can build a dirt track. Grade out the oval, slap up a fence and a grandstand, and, what the hell, you're in business. Call it the Ring of Fire, or the Tallapoosa Speedway, or the Rebel Rally, whatever—stock cars on Saturday, tractor pulls on Sunday, a mud park for the ages."

He caught his breath and then gestured to Junior. "C'mere, son."

A rawboned kid with a killer smile, Junior had dodged the devil on every hairpin curve in West Georgia. He slipped from the hood of his Hornet and ambled up.

"This here's a stock-car demon. So, Junior, tell us, how you're doin' on that?"

Junior's eyes lit up as he shuffled from side to side. "They say I'm on my way. Won prize money here lately at the West Georgia Speedway. Headed fer Dixie Speedway soon."

"Are we all hearing this?" Virgil bellowed, "We got a great location here and lots of local talent that's sure to draw a crowd. This here's a pot of gold!"

Sonny closed his ticket book and beckoned to Alta, pointing to a clearing beyond the dirt track.

Alta turned to Virgil. "Don't run off. I'll be right back."

Sonny's boots disappeared in the red, loamy soil as he marched out beyond the dirt track. He wore a frown when he turned and faced Alta.

Alta smiled broadly, trying to break the ice. "So Sonny, where'd you hide the body?"

Sonny's frown melted as he responded, "So, Alta, where'd you stash the loot?"

Making a quick-draw move with his empty hand, Alta replied, "Just keep your hands where I can see 'em, so I don't have to shoot."

They chuckled for a moment, and then Sonny's face went blank. "Seriously, Alta, the FBI in Atlanta is leaning on me. They're sure you're up to somethin'."

"Hell, Sonny, this is the first I heard about this dirt track business."

Sonny tapped a pen on his ticket book. "I truly doubt it. And there's another thing. What da'ya know about the fire at the Baptist Church in Esom Hill?"

"I heard."

"Someone set it. And you know what we found in the ashes of the basement?"

"I can't say."

"A moonshine still."

Alta shook his head. "Sonny, I can't say it any other way. I'm out of that business. Hell, you know me; my whiskey stills were in chicken coops."

"Look, Alta, I'm tired of hounding you, but the FBI wants a big bust of a big-time operator, and around here, that be you."

"I understand, and I don't take it personally. Say, listen, Sonny," Alta winked, "I could use your help with some other issues. Would you be interested now and again?"

"Now and again," Sonny said and shrugged. "Might be possible."

"Good, good; I'll get back to you on it."

The rolling thunder and the dust storm returned as the boys started runnin' laps again.

———

Virgil caught up with Alta back at his truck. "So, what do you think?"

"You got a good one here, Virgil. But truly, right now I ain't got the time or the money."

Virgil's eyes lit up. "Hell, I got the time…and I got a little surprise for you. I've been down to the Strip in Biloxi, Mississippi talking to Billy Blue-Eyes and the rest of the Dixie mafia boys."

"And?"

"Well, they're a bad bunch and all, but the thing is, they want in on the gas tappin'."

"I've heard that before."

Virgil swung the door open and pulled a large brown bag from under the seat. "Have a look."

Alta peaked inside and grinned. "Woo wee!"

"That's a down payment—ten thousand dollars in laundered cash. They'll have the rest at the end of the month."

Alta rubbed his chin and reflected. He wanted to believe Virgil; he wanted out of the gas tapping; he wanted to make Mandy proud, and Doc Dorothy, and all, but damn…something didn't feel right.

Virgil pounded on the hood. "So, you in on the dirt track?"

Alta shrugged. "Maybe."

CHAPTER 24

Bremen, Days Later

———

ALTA ROLLED UP TO THE Bremen OTASCO store at 3:30 p.m. A red banner stretched across the storefront, announcing the Grand Opening the next day. Curious shoppers strolled by, peeking in the windows.

He switched off the engine and paused before getting out. He had the contract in his pocket but was unsure Mandy would sign off on the deal. She was as skittish as a pony on a foot bridge. He got out and paused again at the front fender. No, he thought, it wasn't a *deal*, and it wasn't a *relationship*. Mandy didn't like either of those words. She wanted to call it an *arrangement*, so that's what he'd call it. He'd made a fortune doing deals, but he, too, was skittish about this one. They both understood there was more than dollars and cents at stake.

He slipped quietly inside and was pleased to see space heaters piled high at the front of the store. Though the cold spell had snapped, space heathers were still in demand. Two young boys scurried about, stocking shelves and sweeping up. Alta stepped behind the heater display and peeked out at Mandy, who was counting money at the cash register. She wore a red OTASCO apron over a long-sleeved pink polyester blouse that matched the floral print in her skirt. She looked wonderful. This appeared to be a dress rehearsal for tomorrow's big opening. She must be pleased to be out of starched white uniforms and bland scrubs.

Alta nodded at Mandy as he ambled down the freshly polished aisles. The old floorboards creaked as he moved along. Rows of hand tools gleamed from one side of the aisle. Nuts and bolts of every shape and size were heaped in bins along the next aisle. Tires were stacked upright on shelves that ran against a side wall. The smell of smoky metal lingered around a secondhand key-cutting machine.

Mandy finished counting, closed the cash drawer, and looked up. "Well, hello there."

Determined to proceed with caution, Alta took a deep breath and replied, "Good afternoon, Mandy; the store looks great. Can we talk?"

She met his eyes with an easy smile that seemed to mask a deeper anxiety. "Well, thank you, Alta. Let's take a break, boys. Go get yourself a Coke out back."

Alta and Mandy stood awkwardly on opposite sides of the counter.

"Mandy, I'm delighted you're here, and by golly, you're doin' it right."

She looked down. "Thank you, sir."

Alta nodded toward the Sewell Mill across the street. "Today's payday. We need to come up with a promotional idea for them."

"I agree. I got somethin' in mind."

"Well," Alta hesitated. "Do we have ourselves an *arrangement?*"

Mandy stepped back and crossed her arms. "Y'know what, Alta? I don't like that word 'arrangement' anymore, and I damn sure don't like the word 'relationship.'"

Confused, Alta paused. Finally, he handed her the contract. "Please read it."

She put on her reading glass and studied every line, then cocked her head to the side. "Well, how 'bout that?"

Alta shoved his hands into his coat pockets and tried to read her thoughts. "You gotta sign all three copies."

"I don't know, Alta. I don't know if I'm doin' the right thing here."

She raked a hand through her hair as her eyes teared up. "Like I told you before, I ain't free and easy, but I damn sure ain't lily white. I've had my share of bright lights and dangerous men. And here lately, I've had my share of gray days and lonely nights."

Alta's jaw tightened as he struggled to remain calm. His heart was a runaway train.

"Let me be honest with you, Alta, love just ain't enough anymore. Countin' on others hasn't worked for me."

She balled her hands into fists. "I'm tired of sittin' in the passenger seat. I've got to have my hands on the wheel. It's up to me to work things out."

Alta smiled weakly as his face flushed. "I believe you'll do fine runnin' the store."

"Hold on, lemme finish." She crossed her arms and looked him in the eye, "I've lost my innocence. And maybe I've gone cold inside. But I've gotta have more control in my life."

They braced against the counter like bookends, blinking away tears, gazing at each other and then down at the contract.

Alta eased around to her side and murmured, "How 'bout we do this? Let's take it a step at a time. Make sure it works for both of us."

Mandy stepped back, shut her eyes, and wrapped her arms around her shoulders, squeezing tight, pulling, it seemed, the broken pieces of her life together. Then her eyes popped open, and an easy smile followed. She looked renewed as she dropped her arms and signed the contract.

———

The sun had set as Alta headed home from Bremen at the end of a long, exhausting day. He forced his eyes open as he gripped and regripped the steering wheel. The smell of new asphalt and the rumble of heavy traffic filled the air. The final section of Interstate 20, the new six-lane highway, cut a wide, black gash across the green countryside. All lanes were open, and the flyovers were finished. Every exit bloomed with new truck stops and strip malls. The spectacle of progress frightened the hell out of him.

He turned onto Route 100 and headed for the home place. Parking out front, he stumbled across the porch and collapsed in a rocking chair. His head felt top-heavy and flopped over on his shoulder. He tried to stand up. Unable to maintain his balance, he collapsed back into the rocker. His heart was in overdrive and he felt flushed.

For some strange reason, his mind went to Vicksburg. As a schoolboy, his history class had taken a field trip to Vicksburg, Mississippi, to visit the Confederate battlefields and the cannon emplacement that perched above the Mississippi River. The mighty howitzers were lined up high above the river to bombard the ironclad gunboats of the Union; the forty-two-pound cannonballs were stacked in pyramids nearby. He reached up and grabbed his head. It seemed enlarged. It felt like a cannonball.

The words of Doc Dorothy rattled through his head: "Only your heart can defeat the demons in your head."

He pondered. *So now my head's a cannonball?*

This frightened him, yet he struggled to be introspective. Part of it, he felt, was the sheer number of issues spinning around in his head: running for mayor, the dirt-track deal, the mysterious arrival of ten thousand dollars that Virgil claimed was a down payment on the sale of his gas-tapping business. And part of it was his awkward yet hopeful *arrangement,* or *relationship,* or whatever the hell she wanted to call it, with Mandy; and part of it was the curse, always the curse, stalking him like a ravenous beast. Doc Dorothy had told him he couldn't beat the curse, but it felt like a race—Alta racing ahead, trying to do good works, while over his shoulder, the beast loped along at half speed; Alta thinking he was winning, the beast licking its chops, knowing it had Alta running in circles.

Alta forced himself to look out on the pasture and took to rocking, both to calm the pounding in his chest and to sort out the clutter in his head. Stripped of their leaves, oak branches swept across the sky, stabbing above the woodlands, searching for the fading light. Solitary leaves tumbled. Out beyond, the afternoon rested for a moment on the Alabama hills. The vane on the barn swung to the east as the evening breeze arrived. He swallowed hard, trying to lose the briny taste in his mouth.

Rocking did the job. Soon he was fast asleep. Childhood dreams streamed through his head. The troubling ones: wetting his pants in the fourth grade, waking up naked at his high school graduation, or being swept out to sea in a rugged undertow. Then came a reprise of Yankee Doodle Dandy, his favorite movie, and his favorite happy dream. James Cagney, the famous song-and-dance man, led the parade on Independence Day, singing:

"I'm a Yankee Doodle Dandy,
Yankee Doodle do or die
A real live nephew of my Uncle Sam
Born on the fourth of July."

But tonight it was different. For the first time, it was Alta wrapped in the flag and leading the parade, not Cagney. Delighted with this version, he snapped awake and began, singing:

"I'm a Yankee Doodle Dandy,
Born on the Fourth of July."

He strutted up and down the porch, repeating the line. Then he grinned broadly and shuffled off to bed. Maybe his better angels had returned. Maybe he'd run for mayor.

CHAPTER 25

Tallapoosa/Bremen, Next Day

UP EARLY THE NEXT DAY, Alta's mind bubbled with prospects. Saturdays were always busy. He'd meet Chester Pope for breakfast, drive him down the new stretch of I-20, do some campaign planning, and then go on to Bremen to help Mandy with her grand opening.

He met Chester Pope outside Friendly's Café, a snug, converted double lane bowling alley. They chatted as Alta guided him to a booth in the back.

"So you had this dream, didya? And Yankee Doodle was in it?" Chester bellowed. "Well, y'know there ain't no good Yankee."

The café was packed with the regulars. Though they looked away, they stayed tuned. Other than the weekly paper, the café was the news center.

Alta winced. "Jesus, Chester, pipe down."

Cupping a hand over his mouth, Chester tried to whisper, "Was *you* in your dream?"

Alta lit up. "Wrapped in the flag and leading the parade."

"Well, gawd damn, that's a sign!" Chester yelped.

Heads bobbed up. Muted laughter washed through the café. Most got a refill of coffee. No one was leaving.

Alta reached across the table and laid his hand on Chester's arm. "Shhhhh."

They finished breakfast in silence.

As Alta paid the bill, a young boy in worn overalls and muddy brogans appeared. He nodded to Alta. "Mr. Alta, I'm Cooter Two. Daddy said I should come see you."

"Sit down, son. You're Cooter Skaggs's boy?"

"Yes sir."

Alta waved the waitress over. "You had breakfast, son?"

Staring down at his muddy brogans, the boy shook his head.

"Go ahead, tell the lady what you want."

His hands sunk in his pockets as he looked up. "Hoecake…ah reckon."

Alta chuckled. "Bring the boy some hoecake, and some ham and grits, and a pitcher of sweet milk, and whatever else he wants."

Chester had nodded off. His head spooled in wide circles, occasionally snapping-up; then he snorted and wheezed; then he was back to spooling.

"So, son," Alta continued, "what brings you to town?"

Young Cooter's eyes widened as he watched Chester's head move about.

"He's harmless, son."

The young boy dug into the hoecake when it arrived. He choked down a mouthful and looked up. "Daddy rolled the hay truck…he's on crutches, and the truck needs work, and…" He took a deep breath and whispered, "And… and we ain't got no money."

"Where's the truck, son?'

He slammed home another fork load of hoecake and chased it with a glass of milk. "Cross the street at Smith's Garage."

Alta jotted on a napkin. "Finish your breakfast; then run this over to Mr. Don at the garage. The note said: 'Put the repairs on my bill.'"

The boy swallowed hard as he wiped away tears, "Thank you Mr. Alta. Thank you."

Alta peeled two twenties from his pocket roll. "Give this to Mama Skaggs for groceries."

Smiles and murmurs of gratitude washed through the café. The regulars gently rapped their knuckles on the counter, casting their vote.

———

After breakfast, Alta and Chester left Friendly's. Alta drove down Route 100 and pulled off just before it went under the freeway at what was now called Exit 5. As they got out, they were buffeted by a fleet of eighteen-wheelers roaring by. Bracing themselves, they wandered around a recently graded and paved ten-acre site. An orange scalloped sign glowed on a towering pole beckoning drivers to fill their gas tanks at the Shell service station. Cars and trucks filled the service lanes; toxic fumes filled the air. A Holiday Inn under construction next door promised clean, affordable rooms with television and air conditioning. The rest of Exit 5 was empty but for a row of power and water hookups poking through a sea of asphalt. Alta smiled. Maybe they've overbuilt. It brought to Alta's mind the land developer's quote in the Atlanta Journal.

Freeway strip malls are the future of retailing, a marriage of high traffic locations and customer convenience. Cutting edge retailers need to be in our prime freeway exit locations. Let me say it loud and proud, we here at Interstate Malls Inc. are open for business. The infrastructure is in and it's time to relocate. Let the gold rush begin!

The gold rush—nice, Alta thought. More traffic, more gas stations. Maybe gas tapping would have worked? Tempting, but no, he was out of that business, headed for higher ground.

"What the hell you smiling about?" Chester barked. "This ain't funny,"

"It ain't funny, Chester; no, it ain't funny. I'm just not sure what to make of it."

They scouted the rest of Exit 5 and were off, ducking and dodging down the freeway, heading east. They pulled in and out of three more exits in the sixteen-mile stretch to Villa Rica, one every four miles. Truck stops and fast-food franchises were bustling. As they pulled into the Villa Rica exit, they passed a Walmart Discount City under construction and parked outside of a newly opened McDonald's. Chester popped out, cane in hand, and stomped in front of Alta's truck. "I tell you," he fumed, "its money leavin' town. There's no way in hell we can compete with this!"

Alta watched the traffic come and go and shrugged. "Yes and no. The tractor-trailers are passing-through freight business. That don't interest me much, but the rest does. Some are local folks, going big-box shopping in Atlanta or into one of these soulless strip malls, and some are families on a road trip, maybe sight-seein', maybe stayin' over. We need to keep all that business on Main Street."

"How they gonna find Main Street?"

"You're right, we need a plan." Alta nodded as promotional ideas burst in his head like popcorn.

Chester whacked his cane on one of Alta's hubcaps. "This'd be a nice-looking truck if you washed the sumbitch."

"You're right on that too, Chester. Buck took it muddin' yesterday. Buck's hard on a rig."

"Gettin' back to this Yankee Doodle business," Chester growled, "all in all, it seems like a bad sign to me. I think ole Yankee Doodle is headed out of town, a-ridin' on his pony."

Alta pulled a rag from under the seat and wiped mud off the front hubcaps. "Here's what I'm thinkin'. My dream, with me bein' Yankee Doodle, all wrapped in the flag and marchin' in the parade—and add to that, the Fourth of July and the Bicentennial bein' right around the corner—I'm thinkin' you're wrong. My dream is a powerful sign."

Alta snapped to attention and threw Chester a salute. "I believe I'm meant to be the mayor of Tallapoosa!"

"Good Lawd, that's clever." Chester puckered his lips. "How'd I miss that one? Born on the Fourth of July and all."

Alta nodded. "It's a powerful sign."

Chester spread his arms expansively to the folks inside McDonald's and crowed, "So, Mr. Mayor, you old jailbird, how you gonna stop these corporate leeches from suckin' the life out of our little town?"

Alta grimaced.

"I been thinkin' on that, too. If you draw a twenty-mile circle around Tallapoosa and set aside Carrolton, you got nothin' but gorgeous farmland and foothills." He paused and then snatched Chester's cane, pumped it in the air, and strutted around his truck. "I'm a Yankee Doodle Dandy..."

Jaws dropped inside McDonald's as they followed Alta's every move. He ran out of steam on the second lap around the truck, arched his head and shoulders back, and threw a deep bow in their direction. Even Chester applauded.

Alta said with a wink, "I am back, I tell you, I'm back…and so…where was I? So, we've got thousands of acres of farms and woodlands right here, some marginal soil, yes, but patches of rich bottomland. And we got solid pioneering stock a-workin' the land…share croppers, small truck farmers, moonshiners, mill hands…and yeah, they like to fight and fuss some…but come Saturday morning, every red dirt road in the county is clogged with folks either bringing their crops to the farmer's market, or comin' to shop."

Chester grabbed his cane back, and was off on his own laps around the truck shouting. "And add to that, ladies and gentlemen, Friday is payday at the textile mills, and come Saturday night, hundreds of thirsty soldier boys are comin' in from Fort McClellan in Anniston and Fort McPherson in Atlanta… all headin' for Tallapoosa, on the border of right and wrong, comin' for a good time. So, I ask you: do we want that money leavin' town?"

"Hell no!" Alta bellowed, throwing his arms in the air like a preacher at a tent show. "Sooooo how we goin' keep money from leavin' town?"

"Woo, hoo, hoo!" Chester howled. "We gotta get you elected, that's how."

The folks in McDonald's rushed outside and flocked around Alta.

Alta was on fire. "Hello, folks. You're tired of them freeway burgers, aren't you?"

"Amen, brother, amen," they chanted.

"Freeway-burgers are tasty, but they ain't wholesome," Alta sang out. "They ain't friendly."

A woman shouted, "So where do we get these friendly burgers?"

Alta's eyes spun like the reels on a slot machine. "Y'all follow me down the hill into Bremen and then go west on Highway Seventy-Eight for nine miles to Tallapoosa. Friendly's Café, right there on Main Street—you can't miss it." Alta paused and then couldn't resist adding, "And there's a farmer's market goin' on right now in Bremen; farm fresh, real wholesome food. You might want to check it out." Alta grinned and started to leave with Chester in tow. "Oh, and by the way, there's a grand opening at the OTASCO store right next to the farmer's market. Lots of bargains."

As they got in Alta's truck, Chester chuckled. "Jesus, son, you are a shameless showman. Why didn't you tell them folks you owned the OTASCO store?"

"Cause it ain't true. Mandy owns a third."

CHAPTER 26

Bremen, Same Day

———

ALTA DROVE CHESTER ON INTO Bremen. He slowed to a crawl as they came into town. The farmer's market filled the town square and cars and trucks lined the shoulders of the road. Alta edged through the congestion and parked behind Chester's bank. They smiled as they looked out on the bustling crowd on the square.

"So, Chester, how 'bout you gettin' an election committee together for me?"

"You sure you wanna run?"

"If Mandy approves."

Chester cocked his head to the side. "You're clean then?"

"Damn near."

"Damn near! Damn near will get you back in the pokey."

"I sold off the gas-tappin' business to the Dixie mafia."

"The Dixie mafia! Them folks from Biloxi? Well, that's civic-minded of you?"

"Virgil's been handlin' it."

"When didya start trustin' Virgil?"

"Gawd damn it, Chester, just get a committee together for me. Tell 'em... tell 'em we'll meet Monday mornin' early at my store."

"Humph!" Chester grumbled and hobbled into his bank.

"Make sure Virgil's on the committee, you hear?"

Alta pushed his political ambitions to the back of his mind and ambled over to the farmer's market. He marveled at the sights and sounds. Fruit and vegetable stalls ran down one side of the square; meat and poultry ran along the other. In the middle, folding tables wobbled under piles of secondhand clothes. A hubbub of sounds filled the air: farmers hawking their goods, teenagers snickering coyly, moms sharing shopping tips, dads arguing football. The smells came in waves. The smoky aroma of boiled peanuts. The sugary sweetness of cotton candy. The tang of pickled okra. Alta mingled, greeting farmers and millhands, hugging their wives, scrapping with their dogs. To most, he was a celebrity, a charming outlaw, generous to a fault.

He'd dressed carefully that morning: two-tone dress shoes, pressed khakis, and a plain white shirt. He enjoyed gatherings: the county fair, a church revival, and all parades. He pinched the crown of his straw fedora, tilted it just so, then strolled on, lingering for a moment at the poultry stall. Stewing hens, broilers, and fryers were laid out in rows; brown and white eggs were nested in star baskets. Yellow pullets peeped in vented shoeboxes. Little children edged up on tiptoes and peeked into the boxes.

The next stall down was loaded with bushel baskets of apples and peaches, and sacks of dry corn and barley stacked and ready for the mill, and finally burlap bags of potatoes. Behind the stalls, farm boys in bib overalls slid crates of produce off their trucks and stacked them high. Alta paused as a wave of joy washed through him. The market was a showcase of rural virtue—simple faith and hard work unlocking the bounty of the land. These were his roots. He felt connected.

He moved on, greeting all comers. Most folks had heard secondhand that he was running for mayor of Tallapoosa. Even those from Bremen and Buchanan pledged their support. He, in turn, promised to bring prosperity to all of Haralson County. Every Baptist church in the county had pews and stained-glass windows with Alta's name on them. He provided a safety net for the community. He helped to forge a tribal alliance, an invisible barrier that kept carpetbaggers and revenuers at bay.

Down the street, Mandy's grand opening was about to get started. Alta looked back on the farmer's market as he left the square. He hoped it could survive the interstates and the strip malls.

Mandy taped a cardboard sign in the front window of the store and smiled out at a line of eager shoppers that stretched down the planked sidewalk and out onto the square. The sign declared:

Grand Opening—Noon Saturday
Winter isn't over,
Great Savings on Space Heaters
Summer's coming on,
Great Savings on Box Fans

While she listened to country music on WPLO Atlanta, Mandy broke coin rolls and filled the change drawer. She wore the same outfit she'd worn the day before: a red OTASCO apron over a long-sleeve pink polyester blouse that matched the floral print in her skirt. A French braid of salt-and-pepper hair fell off her shoulders, and confidence radiated across her face. It had been nonstop for the last week. Alta had helped out, but he'd agreed she was the manager, and she was in charge. She sang along as a favorite country songs came on the radio,

I don't want to hear a sad story,
We both already know how it goes,
So, if you'll be my tall dark stranger,
I'll be your San Antone Rose.

The song perfectly captured her current feelings about love. Let's loose ourselves in the warm glow of romance without getting into any "he done me wrong" stories. She glanced at the line of shoppers on the sidewalk and then at the wall clock. The doors would swing open in five minute. She rubbed her hands together and smiled. She was ready, and the store was ready: shelves were stocked, labels facing out, pricing displayed. Tin buckets of sweet shrub sat at the head of each aisle. The citrus scent masked the sharp smells of motor oil and tires. In the back, near the wood stove, she'd added a display of toys—a woman's touch. The stock room was crammed with space heaters and box fans that she and Alta had bought at the Treasure Island Discounter in Atlanta.

A sales assistant and a stock boy she'd brought on for the day stood at attention in bow ties and starched shop aprons. As the clock struck twelve, Alta came flying in the back door. Mandy shot him a smile and strolled confidently to the front door.

———

Both the space heaters and the box fans were gone in an hour. Most folks were still shivering from the harsh winter. Yet, most were also without air conditioning so they bought fans as well. They'd checked their almanacs and noted that, indeed, this would be a hot summer. By two thirty, the rush was over. Most shelves were empty. They'd sold fifteen cases of motor oil and all the toys.

Mandy turned the store over to her assistant and joined Alta in the back.

Hoisting himself off the sagging couch, Alta stood to greet her. "Well done, darlin'." He grinned broadly. "You're likein' it, are you?"

Mandy's eyes sparkled as she dropped into the chair. "I'm lovin' it!"

"You feel like you're in charge, don't cha?"

She pulled herself forward on the edge of the cushion and smiled. "Alta, you been awful good to me. I feel like I can handle the store. It's a real good feelin' for me, and..." She turned her head to the side as she felt the tears coming. Blinking them away, she looked into his eyes. "And...I thank you for givin' me the chance."

They embraced. Mandy's heart was on fire. This felt right. Their time had come. Slowly, step by step, they'd found each other, comforting and healing one another. As the song she'd heard earlier popped into her head, she stepped back from Alta and sang, "If you'll be my tall dark stranger, I'll be your San Antone Rose."

Alta rolled his eyes. "I don't know that one."

Mandy laughed. "It pleases me."

"Well, Mandy, darlin', whatever pleases you delights the hell outta me. And yes thank you, I'll be your tall dark stranger."

She cocked her head back and put her hands to her hips. "I like the sound of that. Soooooo yes, it would please me to go to church with you tomorrow in Newnan."

Alta paused awkwardly and then nodded. "I'd be delighted, if you'll go to lunch with me later at Sprayberry's Barbecue."

"I accept."

Alta headed for the door and then turned. "You know, today was a day of surprises."

"How so?"

"I forgot to mention it, but ah'm runnin' for mayor. If you agree."

Mandy's head snapped up and she paused. "Are you sure you want this?"

Alta turned away, gathered himself and turned back. "I've got a lot to prove...to you and to this town. I'm more than an ex-con."

Mandy grabbed his shoulders and kissed him on the forehead. "Then you do it, but do it right. And I'll love you for it."

CHAPTER 27

Tallapoosa, Days Later, March 1976

———

MARCH BLEW IN COLD AND wet. Alta got to the store early and hustled around, getting a fire going in the wood stove and making coffee. His campaign team would arrive soon.

He sipped coffee and warmed himself by the stove. Sunday had been a great day—his best day in a long time. He had his first proper date with Mandy Tate and with her approval, made the final decision to run for mayor. He smiled into the fire. This was his time, a time for growth and prosperity. It was all there for the taking. He would defy the curse. He would save the community.

"Sweet Jesus!" he murmured. "I've reached the mountain top, and I'm highballin' it down the road to redemption!"

He greeted his team as they straggled in, grabbed coffee, and gathered around the stove. They were fearless, if not altogether noble, and included his sons Buck and Jack, his wily lawyer Chester T. Pope III, his ill-tempered brother Fred, his sometime business partner Virgil, and Pinkney "Pink" Allen, the Haralson county sheriff.

As they settled in, Alta nodded to Pink, a last-minute addition to the team. He was stovepipe tall, dressed in black shirt and trousers. A gold badge shone prominently above his shirt pocket. Pink wore a wide-brimmed straw hat indoors and out. His patrol car was an armory; his favorite weapon was a Thompson submachine gun, a honey of a M-192. He was known to spray it around when raiding a still—or chasing crows out of his yard. He'd seized plenty of moonshine stills in his day, and he'd overlooked a few as well.

Alta spoke up once they were seated. "As you know, I've decided to run for mayor. It's time for some real growth and prosperity."

"Growth and prosperity," the men repeated and stomped their heels on the rough-cut pine floor.

Alta beamed. "I'm gonna win this election. But I can't do it without you."

Chester hauled himself up from the couch and stamped his cane on the floor. "Alta we're all mighty proud of you. You've been a great big success with the OTASCO stores and your homebuilding. We all want growth and prosperity, but that means bringin' in new industry."

They all nodded in agreement. Alta's brother Fred stood up. "Chester's right, but we gotta clean up the town before we can attract new industry."

Pink Allen popped up instantly. "Give 'em asphalt and gravel. That's what they need. Asphalt and gravel and plenty of it."

Pink had struck a chord.

"Asphalt and gravel!" They stomped their heels on the floor again.

"I agree with you, Pink, the streets need pavin'," Alta replied, "but will that help get me elected?"

"Alta," Pink shot back, "I don't recall anyone losin' an election around here by offerin' to pave the roads and driveways."

"Well, by God, that's what we'll do," Alta agreed. "We'll fill every pothole and crater in Tallapoosa get folks to market."

Alta noticed Virgil fuming in the corner. He was probably pissed off because Alta insisted that he attend the meeting. It had been two weeks since Virgil had given Alta the down payment from the Dixie mafia on the tapping business. Alta stared at Virgil and shrugged as if to say, "You got anything to add?"

Virgil stood slowly. "It's good and all to talk about asphalt, but lemme ask you, how are folks from the south side of town gonna get to the polls? The roads will still be bad on Election Day, and a lot of 'em don't own cars."

The room fell silent. Alta looked around and noticed his son Buck waiting to be recognized.

He nodded. "What 'cha got, Buck?"

Buck smiled broadly. "How about a caravan? I'll get my boys to run folks back and forth to City Hall on Election Day."

Chester remained seated but banged his cane with delight. "Fine idea there, Buck. Legally you can't tell 'em who to vote for. That'd be tamperin'. Just tell 'em your daddy is gonna pave the roads and get the buses runnin' again."

Buck grinned and sat down. His twin brother Jack popped up.

Alta nodded to Jack.

"Well, I ain't hearin' nothin' about mudslingin'. I hear your competition has got a com-mit-ee plottin' against us. I think we ought to sling some mud their way."

"Son, I aim to run a righteous campaign," Alta declared.

Jack frowned, unconvinced.

Alta was pleased with the progress as the morning moved along. They huddled around the wood stove in sagging sofas and rickety nail kegs and came up with ways to pump life back into Tallapoosa. There was general agreement that the hard times were over. The community was the thing. The July 4th Bicentennial would celebrate the birth of the nation as well as the rebirth of Tallapoosa. Glory Hallelujah!

"The phoenix from the fire, the phoenix from the fire," Alta quietly chanted.

They all had jobs to do. Alta's boys would stuff mailboxes, hand out flyers, and perhaps get in some mudslinging. They'd also organize a car caravan to get folks to the polls. Pink Allen would come up with plans to pave streets and to paint the storefronts along Head Avenue. Virgil would check with the Georgia Department of Transportation on road funding and programs for feeding the elderly. Alta and Fred would go door to door, shaking hands and twisting arms. The election was on Saturday, March 6. They had five days to execute their plans.

As they departed, Alta caught Virgil by the arm and said, "Wait here. We need to talk, but Chester's aching to tell me something first."

Virgil shrugged and waited at the back door as Alta hustled back up front to catch Chester.

"What was it, Chester?"

"Alta, this is pretty damn personal," he said as he guided Alta off behind a tire display, "but I believe it needs to be said."

"Say it."

"It has to do with you and Mrs. Mandy Tate. Y'see, you been seen slippin' around with Mandy and folks are talkin'."

Alta's scowled and barked back, "Chester, that's my business!"

Chester tapped his cane on the floor. "The thing is, if you're elected mayor, your business is everybody's business. You gotta start actin' may-or-al."

"May-or-al, good Lawd, Chester. I ain't done nothin' sinful."

Chester struck a righteous pose, arms crossed, head cocked high. "It ain't the sin itself that'll do you in. It's the appearance of sin. You gotta stop slippin' around. Cut bait, or do the honorable thing."

"I tell you what, if I get elected, I'll work on bein' may-or-al."

Alta flushed Chester out the front door and found Virgil out back.

"So Virgil, what're you hearin' from Billy Blue-Eyes on buyin' the gas-tappin' business?"

"Damnit, Alta, I said you'd have the rest of your money by the end of the month. We got another week."

"So where you been?"

Virgil shuffled from side to side and looked across the street. "I been down to Biloxi, Mississippi, tryin' to do the deal with the Dixie mafia. But…" The cords in his neck flared, and his goofy right hand trembled. "But I can't sell what ain't workin', can I? A couple of the gas taps are in and workin'…we're waiting to get a pumping schedule from our snitch at Plantation Pipeline. But truly, Alta, I could be wrong here, but I think it's gonna work. This could be the mother lode."

Alta clenched his jaw and reflected. *He's probably lying. It's hard to tell with ole Virgil. He usually screws things up pretty bad before he pulls 'em out of the fire. But things have changed with me—I'm on the road to redemption.*

Alta's better angels quickly took flight. His reply sound like a nail gun. "Get-your-fat-ass-on-the-next-plane-to-Biloxi-and-do-the-fuckin'-deal. I aim to do right, and I will not be fooled with."

CHAPTER 28

Dryden Home Place, Days Later

———

A SHAFT OF LIGHT FROM the kitchen window cut across the cluttered stovetop. Alta floated in and out of the light, lost in the soothing routine of making breakfast. Humming softly, he reworked the lyrics to "San Antone Rose" as an image of Mandy glowed above the stove.

"Yes, Mandy darlin', I'll be your tall dark stranger, if you'll be my San Antone Rose."

Inhaling the rich aroma of perking coffee, sizzling bacon, and baked biscuits, he gathered his breakfast and moved onto the porch. He did his best thinking at daybreak, rocking on the porch. With the election only two days off, he had a lot to do. Winning the election, he was now convinced, would be the centerpiece of his relationship with Mandy, the key to expanding his legitimate business ventures, and ultimately beating the curse.

The dawn brought with it a clear blue sky. It had rained most of February and the first week of March. The hardwoods swayed on the horizon like witches' brooms, leafless yet budding. Winter lingered; spring was on the way. He smiled and dozed.

As the morning sun rose above the tree line and shone directly on Alta, he awoke and shuffled back to the kitchen, and returned with a second cup of coffee. Then he was off like a hummingbird, skimming and flipping through a stack of newspapers his son Buck had dropped by. He scanned the front page, the business section, the sports section, and then on to the next day's paper. He finished reviewing the last few weeks of the *Atlanta Journal* as his head slumped to his chest.

He awoke with a grin an hour later. Yes indeed, 1976 would be a big year for America, a big year for Georgia, and, hell yes, a big year for Tallapoosa. The nation was celebrating its two-hundredth birthday. Jimmy Carter, a peanut farmer from Plains, Georgia, was running for president, and this would be the year—with the help of "de Lawd"—that the Georgia Bulldogs shut down Alabama. All of this while Tallapoosa celebrated both the Bicentennial and its own 116th birthday, and…and by God, elected a mayor to lead them forward.

As his mind steamrolled ahead, Alta felt a spike in his chest. He pumped the brakes on his freewheeling thoughts and slipped into slow, rhythmic breathing. He'd never reached the high plane of introspection, that Doc Dorothy had preached, but he did however, pay closer attention to what his mind was doing to his body.

He gathered his breakfast dishes and shuffled to the kitchen. After cleaning up, he returned to the porch. He singled out the March 3rd copy of the *Tallapoosa-Beacon* and found an article entitled "Mayoral Candidates Discuss Their Platforms." He chuckled as he read his platform:

I will keep taxes low, maintain law and order, and do my best to make our town a town to be proud of…

Good, good. He read on:

We need to improve our streets and modernize our business buildings. We cannot allow Tallapoosa to become an abandoned wayside off I-20…the key to our survival is growth: growth in our farm production, growth in light industry, growth in civic pride. Prosperity will come if we court it.

Good Lawd, did I say that? He paused, feeling his heart rev up again, and got back to deep breathing.

"I stand behind my platform," he murmured. "I've done well with the OTASCO stores, I've done well with housin', and, as a councilman, and I've damn well led the charge for modernizing the town, though nobody much followed me."

Alta's chief opponent for mayor was a prominent businessman and deacon of the local Baptist church. He'd formed a citizens group to promote himself and expose Alta's past. His campaign pledge ran in a column next to Alta's

I was born in Tallapoosa, and except for the time spent away in school and in the army, I have lived here all my life. My qualifications speak for themselves, and I feel that everyone is familiar with them...certain changes will be made, of course; however, not having been involved directly in city government, I do not presently have knowledge of major changes that should be made at this time."

Alta arched his brows. "Pretty cautious for the challenges ahead."

Alta pulled out a copy of the *Atlanta Journal Constitution* from the previous day. "Woo-wee!" he hooted. "I made the front page!"

The headline blared:

FROM MOONSHINE TO CITY HALL

The subheadline proclaimed:

EX-CON WANTS TO "GIVE PEOPLE SERVICE."

The first line read: "We're going to pave every street in town," Dryden promised, "and we're going to feed our elderly."

Alta grinned. "I guess we can thank my competition for the headlines. Glad I got a quote in there."

Just then the phone rang. He hopped up and hurried into the house. "Alta here."

"Hey Alta, its Chester. Did you see the front page of yesterday's *Atlanta Journal?*"

"I just read it."

"It's not bad. I don't like the 'ex-con' part, but your quote was great. Very may-or-al, Alta, very may-or-al."

"Why, thank you."

"And Alta…"

"I know, stop slippin' around. Bye."

CHAPTER 29

Tallapoosa, Next Day

———

CLOUDS BLEW IN EARLY THAT morning. The air crackled; a storm was coming. Alta parked in front of the store, humming a tune. He strolled to the front
door, stuck the key in the lock, and paused. Withdrawing the key, he turned
on his heel. His eyes moved across the street to Smith's Garage and then up to
the water tank that loomed above town.

Crows flocked around the water tank, screeching, riding an upward draft,
wings extended, soaring, sailing, and then screaming down, spinning in tight
circles, gaining speed, full of fury. Strange, Alta thought, very strange, as he
crossed the street. Don Smith lowered the hood of the car he'd just tuned, saw
Alta coming, and scowled. He wiped the grease off his hands and told his son
to stand by, which was code for have a gun handy.

Don, a bantam rooster of a man, was an upstanding citizen, a prominent
member of the Baptist church, and an altogether feisty fellow. He kept an
armory of well-oiled rifles in the back, and he was prone to talk in parables.

The wind whipped the trees about. Thunder roared beyond the river to
the west.

Alta extended his hand. "Good mornin', Mr. Smith."

Ignoring the extended hand, Don took a stance, pushing into Alta's space:
chest out, arms crossed, chin cocked back. He glared up at a much taller man.
"Mornin', Alta."

Alta smiled, and held his ground. "Don, I understand you've done a lot of
work for the city here in your garage. Am I right?'

"We've done a good bit."

"I'd hate to see that go away."

"Our prices are fair. Our service is excellent. I can't see that happenin'."

Alta rubbed his chin. "Well, y'see, if I'm elected mayor, I aim to do some serious cost cutting."

Don rocked back on his heels. "So that's what this is about. I'm supportin' your competition for mayor, and you're not likin' it?"

Alta pursed his lips. "There's been talk."

Don shot back in a high, reedy voice, "There's also been talk about your boys spray paintin' your opponent's car."

Suddenly, the sky filled with crows, swarming down from the tank, together with a chorus of piercing caaaaaaws. Screeching and swooping, all beaks, wings, and talons, they flocked around Alta and Don, moved on to an oak tree, and then were back again. Amid the swooping, the wind set to howling and gusting, throwing up grit and dust. Rain was on the way.

Alta staggered backward, arms wrapped around his head. "Gawd damn crows, what's with that?"

Don's eyes lit up. "They're mobbing us, tryin' to drive off predators, tryin' to protect their roost like...like a lot of folks here in town."

Alta stumbled back, then slumped against the trunk of a car. He knew a sign when he saw one, and this wasn't a sign. *It couldn't be.* That thought, just a passing glimmer, got lost somewhere between what he'd just seen, what he'd just heard. At the moment, he felt only the violent beating of his heart and a firestorm of distorted emotions. In the past, he'd have dismissed the incident, probably just a red-tailed hawk stirring up a crow's roost. But, he was coming to know his curse, if not control it. Being the mayor was a good thing; he meant to do right. Stupid how he got off track, allowing the boys to spray-paint the car, a silly prank. Yet, he knew there was more to it. Some folks in town only saw him as a convicted felon, not to be trusted, a hawk in a crow's roost. By God, he'd do better. He'd get himself elected. He'd do right.

The rain came in waves. Don didn't move, hadn't moved, hadn't even flinched from the mobbing crows. He understood the meaning. He wiped the rain from his face. "We'll fight you tooth and nail, if it comes to savin' this town."

Alta pushed off the trunk of the car. He moved slowly, smoothing back his hair, cleaning his glasses, letting the fire inside him cool. He pulled on his chin, searching for the right words, and then stepped up to Don. "There's probably no way an old jailbird like me can change your mind, but I mean to do right as mayor, get this town moving again, and," he paused as the words came harder, "and I'd like…I'd like you to give me a second chance."

Touched, but unmoved, Don grumbled, "I won't stand in your way, but I sure won't support you."

CHAPTER 30

Tallapoosa Water Tank, Next Day

LAMAR PARKED HIS HARLEY BEHIND Smith's Garage and strolled next door to city hall. It was Election Saturday, and the polls were crowded. People seemed ready for change and wanted a voice in it. Most were crawling out of hard times and were ready for any promise of prosperity. Streets were jammed in all directions. Buck and Jack Dryden came and went in a rented school bus, bringing the poor and elderly to the polls from the south side of the tracks. Banners taped to the sides of the buses proclaimed, "A Vote for Alta Dryden Is a Vote for Growth and Prosperity."

Lamar cast his ballot and walked down the alley to the foot of the water tank. Half way up the tank, he paused and surveyed the crowd below. A long line strung down Main Street from city hall. Unbidden, like retractable claws that emerged in the heat of combat, Lamar's face tightened: his lips curled back. A switch was thrown in a dark corner of his head and alarms blared, red lights flashed, as this ordinary, badass biker-boy morphed into an apex predator. He was dimly aware of the transformation, but it pleased him.

He hustled up the tank to his "crow's nest." From there, he could see for miles: detect present and potential danger, exploit emerging opportunities, and consider the progress and regress of the human species—and, best of all, plot and scheme. As he watched voters come and go from city hall, he had a rare moment of hope. Perhaps the ecosystem could come together; perhaps a balance of good and evil could be achieved with the election process, a

185

balance that might bring stability to the land. Perhaps democracy was a better way. But then again, the law of club and fang was alwasy lurking just behind the banner of democracy.

He, he, he. Ever since I shoved the Magnum under Virgil's chin, I've been a member of the tappin' team.

He pulled out his binoculars and studied Main Street. In addition to the regular farmer's market bustle, the shops and cafes were overflowing with the Election Day crowd: a mixture of true-blue, bona-fide citizens, occasional offenders, and hardened felons. Local merchants remained upbeat and did their best to compete with the fast-food franchisers and the big-box discounters that lined I-20. In the shaded backstreets, aging moonshiners played cops and robbers with the law, as housebuilders and house burners crossed paths.

The election turnout was impressive. Everyone had a stake in the game. The choice between Alta Dryden and his opponent was substantial, a choice between a good-hearted, pro-growth ex-con, and a law-abiding pillar of the community. The tension between the two different candidates, like a turnbuckle through a collapsing building, strangely pulled them together, providing a measure of stability. Yet, if Alta was elected, he could unite the lawful and the lawless factions, creating a dominant coalition that could disrupt the current balance of power. Weighing all this, Lamar had voted for Alta's opponent.

He set his pack down and shook out his long, blond hair, preening in the sun. The tapping business continued to weigh heavily on his mind. The shootouts had stopped since he and Virgil had become partners. Shootouts were like a delinquency notice that said, "You aren't through paying for what you did to me or...my pappy...or my pappy's pappy." Sure, his relationship with Virgil had always been troubled, but nothing that a profitable business deal couldn't overcome.

He grinned as he studied the Shell station on the east side of town. Nowadays, he was in charge of finding gas-station buyers. So far, he'd contacted stations in Fruithurst, Heflin, and Anniston, Alabama; and Tallapoosa, Buchanan, Bremen, Carrolton, and Cedartown, Georgia. He was also responsible for transporting gas from the tapping sites to gas stations. He'd started by welding a thousand-gallon tank to a white Ford truck; then he had strapped a two-thousand-gallon tank to a red stake side truck. They'd had several successful midnight runs—and several screw-ups. To grow, they needed more trucks and drivers. This required more brains and cash than Lamar or Virgil possessed. Clearly they had to get Alta back in the game, and to do that, they needed to get the business up and running. If Alta saw the money roll in, then he'd join them. With all these "what-ifs" and "if-thens" swirling through his head, Lamar had arranged a meeting with Virgil that evening. He was eager to get on with the tapping and make the big money. Yet, part of him wavered, like a cat on a fence, drifting back to his default mode as an alpha predator.

Lately his reading had turned to the *Book of Exodus* and *The Origin of Species*. He considered cosmic change as a complex riddle, more comic than tragic. And of course, for Lamar, any new concept became a lens to reassess his West Georgia domain. Clinging to the railing, three hundred feet above the quilted foothills, he observed the evolution and devolution of the region. To the north, a green forest canopy shrouded mixed housing: a few proud Victorians with wraparound porches, ornate arbors, and gingerbread trim; and here and there a modest ranch-style bungalow with a carport and a pickup. He reckoned that some homeowners had worked for what they had, and others, the idol privileged class, were born into it.

Suddenly he was dizzy. His mind was never quiet, but with new concepts, he was a gerbil on a treadmill, racing to convert them to hard science and apply them to his role as an avenging angel. He pushed back against the water tank to steady himself. Slowly, arm over arm, he inched around the catwalk.

Gazing down on the town, he focused on the manicured gardens and neatly trimmed lawns; he noticed English ivy quietly choking slumbering oaks and pines; and carpenter bees drilling circular holes in arbors and laying their eggs. He knew pileated woodpeckers would soon arrive to jackhammer the holes and devour the larvae. He also noticed the blooms of moss and mold in every pocket of shade, patiently weaving their tendrils into mortar and siding. He saw the smilax vine had sent a single shoot two to three feet above the ground, shoots with pleasant heart-shaped leaves that hid thorny tendrils—tendrils that twined around azaleas and rhododendrons and choked them off.

And of course, he noticed the rutted roads and weed-filled paths that fanned off the paved streets; paths that led to sagging clapboard shacks overgrown with Muscatine vines.

Yes, human nature and nonhuman nature constantly interacted Lamar concluded. If you blinked, you miss the clash of competing species and the relentless struggle for dominance. He wasn't sure he fully understood Charles Darwin, but felt he understood the concept of natural selection, a silent juggernaut he chose to befriend. He remembered what his father had said about getting rid of kitchen roaches, "You spray them and some die. Those that don't die multiply and you've got to get a stronger spray or the roaches win. That, he concluded was natural selection or close to it. He chanted his latest mantra as a peace offering:

"I'm in your patch, you're in mine,
I'm a flower, you're a vine.
I'll be nice if you'll be nice
Now don't that sound like Paradise?"

Acre on acre of forested woodlands spread to the west and south of town: here, a ragged stand of Loblolly pine had been overcut, bucked, and hauled to the mill; and there, a green, rolling meadow cleared for grazing. Scattered among the woodlands were sections of plowed bottomland, ready for seeding.

Corrugated warehouses jammed the industrial parks south of Highway 78; some were working factories, and some were hollow, rusted caverns. Light winds whistled through the sidings; stronger winds set tin sheets to banging. Polished train tracks cut through the center of town. Just south of town, Interstate 20 gouged a wide asphalt scar through the countryside. Long-haul freightliners snarled down the blacktop, dwarfing family sedans.

As he remembered the day's news, Lamar switched off his mental treadmill and set the binoculars aside. That morning, the DEA, not the ATF, had seized a DC4 from Miami loaded with three thousand pounds of marijuana, not moonshine, on a roughhewn airstrip near Cedartown; it was the first big drug bust in West Georgia and another example of an emerging species—drugs—beginning to edge out an endangered species, corn liquor. Same game, different players, more global. *I may just go global.*

As the sun disappeared behind the Talladega Mountains, Lamar slid his right hand inside his jacket and pulled out his 357 magnum. Idly spinning the cylinder, he checked the six hollow-point bullets and chanted his warrior mantra as he prepared for his meeting with Virgil.

"Bang, bang, shoot 'em up
Grab your gun
Bang, bang, shoot 'em up
Here I come!"

Lately, he and Virgil had declared a cease-fire, but you never knew with Virgil. As the darkness came, and the lights of Tallapoosa flickered on, Lamer let go with a wild-dog howl.

"Aaaaah-ooooooooooooooh…Aaaaah-ooooooooooooooh!
He packed his gear and scrambled down the water tank.

CHAPTER 31

Tallapoosa, Same Day

ALTA POPPED UP, LOST HIS balance, and collapsed back in bed. The roosters had crowed, and the hens were clucking as first light streamed through the window. His shoulders cracked, and the bedspring groaned. He stretched back and seized the spindles, pulling himself up against the brass headboard.

His smile became a frown as he eyed the swayback mattress.

"Bigger than my prison cot," he mumbled, "but just as lonely."

He shuffled into the kitchen, his head spinning with the prospects of Election Day. He'd campaigned hard the day before, posting signs, knocking on doors, shaking hands, twisting arms. Yet, when he fell into bed, he was strangely at peace with himself.

He made coffee and pushed away his concerns about the tapping business. *Maybe I can win this election.*

Then he got to thinking about his own behavior—being introspective, as Doc Dorothy called it. He was superstitious, if not introspective. He'd follow a hunch, a dream, or a prophetic sign. Yet, he maintained an iron grip on his agenda. He made things happen. He couldn't control everything. But he could make *most* things happen. Most of the time his hunches gave him an edge, a sharp edge. In spite of all this willfulness, he still had a lot of country boy romping around in his head. Simple pranks gave him great pleasure. Currently he was pranking Ray Winchester at the Western Auto. They both featured Toro power mowers. He couldn't wait to check it out.

He hustled around the rest of the morning: sweeping up, chopping wood, and making a shopping list. Mandy was coming for dinner, a victory barbecue, he hoped.

He selected his outfit carefully, dressing in front of Shelby's cheval mirror. He considered white linen slacks. They were smart but a little too preppy and privileged. No, he'd go with his standard pressed khakis, the pants of the common man. Tucking in a starched white shirt, he wandered back to the bedroom and fanned through his ties. Red, white, and blue bow tie? Nah, save that for the fourth of July. Enjoying himself, he chose a hand-painted silk tie: an attacking eagle, wings fanned, talons extended. He shrugged playfully, recalling Chester's parting advice at the campaign meeting: "Alta," he'd said, "you gotta start acting may-or-al."

"By golly, Chester," Alta sang out, "ah got me a may-or-al tie."

Standing at the sink, he finished his grooming: shaving with a straight razor, brushing back his hair, adding a dab of Brylcreem and slicking it back with his palm. Polishing his gold-rimmed glasses, he carefully put them on. Smiling into the mirror, preening a bit, he slicked his hair back again and considered a proper hat.

He made one more walk-through of the house: the dishes were done, the bed made, wood was in the fireplace—nice. He scribbled down additional items on his grocery list and headed to town.

———

It was noon when he pulled in front of the store. The sidewalks were crowded with shoppers and voters. Main Street was backed up with cars edging around to city hall. Most recognized him and honked or waved. He caught a glimpse of the Toro lawn mower display in front of the Western Auto store. Grinning broadly, he turned to his mower display in front of his own store and chuckled, "Good, good."

Jack rang up a sale at the cash register and nodded as Alta walked through the front door. "Didya vote, Daddy?"

"I did, son; it was my first stop."

"What'dya think?"

"'Bout what?"

"'Bout the e-lection."

Alta shrugged. "Can't say. So, how we doin' with them power mowers?"

"Daddy, don't you care about the election?"

"I do, but...has Mr. Western Auto been over?"

"Every mornin'. Says he's got the ex-clu-sive franchise for Toro power mowers in Georgia. Says he's takin' you to court."

Alta slapped his thigh and spun around the aisle, crowing like a rooster greeting the morning sun. "Good, good, good. How many we sold?"

"Not a one, not a one."

Alta was off again, two-stepping down the aisle. "So, our prank is workin'."

"How'ya figure? We ain't sold a one."

"Pranks ain't about money; they're leg-pullers."

"Gosh darn, aren't mayors supposed to act respectable?"

"Hell, it's just a prank. Tryin' to drive Mr. Western Auto a little crazy. Him with the only exclusive power mower franchise in Georgia, thinkin' he's losin' sales to us."

"It don't seem so funny, if we ain't sellin' any."

"That's the point. He thinks were taking business away from him. So, just keep on doin' what you're doin'. At the close of business, load our mowers on the trailer and haul 'em back to Virgil's barn. He'll reckon we sold 'em. Then haul 'um back in the morning and set 'em out front."

"But, if we keep tellin' customers our mowers are spoken for, we're probably drivin' business his way."

"That, son, is the full measure of a prank. We're actually helpin' him out, but he thinks we're hurtin' him. That's the prank."

"I love you, Daddy, but that's sick."

———

Virgil stumbled in the back door of the Legion Post, flipped on the lights, and weaved his way to the bar. After casting his vote, he'd stopped off at the

High Hat for a few beers. The streets were mobbed with registered voters, and they'd arrive at the Post in droves if Alta won. He pulled a jar of corn liquor from under the counter, spun off the lid, and knocked down a healthy swig. His eyes narrowed as he looked about the room. Lamar would be by soon, and it could get messy. He fumbled behind the bonded liquor display, fished out his snub-nosed .38, and sneered into the bar mirror.

A man's gotta be prepared.

He slid the pistol into his back pocket, hitched up his pants, and slipped out onto the porch.

"Hey Boo, you out here?"

Boo Thrower emerged from the shadows, a towering giant in bib overalls, reeking of the barnyard.

Boo's jaw shuttled back and forth as he struggled to make words. "Hey... hey-...Vir...Vir-jul."

Virgil winced as the stench engulfed him. "Shee-yet, Boo, you been slee-pin' with the pigs?"

"Pigs...ya pigs...yah...yah," Boo said as he tried to laugh.

Virgil guided him over to a pole light that swarmed with moths and mosquitos.

"Lamar's gonna ride up on his bike...soon."

"Bi-ka...soo...bi-ka...soo."

"Yeah, bi-ka...soo. You stay back in the shadows, and when he comes up the steps, you squeeze him, but don't break him."

"Sa-weeze, don't braa."

"That's it, sa-weeze, don't braa."

Virgil ducked inside and settled on a barstool. The Pabst Blue Ribbon sign blinked off and on above the bar, sending spears of blue light onto the back porch. His eyelids fluttered and then drooped. His eyes popped open, as a muffled cheer floated up from town.

"They must've announced the winner," he murmured. "I hope to hell its Alta."

———

The ragged shriek of an Ironhead Harley announced Lamar's arrival as he fishtailed up the driveway, leaving a cloud of dust and gravel behind. He skidded to a halt and stomped up the porch stairs.

When Virgil appeared on the porch, Boo had Lamar in a squeeze. His face was pale, and his eyes bugged out.

"Don't break him, Boo," Virgil said with a snicker.

Boo loosened his grip, and the color returned to Lamar's face.

"What the hell, Virgil," Lamar gasped. "I thought we were partners."

Virgil pulled the 357 Magnum from Lamar's vest holster. "Well, looky here, looky what Wild Dog is packin.'"

Virgil pulled two chairs over. "Set him down right here, Boo."

"Rye-hair," Boo echoed.

Boo set Lamar down on a chair and stood above him. Lamar glared at Virgil. Virgil smiled. "So who won?"

"Alta won big time, five sixty-nine to the other guy's three seventy-two," Lamar shot back. "There could be big problems."

Virgil's head snapped back in surprise. "You're not happy, Wild Dog? Damn, Alta's our man."

"Alta being mayor could upset the balance of power."

Virgil erupted in laughter. "Wild Dog, that's what you call yerself, right? Well, I can't save you from your fuckin' demons. Shee-itt, I'm as loony as a sailor on shore leave, but Alta, Alta's our man."

"Maybe, but right now nobody's getting' rich tappin' gas."

Virgil shook his head. "Here's the thing: with Alta being mayor, we got more clout. That don't make us legal, but now Alta's got the ear of the sheriff, the district attorney, and the judge. You just gotta hang in there, Lamar."

Lamar raked his hands through his hair. "Hang in there? Damn, look at me, burn scars from them Cajun boys dunking me in the mash vat, patches and scabs all over my head from Fred Dryden's pistol-whipping. Hang in there? I've had my fill of hangin' in there!"

Lamar sulked as the parking lot filled with cars. The town was ready for a party, and the Legion Post was campaign central for Alta. A line was forming at the front door.

"Here, Boo," Virgil said as he handed him Lamar's pistol. "Keep an eye on Wild Dog. I gotta open the bar."

Virgil hurried back moments later and sat next to Lamar. "Look, Lamar, I know you've taken a few licks. Hell, Fred wacked me on the head as well. But here's the thing: we're good on the taps, and it looks like we'll be getting a better pumpin' schedule. We're ready to put the pedal to the metal. So, tell me, you got them tankers and the gas stations set up?"

"I got plenty of gas stations ready to buy our gas," Lamar growled. "And I got three tank trucks up and runnin' and three more gettin' rigged."

"Hell son, that all sounds great. I'll be ridin' with your drivers now and again, and they damn well better know what they're doin'."

"Them boys know what they're doin'. Most of their daddies ran moonshine for us."

"They better."

Lamar jumped up and stomped across the porch. "Look, none of this means a damn thing unless Alta is in."

Virgil eyes tightened as his lips creased into a thin smile. "Alta, hmm? He says he wants out. Does he mean it? Maybe. Is he out? No. Does he think he's out? I doubt it."

Virgil glanced through the back window of the club. Alta's supporters had made their way to the bar and were serving themselves.

Virgil took Lamar's pistol back from Boo, pointed it at the sky, and spun the cylinder. The bullets dropped on the deck. He grinned and handed it back to Lamar. "Alta thinks I'm doin' a deal with the Dixie mafia in Biloxi this week." He chuckled. "Are we runnin' out of time? Yes! Do we need to make the tappin' work? Hell yes! Are you a dead man if you snitch? Oh, hell yes!"

Lamar growled. "Any asshole can sound threatening when he has the upper hand!"

Virgil roared with laughter. "OK. Let me see if I can do better. Boo here is going to flatten your Harley and your singlewide with a bulldozer if you snitch!"

CHAPTER 32

Tallapoosa, Same Day

———

MANDY'S ELECTION DAY PROMOTION FOLLOWING on her Grand-Opening was a great success, and tonight, tonight she had a date with the mayor. The election results were announced on the radio at five; Alta won by a landslide. He was delighted when he got her call, and said he'd pick her up for their victory dinner. She cautiously elected to drive.

She took her time dressing, combining a sheer silk blouse with a print skirt. "Modest yet festive," she giggled. Though she rarely wore makeup, tonight was special. Puckering her lips, she applied a ruby-red color and added a splash of rosewater cologne, then sorted through her jewelry box and found a pair of small pearl earrings—nice. She considered wearing her lucky charm, her college basketball ring that hung from a necklace. She held it in place in front of the mirror, set her jaw, and dismissed the idea. *I'm through with lucky charms. I'm in charge of my life.* She still remembered the words of her basketball coach. "Mandy, don't worry so much about pleasing others. You decide what's right for you and go for it." That's right, she nodded. I'll decide what's right for me.

Tonight was special. Excitement bubbled through her. She nervously brushed her hair back a final time, and slid the lucky charm in her skirt pocket.

———

Alta set the table out on the porch as he awaited Mandy's arrival. The champagne was chilling in a milk pail. Two long stemmed glasses stood at the ready. Neither the dishes nor the utensils matched, but it all looked snappy.

He lit the charcoal in the grill and hurried back to the kitchen. The steaks and corn lay on the counter, seasoned and ready for the grill. His first-ever green salad cooled in the refrigerator. With the coffee ready to perk, Alta was beaming.

By eight o'clock he'd finished the preparations. Mandy was due any minute. The phone rang, and he rushed inside. "Hel-lo."

"Alta, this is Chester. Congratulations!"

"Woo, hoo, hoo!" Alta howled. "Thank you, Chester. You deserve a lot of the credit."

"That's so true. Say, Alta, you got your radio on?"

"I do."

"Are you listening' to country music out of Atlanta?"

"I am."

"Stay tuned, pard-ner." Chester said, laughing, and sang, "Slipppppiiiiinnn' around, afraid we might be found."

Alta shuffled over to the Philco and turned up the volume.

The DJ was thrilled as he announced, "I got a special request goin' out to the brand new mayor of Tallapoosa, Mr. Alta Dryden. It's an old favorite by Ernest Tubb and the Texas Troubadours called 'Slipping Around.'"

Alta chuckled as he two-stepped around the kitchen. *It's true, Mandy and I have done some slipping around, shared a few secret Sunday afternoons together, but it's been on the up and up.*

Mandy drove up in her Plymouth Fury and laid on the horn. As he headed for the door, Alta paused at the hall mirror. He hitched up his pants, straightened his tie, and set his straw hat at a rakish angle. Then changed his mind, set it straight and smiled into the mirror.

May-or-al, damn, may-or-al.

Mandy bounded up the stairs with a bouquet of roses cradled in her arms.

"Congratulations Alta, congratulations!"

"Roses, yes roses are special," he said with a wink. "I'll damn sure be your tall dark stranger, if you'll be my San Antone Rose."

Mandy edged forward cautiously and hugged him. "I am mighty proud of you."

For the first time in a while, Alta noticed that Mandy was an inch or so taller than him. Gawd she looked good. "Well, I'm mighty proud of you, Mandy. You've become quite the shopkeeper, and you look real fine with the lipstick and all."

"And look at you, Mr. Mayor, with a straw hat and pressed trousers, real nice. But please, get rid of the painted tie."

He slipped it off and in his pocket. "It's gone."

"Way better."

"And now, my dear," Alta proclaimed in a raspy drawl, "please join me in a cel-e-bra-tory toast."

He pulled the champagne from the milk pail and fumbled with the closure.

Mandy watched and broke up laughing. "It's not a screw-top, daw-lin'. Peel off the foil, undo the metal loop, and gently pull out the cork."

He shrugged playfully and finally pulled out the cork. "I ain't so good at this stuff."

She flinched somewhat as he stepped forward to pour but then extended her arm. "It ain't your best feature."

"So, here's to you, dear Mandy, for..." his voice cracked, "for keepin' me on the straight and narrow."

She stepped back and sipped her champagne. "Alta, you've helped me more than you'll ever know," she sighed.

"I mean it, Mandy."

"And here's to you, Mr. Mayor, your honor, sir," she toasted. "May you bring prosperity and decency to our little town."

She sipped champagne and skittered off like a water bug. She fingered the family heirlooms as she puttered about, stopping at a framed picture of Shelby. "Y'know, I've only been in the house that once, after Shelby's funeral. You keep a nice house."

He caught up with her in the kitchen. "I cleaned it up for tonight. Say, you hungry?"

She leaned back against the refrigerator. "Let's visit. So, tell me truly, how happy are you?"

"I'm happier than a butcher's dog," Alta declared, shuffling up and down the kitchen floor. "I can't wait to get things movin'. The key to our survival, y'see, is growth: growth in our farm production, growth in light industry, growth in civic pride."

Mandy smiled politely as he went on.

"To conclude, and this is what I told the folks from the *Atlanta Journal* when they called, "we're gonna feed the elderly and pave every street."

"Well, big boy," she said as she tapped him on the chest, "now you got to do it. What's the first thing on your agenda?"

The first thing?" A sly smile flashed across his face. "That's not counting you—."

"Behave."

"Well, you know Rhubarb Jones? Well, his grandma's driveway washed out, over on Lyons Street. Po' lady has to park down the street and lug groceries up to the house. The first thing I'm gonna do come Monday is to get Pink Allen—he'll be runnin' the Streets and Waterworks Department—to take a load of asphalt and gravel over to Lyons Street. Ole Pink is hell on asphalt and gravel!"

"That's been approved, has it?"

"In concept."

"Yessir," Mandy said as she arched her brow, "you'll make a fine mayor."

As the evening unfolded, they moved back out on the porch to eat. The grilled corn and steak were overcooked but delicious. Something, however, went terribly wrong with Alta's first salad. The chopped kale was miserably thorny. He shrugged it off and refilled their champagne glasses.

Alta pushed his hands out with open palms. "Soooo, enough about me. How you feelin'?"

Mandy wrinkled her nose. "Happier than a prom queen."

Alta broke in, "With the football captain at your side."

Mandy popped up and circled the table. "With a case of beer in the trunk of his daddy's car. And to conclude, sales were brisk and steady at the store. The space heaters are still selling, but the box fans, what with summer coming on, sold out, and I'm holdin' back orders for twenty more."

Alta's lips puckered. "Your take-home on the box fans?"

Her eyes sparkled as she sat down on the porch swing. "Well over a thousand dollars."

"Whoa!"

"Best ever!"

Alta sidled up. "Say, Mandy?"

"Yes?"

"Mind if I join you on the swing?"

"Just behave."

The evening was peaceful yet full of night music—the drone of crickets joined the ardent croaking of tree frogs. Fireflies buzzed about the porch as the crescent moon settled into a corner of the sky. Hand in hand, they swung quietly.

Alta felt Mandy's shoulders shake and was surprised to see her tears. "What's wrong?"

"I don't know if I can explain it."

Alta looked on helplessly. "Did I do somethin' wrong?"

"No, this time I did it to myself. Like I said when I signed that contract… I've had my fill of bright lights and dangerous men. And I've damn sure had my fill of gray days and lonely nights…and well…our arrangement helped me put some order in my life, but somehow, in doin' it, I built a wall around my feelings."

"Uh-oh." Alta blushed, searching for a response.

"Our business arrangement isn't the problem. The problem is here and now. The wall is startin' to crumble. Like I've said before, I gave up on romantic love a long time ago, and yet, and yet…I'm still a woman."

Hearing the words but missing the meaning, Alta nodded. "That you are."

"Shut up Alta. Just shut up."

His head dropped like a scolded hound.

Mandy jumped up and paced back and forth in front of the swing. Alta noticed she was rubbing her basketball charm against her side. *Good Lawd, she's on the war path.*

"You know Alta, I was all-conference forward on my college basketball team."

"I do."

"And, you know I'm bigger and stronger than you."

"I do."

"And I can damn well kick your ass if you cross me."

Alta winced. "That you can."

"But I just don't know if I can trust you."

Alta jumped up and sputtered. "Hold tight. Coffee's ready." He disappeared into the kitchen.

He grabbed the coffee pot and two cups, braced against the kitchen sink and looked out at Mandy. He was lost in a crossfire of emotions. He hadn't felt the warm glow of love in years. Yet, he also felt a drumming in his chest or was it a judge hammering a gavel. His thoughts drifted back to his many court trials. The bailiff held out the Bible. He placed his hand on it and swore an oath. Tonight, Mandy wanted him to swear an oath to her, and oath to do-right—an oath he'd never kept.

He returned to the porch with the coffee. Mandy joined him at the table. They sipped coffee in silence. Alta struggled to find the right words. Eventually, he stammered. "Mandy, I've come to care for you, but I won't make false promises. I want to do right, but I've been wrong before."

Mandy shook her head. She seemed bewildered. "Jesus Christ Alta, I don't know whether you lack passion or commitment?"

His eyes glazed over as his brain ramped up. "Probably both."

Doc Dorothy's haunting prescription seared through him: "Alta, you've got to find someone to love that's more important to you than being the smartest man in West Georgia." He knew she was right. Why, he wondered, why am I so good with numbers and so bad with feelings? *I'll be damned if I lose Mandy.*

He stood and extended his hands to her. They walked to the edge of the porch where the moon glimmered through the treetops. For the first time, he smelled her perfume. The night music encircled them as they embraced. Mandy held him tight as they kissed—a gentle kiss of innocence. Alta nestled his head in her hair. He felt a stirring down his spine. A wave of passion washed over his doubts and fears. He returned a long lingering kiss as they swayed in the dappled moonlight. Her easy purr became a moan, a sweet dovelike moan, as she locked her arms around his back. His chest thundered, not the harsh rumble of a lonely heart, but the crackling tremolo of two hearts on fire. They were home at last in a nest of their own making.

Suddenly, Mandy broke away and stepped back. Her lips moved from a smile to a smirk. Her eyes flickered; there seemed to be a devil dancing inside her. She glided over to the dinner table, pulled a rose from the vase and placed it behind her ear. Turning to Alta, who watched in amazement, she taunted. "Well, giddy up, cowboy! Giddy up! If you'll be my tall dark stranger, I'll be your San Antone Rose."

Alta's face lit up. Arm in arm they swayed back to the house. Then it hit him. *Gawd damn, I gotta do-right.*

Part 3

Charlie and Mattie Dryden, Alta's parents.

Thousand gallon still, Haralson County

ATF agents dumping mash barrels.

Still hands arrested.

Still hand going to jail.

Sheriff Pink Allen.

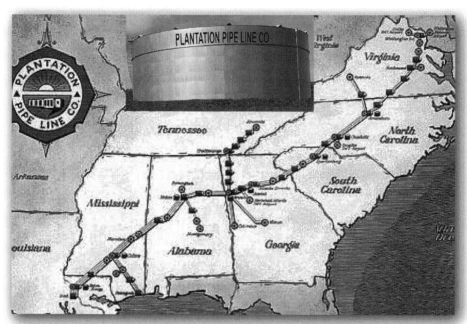

Plantation Pipeline.

Welding a hot tap.

Guests at the Nutrition Center's Open House included Mrs. Ayers, supervisor of the Nutrition Program in the area and Leon Skidmore of Coosa Valley Authority, (not pictured) and left to right Jess Newman, Rep. Tom Murphy, Dr. Henry Fields, Commissioner of Roads and Revenue Jim Frank Smith, Bremen Mayor Robert Ritchie and Tallapoosa Mayor Alta Dryden.

Tom Murphy, Speaker of the House, July 4th parade.

One of the pageant scenes was the signing of the Declaration of Independence - Playing roles in the scene were, from left, Pete Mobley, Tax Commissioner, Judge Harold Murphy, Sen. Nathan Dean, Rep. Tom Murphy, Mayor Alta Dryden and J.F. Smith, Road Commissioner.

TAP SITE SOUTH OF MUSCADINE, ALABAMA

CHAPTER 33

Tallapoosa/Atlanta, A Month Later

ALTA ROLLED OVER TO CHECK the clock, 6.00 a.m. Good. He rolled back and gently hugged Mandy. He loved her silk negligee. She was warm and soft, smelled of red rose perfume and purred like a kitten. Morning sleep was pure gold to Mandy. He loved her in the morning. He slipped out of bed, pulled on his robe and was off to the kitchen. Grinning like a schoolboy, he looked back to see her snuggled in the covers.

Gently closing the kitchen door, he headed for the back porch. The hummingbirds ducked and dodged around the hanging baskets. They liked Petunias and Impatiens, but adored Alta's sweet concoction—one part sugar, four parts water, a teaspoon of brown sugar and a tablespoon of moonshine. After filling the feeders, he cut a bouquet of white Gardenias. *Good lawd they're intoxicating.*

Breakfast started with biscuits—preheat oven to 450°F, one egg, one cup of Bisquick flour, one cup of milk, mix, pour into muffin pan and into the oven for ten minutes. Next, he got the coffee brewing and the bacon sizzling in the fry pan. The blend of breakfast smells and Gardenias was overwhelming. He rubbed his hands together and chuckled, eight more minutes on the biscuits.

When the biscuits were a gold brown, he turned off the oven but left the oven door open. Finally, he cracked four eggs into the fry pan and opened the bedroom door. As his love potion drifted into the bedroom, Alta watched the second hand on the oven clock…five seconds…ten seconds.

"Ooooooooh, Alta I love you!"

"And I love you Mandy. Stay where you are. Breakfast is coming."

"Breakfast in bed! Oooooooooh, I do love you! Are those Gardenias I smell?"

"Yes darling."

"Ooooh, Alta get in here."

———

Mandy and Alta took their second cup of coffee out on the porch. Their routine was simple. They rolled out of bed about 6:30, ate breakfast and planned their day. Mandy loved everything about managing the Bremen hardware store which was morphing into a gift and toy shop. Alta having delegated most of the management of the Tallapoosa store to his son Jack, focused mainly on his plans for the day at city hall. His first month as mayor had been a nonstop campaign against bad practices and bureaucratic shenanigans. He'd fallen into an exhausting yet engaging routine, not a sprint, not a marathon, but a good deal of both. He was thoroughly energized.

At 7:30 a.m., they kissed goodbye and headed in different directions.

Mandy smirked. "Say Alta, that was some breakfast this morning. I do love you."

"Yes it was, and I do love you too."

———

Alta met Jack at the store. They sipped coffee on the back couch, discussed shop retailing, profit margins, and seasonal promotions. At eight, he charged across Main Street to city hall.

After a morning of committee meetings, Alta retreated to his office, sank deep into his tufted leather chair, and yawned. Crossing his feet on the battered oak desk, he stretched his hands down the cushioned arms and tapped the nail-head trim. He loved the chair. It had that new-leather smell and that old-leather feel. It was clearly a power chair. So far, he felt he had used his power wisely, getting many programs moving. His plan to feed the elderly, however, was stuck. As his eyes closed, he wondered if his favorite chair might become a hot seat.

For a week now, he had called, and awaited a call back from Tom Murphy, Georgia's speaker of the house and the political kingpin of Haralson County. He needed Tom's support for a nutrition center that would deliver meals out to the elderly. It wasn't like Tom to keep him waiting. *Maybe I pushed too hard.*

Last week, at the closing session of the Georgia General Assembly, Tom had been presented with a brand-new Ford LTD and little else. Most of his prized legislation had been blocked by urban county legislators. Rural counties were losing power, and Tom was fighting it tooth and nail. Violet, Tom's secretary, had promised he'd return Alta's call at nine sharp that morning. Alta's eyes snapped open, and he glanced at the wall clock. It was half past eleven.

He jumped up, stomped across the hardwood floor, and hollered down the hall, "Robert, get in here."

Robert, a fussy young clerk, was preparing to leave for the day. No one worked on Wednesday afternoons, not in Tallapoosa, not even during the Civil War. Robert ambled down the hall with his briefcase in hand. "Can it wait 'til tomorrow, Mr. Mayor?" he replied curtly. "It is Wednesday afternoon, y'know."

"No it can't. Did ya get anything back from your man in the nutrition office?"

"Not yet," Robert snapped. "I sent another memo."

"A memo? Have you called him?"

"No sir," he replied, the edge coming off of his voice.

"Well, go on, son, get on it."

Alta frowned as he paced back and forth across his office. On Election Day, his campaign team had bused hundreds of elderly folks to the polls. Those folks were counting on the nutrition program. His frown became a smile as he paused in front of his prized bulletin board. Covered with news clippings, it was the high altar of Alta's crusade for growth and prosperity. All in all, things had gone well since he was elected. Pinned to the top of the board was his favorite clipping, a March 6th front-page headline from the *Atlanta Journal*: "FROM MOONSHINE TO CITY HALL," it proclaimed. The subheadline announced: EX-CON WANTS TO GIVE PEOPLE SERVICE. Alta was quoted in the text: "We're going to pave every street in town," Dryden promised, "and we're going to feed our elderly."

The paving was well underway, thanks to Pink Allen and his crew, yet the nutrition program was ankle-deep in bureaucratic red tape. Below the *Atlanta Journal* article was a March 17 front-page clipping from the *Tallapoosa-Beacon* announcing: "Mayor Dryden Appoints Department Chairmen" at the first council meeting. On the same front page was a picture of the mayor awarding the grand champion ribbon at the 4-H Steer Show.

The next clipping splashed across the front page of the *Beacon* read: "Mayor Proclamation. The mayor proclaims May 1st as Loyalty Day as an incentive for every red blooded American to reaffirm their love of flag and country and to proudly display the flag."

He grabbed one of the miniature flags displayed throughout his office and waved it about. The front page of the May 4th Beacon showed a picture of the mayor throwing out the first pitch of Little League season. Then on May 11th, another of Alta's prized clippings, showed him throwing out the first pitch at Atlanta-Fulton County Stadium— "Tallapoosa Night" at Braves' field.

Alta smiled. *The only convicted felon in history to throw out the first pitch.*

Below that was a June 23rd clipping from the *Beacon* announcing: "Tallapoosa Clean-Up Day Scheduled Next Wednesday." The text read: "Mayor Alta Dryden said that he and the council were concentrating on getting the streets in tip-top shape for the Bicentennial celebration July 2nd, 3rd, and 4th."

The last clipping on the board, from the June 30th *Beacon*, announced the expansion of the Stoffel Seal Plant, a major business in town. The accompanying picture showed Mayor Dryden removing the first shovel of dirt at the groundbreaking.

Alta grinned broadly as he turned from the bulletin boards. "Patriotism, pavin', and paint, I like the sound of that…and new plants and new business. We'll damn well keep money from leavin' town."

Robert appeared at the door. "I couldn't get through to the nutrition office. They aren't takin' our calls."

Alta frowned. "You got a full tank of gas in your car?"

"I do."

"Good, you're driving. We're going to make an office call on your nutrition man at the state capital in Atlanta."

"Mr. Mayor, if you don't mind, I think that would be a mistake. He's very powerful. It wouldn't pay to upset him."

"Good Lawd, Robert, he's a public servant."

Robert pouted as he drove. Alta reviewed the nutrition file. As they passed the Mableton exit on I-20, he closed the file and said, "Let's review our request. We've got a lot of folks in town who are going hungry. In the last census, it says, thirty percent of those over sixty-five are livin' below the poverty line."

"Yes, but," Robert said quickly, "twenty percent of those below the age of thirty are living below the poverty line as well."

"Young folks need jobs, not welfare, and we're bringin' plenty of new jobs to town. So Robert, am I right on them numbers? Thirty percent of our elderly are living in poverty."

"That's correct. As are thirty percent of the elderly in Bremen, Buchanan, and Cedartown."

"Damn, son, that's my point. They all have nutrition centers to prepare and distribute meals to the elderly."

Robert grinned smugly. "Then, clearly, it's our turn."

"Son, I know I do things differently. And I do want your help. But our days of waitin' in line, and takin' our turn are over. You hear?"

"I hear what you're sayin', I do," Robert said nodded submissively, having no idea what Alta was saying.

"Good, good."

Alta tapped his finger on the dashboard as they parked below the golden dome of the Georgia capitol building, "I'm gonna go see the speaker, if I can get in. And I want you to camp in the lobby of Mr. Nutrition, whatever the hell his name is. Tell him that Mr. Murphy, the speaker of the house, who comes from Bremen just nine miles down the road from Tallapoosa, will be giving him a call directly."

"Yessir"

Alta made his way to the speaker's office and poked his head in the outer door. "Hello, sugar," he whispered to Violet, Tom's secretary. "Got a minute?"

"Well, by golly, hello, Alta. I guess it's Mr. Mayor these days."

Violet popped up and gave him a hug. "Sit down, darlin'. It's crazy around here this time of year. He's got two calls on hold, and he's been on this one for fifteen minutes."

Alta sat on the couch and folded his arms in his lap. "I can wait. I only need a minute."

She pushed her glasses back on her head. "I know he wants to see you, but he truly is in a hell of a row with the budget committee."

Through his office door, the speaker could be heard hammering his gavel and hollering, "What is it you don't understand about hell no?"

Violet and Alta shrugged with a grin.

"I understand, Violet. Promise me one thing. Have Tom phone this nutrition guy and set up a meeting for us this afternoon."

"Yes, I truly promise. And Mr. Mayor," she added, "he's called the nutrition commissioner."

Alta snapped to attention and saluted her. "Then, by golly, that's what we'll call him."

Alta joined Robert in the cramped outer office of the nutrition commissioner. When she wasn't working on her hair, his secretary shot them the evil eye. She was a skilled gatekeeper who knew the drill. At five fifteen, Alta started to wonder about Tom Murphy. Over the years, Tom had hit him up for every charity event in Haralson County, from summer-league softball to hayrides, and Alta had always given big. Was Tom just busy, or was he pissed off at him? Alta decided he'd wait five more minutes for Tom's call. Then, by God, he'd march back down to Tom's office and confront him face to face. When it came to head-butting, bull elks in rut were no match for Tom Murphy and Alta Dryden.

Several minutes later, the phone rang inside the commissioner's office. Alta exhaled as the door swung open and they were ushered in. It was quickly apparent that the commissioner, a buttoned-up bureaucrat in an Ivy League suit, was going through the motions. After half an hour of wrangling, he conceded they might qualify for funding, but they needed to submit a request, and that needed to be reviewed. If approved, they could move ahead early next year. Alta's eyes glazed over.

He stood up, carefully set his wire-rimmed glasses in their case, and snapped it shut. With little conscious effort, a solution came to him. He knew what he had to do. Robert was deferential, fussing about the commissioner like a valet as they departed. He gathered a handful of request forms and vigorously pumped the commissioner's hand.

As they got in the car, Robert turned to Alta. "So that went pretty well, don't you think?"

"You think so?"

They didn't talk much on the ride home. Alta buried his head in a stack of Atlanta trade magazines. "Accordin' to the *Almanac*, it's gonna be a damn hot summer," he mused. "I've got to get me another truckload of them box fans and some swing sets."

Robert forced a smile and kept quiet. Occasionally he stole a glance over at Alta but didn't dare disturb him. As they pulled into Tallapoosa, Alta finally looked up. "Robert, I want you to call up the local newspapers before you go home. Tell them to be here tomorrow at ten thirty sharp. We're gonna have us a press conference. Also, call Nathan Dean, our esteemed senator, and Mr. Tom Murphy, his highness, and get them on the phone at ten thirty."

"Can I ask what this is about?"

"Son, Tallapoosa's gonna get us a nutrition center."

———

By ten fifteen the next morning, the local newspaper reporters were standing by in the city hall lobby. The mayor greeted them graciously and then excused himself, promising to return in five minutes for a press conference. He stepped into his office and closed the door. Holding the phone in one hand, Robert braced himself against the desk to keep from shaking.

Alta winked at Robert. "Ya got 'em on the line?"

"Nathan can't make it, but he said he'd support you. Said it was Tom's call. Tom's on the line, and he's hot."

Alta flashed a wicked smile and took the phone. "Good mornin', Tom. What the hell am I doing'? Well, as you know, we, the po', unwashed folks from Tallapoosa been tryin' to get us a nutrition center. Hold on, Tom, let me finish."

Alta put his hand over the earpiece and held the phone at arm's length. Moments later he pulled the phone back and bellowed, "Did I say that Tallapoosa, the oldest city in Haralson County, is the only city without a nutrition enter? Now, Tom, will you listen for a minute?"

Again Alta put his hand over the earpiece and shuffled back and forth. By now, Robert was trembling.

"Mr. Speaker, let me be clear. We got newspaper reporters from Bremen, Buchanan, and Cedartown sittin' out in our meeting room. What are they waitin' for? That's a fine question. They're waitin' to hear about our new nutritional center. What am I goin' tell 'em? Well, that's up to you. I can tell 'um that the mayor of Tallapoosa is going to fund the center out of his own pocket. Now wouldn't that make great copy? Or, I could tell them that we are delighted to hear that the state of Georgia has just approved funding for the center. No, I ain't kiddin', your honor. Can I put you through to them? I don't know, let me check." He looked at Robert. "Say Robert, Can we transfer this call to the speaker phone in the meeting room?"

With his eyes fully dilated, Robert nodded yes.

"Hang on, Tom, we'll do just that." Turning to Robert, he said, "Go tell the reporters I'll be right in."

Alta strolled down to the meeting room wearing a grin and picked up the phone. "Hello, Tom, you there? I'm switchin' ya on speaker."

Tom Murphy's voice boomed out of the mounted speaker, sending cobwebs flying. "Good mornin', gentlemen, this is Tom Murphy, and I've got some really good news. I just approved a first-class nutrition center for Tallapoosa."

The room erupted in applause. Alta put his arm around Robert's shoulder. "Tom's a crackerjack, ain't he?"

CHAPTER 34

Muscatine, Alabama, Days Later

AT ONE THIRTY ON A dark, moonless night, Virgil leaned against a workbench in an abandoned barn in Muscatine, Alabama, a pencil in one hand, a flashlight in the other, trying to tally the gas-tapping accounts. He closed one eye to keep the columns from doubling and took a long pull on a jar of moonshine. Since Alta's return from prison, Virgil's life had been crazy. From six to twelve at night, he ran the bar at the Legion Post; then he hauled gas until sunup or ran gas tapping gear out to new tap sites. A steady diet of moonshine and countless bags of pork rinds kept him upright, if not amiable. His teeth were yellow, his eyes were red, and his shirt looked like a bar towel.

As the winds shifted, the smell of moldering hay drove off the gas fumes, a bouquet of vaporized hydrocarbons. A red Ford flatbed truck with a two-thousand-gallon tank chained to the bed was parked in the back of the barn. A three-inch rubber hose ran from a manhole coupling on top of the truck out the side of the barn and across the yard to the hot tap on the twenty-six-inch Plantation Pipeline.

Several weeks earlier, when Virgil had started tapping, he'd fully opened the nozzle on the hose. High-pressure gasoline had ripped the nozzle from his hands and blown off the barn door. These days he barely cracked the nozzle. Gas shot into the tank, and fumes filled the barn. The slightest spark of stray electricity would have taken out the barn and several acres of rural Alabama.

Tonight was Virgil's turn to ride shotgun with a new driver. Once the tanker truck was full, they'd be off on a delivery. They needed to slip into the gas station just after two a.m. and slip out in no more than ten minutes. No lights, no noise, just connect the hose from the tanker to the underground storage tank and open the valve.

A sly smile crossed Virgil's face as he finished his numbers. It was working; the money was coming in. Sure, they needed more trucks, more tap sites, and, yes, they needed more cash to fund the deal. But on a good night, they were delivering over seven thousand gallons of gas and bringing in about three thousand dollars. Still, he worried about keeping Alta and his money in the game. Alta still thought the deal with Billy Blue-Eyes and the Dixie mafia was going through. Since becoming mayor, he was consumed with going straight and getting the town moving. Yet, Virgil knew a showdown was coming.

He eyeballed Jimmy-Lee, the new driver, as he topped off the tanker and lowered the filling hose.

"C'mere, son," Virgil snarled.

Jimmy-Lee, a rawboned kid with a tattoo around his neck, climbed off the truck and joined Virgil in the beam of his flashlight.

"How you doin', son?"

Jimmy-Lee shot a smile into the light beam. "I'm hanging in there like a hair on a biscuit."

"You some kind of comedian, are you?"

"Nossir."

"Lamar Tate hired you, right?"

"Yessir."

Virgil grabbed his shirt collar. "You know better than to trust that no good sumbitch, don't you?"

Jimmy-Lee flinched. "Nossir...I mean yessir."

"You understand what we're up to here?"

"Yessir...haulin' gas."

"Where to?"

Jimmy-Lee looked up with a smile. "Union Seventy-Six in Tallapoosa."

"Who's our contact?"

"Travis."

"Did you talk to him today?"

"Yessir."

"How much does he need?"

"A…a full load?" Jimmy-Lee's voice broke.

"Did you see him check the storage tank with a dip stick?" Virgil barked.

Jimmy-Lee cringed. "Yessir, well, nossir. He said he did. Said it was near empty."

"It better be." Virgil scratched his head and changed course. "How much we haulin' tonight?"

"Two thousand gallons."

"That's right, son; now have a look at that tank truck. What d'you see?"

Smiling over broken teeth, Jimmy-Lee replied, "A pile of shit."

Virgil chuckled. "Yeah, but it's our pile of shit. How 'bout them tires?"

"They look flat."

"They're low, all right. Two thousand gallons of gas comes to around twelve thousand pounds, that's six tons. And that's a hell of a load, and the tank has no baffles in it."

Virgil handed him the keys to the truck. "What's that tell you, son?"

"Slow down?"

"That's right, take her slow. Without baffles, you'll have six tons of gas surging from side to side on the curves."

Impatiently rattling the keys, Jimmy-Lee appeared ready to go and tired of the lecture.

"OK, son, let's go. You better be right about the Seventy-Six needin' a full load."

Fighting sleep, Virgil slumped back in the seat. With only running lights to guide him, Jimmy-Lee dodged potholes on the winding backroads. On the curves, the fully loaded tanker swayed violently from side to side; the chains tying the tank down rattled under the strain.

Half asleep, Virgil mumbled, "Easy, son."

The road straightened out slightly as Jimmy-Lee turned on to Route 4, a graded gravel road. Several miles later they pulled onto Highway 78, a paved road with a white line. Lights from passing cars snapped Virgil out of his stupor just as the truck went sideways on Dead Man's Curve.

"Holy shee-yet, son! Straighten her out! Do not hit the brakes!"

As they skidded sideways around the curve, gas slopped out the top of the truck and poured onto the road. The rear wheels slid across the gravel shoulder as Jimmy-Lee pulled her back on the road again. His eyes looked like silver dollars.

"Slow the fawk down," Virgil yelled. "Any sign of the law?"

Jimmy-Lee swallowed hard, wiped his forehead with his sleeve, and said, "Naw. Not much traffic this time of night."

Virgil looked over and saw Jimmy-Lee's face twitching and knew he was lying. "Keep an eye out."

———————

At ten after two, they coasted into town. Other than the Burger Inn and the High Hat, the town was dark and empty. The Burger Inn was bustling with the going-home bar crowd looking for a burger and a cup of coffee. The dimly lit High Hat was the only place you could buy an after-hours drink. Virgil was dying for a cold beer but dismissed it. Hanging his head out the passenger window, he whispered, "Kill your lights and pull off there behind the Seventy-Six station."

"Yessir," Jimmy-Lee chirped. "The fitting for the storage tanks is right outside the restrooms."

"Good boy, pull around and park there."

"I can hook up the hose," Jimmy-Lee said proudly. "I done it before."

"Shut up son. Sit tight and leave the engine running."

Ten minutes passed, and only two cars drove down Main Street.

Virgil looked up and down the highway. "All right, Jimmy-Lee, quiet like, set up the hose, open the vent on top of the tank, and start dumpin'."

"Yessir."

"Say, where's your boy, Travis?"

Jimmy shrugged. "Don't know. Said he'd meet us."

"Get started and then find him, quick like."

Virgil waited in the truck. A neon sign above the West Georgia Bank across the street flashed the time and temperature: Fifty degrees Fahrenheit, 2:15 a.m.

Virgil yawned and cracked the window. "Two-fifteen, that's about right."

He took one last pull on his jar of moonshine, leaned back in the seat, and dozed.

A while later, Virgil jerked awake, overcome with gas fumes. He rubbed his eyes and looked over at the bank sign. It now flashed 2:30 a.m. "Shee-yet!"

He snapped forward and looked out the window. Gas gushed out the end of the hose, flooding down the gas pump lanes and washing across Main Street.

"Ho-ly shee-yet!"

He jumped out and shut off the hose. Jimmy-Lee stumbled up with a bottle of beer in his hand as Virgil uncoupled the hose.

"Get in, you little sumbitch. So where the hell is Travis?"

Jimmy-Lee trembled as he tried to hide his beer. "I couldn't find him."

Just then a Tallapoosa police car cruised down Main Street and screeched to a halt in front of the gas spill. A red spotlight flashed on and swung up from the road, following the spill to the gas station. It caught the front of the tanker and then swept back to the street and went off. Seconds later the police drove off.

A smile of relief crossed Virgil's face as he pulled out the back of the station and disappeared into the night. "Thank Gawd them boys are on the take."

CHAPTER 35
Tallapoosa, Same Day

———

A ROADSIDE STREETLAMP THREW A shaft of light across the bedroom of Lamar's trailer It was four a.m., and he was still awake. Last night, his night off, was playtime. Every other night he rode shotgun with new drivers, hauling gas from the tap sites to various service stations in West Georgia. He'd partied hard last night and brought home a trophy. Rondell—or was it Shirley?—purred beside him: a bank teller by day, a pole dancer by night, all in all, a ravenous love machine.

He bounced out of bed in leopard-skin boxers, skidded down the linoleum hallway into the kitchen, and gulped down a quart of milk. The gas-tapping money was rolling in, and he was back in high cotton. Belching loudly, he fell back on the couch, admiring his treasured painting of an African wild dog.

Lately, he'd expanded his whole apex predator–avenging angel image. Gas tapping! Shit-fire! He'd hit the motherlode. Way better than racing his Harley or running moonshine, and he loved the political angle. Grinning wildly, he imagined the headlines in the newspaper:

West Georgia Vigilantes Take On Big Oil.

And he would add: **Think Globally, Tap Locally**

His eyes narrowed as he curled back his lips. This was much bigger and far nobler than stabilizing a single ecosystem. Gas tapping, and what it symbolized, was a major geopolitical statement. He knew his mind worked

225

differently than most, more cosmic perhaps. His sphere of influence had broadened. Now he focused on international issues.

In a relentless search for global predators, Lamar had zeroed in on the OPEC Oil Embargo of 1973. He had endured the gas shortages, the endless lines at the pumps, the high prices. He was still pissed off at what it had done to the nation and the planet. No ecosystem was safe from Big Oil.

He didn't understand the full impact of the oil embargo. He'd heard it caused both inflation and stagnation. Corporate assholes! Then, once America's oil reserves ran low, a cartel of East Texas oil producers, Big US Oil, raised their prices. These were the same boys who ran their pipeline through West Georgia.

"Standard business-school practices," he moaned.

Add to that, the boys in Washington, that's Big Government, made the decision to float the dollar on the international exchange, further feeding inflation.

"When Big Oil exploits po' folk and pollutes the land, its old-fashioned capitalism," he growled, "but if we tap a few barrels from Big Oil, it's a felony!"

"La-mar? What's wrong?" hollered his new friend.

"Nothing, Shirley, go back to sleep."

"It's Rondell, asshole."

Down deep he wondered: was the gas-tapping campaign his finest hour or another fantasy? Since Alta got out of prison, Lamar's life had spiraled downward: Alta had sold the moonshine business out from under him; he'd been scarred, parboiled, and damn near drowned by Billy Boudreaux and his merry pranksters; and Mandy, his ex-wife, was now living with Alta. And there was Virgil. What could you say about Virgil? A truly violent man with a gun. And tonight, Rondell. She was truly insatiable, way more woman than he could handle. Surely all of this was a sign of some sort.

Shaking off his doubts, he popped a beer and winked in the mirror as he combed his gold locks over the scars on his head.

I'm still a handsome sumbitch. I got that workin' for me. And they say I'm a bona-fide sex object.

He wondered what the honest, hardworking people believed in. How did they define the good life?—a mountain to climb, an ocean to cross, overcoming obstacles, enduring setbacks, sin, redemption, forgiveness…always moving on to higher ground? How would that be? He wondered. And why was his life such a roller-coaster ride? Staggering ascents, breakneck speeds, astounding highs, terrifying lows, again and again, wheels locked in a closed loop. Or maybe he was through the worst of it and on his way to the good life?

A little after five o'clock, as he lingered on the edge of an epiphany, the phone rang.

"Lamar here."

A husky baritone whispered, "You got a problem."

"Who's this?"

"The police, stupid."

"Oh shee-yet! What's up?"

"Your ass, if you don't get down here. Your boy Virgil just flooded the Union

Seventy-Six station."

"I'm on my way."

"If this gets out, we ain't coverin' for you."

As Lamar yanked on his trousers and searched for his bike key, Rondell scurried out of the bedroom buck naked, her red hair flying in all directions, her pendulous breasts swaying to and fro like beagles on the prowl. "Hey, big boy, we ain't done here!"

Lamar's eyes widened as he bolted out the door. "Gotta run."

Lamar coasted the last three blocks to the Union 76 station, keeping the Harley idling quietly. Parking behind a nearby warehouse, he slipped into the gloom. It was five twenty, and the sky was starting to lighten. An iridescent blue-green haze shimmered on the pavement surrounding the station. The gas fumes were sweet yet stung his eyes. Though it faded as it evaporated, a distinct gas stain stretched across Main Street, yet there was no pooling in the gutters that led into the storm drain.

Traffic was light and ran smoothly along Main Street. No one was stopping, not now anyway. He considered hosing off the pavement but was afraid he be seen. Someone in addition to the Tallapoosa police had seen something. Lamar's current scheme of bringing down Big Oil disappeared. His face burned. His body shook.

"Fuckin' Virgil."

———

Lamar looped down Main Street and up the hill to the Legion Post, quietly parking his Harley behind a World War II Sherman tank. As he expected, the red Ford tanker was parked up behind the clubhouse. Virgil had probably crashed in the back room. Lamar pulled his 357 Magnum out of his saddlebag and considered his options. The gas-tapping business now seemed doomed. Alta was damn good at damage control, but news of the spill would surely get out, and the law would start circling like sharks—the sheriff, the ATF, the FBI. Hey, Alta was a big catch.

He debated. He could simply disappear, get away, and start over, maybe go straight like Alta was trying to do. Would that work? That would be the right thing to do. Then he'd be clean, redeemed, saved. Tempting, very tempting. His mind turned dark as he spun the cylinder of the 357 Magnum. When it came to crime and punishment, the privileged had an unfair advantage. Chester Pope, Alta's legal and financial adviser, was a case in point.

Chester was privileged. He'd never spent a day in jail. Born to a wealthy planter, he was whisked off to military school at a young age to expand his mind and connect with the leaders of the New South. A prestigious law degree and four years as a defense attorney produced a cunning mind beneath a veneer of righteousness. He made his fortune in shaky loans and flaky land deals. Chester learned that the adversarial system of justice, while reducing the chances of convicting the innocent, provided a major advantage to the guilty. With a top-quality lawyer, those in the privileged class were usually acquitted or plead out to a lesser crime.

Then there was Alta Dryden, born to tenant farmers during the hard times. Alta was certainly not privileged. Yet by some genetic accident, he was clever, damn clever, and found his calling stealing cars and running moonshine. He quickly learned that moral qualms were a distraction when survival was at stake. He also learned that big money, for privileged and non-privileged criminals alike, was made "out there on the tight wire." If the privileged fell, they usually fell into a safety net. Others hit hard and landed in jail. Alta had spent over ten years off and on in the "big house" in Atlanta. He seemed to have concluded that there were major opportunities on the criminal side of life for a po' boy if he was willing to do a little hard time to repay his debt to society.

He remembered Alta telling him, "If the game is rigged, you do what you can to survive and accept the legal consequences." And here lately, to his credit, Alta had engaged several top-quality lawyers like Chester.

A passing truck jarred Lamar from his reverie. His anger had passed. He was into a raw predatory mode, beyond fear, guilt, or any elegant justification of his conduct, well beyond reforming Big Oil or saving the planet. He simply wanted to get away with a piece of the action. He'd listen to what Virgil had to say rather than shoot him outright. He tucked his 357 Magnum in his vest holster and crept up behind the Legion Post.

———

Virgil tossed and turned on a narrow army cot in the backroom of the Legion Post. The smell of stale beer and cigarette smoke hung heavy. He desperately tried to put the gas spill behind him. The police were in Alta's pocket. The gas would evaporate; nobody would notice. Or so he hoped.

He heard the floor creak and whipped around, his .38 revolver in hand, to discover Lamar standing in the dark.

Lamar threw his hands in the air. "Don't shoot, it's me, Lamar."

"What do you want?"

Lamar stepped back. "I got a call from the po-lice. What the hell happened at the Union Seventy-Six?"

Virgil swung his legs to the floor and sat up, shaking his head. "Your boy Jimmy-Lee blew it. Said they needed a full load."

"Damn, Virgil, it ain't that hard. You turn off the gas when the tank is full. If you listen, you can hear it gurgle."

"It was supposed to be empty."

"I also got a call from Jimmy-Lee. He said you smacked him up good. He also said you fell asleep."

"Yeah, and he ran off." Virgil stood up quickly and shoved the barrel of the .38 in Lamar's chest. "Hey, it's over. Let's get on with it. We're fine."

Lamar's eyes blazed as he stepped back. "The hell it's over. The police know, and when gasoline floods across Main Street, someone else damn well knows."

Virgil struggled to hold the gun steady as anger erupted inside him. He knew Lamar was angling for something, but he hadn't figured it out. He also was trying to recall Alta's sermon on anger.

Virgil, when you're angry, you ain't thinkin'. And that's when you get violent, and that's when you start shootin' people. Its somthin' you need to work on.

He stepped back from Lamar but held the gun steady as Alta's sermon continued to spin through his mind.

You see, when you're angry at a fellow and want to shoot him, I say, slow down and find a way to put a rock in his shoe.

Virgil knew it was good advice, but he wasn't as smart as Alta. He needed to find a rock to put in Lamar's shoe.

Lamar waited patiently with a smirk on his face, noting Virgil's uncertainty.

Virgil, still confused, started over. "So, you got any bright ideas?"

"Well, uh…let me ask you, is Alta still in?" Lamar shot back.

A smile returned to Virgil face. "Oh, hell yes, he's in. If you don't pull out, then you're in! Them's the rules, and that's the way the law sees it as well."

"That's bullshit. If he thinks he's in, and word of the spill gets around, he'll be out."

Virgil shook his head. "I don't believe it."

"If he's out, this ain't gonna work. We need more trucks, more taps, more drivers, and Alta's the only one that's got that kind of money," Lamar argued.

Virgil puckered his lips. "So, as I said, you got any bright ideas?"

Lamar's eyes lit up. "The criminal part of tappin' ain't so bad."

"What do you mean?"

"You see, tappin' ain't so bad when you consider that Big Oil is the real problem, the real criminal. They're what I call a privileged class of criminal: price-fixing, gas spills, and pollution. Hell, they spill more than we'll ever steal from them."

"Slow down, Lamar, what in hell you talkin' about? Privileged class of criminal? Big Oil?"

"Here's the math on what were doin'," Lamar snapped. "We're tappin' five or six tanker loads a night; that's roughly seven thousand gallons of gas, or as the Big Oil Boys' count, that's a hundred and ninety barrels a night, OK?"

"Seven thousand gallons, that sounds right."

"I been doing my homework here. Plantation Pipeline runs up to seven hundred thousand barrels a day through that line. So we're tappin' point zero three percent of their daily volume. What the hell, point zero three percent is below their systems-loss standard...what they expect to lose from leakage and evaporation."

Virgil struck a poker face as the numbers spun through his head. "So what?"

"Are you payin' attention? Point zero three percent is *nothing*, and that's just what goes through the pipeline. If you add the gas storage tanks at the pump station in Bremen, it comes to over a hundred million gallons. So what, you say? So globally, if we get caught, it's a dribble. If Big Oil makes a mistake or gets it right, the world suffers. Damn, Virgil, whose side are you on?"

Virgil dismissed the global impact. That was Lamar's thing. But, good Lord, the numbers were staggering. Unconsciously he lowered his pistol. He sensed he'd found a rock but wasn't sure whose shoe to put it in. "You think Alta will buy your argument about Big Oil? You know him, bein' mayor and all, and his connections in high places."

Lamar suddenly snatched Virgil's pistol in one hand and pulled out his 357 Magnum with the other. "Oh, he'll buy it, if you put it to him right."

Virgil fell back on his cot and snarled, "You sum-bitch!"

Lamar snickered. "Or, I could go to him myself and tell him what you been up to. Tell him how you screwed up the Union Seventy-Six delivery. Tell him that you never aimed to sell the business to Billy Blue-Eyes. Tell him he'd better shut this thing down and wash his hands of it."

Instantly, Virgil felt a rock in *his* shoe. "Aw no, don't do that. That would kill the whole deal!"

"Or…you could pay me for my silence, and I'd be gone."

"Really?"

"Yeah, just give me five thousand dollars. Hell, I've earned that much by now."

Virgil's jaw went tight and his eyes narrowed. "I'll give you twenty-five hundred and a fast train to hell."

"I'll take the twenty-five hundred. You can have the fast train."

"Come by the Legion Post tomorrow at closing time."

Lamar poked the barrel of the Magnum against Virgil's forehead and grinned. "If I don't get the money, I'm going to Alta or the law, whoever pays the best."

CHAPTER 36

Tallapoosa, Same Morning

———

DAWN WAS BREAKING WHEN LAMAR finally roared off down the road. Virgil stumbled from the back room of the Legion Post into the bar and settled up on a bar stool. His reflection in the bar mirror was scary. His jowls sagged, and his eyes glowed like red beacons.

His head lurched like a car running out of gas. The labels on the whiskey bottles jumped in and out of focus. He placed his index fingers at the ends of his lips and pushed them up, creating a momentary smile that soon collapsed. Reaching over the counter, he fished out a bottle of beer. Warm beer shot up like a geyser as he popped off the cap on the corner of the bar. He wiped his face with his sleeve, shrugged into the mirror, and downed what was left. His head moved from an out of gas lurching to a hammering flat tire pain. Clunk. Clunk. Clunk.

He fished out another beer, opened it carefully, and tried to reconstruct recent events. A blur of images seared through his head: Alta's election, the tapping business starting to take off, the gas spill at the Union 76, the barrel of Lamar's 357 Magnum shoved against his forehead, then a river of gasoline pouring into the storm drain—an enormous explosion, and a mushroom cloud hanging over a crater that once was Tallapoosa. Time to forget this whole business of putting rocks in shoes—*time to get back to good old-fashioned violence.*

He tried to dilute his anger with another beer. Slowly a plan of sorts emerged: check the Union 76 station, see if the gas had gone away, somehow deal with Lamar—*I may have to take him out for good.* An evil grin appeared in the mirror. Then I need to have a word with the local police, check the four tapping sights, get more tanker trucks, and somehow deal with Alta. He flipped on the radio to check the weather.

Dad-gummit!

A storm was swinging east down Tornado Alley. You never knew if it would turn south. The big ones wiped out trailer parks and anything else that wasn't bolted down. The sky had darkened as storm clouds rolled in from the west, by the time he finally got going. He grabbed his ten-gauge shotgun, a box of Winchester slugs, a premium jar of kickass moonshine, and headed for the Union 76 station.

He cruised slowly by the station and circled back. It all looked pretty normal: cars pulling in and out of the gas lanes, no pooling of gas on the blacktop apron or in the gutter, no major fuel stains on the highway. Three stores down from the station, the gutter ran into a storm drain. He parked there. Slowly turning his head left and right, he stole a glance out the rearview mirror. No one seemed to be paying much attention. Hoping to become part of the landscape, he waited.

He got out slowly. Keeping his head level, he edged over to the storm drain and peeked down. Several feet below the metal grating, he saw a pool of standing gas covered with an iridescent film. It looked as if gas had backed up in the storm drain. The fumes were overpowering. *This ain't good.*

But, no sign of gas in the street."

He eased back to his truck and headed west to check on the tapping sites. Winds gusted as dark thunderclouds rolled in. In less than a mile, a police car was on his tail with its red lights flashing. He turned up the first side road and stopped. The police pulled behind him.

Virgil grimaced and rolled down his window as Sonny Hoyt lumbered up. Sonny swiped a wooden match across his butt and held the flame close to Virgil's face. "One match down the storm drain, and *boom*! And the whole town is gone. Yessir, quite the operation you boys are runnin'."

"Well, *boom* back at you!" Virgil growled. "Nobody saw the spill."

Sonny let the match burn down and flicked it away. "The hell. We wrote it up as a gas pump leak. But Margaret, from the *Tallapoosa-Beacon*, came by.

She didn't buy it. It'll be in the paper this week. Floyd down at the waterworks says there's hundreds of gallons of gasoline in the sewer system." Chief Hoyt stepped back and winked. "But ole Floyd says his lips are sealed.'"

"Let it go, Chief. It won't happen again."

Sonny anchored down his wide-brimmed trooper hat and growled, "And one more thing, your boy Wild Dog..."

"La-mar."

"That's him. He's got a mouth on him. Seems to be buddy-buddy with them ATF agents that hang out at the Burger Inn."

"Don't you worry, Sonny, I'm fixin' to put a muzzle on Wild Dog."

"One more thing: if word gets out on the spill, you boys are on your own."

Virgil nodded with a sly smile. He knew Sonny was knee-deep in the gas tapping business as well. "Well butter my butt and call me a biscuit. I'm talking to the number one crime dog in Tallapoosa."

———

Gusting winds shoved Virgil's truck from side to side as he bounded down the road to the first tap site south of Muscatine. Rolling thunder pounded the backwoods of Alabama.

"Storm's a-comin'," he declared to himself.

His mind looped in circles as he wrestled with the moving parts of the tapping equation. OK, he considered, as far as the gas spill went, it seemed as if Sonny and the local police would cover for them. Then there was Alta. Hell, maybe Lamar was right. Maybe he should sell Alta on the evils of Big Oil and show him the big profit potential. Get him to double down on the tapping business. Maybe, just maybe, he would go for it. Alta loved to outsmart the big boys. But first, he had to make damn sure the tapping business was running smoothly.

As he turned onto Zion Road, a rough gravel lane leading to the tap site, he reviewed his operation: *We got four working tapping sites, two more on the way; and we got two more gas trucks being rigged with big tanks. We need to get a few more drivers. We're hauling to fifteen gas stations. That's seven to ten thousand gallons a night. That part is working, but we need a more accurate pumping schedule from Plantation Pipeline.* Their current snitch had been taking the money, but he hadn't always been right. Virgil had learned that you couldn't sell jet fuel to a gas station more that once. *We need a high-level snitch at the corporate office, and they cost plenty. We need Alta's bankroll for sure.*

Virgil coasted up to a large, rectangular shed just past the Grizzard place and cut the engine. The new interstate highway and the Plantation Pipeline skirted the heavily wooded property. Bolts of lightning spiked nearby as the rain came. He spun the lid off the whiskey jar and had the first nip of the journey, then slipped from his truck and quietly scouted around. The tap hose coming off the Plantation Pipeline had been trenched and covered. Nice. Inside the shed, two tank trucks were loaded and ready for delivery that night. Everything seemed in order.

The wind howled and the rain pelted him as he sloshed back to the truck. *So far so good.* But the image of Lamar and his 357 Magnum returned. Despite his preference for violence, Virgil still searched for a way "to put a rock in Lamar's shoe," to somehow get the upper hand. So far nothing came to mind. He damn sure wasn't paying Lamar twenty-five hundred dollars in hush money when the snitching bastard could still run to the law for a second helping. That's the hog in him. Virgil chuckled. *Pigs get fed; hogs get butchered.*

It took Virgil the rest of the day to check the three other tap sites. He was pleased to find them working and ready for the nightly gas haul. For some reason, as he drove through Bremen, he pulled over at the Plantation pump station. It was turning dark, and the rain continued. He'd heard the eye of the storm would hit Georgia later that night. Trees were down on the road, and several stores along the way were without power.

Some of what Lamar had said about Big Oil was coming back to him. The wooded hills of the pump station yard had been cleared and were covered with enormous cylindrical storage tanks surrounded by a cyclone fence with rows of concertina wire strung on top. The tanks stood several hundred feet off the ground with catwalks winding up the sides.

"Sum-bitch! It's a damn fortress," Virgil whispered in amazement.

What was it Lamar said? "Each tanks holds one hundred thousand barrels of gas, and that's just for temporary holding and transfer." Virgil pulled the jar of moonshine from a brown bag, spun off the lid, and had another jolt. His head was clear, and his brain was clicking. He tore off a piece of the bag and began doing the numbers.

"I need to make a case to Alta on Big Oil," he mumbled. "Let me see here, there's forty-two gallons in a barrel of gas, so a hundred-thousand-barrel tank holds over…hmm…four million gallons of gas.

Good lawd!

From the road he could only see one side of the enormous pumping station, but counted twenty storage tanks. *Hell, I can do the math on that in my head. Twenty tanks, each holding, say, four million gallons of gas. That's eighty million gallons of gas just sittin' there.*

He licked his lips and had another jolt of whiskey.

"And what was it Lamar said? The pipeline itself is pumping over seven hundred thousand barrels a day. That's…hmm…" He did the numbers — another twenty-nine million gallons of gas. "All in all, over a hundred million gallons runnin' in and out of here on any given day, and we are taking maybe seven thousand gallons a night. A hundred million versus seven thousand, that's nothin'."

Virgil slumped back on the seat, drained the jar, and wolfed down his last bag of pork rinds. *Well, well, well, I do believe I can sell Alta on the benefits of Big Oil, a privileged class of criminals.* He wore a goofy smile as he dozed off across the road from the pumping station.

Several hours later, Virgil slammed forward and smacked his head on the steering wheel.

"Damn Lamar," he hissed and checked his watch—two a.m.

His nightmare had ended with Lamar's 357 Magnum aimed at this head. He shook himself awake and rubbed his head. His mouth was dry and nasty. He pulled an "emergency" jar of moonshine from under the seat, took a sip, and pondered. What to do? He looked over at the shotgun and the box of slugs that lay across the passenger seat. The tapping business was working; he had a good case to make for Big Oil. Surely Alta would buy it. But what of Lamar? He rolled up the window as a blast of wind rocked his truck. Trees bent double; the big storm had arrived. He paused and then nodded decisively. The truck lurched forward as he gunned the engine and rapped out the twin glass packs. He roared off into the night, weaving back and forth across the road.

———

At two-fifteen, Virgil swerved across the road and lurched to a stop behind the Lucky Star Trailer Park. Two cans were missing from the six pack of Pabst Blue Ribbon that sat on the seat. The tornado had blown through, leaving a trail of debris. On the west side of the trailer park, two single-wide trailers were blown off their blocks and lay on their sides. Aluminum siding had peeled off many trailers and banged in the wind.

He fumbled with the box of slugs as he mumbled, "It don't seem to matter. I know damn well the gas tappin' will be a bonanza. I'm sure I can sell Alta into doublin' down. But if I'm right, Lamar is set to play both ends against the middle—press us for hush money or snitch to the law."

He popped another beer and chugged it down. Finally loading the shotgun, he staggered from the truck. The power line to the trailer park was down, and it was pitch dark. He stumbled from trailer to trailer, not sure which was Lamar's. Finally, he spotted the Harley parked outside the end trailer. He kicked over a garbage can as he tried to look inside the window.

A flashlight flickered on, and what looked like Lamar's profile appeared in the window. Virgil jerked the gun up and fired instantly.

Boom! Splash!

A high-pitched scream and the sound of shattering glass echoed through the trailer park as Virgil stumbled away.

CHAPTER 37

Tallapoosa, Same Morning

———

MANDY ROLLED OVER AND NUDGED Alta. "Wake up, Alta, it's the phone."

"Again?" He sat up in bed. "Good Lawd, what time is it?"

Without stirring, Mandy peeked over at the alarm clock. "It's five in the mornin'. Night calls are never good."

Alta yawned. "A tornado blew through early this mornin' while you were snoring."

He switched on the light and shuffled into the kitchen for the phone. Mandy smiled and disappeared under the covers.

"Hello, Alta here."

"Hey, hey, it's Vurrrr-gilll," slurred the voice on the other end.

Alta scowled and lowered his voice. "What in hell d'ya want? It's five in the mornin'."

"We need to talk; it's important."

"So, talk."

"No...we need to meet. I want to show you somethin'."

"You been drinking?"

"Just a nip here and there."

Alta winced. "D'ya close the deal with Billy Blue-Eyes?"

"This is a bonanza. It could be the..."

"I know, the motherlode. Where are you?"

"Parked behind your store."

"I'll be there in ten minutes. This better be good."

He slipped back into the bedroom and got dressed, trying not to wake Mandy.

"Alta, who was that?"

Alta seized up. Virgil was not the right answer. "Oh…it was nothin'."

Mandy sat up in bed. "Nothin'? You spent awhile on the phone for nothin'."

"Yeah, well…it was…it was the Red Cross; they need more blankets and cots down at the gym. A lot of trailers blew over."

"Oh dear, can I come?"

"I'll be back in a bit, and then we'll go out and survey the damage."

Mandy nodded as the phone rang again. Pulling on his shirt, Alta ran for the phone, "Hello," he said wearily.

"Hey, this is Bridget down at the ER. Can I have a word with Mandy?"

Alta rolled his eyes. He was surprised that she knew Mandy had moved in. "Hang on, I'll get her."

He hurried back to the bedroom to finish dressing. "Hey sleepyhead, Bridget's on the phone."

Mandy grabbed her chenille robe and scurried for the phone. Alta pulled on his shoes. A moment later she eased back into the room and slumped on the corner of the bed, wiping away tears. Pain like stray voltage shot through Alta's chest as his heart roared into overdrive. "What's wrong?"

"A young girl, Rondell something, was shot and killed at the Lucky Star Trailer Park. She'd been staying with Lamar.

"Oh Gawd." Alta seized his chest. *Had the curse returned? Am I havin' the big one?* Collecting himself, he asked, "Was she dead on arrival?"

"Died instantly from a shotgun wound. Lamar reported it to the police."

"Who do they think…?"

"According to Bridget, Lamar claims the shot came from outside the trailer," Mandy said as she squeezed her eyes shut. "Who do you think?"

Alta arched his brows. "Lamar plays a dangerous game."

"Virgil, you think?'

"I can't say. I gotta go."

They embraced. Then Mandy held him at arm's length. "Alta, tell me true, do I have anything to worry about?"

"Hell no, darlin'."

He swung by the bathroom on his way out and grabbed his heart medicine. As he reached the front door, the phone rang again.

"Ah got it!" he yelled up to Mandy.

Lifting up the phone, he shook his head. What next? "Hey, this is Alta."

"Alta, this is Pink Allen down at the waterworks."

"Yeah Pink, make it quick."

"We had a flood of gasoline comin' into the drainage system last night. Several hundred gallons. Mighty damn dangerous! We're releasing it as fast as we can into the river. Just thought you should know."

"You think a gas main broke somewhere?"

"You don't want to know. I'm hearing through my contacts that Virgil and his gas-tappin' boys had a big spill at the Union Seventy-Six."

"My Gawd. All right, Pink, keep a lid on it. I'll be there soon."

As he ducked out the door, he saw Mandy glaring down at him from the top of the stairs. "Alta!"

CHAPTER 38

Plantation Pump Station/ Bremen, Same Morning

————

ALTA'S HEADLIGHTS WERE LOST IN the ground fog as he crept up Main Street and parked behind Virgil's Ford truck. It was 5:20 a.m. Alta flashed his high beams on Virgil's truck. Nothing. He walked up to the driver's window to find Virgil slumped over the steering wheel. Alta tapped on the window, then wished he hadn't. A goofy smile appeared as Virgil jerked awake and cracked the window. A lethal dose of whiskey breath washed out.

Alta winced as his knees buckled. "Damn son, you gotta work on your hygiene."

Virgil's head swayed back and forth like a flagpole in a windstorm. His words were mangled. "A win-dow...a win-dow of opera-tun-ity is...is open... is wide open...eh?"

Alta wiggled his nose. "It don't smell like opportunity."

Virgil grinned. "Yeah but, before you give me hell or whatever, I need to show you somethin'. Then you can shoot me."

Alta stood firm. "Just say what you gotta say."

"Y'see, Alta," Virgil managed a wink, "I just don't want this gas tappin' to blow up on you."

Alta's eyes narrowed to slits as a bolt of lightning shot through him. His jaw clamped shut as he struggled to maintain his composure. Yes, by God, Virgil had said it: "I don't want this thing to blow up on you." The message

242

was clear. Virgil was threatening to rat him *out* if he didn't stay *in* the gas-tapping business.

Good Lawd! I should've seen this coming, Alta fumed. *The sumbitch put a rock in my shoe.*

Alta smiled as though nothing had changed. "All right, scoot over; I'm drivin'. Where to?"

"Plantation's Pump Station in Bremen."

As he got in, Alta noticed an empty shotgun shell on the floorboard. While Virgil was busy popping another beer, Alta slipped the shell into his pocket and tried to calm down as he drove. The fog still hung heavy on the ground as dawn broke through the gloom. He did have a few cards to play, but he needed more information. "So, whatever happened to the Billy Blue-Eyes deal?"

"Lot-ta opera-tun-it-ees on the table," Virgil said with a cackle. "That's why I called you."

Virgil's eyes lit up as they approached the pump station. "Pull over next to the fence."

Alta looked out. Fog covered the yard, but it had started to thin out. Row on row of huge gasoline storage tanks loomed through the mist up on the hillside.

"Spooky," Alta whispered.

Virgil grinned. "That's exactly what I wan-ted you to see."

Alta was entranced. The gasoline tanks seemed to rise up to the high heavens like stone monoliths—an amazing sight. He turned to Virgil. "So?"

Virgil, apparently going for a strong opening statement, finished the can of beer, smacked his lips together and began, "Listen carefully. There are a lot of things going on locally and globally that you need to understand."

Alta bit his lip and listened. He still felt he had the upper hand, but maybe, just maybe, Virgil had something new to add.

Virgil continued, "I know, at first them storage tanks look like tombstones in a graveyard, or then again like pagan temples at the dawn of civilization, or like say Stonehenge, or Easter Island."

Alta furrowed his brows. Virgil loved to throw in mangled bits of history to support a pitch.

"Them storage tanks shimmering up there in the rising sun are the second coming of Big Oil…eh? A new order of global capitalism; the end of life as we know it. I tell you, Alta, we gotta move with the times. We need to get on-board, get together with the big boys…a merger…an acquisition…or maybe we can franchise the gas-tappin' business? Lots of opportunities available in the global marketplace."

Alta eyes lit up as a smile crossed his face. Something Virgil said had clicked somewhere deep in his head. He searched for a concept. It wasn't a merger, and it wasn't an acquisition. It was something bigger.

Virgil caught the smile on Alta's face. Sensing he had struck a chord, he moved on. "So first off, let's dispense with the notion of criminality. All of us have suffered through the recent fuel shortage, the endless lines at the pumps, the obscene prices."

Alta pursed his lips, he'd never heard Virgil talk this way. He must have read it somewhere.

"If you recall," Virgil continued, "that was brought on by the OPEC Oil Embargo of 1973. Then, when US oil reserves ran low, a cartel of East Texas oil producers, let's call them Big Oil, ratcheted up their prices. These were some of the same boys that built the Plantation Pipeline and the storage tanks we're lookin' at."

Alta began to recognize Virgil's story line as something he'd lifted from Lamar Tate. Yet, he was fascinated. "Say Virgil, this pitch I'm hearin'. You ain't just pitchin' your own tent here, are you?"

"Oh nossir," Virgil said with a grin. "This here deal is for all of us."

Virgil fished under the seat for another can of beer with no luck. "So Alta, as I was saying, let's dispense with the notion of criminality. Let's be clear, Big Oil is the real criminal in all this. They're what I call a privileged class of criminals, with their price-fixing, their oil spills, and pollution. Hell, they spill more than we tap."

"Speaking of spills," Alta jumped in, "what happened at the Union Seventy-Six the other night?"

Virgil shuddered. "Minor hiccup, nothing serious."

"The hell. Pink Allen called me from the waterworks, says we got hundreds of gallons of gasoline in the sewer system."

"We got that fixed, Alta. Let me go on. Let me paint the big picture for you. As you look out on the hillside, how many storage tanks do you count?"

"Twenty, ah reckon."

"That's my count, and there's twice that many beyond the hill. But let's go with twenty. So, real quick like, you got twenty tanks; each one holds, say, four million gallons of gas...and bingo! That's eighty million gallons of gas, just sittin' there restin', or evaporatin', or pollutin'. Trust me on the numbers, Alta, I done my homework."

Alta paused, cocked his head to the side, and ran the numbers. Then the word *franchise* popped back in his mind. *That's the concept that got the buzz going a minute ago. Or was it a merger?*

Virgil took this as a positive sign. "Trust me, I'm right. And add to that, the pipeline itself is pumping over seven hundred thousand barrels a day. That's another twenty-nine million gallons of some sort of gas. All in all, over a hundred million gallons runnin' in and out of here on any given day, and we're takin' maybe seven thousand gallons a night, eh? Seven thousand versus one hundred million gallons, that's nothin'. Drips and drabs, drips and drabs, point zero three percent."

Alta nodded. "You mentioned gas franchising earlier?"

"I did. Great way to grow the business, eh?"

"Yeah, maybe." Alta rubbed his chin. "There's over five hundred miles of pipeline from here to the refineries in Baton Rouge, Louisiana. Interesting. So, how would that work?"

"Well, let's see. We could franchise sections of the pipeline and sell 'em our tappin' technology, and," he paused and scratched his head, "and...and they'd give us a cut on the gallons they tapped."

Alta shook his head. "So, they're gonna tell us how much they tapped and give us a cut? Virgil, I don't like your business model. You're askin' criminals to be honest, and that don't work so well. Y'know, my only regret with my moonshining business was I didn't control the whole process. I should have got me a chain of juke joints and honky-tonks, so I controlled the whole thing, from our sweet whiskey stills to their thirsty lips. No sir, I ain't so sure about franchisin'. The big boys usually get beyond franchising; they like to control the whole supply chain."

Virgil pushed on. "So, as I was sayin', there's plenty of gasoline to be tapped, but gettin' back to the criminality issue, and you bein' the mayor and wantin' to go straight and all...Have you ever heard of any of the Big Oil boys going to jail? No, you haven't. Why? 'Cause the Big Oil boys are a privileged class of people, with them high-priced lawyers buzzin' around 'em like blow-flies on pile of shit. And them lawyers get 'em acquitted or plead down to a lesser charge. So, what the hell, Alta, we can play that game, too."

Alta was half listening, when it came to him...vertical integration. *That's the concept I been searchin' for. That's what the Harvard boys are pitchin' these days, and by golly, that's the answer. Control the whole process from drillin' crude, to refinin', to selling gas at your very own chain of service stations. That's the ticket, and it's perfectly legal, I'm told.*

Virgil saw that he had lost Alta's attention and rapped his fist on the dash. "Damn it, Alta, you're gettin' ahead of me."

Alta shrugged. "That ain't so hard."

Virgil continued. "For now, let's just focus on growin' the tappin' business. So, we got us plenty of gas to tap, and legally if we're clever, and get us a fancy lawyer, we're above the law...and here comes the kicker. The tappin' is un-trace-able. If we had fifty taps on the pipeline, it wouldn't amount to a pimple on the butt of a fly that's restin' on an elephant's ass. Y'see, Alta, Plantation Pipeline just don't have a measurement system that can detect our little drips and drabs. It's un-trace-able! Now, lemme finish up. Our current gas-tappin' business is workin' well. I just checked out all our tappin' sites last night, or was it this mornin'? Anyway, they're all up and workin'."

Alta stared out at the storage tanks. He, too, was caught in a window of opportunity, not knowing which way to move. He desperately wanted out of the tapping business. He may have been kidding himself, but he thought he was out. Time to get back with Mandy. Time to get on with his mayoral duties. Time to save the town from the strip malls out on Interstate 20, and high time he put the rock back in Virgil's shoe.

"Sooooo, lemme ask you, Virgil, Lamar has always been a problem with whatever we do. Will he be a problem if we expand the tappin' business?"

"Don't you worry; he won't be a problem."

"How's that?"

"He's gone away."

"You're sure about that?"

Virgil flashed an evil grin. "Oh yeah, I'm sure?"

"Well now, that's strange. Cause Lamar's girlfriend, Rondell, was killed last night in his trailer."

Virgil's jaw went slack. "No way."

"Oh yeah, someone outside the trailer shot her with a ten-gauge shotgun."

Virgil started to tremble. "It musta been Lamar."

"Maybe, but I thought you said Lamar had gone away?"

"I guess he's back."

"Oh yeah, he's back."

Alta pulled the empty shotgun shell from his pocket. "And here's my guess: you shot Rondell by mistake with a shell like this."

Virgil's head dropped to his chest. They sat in silence for a moment; then Virgil jumped out and slammed the door. He stomped around the truck several times and came to rest on the driver's side. Alta rolled down the window, shaking his head.

"Y'know, Alta, your prints are all over that shell. And if the story gets out about the honorable mayor of Tallapoosa and his gas-tappin' business, well… they'll figure you done the killin' as well."

Alta's head snapped back as his thoughts tumbled to the darkest corner of his mind. *Sumbitch! Virgil's put a rock in my shoe, and he's got a boot on my neck. Think Alta, think! If I do the right thing and walk away from the tappin', I'll have both Virgil and Lamar to deal with. Lamar will be tryin' to kill Virgil or snitch to the feds. And Virgil—shee-yet, Virgil! He'll snitch as well before he goes down. Damn it! Goin' straight just ain't an option, not right now anyway. It's survival time!* A fleeting image of Mandy and their budding relationship vanished in the fog. *My only chance of stepping away from the gas tappin' is to make the deal work for Lamar and Virgil, which is like tyin' two scorpions together. I'll have to look into the vertical integration business with Chester. Virgil may be right; Big Oil and big money could solve a lot of our problems.*

And then, and then—I'll get back to goin' straight.

Alta got out of the truck and put and arm around Virgil's shoulder. "So Virgil, good buddy, let's sit tight. Lemme discuss your Big Oil deal with Chester Pope. And you'd better get out of town for a while till the shootin' blows over. I'll deal with Lamar. By golly, Big Oil has gotta be the answer. I damn sure want to be in on that."

Virgil smiled like a fox in the henhouse.

CHAPTER 39

Tallapoosa, Same Morning

———

MANDY SWERVED BACK AND FORTH, dodging broken branches and debris as she hurried down the highway. Sometime during the night a plank of siding from the barn had let go and smashed out the rear window of her Plymouth Fury. She trembled as the wind howled through the broken glass. The tornado had passed around two in the morning and left a path of destruction through Tallapoosa. Gale-force winds ripped off roofs, flattened barns, and uprooted fences. Liberated cows wandered through cornfields.

She'd had a sleepless night with the tornado blowing through and the phone ringing off the hook. At five o'clock, Alta got a call and left the house, saying he had to help out with the tornado relief effort. Ten minutes later, Bridget Mulligan, the night nurse at the Carrolton ER, called. A fatally wounded girl had just arrived at the emergency ward. Bridget, who knew all things at the hospital, said the girl was shot in Lamar Tate's trailer. Lamar it seems, had been inside the trailer when the shot was fired from the outside; then Bridget called back at eight o'clock, insisting that Mandy meet her at her farm as soon as possible.

"Christ almighty!" she screamed, slamming the horn and the brakes. Mandy's Plymouth Fury skidded sideways, narrowly missing a hapless cow. Though the tornado had passed, a storm still swirled through her head. Changes, so many recent changes in her life: giving up on Lamar; ending her stressful nursing career in the ER; starting over as the manager of the Bremen OTASCO; signing a "business contract" with Alta Dryden, the ex-con, and finally falling in love with the reformed Alta Dryden; moments of true happiness; and now, all these confusing signals.

She turned into Bridget's driveway, bounced down the washboard drive, and skidded up to the farmhouse. She'd beaten Bridget home. After years of subsistence farming, the Mulligan's had sold off all but five acres of the farm. Sean, her husband, had moved into assisted living a year later. Mandy parked her Fury and made her way to the back porch that looked out on the river. The sky had cleared, and the wind had died down. Brown and swollen, the river raged. Mandy was glad to collapse on a bench. She knew Bridget had more to say on the girl who'd been killed. But what did it have to do with her?

Bridget honked as she roared up the driveway and parked. She charged across the porch, all round, white, and starched.

"Hello, sister!" she exclaimed with open arms.

They embraced. Mandy forced a smile, but her swollen eyes gave her away. "Thanks, girlfriend, thanks for calling...both times."

Bridget held her at arm's length. "We'll talk, but let me change." She disappeared through the back door, hollering, "What're you drinkin'?"

Mandy wiped away tears and shouted, "Coffee, hot and black."

Bridget had grown up on the farm, raising steers and roping in local rodeos. She had a gentle hand with livestock but the iron grip of a bull rider. She returned moments later in faded jeans, a red flannel shirt, and a Stetson that her horse must have sat on. She held a cup of coffee in each hand.

"Let's have coffee and a good cry; then we'll get down to business."

ER would have been a house of pain without Nurse Bridget. She'd taught Mandy to deal with the agony and heartbreak of patients and loved ones. She could charm righteous citizens as well as scoundrels, and she could bully them as well.

"Drink up, girly," she said, handing Mandy a cup.

Mandy's eyes popped out as she gulped down the coffee. "Whoa! Whiskey in a coffee cup."

"Irish coffee. Fights depression!"

They sipped in silence for several moments; then Bridget began, "Here's what I know. The girl, Rondell Parks, was dead on arrival. Her head was blown off by a shotgun slug at close range. Lamar reported it and was escorted to the hospital by the police. From what I hear, they were both inside his trailer. She heard something outside, went to the window, and ka-boom."

Tears rolled down Mandy cheeks. "Is Lamar under arrest?"

"He's under investigation but hasn't been charged. He was inside the trailer and got cut up by the glass, claims the shot came from outside."

Mandy sighed deeply. "It must have been Virgil Pettimore. Lamar and Virgil have been feuding for years—a lot of bad blood between'em. Both of 'em ran moonshine for Alta in the old days."

What, Mandy wondered, was this about? Thank goodness Alta was out of the whiskey business for good.

Bridget patted Mandy's hand. "Another cup of coffee?"

Mandy nodded. "But leave out the coffee."

Bridget returned moments later with two cups, no steam and no coffee.

Mandy bit her lip and grabbed the cup. "Anything you ain't tellin' me?"

Bridget sighed. "There's been talk. Didya hear about the gas spill at the Union Seventy-Six station?"

Mandy froze.

Taking a big gulp, Bridget continued, "Weeelll, it seems the boys have been tappin' the Plantation Pipeline and sellin' it to local stations."

Mandy's heart sank. She lurched up and stared out on the muddy river. She'd heard the whispers. Just gossip, she thought. Alta promised he was well out of it. Turning back to Bridget, she asked, "Anything else?"

"You better sit down for this one."

Mandy stepped back and steadied herself on the porch railing. "I know what you're gonna say, and it's just not true."

"Look, I can't prove a darn thing, and I hope I'm wrong, but this gas tappin' is a thriving business: four or five tap sites, they say; half a dozen sad-ass tanker trucks runnin' through the night; most of the gas stations from here to Villa Rica are in on it."

Bridget nudged up against Mandy and wrapped an arm around her. "I'm on your side, but you gotta ask yourself: who else around here has the money to bankroll this?"

"It's just not so! Alta and I have an agreement. He's never let me down. Truly, look at what he's done: elected mayor, making honest money at his stores and what all, doin' good for the town. No Bridget, ah don't believe it. We all know he's tryin' to change. I believe he has."

"Fine; you look into it. As a friend, I felt I had to say somethin'." Suddenly Bridget pulled a cigar stub from her shirt pocket and stuck it in her mouth.

Mandy's eyes popped open. "What the hell?"

Bridget grinned, holding the cigar between her teeth. "My little secret. It's a stogie, what's left of a fine Marsh-Wheeling cigar from Wheeling, West Virginia."

Bridget jostled Mandy. "Just ask yourself one question: what do you want out of the rest of your life?"

"I want Alta."

Bridget lit the stogie with a kitchen match, inhaled deeply, and blew smoke out her nose.

Mandy grinned. They were girls for a moment. "That's disgusting, but I love the smell."

"My little secret." Bridget winked. "Sean won't allow it. Look, we all got our flaws; no need to make 'em fatal. You're my best friend and a damn fine woman. Flawless? No, not all together. Your flaw—don't hit me now—*your flaw* is you're a sucker for a dangerous man...and...and you're a pleaser. Now *that* combination can be fatal."

CHAPTER 40

Plantation Pump Station/
Bremen, Same Morning

———

ALTA RACED BACK TO HIS store from the pump station in Virgil's truck. Across the seat Virgil snored, still wearing a crooked smile and stinking to high heaven. "ZzzZZZ-aah! ZzzZZZ-aah!"

Alta had to move fast. If the Big Oil deal fell through, he'd be back in jail. First, he'd run over to city hall; then he'd meet with Chester Pope at his bank in Bremen; then he'd try to get back with Mandy. He poked Virgil in the gut as he pulled in behind the store. "Stay close to the phone. I'll call soon."

Rubbing his eyes, Virgil snickered, "Is the Big Oil deal on?"

"You asshole!" Alta snapped. "Don't you get it? You spilled hundreds of gallons of gas at the Union Seventy-Six station, enough to blow up the whole town, and then you killed that young girl! Just keep your head down and your mouth shut. And while you're at it, take a bath."

Slamming the truck door, Alta paused, straightened his tie, and hustled across Main Street to the city hall. After signing off on emergency funds for tornado relief, he hustled back to his truck. He began to tremble as he put the key in the ignition. His heart revved up. No longer was he the predator. He'd become the prey. His mind swung between fight and flight. Gripping the steering wheel, he thought, *Can I do right and survive?*

———

Alta pulled behind Chester's bank at nine o'clock without an appointment. Verlene, Chester's secretary, met him at the back door with a handful of messages, "Good morning, Mr. Mayor."

"Mornin', Verlene, is Chester in?"

She rolled her eyes. "He's in and out, and he's been real nasty. He's over at the courthouse now."

"That's fine; I'll wait."

"Oh here, I almost forgot," she said, handing him his phone messages. "A lot of folks been tryin' to catch up with you, Mr. Mayor. Margaret from the Tallapoosa-Beacon wants a statement from you on the," she put her hands on her hips and winked, "on the gas spill at the Seventy-Six. Soooo, what do you think was goin' on there?"

Alta smiled wearily. "That's N-Y-B."

"N-Y-B?"

"None of your business."

Verlene blushed. "You're right, Mr. Mayor, it's none of my business."

She led him into Chester's office and disappeared. Alta paced back and forth, inhaling and exhaling deeply as he read the other messages: Mandy called and said she'd moved out. She'd be staying with Bridgit. *Gawd dam, this can't be happening.*

Lamar's message was coded: must invest now to grow big oil and Sonny Hoyt, the chief of police's message said, "Callback urgent." Alta grabbed his chest as he continued to pace the floor. "My heart feels like a pile driver, and my life is in shambles."

He paused at a shelf of Chester's library having to do with prohibition. Pulling out a book titled *Prohibition: Modification of the Volstead Law*, he sank into the tufted leather couch, the "client's couch," and skimmed through the book, reading a page or two here and there. He closed it with a sigh. He knew the whiskey story. He'd grown up with it. Without prohibition, moonshine would not have amounted to much. It had been around forever, mostly harmless, a staple of every Southern farmer. He leaned back on the couch and tried to remember the first time he'd heard about the whiskey business. He must have been ten.

———

"*Say Daddy, what's happened to our cotton?*"

"*The boll weevil done took it, son.*"

"*How we gonna get by?*"

"*Got us a new crop, called likker.*"

"*So the boll weevil took the cotton, and we're turnin' to likker?*"

"*Sort of. Y'see the guv-ment don't want nobody drinkin' likker no more. Its call Pro-hib-it-ion.*"

"*But Daddy, you been makin' likker out back fer-ever. And now you can't drink it?*"

"*More or less. Y'see, the boll weevil took the cotton, and big business took the jobs. They call it the Great Depression. Likker, y'see, is our main crop now. We trade it fer groceries and stuff. Just to get by, you understand?*"

"*And that part is legal?*"

"*Well, nowadays, big guv-ment says it ain't. But y'see, it beats starvin'.*"

Alta never figured out the illegal part. When he turned thirteen, he heard that Prohibition was over. That confused him, too.

"*So Daddy, is likker legal now?*"

"*More or less, son. Big guv-ment changed its mind. Now, it's legal to drink likker, but it ain't legal to sell it, unless you pay taxes on it to big guv-ment. That's the law.*"

"*Laws ain't so easy to understand, Daddy.*"

"*You're right, son. Now, you take good and evil, they're easy. They don't change so much. So, let me ask you, son, what's good and what's evil?*"

"*That's easy, Daddy. Robert E. Lee is good, and William Tecumseh Sherman is evil.*"

"*That a boy.*"

"So if you sell likker and don't pay taxes on it, is that good or evil?"
"That's good, son! That's reeeeeaaaaalll good!"

———

Alta sat back down on the "client's couch," and scowled. He still wasn't sure what was good and what was evil. He felt Big Oil might be the answer, yet he struggled with the concept of vertical integration. Moments later, Chester hobbled into his office, bent over his gold-handled cane.

Alta stood awkwardly. "Good mornin', Chester."

Marching over to the window overlooking the courthouse, Chester fumed. "Good lawd Alta, I don't know where to start."

"Truly, Chester, I thought I was out of the gas-tappin' business," Alta offered lamely. "That's what Virgil's been tellin' me."

Chester stomped back to Alta, drumming his cane on the hardwood floor. "Oh yeah, that'll play well in court."

He gazed up at a framed photograph of Thomas Lawson, Esq., the current Haralson County judge, and continued, "You see, your honor, my client, a convicted felon with the deepest pockets in Haralson County, was told by his business associate, a Mr. Virgil Pettimore, another convicted felon who is under investigation for the murder of a young girl here in Bremen, that…that what, Alta?"

Chester turned to Alta. "That Virgil did you wrong? That Virgil misled the all-knowing and all-powerful mayor of Tallapoosa?"

Chester hung over him like a praying mantis. Alta sank deeper into the couch.

"Would I defend you?" Chester roared. "Not on your life."

Alta absorbed Chester's opening salvo, eyeing his credentials on the far wall: the BA Vanderbilt, the MBA from Duke University, and the law degree from the University of Georgia. Cultivated. Prestigious. Then, Alta took in Chester's impeccable glen plaid suit and his polished penny loafers. The penny loafers were the key, the giveaway. Chester tolerated rednecks with fistfuls of cash, but he simply adored old Southern money, the Ashley Wilkes type, and Yankee carpetbaggers—the privileged class.

Pulling himself up off the couch, Alta walked to the window, overlooking the courthouse. "Cool your heels, Chester. We aaalll know you are a first-class lawyer who mingles with the privileged class. That's clear to us all, but…"

Chester nodded ruefully.

Alta spun on his heels, jamming his thumbs under his belt "But I seem to recall, when you were serving on the school board, you bought up all that land north of town, just before it was condemned for the new high school. I believe you made a healthy profit on that sleight of hand. And then here lately, somehow you got that plot of land you sold me rezoned commercial, despite a county ordinance to the contrary. And when I got your legal fees, which were substantial, you said something to the effect, 'It always cost more when you're breakin' the law.'"

"It's not breaking the law!" Chester howled. "It's circumventing draconian measures!"

"Now, I wouldn't want any of that to get out."

Crossing his arms, Chester arched his head up at the crystal chandelier. "Absolutely not."

Alta's lips narrowed. "So I'm thinking a man with your extraordinary legal gifts might find a way to have any gas-tappin' charges that might arise, dismissed, for…for the sake of…an aging public servant who innocently lost his way on the road to redemption."

Chester leered at Alta. "Perhaps, but it won't be cheap."

The office door creaked open slightly. They both looked up and waited. Finally Chester eased over and threw open the door. Verlene, the office snoop, was caught red-handed.

"Sorry." She blushed as she stood up straight. "I didn't want to interrupt."

"Knock and enter, Verlene, just knock and enter," Chester fumed. "Now what is it?"

"Sonny Hoyt, the police chief, is parked out front, He wants to meet with the Mayor Dryden right now."

"Thank you, Verlene; tell him to wait."

As she closed the door, Chester turned to Alta. "Is Sonny on the take?"

"NYB."

"I'll take that for a yes."

Alta sat on the arm of the couch. "Say, Chester, can a client get a cold Coke around here?"

Chester scowled impatiently. "Hang on, Mr. Mayor."

As Alta sank back down on the couch, he felt the wave of fear return. He was no longer the aggressor, the pursuer, the snarling alpha dog. Sonny Hoyt, Lamer Tate, and Virgil Pettimore were snapping at his heels. The inside of his head became a theater marquee. A red neon message scrolled across the marquee: Going Straight and Doing Right Is Bullshit. Another bigger, bolder message followed: YOUR CURSE IS BULLSHIT. SURVIVAL TRUMPS INTEGRITY.

He dug his fingernails into the arms of the tufted leather couch. He had to fix this mess; then he could turn it around and then he could do right. He felt Mandy would understand. He hoped.

Chester reappeared and handed him a bottle of Coke.

"Ice cold Coca-Cola, thanks." Alta took a sip and then it hit him. Within arm's reach of desire, that was it—the old Coca-Cola ad. That's what he wanted to do with gasoline. That was vertical integration.

Alta eyes lit up as he jumped up and strutted back and forth. "Now then, I got one other option on the gas tappin'. Let's call it the Coca-Cola solution."

Chester sipped his Coke, leaned back on the edge of his desk, and smiled. "Truly Alta, I like the way you worked that in."

"Amen, Chester, it just came to me. Remember the old Coke ad, 'Put Coca-Cola within arm's reach of desire'?"

Chester took another sip. "That, my friend, was a classic."

"And that's the solution. Put the product within arm's reach of desire. You've gotta control the whole process from creation to consumption, no middlemen. It worked for Coca-Cola, and it'll work with gasoline."

"Gasoline?"

"Yes, gasoline! Listen to this." Alta trotted out what he'd just heard from Virgil. "The Plantation pumpstation right down the road, here, has eighty million gallons of gas just sittin' there restin', or evaporatin', or leakin' in them storage tanks. Add to that, the pipeline itself is pumping over seven hundred thousand barrels a day. That's another twenty-nine million gallons of gas. All in all, over a hundred million gallons runnin' in and out of here on any given day."

Chester eyes lit up. "That's a whole lot of gas. So, you get bigger, but as I recall, stealin' gas is still illegal."

"Hang on, here comes the kicker."

"The what?"

"The kicker. The boys up at Harvard call it vertical integration; I call it the Coca-Cola solution: control the process from conception to consumption."

Alta watched Chester pace back and forth down the hardwood floor, a sure sign both the legal and illegal sides of his brain were firing.

"*Vertical integration*? Sounds like *a monopoly* to me," Chester shot back. "Don't sound legal."

"Hmm, maybe let's call it something else. Let's call it a merger. Anyway, as I said earlier, there's plenty of gas to be tapped from Plantation, and for the time being, it's untraceable. They can't measure what we're tappin'. Soooooo, that's the current deal, but it's time to move to higher ground. Y'see, we got some feuding partners, namely Virgil and Lamar. They're not sure if they are *in* or *out*, not sure if they want to kill each other or not; and I suspect they think they can make more money snitchin' to the law than continuing to tap gas."

Chester plopped into his tufted chair behind his massive mahogany desk. Another good sign, Alta thought, that he was conspiring.

Ambling slowly across the room, Alta stopped at the window and noticed the police chief parked below. He winced as he turned back. "So this, a… merger allows us to go legit, make a hell of a lot more money, and keep Virgil and Lamar in the game."

"I hear the sizzle, but I can't taste the steak."

"Like I said, the big money comes from controlling the process, from the kitchen to the dinner table, from production to consumption—from the oilfield, to the refinery, to tanker trucks, and on to gas stations throughout the South."

"Yes, yes, get to the steak."

"So, I want to buy a wildcat driller and a couple of wells, say, down on the gulf coast, and then buy a small refinery that can make gasoline out of crude oil. You with me, Chester?"

Chester fingered his gold fountain pen, his contract-signing pen. "I'm tastin' the steak."

"Then, we buy a fleet of delivery tankers, maybe just lease 'em. And finally, we buy, say, half a dozen independent service stations here in the Southeast. That's it. That's the deal…from drillin' to fillin', puttin' gasoline within arm's reach of desire."

A wry smile washed across Chester's face as he did the sums with his gold pen. "This is gonna cost you big time, legal fees and all."

"It always has, Chester; it always has." Alta grimaced. "Virgil and Lamar come after me with guns, and you, my distinguished attorney, come after me with a fountain pen."

"I suppose you want this done overnight."

"Here's the deal. I want to be shipping legal gas from my refinery to all the service stations we are currently serving within the month."

"Nossir, I can't do it that fast."

"Just do it. I'm prepared to pay a premium to get outta this mess," Alta growled. "And make damn sure it's legal."

CHAPTER 41

Tallapoosa Water Tank, Next Day

———

HIGH ABOVE TOWN, LAMAR CROUCHED on the catwalk that circled the water tank. Biting hard on his lower lip, he tried to stop shivering. A summer shower had just blown through, soaking his clothes and leaving his long hair in a tangle. Out to the west, the Tallapoosa River raged. Sections of the bank had washed out, and bottomland had flooded. He squeezed his eyes shut and then snapped them open; shut then open; shut then open, trying to separate the real world from his fantasies. It wasn't working. Blurred images churned through his head. They were important, but he couldn't read them. His crusade against Big Oil would probably have to wait.

"Sumbitch!" he exploded. "Someone tried to kill me."

He pulled out his 357 Magnum and spun the cylinder. Loaded and dry. Ready. Down below, the Sunday morning train rumbled through town, setting the water tank to shaking. Two lashed-up locomotives spray-painted with graffiti pulled a long line of container boxes east to Atlanta, an endless conveyor belt moving Japanese cars from coast to coast. Trains sounded their alarms as they roared through town, but they no longer stopped. The depot had been torn down years ago. Tallapoosa wasn't much of a train town anymore.

As the train passed, Lamar caught sight of the decent folks walking their families to church. He wondered, *Could that be me? Could I save the town? Could I be saved?* The Presbyterian Church had a white, angular nave with a cluster of stained-glass windows joined to a tower that stretched skyward from its belfry to a needled spire that, Lamar thought, that guides our soul up to the high heavens.

Just across the street, the United Methodist Church, a stout, sensible, one-story structure, was firmly anchored to the earth. Horseshoe stairs led up to Greek columns and a grand portico—no tower, no belfry, and no spire. Off and beyond, the simple wooden crosses of country Baptist churches spiked above the tree line. So many paths to the good life, so many good people. Tallapoosa was a good town, just flawed. Border towns were like that: pockets of solid citizens in town, with commercial opportunities lurking on the border between Georgia and Alabama—both the legal and the illegal kind. Lamar's face lit up. "Maybe I can save the town!"

By now, the rain shower had passed, and it had become muggy. Steam came off his shirt and pants. He swung his head back to the west of town, taking in the Union 76 station. Faint stains from the gas spill ran across the highway and into the storm drain. He slumped down on the catwalk, bracing his back against the water tank. The blurred images that churned through his head had slowed down, lined up, and fell into place. Each posed a question; none gave an answer.

First off, who shot Rondell, and was it meant for me? Was it Virgil that evil shee-yet? Probably. Did he want me out of the way so he could cash in on my idea, my crusade against Big Oil? Not likely. Virgil ain't much of a patriot.

Or maybe Virgil figured the gas-tapping business was crashing, and he wanted to be the first in line to snitch on Alta, now that he was mayor and acting righteous. Then again, if Virgil didn't shoot Rondell, who did—and why? The gas spill had sent all hands scurrying like rats on a sinking ship. Probably over thirty rats involved in the tapping business these day—welders, tank truck drivers, gas station owners and a few in local law enforcement.

He winced as he saw an ATF patrol car pull into the Burger Inn. Too many moving parts, too many unknowns coming at him. If Virgil shot Rondell by mistake, then he'd be back to finish the job. *I don't mind shootin' Virgil, but that can wait.* "It's time I got out."

He grabbed the rail of the catwalk and snapped up. His lips curled, and his eyes narrowed as he threw back his head and let out his wild-dog howl, louder and louder.

"I'm back!" he hollered. "And I got a plan!"

He scrambled down from the tank, revved up his Harley, and coasted slowly down Main Street chanting. "I'm a man with a plan."

He paused for the longest time at the corner between the Presbyterian Church and the Methodist Church, then eased behind the Burger Inn.

CHAPTER 42

Tallapoosa, Same Day

———

MANDY BRACED AGAINST THE PORCH railing as the river, an angry torrent of mud and debris, flooded over its banks. Dead chickens floated by as banded water moccasins slithered up laurel branches. The sky was steel gray, and Bridget's lower pasture was swamped. Water lapped against sand bags stacked below the porch. It had rained most of Sunday, but the radio said it was due to blow through sometime later that morning.

Alta arrived unannounced earlier, and they had argued. She'd walked away, convinced he was lying. She counted to twenty and turned back to him. "You're knee-deep in the gas-tappin' business, aren't you?"

Alta swallowed hard and tried to smile. "It's not that simple, not when you're dealin' with a curse."

Mandy felt her jaw tighten. "I'm so damn tired of hearin' about your curse. Good Lord, I've got flaws, but I don't blame every setback on them."

"Hold on, Mandy," he said as he threw up his hands. "A curse ain't the same as a flaw. Let me try to explain: y'see, I ain't always conscious when I'm do somethin' wrong. As you well know, ah have my share of golden moments where I'm absolutely doin' right…you've seen 'um, like runnin' the store, like my housin' business, like bein' mayor and all. That's all proof that I'm beatin' the curse…but then…now and again…I lose track of things. That's the nature of a curse. It plays tricks on you. And then things happen that I'm not conscious of…soooooo, at those brief moments," he sent an index finger flying in the air, "at those brief moments, you couldn't really say I was guilty of a crime…more the victim of a curse."

"You're guilty in the eyes of the law," Mandy said, glaring at him.

"Well now, speaking of the law," Alta slid down the railing next to Mandy. "Let me say this: I'm in transition, movin' on to the legal side of life. It's called—."

"It's called," he continued, "vertical integration, taking the gasoline directly from the kitchen to the dinner table—from drillin' to refinin', from refinin' to delivery at my very own gas stations."

Mandy turned away and watched as the river edged above the sandbags. *Maybe Bridget was right. Maybe I am a sucker for a dangerous man.* Good Lord, Alta was certainly dangerous: from moonshining, to gas tapping, to being mayor of Tallapoosa, and now this vertical integration bullshit. Part of it was downright thrilling, and part of it was a train wreck. He was so pathetic, amusing in a weird way, but pathetic when he lied. She felt it couldn't last, but…But what? According to Bridget, she was also a pleaser, and it pleased her to be around Alta, and it pained her to think about the future and what she truly wanted out of life.

Mandy crossed her arms. Her pain hardened into irony. "So how do you know if you're consciously doin' right or unconsciously doin' wrong? Y'know, you bein' the sad-ass victim of the big, bad curse."

He shrugged. "I don't, but I'm workin' on it."

"I have great affection for you, Alta, but I've got to have more control in my life. I'm goin' miss you."

She extended a trembling hand to hold him back. "The best part of me knows this is over. I believe you're headin' for more jail time, and I just don't want to be left alone…again."

"That's not happenin'. You'll see. Vertical integration is honest business."

Mandy stiffened and stepped back. "And how's the store gonna work out for me, if you're back in prison?"

They both turned to the sound of Bridget honking her horn as she roared up the road.

"Alta, you better get outta here. Bridget don't much like you, and she carries a shotgun in her truck."

Alta's eyes widened. "You're kickin' me out?"

"You better go. Go on now, git!"

Mandy felt utterly miserable. She looked into Alta's eyes. She could tell he felt equally miserable. Neither knew what to do about it.

CHAPTER 43

Tallapoosa, Same Day

———

ALTA HIGHTAILED IT BACK TO his store, doing his best to tamp down his feelings. His head snapped back then he felt a jolt of pain in his chest. *I got no time to deal with a heart attack. Yet, he wondered, am I fighting mad or hurt?*

"Hell if I know," he growled to himself.

He'd never spent much time on his feelings. And this certainly wasn't the time to start. Twice now in the last year, he'd been rejected by women he cared deeply about. He would not lose Mandy, and that was that. Yet, if he didn't deal with the tapping business, he'd lose everything. He shrugged and did what he always did; he shoved his feelings down a rabbit hole and tried to outsmart his opponents.

It's time to put the curse of genius to work.

His brain roared into action like a chainsaw on a Georgia pine. The Union 76 gas spill had to be covered up, or it would become the subject of an exposé by the *Tallapoosa-Beacon*. However, the odds of that happening were fairly low. But then, there was Virgil. He might rat out and become a government witness, but Virgil could count. He knew if the vertical integration deal worked out, he'd be filthy rich.

I've got to do the Big Oil deal!

Now it was all in Chester's hands, and when the fees were substantial, which they would be, Chester could move heaven and earth. And finally, there was Lamar. No telling what he was up to. He was way more cunning than Virgil but a full-blown wacko, one day an apex predator saving the planet, the next a greedy capitalist trying to corner the global oil market. Yet, Lamar just might decide to shoot Virgil for killing Rondell and then go on to rat out the whole tapping deal. Yet, Lamar was more about shooting than killing. Killing was Virgil's thing.

———

At ten thirty in the morning, Alta pulled behind his OTASCO store. Chester Pope was due any minute. He glanced in the rearview mirror, alternately smiling and frowning. He needed to calm down. He needed to exude confidence.

He slipped in the back door and paused. His son Jack was ringing up a sale at the cash register. As usual, he had the country music station at full volume.

Alta forced a smile and joined Jack at the counter. "Good mornin', son. Could you turn down the damn radio?"

"Hello, Daddy. Hang on a minute; the new song about the gambler is coming up."

All Alta could make out was something about *know when to hold 'em, know when to fold 'em.* Sure he winced. But how do you know *when?*

"All right, son, now turn the damn thing down."

"Yessir. Are you in for the day?" Jack asked.

"In and out, busy times with the tornado and all."

"Say, Daddy, can I show you somethin'?"

"Sure."

Jack walked to the front of the store and pointed out the window. "See that train car on the siding over there?"

"I do. That's where the crew stays when they're out fixin' the Georgia-Pacific Line."

"I don't remember seein' it parked there before."

Alta shrugged. "I think it's all right."

"Lot of folks in overalls goin' in and out of it the last few days."

Alta wandered over to the lawn mower display and snickered. "How we doin' on them Toro mowers?"

"Haven't sold a one," Jack said, laughing. "But we're drivin your man at Western Auto crazy." Alta let out a loud cackle.

───────

Chester roared up in his Coupe de Ville, lurching to a stop in the mayor's parking space, then revved the engine to a shrieking pitch. Sleeping dogs ran for cover. Old-timers on the bench outside city hall just chuckled.

Alta hurried out of City Hall. "Goddamn, Chester. Shut the sumbitch down."

Chester gripped the wheel and continued to rev the engine. His eyes glazed over as his head swung back and forth.

"Oh, hey Alta," he said with a sheepish grin. "Got to keep the battery charged."

"Damn, Chester, when they go, they go. We sell new ones across the street."

Chester straightened his bow tie. The tie was a sure sign he'd been in court that morning. "I'll look into it."

Alta walked around the car, noticing the dented fenders. "You hit anything on the way over?"

"I had a road hen dead to rights, but I gave her life without parole."

Though his heart was still pounding, Alta knew the drill. Shoot the shit. Take your time. Don't panic. The banter continued as they shuffled into the mayor's office.

Alta sat in his tufted mayor's chair as Chester stumped around his office, drumming his cane on everything he passed.

"So, what'ya got for me, Chester?"

"A pig in a poke."

"Nothing new there."

Chester pulled out his gold fountain pen and a handful of contracts. "We can pick up two independent gas stations that are goin' broke. They say they can't get enough gas from the Big Oil companies."

"Independents can't get gas? I like that. Sounds like were gettin' in the right business. And the oil wells?"

"Got a small wildcatter in Louisiana, way down on Bayou Lafourche. He's pumpin' two thousand barrels of crude a day."

"Bayou Lafourche, that's coon-ass country, ain't it?"

"They're called French Arcadians or Cajuns," Chester snapped.

"Don't preach to me, you miserable coot. And what about the refinery?"

"No luck yet."

Alta tapped his index finger on the desk. "Chester, this has to go down real soon."

"Well, it ain't gonna happen real soon. It'll take a month or two if you want it clean."

Alta leaned back in his chair, pursed his lips, and exhaled like he was blowing out a candle. "Can we backdate the titles? I just want a small piece of the ownership and a document to prove it."

"So," Chester arched his brow, "you want it now and you want it clean?"

Alta swallowed hard. "I do."

Chester chuckled and pulled a letter from his pocket. "How do you want to handle Mandy's contract?"

Alta's heart throttled up again as he reviewed the contract.

"You aim to do right by her?" asked Chester.

Alta nodded slowly. "I do."

"It says she'll own a third of the Bremen store with an option to buy up to fifty-one percent. Now if you go back to prison, any property with your name on it will be challenged in court. They'll say you bought it with whiskey money."

Alta shrugged. "You think I should sell it to her outright?"

"Whatever. You decide. Just amend it and get it back to me. I can bury the title so no one comes after her."

"That would be good." Alta shoved the contract in his pocket and stood up. "So what's the bottom line on the gas business?"

Chester paced back and forth. "You got two gas stations for, say, twenty thousand apiece...that's forty. For another forty, you can get yourself a fifty-percent share of a wildcat driller down on Bayou Lafourche. And maybe, if we get lucky on a refinery...I'd say you could get a small share of a small refinery for, say, sixty grand…so you're talking about a hundred and forty thousand out of pocket."

Alta's eyes popped open. "Holy shee-yet! And how soon can this come together?"

"Soon."

"Is that today-soon?"

Chester cocked his head back. "It'd have to be a cash payment. We'd backdate the documents, and of course they'd want a premium payment for signing early. Could happen in a week or so. But, we still don't have a refinery. So, it all depends."

"Depends on what?"

Chester toyed with his gold pen. "You want it soon, or you want it clean?"

Alta popped his knuckles and sighed. "You remember Captain Billy Boudreaux?"

Chester paused, then grinned. "Billy Boudreaux from Thibodaux. He bought your likker business."

"Cajun mafia." Alta smiled and handed him the phone. "Give Billy a call. See if he can find us a refinery. This has to go down soon."

Jack Dryden appeared at the door, looking worried. Alta joined him in the hall. "What's up, son?"

"It's Virgil," he whispered. "He's at the store, stinkin' of whiskey and packin' a pistol. Wants to see you *now!*"

"All right, son, go grab your deer rifle and back me up. Stay out of sight; just be there if I need you."

As Alta slipped back into the store, Virgil practiced his quick draw. Whipping his .38 from a newly acquired vest holster, he aimed at the cash register, clicked the trigger, blew imaginary smoke from the end of the barrel, and slipped it back in his holster, only to start over. Flaming red eyes burned through his deathly pallor and he still had the skunky smell of road kill.

His eyes narrowed when he saw Alta. "So, mish-ta may-or," he slurred, "you gonna ramp up the gas tappin'?"

"It's moving along," Alta lied, "coming together?"

Virgil shook his head. "Wrong answer, mish-ta may-or. Ever' buddy wants to know if you're *out* or you're *in*. And when I say ever' buddy, I mean ever' buddy—let's call 'em Alta's Outlaws: welders, pipe fitters, haulers, gas-station owners, and a gang of crooked cops in five counties!"

Alta noticed the .38 wasn't loaded as Virgil repeated his quick-draw routine.

"Cause..." Virgil continued, turning back to Alta, "if you're out, this whole thing is comin' down. Any of your outlaws could rat you out if they think you are out. And believe me, they're are all waitin' to hear from me."

Alta shook his head with concern. "So what'll it take to ramp up the tappin'?"

A goofy smile spread across Virgil's face. "With fifty thousand, we could double our current output, deliver fifteen thousand gallons a night; and at forty cents a gallon, that'll bring in about six thousand dollars a night. You'd get your money back in a couple of weeks. And if you chose, we'd buy you out. Then, Mr. Mayor, then you'd be back on the high road again, holdin' Miss Mandy's hand and savin' the town. One hell of a package, my boy!"

Alta paced down the aisle sifting through his options. He loved the way Luther pitched a deal. The sumbitch ought to be in show business. Fifty thousand dollars sure beat the hell out the hundred and forty thousand Chester wanted...and by God, Virgil could be right. *If it works, they could buy me out in a month or so.*

Alta stepped up to Virgil and jabbed him in the gut. "Are you *in*, if I'm *in*?"

"For sure, Mr. Mayor, you're the guy with all the brains and money. Course I'm *in*."

"So you'd be happy with the deal?"

Virgil eyes glazed over as a goofy grin spread across his face. "Happy?— I'd be happier than a tick on a fat dog."

Alta stifled a smile. "What about Lamar?"

"I'm gonna kill that twisted little pissant."

"No, no, don't do that. Y'think he'll be *in*, if we're *in*?"

"Maybe."

"He won't rat us out?"

"Not if he's dead."

"Don't kill him, you hear me? Not yet."

Alta sauntered over to the cash register and struck the no-sale key. As the drawer slid open, he grabbed his lucky silver dollar and flipped it. He caught it in midair and slapped it on the counter. "So, Virgil, you feelin' lucky?"

"Hell yes!"

"Call it."

"Tails."

Alta removed his hand. "Tails it is. You win. Your call. You really want to ramp up the gas tappin'?"

"Hell yes, let's do it."

"Say, Virgil, is your gun loaded?"

"Not yet." He snapped it out of the holster and laid it on the counter.

"Good, good. No more shootin', you hear?" Alta reached out and gave him a bear hug. He felt Virgil meant it when he said he was in. He also felt that Virgil would rat him out if something better came along. Despite that, he was still not ready to act. He knew time was running out. He also knew this was the time when really smart guys made their money. A time when you could outfox the opposition, and, if you got too damn clever, you could outfox yourself. By now, honorable solutions were off the table. He must decide. "OK, Virgil, you hold tight. I'll be back soon."

Turning to the rear of the store, Alta shouted, "Come on out, Jack."

The storage-room door swung open, and Jack strode out, a smile on his face and a rifle in his hand.

"Just keep an eye on him, son. We may have a deal."

Virgil's eyes bulged as he shook with rage.

Jack pulled up a chair next to Virgil and snickered, "Hey there, good buddy. Say, Daddy," he continued, "are they runnin' war games again over at Fort McClellan?"

"Can't say; why?"

"There been a small plane buzzing around here lately, sounds like a single-engine Piper Cub."

"You still want to be a pilot, eh?"

"I do."

Turning to Virgil, Alta declared, "We've got us a deal. Just sit tight. I'll be right back."

Virgil heaved out of the chair. Jack rammed the barrel of his rifle against his chest and shoved him back down.

"Any fool knows you're playin' me," Virgil snarled.

Alta's head shook uncontrollably. He felt his heart ramp up. "The deal, gawd damit, the deal," he stammered, "is still in play."

Turning to Jack, Alta continued. "If he tries anything, shoot the sumbitch. Just wing him...don't kill him"

CHAPTER 44

Bridget's Farm, Tallapoosa, Same Day

––––––

BRIDGET SAT NEXT TO MANDY on the back porch. "So you ran him off? Is that the end of it?"

Mandy looked away. "Yes."

"You sure?"

"No."

"Tell me again, what he said?"

"He said he's got a curse. Says when he's doin' right, he truly knows he's doin' right, but when he's doin' wrong, he's not always conscious of it."

Bridget chuckled. "That's easy. He's a crook. Hell, you guys are made for each other, just like Bonnie and Clyde. You, fallin' for dangerous men and then tryin' to please 'em, and him with his godforsaken curse, a perfect match."

Mandy pursed her lips and turned to see Alta barreling up the drive.

Bridget squeezed her arm. "Here comes trouble."

"Uh-huh."

"Do what's right for you darlin'," Bridget said as she headed for the barn. "Either way, you're my girl."

––––––

Hat in hand, Alta edged across the porch. Mandy saw him coming and looked away. The storm had blown through. The river had crested at noon and now ran slack. Brown sludge oozed down the main channel, coating the banks in glistening clay, here a mound of fertile soil fallen from the undercut bank, there an eroded bomb crater. The change was ominous.

Is it a sign Alta wondered. A beginning? An ending?

Mandy held her hands to her hips, as she turned to face him. Her face was drawn and a scowl emerged. "How do'ya know, Alta? How do'ya know?"

His mouth fell open as his brows furrowed.

"How do'ya know if what you want is the right thing to do?" she continued. "Maybe you ain't conscious of what you're sayin', and deep down, what you really want is to make a killin' on all your gas deals."

"No, Mandy, I'm not wantin' that."

"That don't mean it's not lurkin' in your crooked head."

Alta stepped back and deliberately listened for voices in his head. Was he listening to the wrong voices with the wrong answers? Or to the right voices with the right answers? Was this how you break the curse? He stopped to listen. He heard no voices, just the drone of his mind running the numbers and spewing out the odds.

"There's no tomorrow, unless I get through today." His voice was ragged. Full of desperation. "Either way, there'll be risks, whether I ramp up the tappin' or get into a Big Oil deal. This is the honest truth. I believe these words are coming from the best part of me."

Mandy nodded sadly. "I believe you're talkin' straight Alta. And, I believe you ought to go."

"Hold on," Alta threw his hands in the air. "Before you run me off, let me show you somethin'." He pulled the contract from his pocket and handed it to her. "I changed some things."

Mandy bit her lip as she read it.

Alta rocked nervously from side to side. "You always said it was about control for you. This contract gives you total control. Now you own the store, free and clear; it's yours. Whatever you decide about me, you don't have to worry about losin' control."

She turned away, fighting back tears, then faced him. "Alta, that's the most decent thing you've ever done. God bless you."

He smiled and put his arm around her shoulder. "So?"

"So," she sighed, "either way, you're headin' back to jail."

"Maybe, but you're in control."

"Yes, but you see, I've come to realize there's more to life than bein' in control. Hell yes, I want you!" she shouted as she jabbed him in the chest. "But I can't have you if you're in jail? And yes, it's breakin' my heart, but it's over."

"It's over?"

Mandy paced to the far end of the porch and stared out at the muddy wreckage of the river. After an awkward pause, she turned back to him. Tears and sadness streaked her face. "I ain't over you Alta. I may never be over you. But, I'm damn sure over your lawlessness."

Alta threw up his hands. "So, I lose my girl, my store, and I go directly to jail."

Mandy tried to smile through her pain. "I guess. I have only one question for you. It's one I can't answer. Why Alta, for Christ sake, why?"

Alta shrugged, not sure he knew the answer and started to leave.

Mandy grabbed his arm. "C'mere, cowboy. Give me a good-bye kiss. I do love you somethin' awful."

Alta rushed back to the store to do the deal with Virgil.

CHAPTER 45

Tallapoosa, Later that Evening

———

"HELL YES, I'M LOVIN' IT," Lamar snickered to himself on the floor of a darkened train car parked on the siding across from Alta's store. Agent Buster Tatum sat beside him on their gas tapping surveillance. Lamar had been paid big money by the feds and the pipeline and granted protection and immunity for any criminal involvement in the gas tapping.

From the jukebox over at the High Hat bar, Willie Nelson warbled the "Party's Over"—a last call for drinks and a reminder that every party has to end. Buster whispered into his mobile radio to the surveillance plane, "What's your ten-twenty? Roger that, I repeat your last, you're passing over the tap site in Fruithurst, Alabama. That's it, good buddy...stay high, don't let 'em hear you...roger that...follow the gas tanker to the Union Seventy-Six here in Tallapoosa. It's a clear night. We need some good photos. We're leavin' now... ten-four that, we'll be across the street from the station with our camera. Roger that. Time check: I've got two a.m. on the button; what's yours? Same, same, over and out."

Buster shoved the radio in his pocket and turned to Lamar. "Let's go, hotshot. I need to get photos of the gas truck with the hose going into the storage tank, and you need to ID the bad boys. "

Lamar furrowed his brow. "We'll have to be directly across the street from the station to get that shot."

"Roger that."

"How do we stay out of sight?"

Buster pulled out a ballast coated tarpaulin from behind him. "Under this."

Lamar snorted. "I get it—undercover."

"Shut up, Lamar; even the law don't like a snitch."

"Yesirr."

Buster carefully loaded his backpack: a pair of night vision binoculars, a night vision camera, a canteen of water, a pack of saltine crackers, and a can of Vienna sausages. He turned and whispered to Lamar, "You got your food and water?"

Lamar pulled on his pack. "I do."

They slipped out the back of the train car and crawled along the tracks on all fours, pulling the tarpaulin over them as they went. They scuttled over gravel beds and greasy ties, caught their breath for a moment under the tarp, and then continued. Everything smelled of creosote. At one point a mangy dog sniveled by, lifted his leg, and let go.

Lamar ducked under the tarp and hissed, "Shee-yet."

Buster chuckled. "You been baptized, son."

Lamar started to laugh and then stopped abruptly as he heard the whistle of a train. "You hearin' what I'm hearin?"

"I am. Grab the edge of the tarp and roll away. Roll away!"

"Summmmmmbiiiiitch!" Lamar yelped and tumbled.

The tracks groaned and the ties rumbled as the locomotive roared by, creating a windstorm that heaved them into the air. As the tarp ripped away, they were stung by flying grit. They landed in a clump at the bottom of the track bed, covered in soot. Lamar felt Buster's phone vibrate in the tangle.

Buster dragged himself up and fished out his phone. "Come on, roger that, I repeat, you're heading into town. Roger that. We'll be in position down here in one minute."

As the faint sound of a single engine plane came into range, Buster and Lamar crawled behind an old warehouse across from the Union 76, edged up a side alley, and got into position behind a dumpster. The gas truck had arrived at the station, but it was too dark to tell much else.

Buster handed Lamar the night-vision binoculars as he pulled out his camera. "You know any of them boys?"

"They're parked over the storage tank," Lamar replied. "I see Travis, the boy from the station, I see Jimmy-Lee, the little shit-ass that helped cause the spill, and I'll be! I see someone wearin' a mangy Auburn ball cap. That's gotta be Lonny James, the welder, runnin' shotgun. They got a hose running under the truck and it looks like it's connected to the storage tank."

Buster focused in with his camera. "Them boys are either damn smart or damn lucky. From this angle, I can't see the gas hose going down under the truck and into the storage tank. It looks like they pulled off the canvas they had over the tank, and it's blockin' the view. To prove they're tappin' and dumpin', we need a smoking-gun photo of the hose goin' into the storage tank."

Lamar grabbed his binoculars. "Maybe you can get a better angle down the street."

Buster grabbed the tarp. "Hold tight; I'll give it a try."

As he waited, Lamar gazed up at the full moon and chuckled. *Yessirr. Main Street looks real good these days: potholes filled, storefronts painted, buses runnin' on time, and new industry comin' in. As border towns go, Tallapoosa is doin' just fine. Where else could a fellow like Alta Dryden, who started with nothing, do so well? He really had started with nothing, well, nothing more than a brilliant mind and an outlaw's cunning. And by golly, this year's Fourth of July parade and picnic were the best ever, add to that, it was the Bicentennial of America. Let the good times roll!*

He raised the binoculars to find the boys still dumping gas at the station and Buster on all fours down the block, trying to get the smoking gun photo. Just then a police car eased down Main Street, paused in front of the 76, and drove on.

Yet again, Lamar found himself at a crossroads of good and evil. The predatory demons that haunted him were loose. His eyes narrowed; his lips peeled back; he was an apex predator again, seeking to right all wrongs, seeking to balance the ecosystem. It was his moment to decide. Should Big Oil survive? Should Big Tappin' survive?

If he banged his pack against the Dumpster, the gas tappers would be off. The surveillance would be blown, and what? What was best for the planet? What was best for the town? What was best for Lamar? Maybe the witness protection program?

Buster slipped back to the dumpster. "I got the photo; let's go."

CHAPTER 46

OTASCO Store, Tallapoosa, Early the Next Morning

———

ALTA BOLTED UPRIGHT ON AN army cot. A jackhammer pounded in his head, and his heart was at full gallop. He groped for his pills and found the small vial, his nitroglycerin pills. Empty. Shit! Then he found the larger vial of sleeping pills. Nearly full. Thank God. He'd crashed that night in the back room of his store, losing himself in sleep, then tortured by frightening dreams, then waking to an even more frightening reality. He checked his watch, 1:00 a.m.

Flopping back on the cot, he considered his fate.

Hours earlier, he and Virgil had agreed to a shaky new gas tapping deal. Alta would pony up fifty thousand dollars for more tankers, more tap sites, and more hush money. They'd go big, double the tapping volume to fifteen thousand gallons a night, make a killing, then Virgil would buy him out, and maybe, just maybe Mandy would have him back. He tried to smile, closed his eyes and drifted off.

He woke at 2:00 a.m., woozy and rattled. Pulling himself up, he staggered to the front of the store. Was the faint buzz he heard in the sky, a single engine plane, or maybe not? It could be some local yokel working on night flight training, or it could be the FBI "sky boys" on air surveillance. He rubbed his eyes and looked over at the train yard. A lone street light threw a faint shaft of light on the railroad trailer. There seemed to be shadows moving around the trailer. Maybe the wind was blowing tree branches back and forth below the street light? Or the Georgia-Pacific night crew leaving on an emergency repair? He crumpled into a rocking chair near the front window.

The Union 76 gas spill had triggered a swarm of agents searching for answers, but so far no one had cracked. Agents continued to chase gas tankers through the West Georgia backwoods only to get lost in a maze of dirt roads and a jungle of kudzu vines. Alta was sure it would blow over. After all, the Tallapoosa police, the Haralson County sheriff and the right honorable Mayor of Tallapoosa couldn't all be wrong. Just then a night train thundered through town. As the blur of boxcars flashed by, a rush of wind buffeted the front windows setting the panes to rattling. Once the train had passed, Alta looked back over at the railroad trailer. Dark shadows continued to play in front of it.

Settling back in his rocker, he deliberated. Perhaps it's true, we all have a measure of good and evil coursing through us, whether its call original sin, bad luck, or a curse. In a moment of rare candor, he admitted: *I am what I am. I grew up in hard times and learned at an early age that the game was often rigged. And when it was, I couldn't play by the rules and win. Not much of a moral principal, but that's the way it is for have-nots in hard times. Sure, you say, not the sort of thing you'd see in a Chamber of Commerce manual. But let me say on my own behalf, I'm only talking about property crimes not crimes of violence.*

Yet, he concluded, being a creature of free-will, I accept the legal consequences of my actions. That said, even when you pay for what you've done, it still doesn't make it right. He drifted off again, hoping the new tapping deal would go well, hoping he could sell off the business, hoping he could go straight.

Virgil called at 5:45 a.m. He'd just gotten off the phone with Slick Duffy, the owner of the Burger Inn. "Listen Alta, listen" Virgil screamed, "Slick said there are twenty or so unmarked cars parked behind the Burger Inn. He said they looked to be FBI agents. They drift into the café in twos and threes, get their coffee in paper cups and drift out. Big men in dark fedoras packing heat. Slick peeked out the back door. He said they stood in a circle. The Lead Agent opened a suitcase full of search and arrest warrants and handed them out and said, 'The names and address are different but the warrants are all the same—charging conspiracy to steal interstate gasoline. Close in on your suspect, but don't serve the warrant until 6:00 a.m. sharp.'

Alta bolted upright. "Good God!"

"The jig's up Mister Mayor," Virgil growled. "Their comin' for us. Someone ratted us out, probably that fuckin' Lamar."

"Where are you now?"

"At home, but I'm headed for the high hills of Alabama. Adios."

Alta hung up and crept to the front of the store. Suddenly police cars streamed down Main Street, single file, bumper to bumper, without lights. The cars peeled off at every cross street heading in different directions.

Alta breathed a sigh of relief as the last of the convoy disappeared down the street. Maybe his political connections were working. The dawn was breaking on the eastern skyline as he grabbed his keys, locked the store, and hustled over to City Hall.

Once inside his office, he spun around and froze. *What the hell am I doing here? I'm not running away. I'm not hiding.* He stumbled then steadied himself on the edge of his desk. He broke into a cold sweat as he felt the burning in his chest return. He knew what was coming. Yet, his mind raced in circles. Above it all thundered Mandy's simple question. *Why Alta, why?*

Unconsciously, he shifted to damage control, inhaling deeply, exhaling deeply. He turned to admire his glory board, the bulletin board filled with news clippings of his great deeds as mayor: the painting, the paving, the new industry, the new jobs, the Nutrition Center, and the Bicentennial Celebration. *How* he wondered. *How* can I be both good and evil?

It was similar, but different than the question Mandy had asked him. Her question, "*Why Alta, why?* Implied he had a choice. Why didn't *you* choose good over evil? Then he got it. His head snapped back. *Now I understand. How questions, are poor me questions. How could the Gods conspire against poor me?*

He edged around his desk still trying to control his breathing. The burning in his chest had passed. He looked out the window to his store across the street. All seemed quiet and peaceful. Maybe he was safe.

As the wall clock struck six, all hell broke loose. With red lights flashing and sirens screaming, a dozen patrol cars encircled his store. Within seconds, a phalanx of agents stood tall outside. Some disappeared behind the store. Others moved to the front door, quickly broke through the lock, and raced inside.

Alta gripped the edge of his desk. The burning in his chest returned as did the cold sweat, followed by an illuminating moment. The searing light of truth suddenly shone through veils of bullshit and self-deception. *Why do I do evil things? Why? Because I can. And because, I do them better than most. And that, that is all on me.*

The agents had regrouped in front of OTASCO. The Lead Agent pointed to City Hall and they headed over to arrest Alta.

Smiling grimly at Mandy's picture on his desk, Alta impulsively called Bridget's number. He was in luck, Mandy answered. "Mandy, this is Alta. Please don't hang up."

"Yes Alta, I'm listening."

"Mandy, I love you."

"And I love you."

"And Mandy, it looks like I'm headed back to prison."

"Oh! Well now. Well, I'm gonna miss you."

"And I'm gonna miss you, but listen Mandy, you need to get on with your life. And Mandy, throw away that lucky charm. You don't need it anymore."

"Yes Alta. Goodbye."

Alta hung up and walked across the street to meet the law.

Epilogue

THE ACCUSED

ON AUGUST 31, 1976, FBI and ATF agents began seizing the gas tapping equipment and making arrests. Thirty-two people were arrested over the next two weeks including the mayor, the chief of police, the assistant chief of police, and a city councilman. The arrest warrants charged them with conspiracy to steal interstate gasoline.

Leading up to the trial, things got crazy. The home of policeman Joe Williams, a government witness, was the target of a burst of gunfire. When Chief Seagle, the new chief of police, tried to follow up on the men who shot into William's home, the patrol car was rammed by an unidentified man. Chief Seagle resigned after serving for six weeks. Mr. Walter Abercrombie, a government witness, drowned under suspicious circumstances in a private lake near his home. The American Legion Post that Virgil Pettigrew operated burned down.

On January 12, 1977, thirty-two defendants pleaded not guilty. On August 18, 1977 seventeen defendants were found guilty.

SAM ALTA DRYDEN

In a memo to Mayor Dryden and the City Council of Tallapoosa on January 3, 1977, the Concerned People of the City of Tallapoosa and Community request those indicted or charged, to voluntarily remove themselves from their elected or appointed positons. The mayor resigned on July 7, 1977. On the same day, the OTASCO store in Tallapoosa burned down. On August 18 Alta Dryden was sentenced to serve a twenty-year prison term.

AKA Lamar Tate

Lamar Tate met with ATF Agent Vance Posey and Roy Stancil at the Burger Inn in July 1976. Thereafter, the FBI and the ATF began extensive air and ground surveillance of the gas tapping operation. For his participation as a government witness, Lamar received approximately $5,000 in monthly installments from the government and the pipeline companies. He lived in the witness protection program for years, then moved back to Tallapoosa for a time. He is thought to have died of hypothermia as a homeless vagrant in Florida.

AKA Virgil Pettigrew

Virgil was found guilty and sentenced to ten years in prison. He appealed his conviction and while the appeal was pending, he hired Kenneth E. McEachern to kill Lamar Tate in order to prevent him from testifying again in the event that the court should reverse the judgment and remand the case for a new trial.

On February 13, 1980, Virgil's body was discovered in the prison machine shop. From all appearances, he'd committed suicide by hanging himself.

AKA Mandy Tate

No one knows what became of Mandy Tate. She is said to have done very well with the OTASCO store in Bremen, sold it, and bought a chain of gift stores in Birmingham. Her friends say she threw away her basketball charm and got on with her life.

Acknowledgments

———

First, I want to thank the people I interviewed from Tallapoosa and Haralson County: Judge J. Edward Hulsey, Probate Court, Haralson County, Georgia; Judge Michael L. Murphy, Superior Court, Haralson County, Georgia; Judge Donald B. Howe Jr.,Superior Court, Douglas County; Becky Robinson, Clerk of Superior Court, Haralson County; Sammy Robinson; Buck and Jack Dryden, Alta's sons; Sandra Dryden, Jack's wife; De Laine Jones, Buck's ex-wife; Mary Tolleson, who moved mountains for me; Betty Lipham; Violet Godwin; Phillip Pope, author of *Tallapoosa 20;* Mark Allen, Pink Allen's nephew; Don Smith; Rhubarb Jones; Janice R. Nichols; Johnny Cantrell; Betty Joe Newman; Jerry Sue Muse; and Sharon Sewell, mayor of Bremen.

Next, I want to thank those who were directly or indirectly involved in the case: Jerry Froelich, Prosecuting Attorney in the gas tapping trial; Bob Fay, Head FBI Agent on the gas tapping case. The following retired ATF agents worked in the Southeast Region and Newnan, GA: Charlie Weems, Head Agent and author of: *Agents That Fly;* Agent Jim Arey; and Agent David Greer.

Next, I want to thank all the great folks that helped me research and put the book together: Blin O'Livere, Archival Librarian, West Georgia College; Tallapoosa librarians; Judy McMahon, librarian, Bremen; Regina Mildedge, ATF National Archives, Atlanta; Paul Martin, contributing photographer; Morris Stephenson, author of: *A Night of Makin' Likker;* Garland Robinson, contributing photographer; Graphic Support, Post Net Atlanta: Michael

Martin and Kevin Center; The Atlanta Writers Group, Benson Center: Alice Godbolt and all of the group that gave me great feedback; Developmental Editor, Ann Fisher; Steamboat Springs Writers Group: to all of the group that helped at the meetings and special thanks for those who provided additional help outside the meetings: Harriet Freiberger, Bobbie Beale, Don Moss, John Gatsby, Chuck McConnell.

And finally, I want to thank my golf buddies and friends who provide input: Dr. Bob Albee, Dr. Bob McDonald, Gene Godbolt, Richard Freeman, Tom Benson, Mike Maffett, Dan Haas, Cliff Thompson and his oldest daughter, Patti Pate.

And final, final thanks go out to my patient wife and ferocious editor, Joan.

Music Attribution

- "Don't Give Your Heart to a Rambling Man," Jimmy Skinner, Hal Leonard
- "Midnight Rider," Gregory L. Allman, SONY/ATV
- "Jambalaya," Hank Williams, Hal Leonard
- "Thunder Road," Robert Mitchum, Universal Music Corporation
- "Wabash Cannonball," Pubic Domain
- "White Lightening," J.P. Richardson, ASCAP Publishers
- "Silver turns to Gold," Public Domain
- "Will there be any stars in my crown," Public Domain
- "Shall we gather at the river," Public Domain
- "Wabash Cannonball," Public Domain
- "Yankee Doodle Dandy," Public Domain
- "San Antone Rose," Clark Susanna Wallis, ASAP Publishers
- "Slipping Around," Floyd Tillman, Hal Leonard
- "Gambler," Don Schiltz, Hal Leonard
- "Party's Over," Jule Styne, Adolph Green, Betty Comden, Hal Leonard

Image Attribution

1. Hot Pursuit, Courtesy of Paul Martin Collection
2. Lloyd Seay, Courtesy of: stock car.reacerunio.com
3. Groundhog Still, ATF Archives
4. Charlie and Mattie Dryden, Courtesy of Dryden Collection
5. Thousand Gallon Still, ATF Archives
6. ATF Raid, Courtesy of Paul Martin Collection
7. Still Hands Arrested, Courtesy of Paul Martin Collection
8. Still Hand, Courtesy of Paul Martin Collection
9. Pink Allen, Courtesy of Garland Robinson Collection
10. Plantation Pipeline, Graphics8.nytimes.com
11. Hot Tap, Hottap
12. Nutrition Center, Tallapoosa-Beacon
13. Tom Murphy, Courtesy of Garland Robinson Collection
14. July 4th, 1976, Tallapoosa-Beacon
15. Gas Tap Site, Atlanta National Archives

Made in the USA
Columbia, SC
14 April 2017